White Pigeon

A MAN WHO STAYED, WITH A WIFE WHO STRAYED

BY

GEOFF TYLER

Copyright © 2025 by – Geoffrey Tyler – All Rights Reserved.

It is not legal to reproduce, duplicate, or transmit any part of this document in either electronic means or printed format. Recording of this publication is strictly prohibited.

Table of Contents

Acknowledgment iii
About the Author iv
Introduction 1
Prologue The reason for my story 3
Chapter 1 Early years 6
Chapter 2 Paris & internet search for women 24
Chapter 3 Meeting with Monica in southern France on holiday 39
Chapter 4 Historical stories & the truth 48
Chapter 5 Monica moves in. Geoff gets dad to change will. 51
Chapter 6 Getting marriage 2003 61
Chapter 7 2003: Monica starts work 66
Chapter 8 Showdown on discovering affair with Paul 74
Chapter 9 Lady with two mutual lovers 79
Chapter 10 When the cat is away, the mice will play (Monica alone with Paul) 101
Chapter 11 Question marks on our marriage 139
Chapter 12 167
Chapter 13 214
Chapter 14 250
Chapter 15 277
Chapter 16 349
Summary of proceeding months of divorce & information 464
Note 1: Lyn, my first wife 471
Note 2: Anne #1 473
Note 3: Monica's real Rwandan story. 475
Note 4: Rwanda 485
Note 5: Monica's affairs, men & women 487
Note 6: Business trips catalogued 489

Acknowledgment

I want to thank all of Monica's female friends I knew that gave me inside information of what she was doing behind my back! Gathering some of the information would have been too difficult without them. Perhaps my good nature & honesty won through, whereby even though I was white & not Rwandese they confided in me. They too were shocked by Monica's behaviour with me.

I also want to thank Nicole for all the support when I was really stressed & getting depressed about my situation with both Monica's many men & affaires, plus financial ruin looming, if I did not do something.

About the Author

My background is science & specialised in atomic spectroscopy living in England, Australia & France before retiring back in England. I have four adult children, one of whom is adopted, plus one who died at infancy. Twice divorced. I am now with a long-term partner. I have been an international standard discus thrower & still throw as of 2024 in international masters track & field championships.

My inspiration was the truth

How you spend time is more important than how you spend money. Money mistakes can be corrected, but time is lost forever

Alfred Tyler

This my love story with a Rwandan lady with some embellishment in events and some intimate parts where I got carried away with details

Introduction

This is a true story, with sometimes some embellishment, of a European white man taken in by a clever, intelligent, devious, but not intellectual African woman, intent on having a good life at his expense & maintaining an image she wanted to create.

I have changed people's names & some details, redacted names & e-mails addresses to prevent embarrassment for those involved and a few fictional events added are wishful thinking.

A story of a beautiful Rwandan woman involved in many devious plots, hiding sex affairs with multiple men & women, wanting money and job positions by sex while having the security of a white husband, a home & maintaining an image of success in life & business.

Was she a typical beautiful African woman using her sexual assets to get what she wanted, or was she not typical? Some of my friends have said her poor & Rwandan genocide African background could make you desperate to achieve a good life & if that means seduction & affairs with many men, why not?

I have had some friends say that in her position, they may have done the same & used their female wiles to seduce & have sex with men who may help them financially or with job prospects.

White Pigeon is very close in this respect to a true, unexpurgated story. Only some details may be missing or added from memory. I used to make copious notes most mornings at work at the time, as one normally does being a scientist. Certainly, this is also true of my exploits with different women between stable relationships. Maybe memories & imagination of some wonderful sexual events blurs with some of the numerous women I have met from those **copious** morning notes & "post-it" notes written at different times.

To be a scientist, one does need to have a logical brain that is open to all ideas & open to brain-storming. If intellectual enough, one can see "bullshit" that can be uttered by ignorant people, it can also help when comments just don't sound right, but you don't have the evidence to disprove at the time. It is then the scientific brain starts making copious notes on a regular basis to make sense of events & to research the truth.

This is that story of patience, deep love for my wife, acceptance of multiple affairs, yet deep distrust, only wanting her to tell me the truth. I would find out things by looking up those copious notes & comparing what I found out much later using my longer-term research, and this uncovered something much more than I had uncovered at the time.

Throughout, one has to keep asking myself questions, questions, questions & all of you reading my story will ask, "WHY did Geoff stay with Monica when all the evidence showed she was bad, very bad for him with regards to money, men & occasional violence?".

I suppose the quick answer was "blind" love or deep love.

I was willing to put up with her numerous men IF ONLY she would admit to me each time she went with a man and the exploits. What I could not accept were the constant lies, lies, lies about her men & of course, the extraction of money from me.

In this account, sometimes the description of events with some of the many women in between relationships gets steamy as the imagination of my time went wild as I wrote from those notes.

Prologue
The reason for my story

Men always want a partner, whether female or male. It is natural to spend time & experiences with someone who can appreciate the moment. Alone, one feels empty. Men & women seek partners to share their lives. Singles clubs, while still popular, are now increasingly being supplemented by internet sites for lonely hearts. One can find whatever kind of partner one wishes, whether Americans wanting another American or European-speaking English, gorgeous Russians, African, Oriental or more recently Ukrainian women wanting a better life in the West, desperate Africans want money, a white man or both. Of course, some sites cater for other types of people who just want their sex, with no attachments or contacts just for company. With all these sites, photos & details give one a better chance to make a good chance for a good meeting.

Me? Ah yes, I tried all types of sites, but one particular site, "AOL at Love," looking for English-speaking women. I was amazed to find women all over the world interested in me & wanting to meet me. I met so many Americans visiting Paris, so a short time together was usually it, with e-mail contact kept as friends. But many "relationships" were literally cyber relationships, and even though we conversed for many hours at unearthly late hours for me, for several, we had cyber sex, making at least one woman have an orgasm with what I was saying via "chat." However, few materialised for more than that....a cyber relationship. One lady, however, did stand out, though. We met in Paris, "chez moi", & holidaying together in Paris & England she lived in Alabama.

This story of my life, my nightmare, is summed up with a book titled* "Women Who Stay, with Men Who Stray" by Dr Debbie Then

(Thorstons - Harper Collins publishers 1998). However, this could be changed in my case to: "men who stay, with women who stray". This is my story of events & my thoughts both at the time & retrospect.

Some people need sex all the time to keep their equilibrium; others need it seldom. Some people are not sure whether they want sex with a male or female, and some find they want both. Sometimes, they find out later in life, maybe in a war situation or maybe just chance circumstances that pose questions for the person themselves. In this, I saw what initially shocked me & later accepted as part of life being married to Monica.

In my story, firstly, I give my background in chapter 1, which always gave me a job I loved & also gave me, as a scientist, the background to be a good detective. Being relatively intelligent & intellectual, it gave me insights to see random comments or excuses by different women to be not possible or implausible and, therefore, needed investigation. I have found some women who lack higher education try to impress by lying & making up stories about their past & what they were doing. As you will read, I was mesmerised by Monica. Even though I investigated her lies & stories, I was initially faithful & accepted her various affairs & liaisons with men & women. However, later, with her permission, I was encouraged to "try" other women.

Being a scientist, I document everything and am effective in making notes of key points to jog my memory to expand later my thoughts, actions & plans. I can look back to find something useful in past experiments and notes to help the present or future. My life became embroiled in subterfuge, intrigue & brain-teasing that needed copious detailed notes to remind me of snippets of information that eventually made sense. I would make notes for maybe 15 minutes or more when I arrived at the office before starting real work. From these notes, I have collated & expanded them to make this autobiographical novel. **I have changed the names of people & companies so that** "innocent" people are kept anonymous & that their lives may continue without interruption from this book.

* I say "novel" due to time, memories, good or bad, fade, and sometimes, perhaps, one needs to use poetic licence at steamy times; the basic facts are there, and the dates are quite accurate.

Whether my work superior, college head of department or international athletics coaches, all have said, "…**you succeed NOT BECAUSE of the system, you succeed INSPITE of the system….**" at college, sport & work. If only I had the support, what could I have been? But then, perhaps, it is in my nature to have adversity to be able to overcome the problems.

Problems are there to be overcome, without problems, life would be boring !!

If you don't want to read my precis on my background & career, skip to Chapter 2.

Chapter 1
Early years

Abbreviations:

1   Atomic Absorption spectrophotometers (AAS)

2   Inductively Couple Plasma Atomic Emission Spectrometers (ICP-AES)

3   Inductively Couple Plasma Mass Spectrometers (ICP-MS)

How can I describe myself? I was, at the time, a middle-aged Englishman with a chemistry degree level science with a background in sales & marketing, successful at what I did, not poor nor rich. A man who has made a number of mistakes, and I will make many more before I die. In all I do, I want to excel, and I am very determined, as I have always been in sports. This, my story, is one of the big mistakes I made, the amazing world I discovered & things I learnt about what being naive in some things can cost you. I think I can sum up my experience as what my father said to me "*....How you spend time is more important than how you spend money. Money mistakes can be corrected, but time is lost forever ...*". It makes me feel better to think of those words & hope my "good" health does not desert me because that is something you cannot buy.

I have always been able to focus when required. I chose athletics in my leisure time after I realised I would be an "also ran footballer" (for Americans = soccer). I achieved the international standard in the discus, ranked 4th twice in the UK, 3rd in UK champs & top 10 UK position in the shot putt until a special injury curtailed the shot put. Athletics has always been, since I was 17 years old, a means of both achieving targets & fitness. At 75+, I am still training, coaching &

competing in world Athletics masters competitions as well as open-age competitions. I have achieved UK M70 records for both discus & shot & came 2nd at the Venice European Masters Champs & 4th in the shot. Talking of the UK records, I broke the British & Australian M45 records **in 1994** and as of 2025, my Australian M45 discus record still stands!

In 2021 (73 years) , I was bench pressing 135kg, & friends in the USA & UK suggested I start powerlifting. In 2022, I started powerlifting bench press-only competitions. I cannot compete in squats or deadlifts due to an artificial hip, so I should not load the hip with more than, say, 50kg. I won in 2022: England, UK, European & World M7 titles. As a coach I have realised that most athletes do not have the drive I have.

By pushing myself, I am able to understand my body & mentality. This is a characteristic that is required for sales & helped me be successful in both, as well as dedicated to learning the technicalities of the atomic spectroscopy products. I was to sell & manage & later define software interface, hardware and product development as a worldwide ICP product manager with two companies.

Married life – first version Lyn (Note-1)

Where do I start? Well, I met Lyn when I was 20, and we got married 4 years later. I was married **for <u>some 10 years</u>** of relative happiness until the wife gradually decided she would do little & just enjoy life with TV & reading "Noddy books" as I called them, you know, the "Mills & Boons" books on love, romance & whatever. Gradually, she did not do anything except shout at the kids & get them to be her "little slaves". I worked hard in my job and trained hard in athletics at an international level while trying to be a father to my three kids. Moving to Australia I discovered Lyn had an affaire on a pre-visit before we moved & also a colleague's wife discovered she was a drunk.

I do not want to give you the hard luck story; there are billions with a harder story, but it helps you later on in understanding my position & eventually understanding "white pigeons" like me looking for beautiful women & loving wives, but more of that later.

After working "on the road" in selling an array of scientific instruments, I would train & return home to find the kids asking, "What's for dinner, dad? Mum has gone to bed." I would "rustle up" something by de-frosting whatever I could find in the freezer quickly in the microwave & cooking the meat with some tinned veg like sweet corn bits, peas or tinned carrots. Now, being English, I have to uphold a certain reputation for cuisine....I have excelled in maintaining this extremely LOW standard of culinary skills. I would constantly remind my kids that tinned food was very fresh; it was fresh when it went into the tin. Certainly, my son agreed that's the only veggies he eats, unless it is given to him in his pub meal. While both my daughters (thankfully) disagree completely with this (bad) attitude, they both buy fresh veggies the same day, or maximum, the day before & feed the family healthy food.

My experience in cooking started when my mum & dad said they were going out for a ride in the Essex countryside, so they had left some lamb chops in the saucepan ready for me to cook. With typical knowledge of cooking at that age, I put the frying pan on full & went down to the garden to do some gardening for maybe ½ hour, as I thought. However, after some time, let's say 20 minutes, I noticed smoke pouring out the small kitchen window, and I rushed up the garden to find, when I opened the door, smoke choking me. I fought my way through the thick smoke to the frying pan by intuition & not by sight. With a towel, I took the frying pan, went outside & placed it on the driveway. Eventually, when the smoke subsided, I discovered an interesting observation: my lamb chops were little pieces of charcoal. As the Americans would say, "Where is the meat?" Being a chemist, knowing that "matter can neither be created nor destroyed", I decided the meat was still floating in the air as carbon particles! So here you have my first experience of cooking. You would think things could only improve, but you forget I am a determined man, & sometimes, I am impatient, so when another opportunity arose with sausages, my skills did not desert me — similar scenario, more charcoal!

When I first started grammar school at Braintree County High School, I was next to last in chemistry, things started to change in the summer when a student teacher dissolved things, now that's more interesting. However, in the 2nd year, we had an interesting female teacher who had spent time in Peru. By the end of the 2nd year, I was first in the class & never looked back at my interest in chemistry & the things I wanted to do in chemistry, which has stayed with me for my life.

Having achieved two "A" levels in chemistry, physics & later ONC in Maths, I did not want to go to university & waste time & money as I thought, enjoying myself. I decided to get a job & get my higher qualifications equivalent to a university degree part-time, earn money & get experience. I achieved an LRIC (Licentiate of the Royal Institute of Chemistry, based in posh central London) qualification after HNC. For employers, this was worth more than a simple university degree. **I am glad I did** because the experience I gained in a multitude of different types of analysis & atomic spectroscopy in my first job at Hoffmanns played an important part in my success with all the jobs I was to have had in my career.

Skip through the years, and I found a job in a laboratory making ball & roller bearings in Chelmsford, Essex (for my American readers, this is the original Chelmsford in Essex, not the **one** in New England). Here, I learnt about the analysis of metals, oils & a multitude of things, including a cutting-edge technology at the time in 1967 called "Atomic Absorption Spectrophotometry", AAS for short, that helped me in my future life. The chief chemist, Max, played with calibration graphs with simple solutions & then said, "Done; we can now start the routine analysis."

Never to take things for granted, I checked the results by duplicating with the old routine analysis method & the results were wildly different, with AAS results out of specification. Gathering technical papers & experimenting, I found I needed to calibrate with certified standards: steels, brasses & bronzes. This research & experimentation would help me in all future work; never assume other work is correct. IF you <u>assume</u> (AssUMe) it can make an Ass of U & Me. It was here that I honed my skills to experiment, make detailed notes & be systematic in everything I do. When I say systematic, we often use the terminology "scientific approach", which means that you collect all information, even if at the time it does not seem relevant, & try to analyse the information not only immediately but also periodically later, if the problem has not been resolved. I found this very useful when analysing events, comments & information regarding my 2nd marriage with Monica. I also use the same principle with my athletics training diary to help me with future training & getting over injuries.

I always keep a pen & notepad by my side in bed, so when I have thoughts, I can make notes & have peace of mind to sleep without worrying all night that I might forget (which one does). The brain still works hard when we are sleeping. One good example was as a product manager; some years later, I had a problem that bugged me for some 3 weeks. One night, I woke up in the middle of the night with the answer made notes, in the morning the notes made sense & solved the problem. You will see later the significance of this trait of mine because scientists make good detectives & oh boy, did that help me!

After some 2-3 years at Hoffmann's, I decided I had learnt enough to move on. I realised I needed to get into sales & marketing if I wanted to get on in life. However, I was always "inexperienced" in the future direction I wanted to pursue. I made a number of job applications, but

I was rejected usually before the interview & always at the interview. Later, I was made redundant, which was probably one of the better things to happen to me. This helped me because it FORCED me to look hard all day, every day, for another job. I decided to research in the library using a directory called "Kompass", I made a list of potential scientific instrument makers in England. With 15 on the first batch of prospective letters I sent, I got 6 positive replies. On my first interview, having had experience with AAS, one of the instruments they made, I was offered a job as a salesman for scientific instruments, including atomic absorption spectrophotometers (AAS), involving and covering the north of England.

I started with an instrument company, Shandon Southern Instruments Ltd., based in Camberley, Surrey, making Atomic Absorption Spectrophotometers (AAS), which is a technique for elemental determinations in basically anything, be it; rocks, metals, water, food, oils etc. Being inexperienced in sales, I had to make up extremely hard work until I learnt the skills for selling. Remember, I succeed in spite of the system rather than because of the system. I remember, after 9 months, I went on a sales course that helped me for life. The tutor, John Fenton, who ran the course, became a multi-millionaire running sales courses & sales training conferences throughout the world. I enjoyed my job, but after some 3 years, it was apparent to me that the company was going to implode. One had a choice either to find something else or stay & pick up the pieces by starting my own company as some colleagues did.

During this time, I did an AAS demonstration in the Carlisle sewage works lab in the presence of a competitor salesman. He had done a demo the previous day but had not finished all the sample analyses requested by the customer. He asked whether he could do more work to give the required results to the customer the next day before he left with the instrument. I did my demonstration several benches away from him, did not notice, but he was listening to everything I was saying. Several months later, he got promoted &

recommended to the managing director I should be pursued, so by pretending to be a customer, they got my home phone number (I used my number almost like the northern office) he rang me one night, offering me an interview for a job.

The new company, Instrumentation Laboratory Ltd., was based in Altrincham, Cheshire, & probably these were my happiest years in business. I had a good sales manager, Doug Milroy, who would buy the pints when we had our weekly "sales meeting" in a local pub. My darts playing improved, and I also learnt from his example how to be a good sales manager. People will follow a good leader in war or business if the person believes in the capabilities of their boss or commander. Respect is everything. I have always aimed to emulate my sales boss & be a good manager, caring for my subordinates & helping where I can, so I suppose that gives me an advantage in identifying poor bosses who may bark, shout, & bully subordinates but gain little or no respect, therefore, get poor returns on the required workload. A famous saying goes, "…remember you may meet the people going down, that you met going up". I have seen this several times in past years & can vouch for this saying as I saw them fall.

Atomic spectroscopy becomes my life's career.

Having served an "apprenticeship" with AAS, I was introduced to a new cutting-edge technique in 1979 that I was to head up for the UK subsidiary company as product manager for Inductively Coupled Plasma Optical/Atomic Emission Spectrometry (ICP-**O**ES / ICP-**A**ES). Nobody ever standardised the terminology; hence, all books, technical papers & brochures on the subject can use either terminology, confusing some customers.

After specialising in ICP-AES for 7 years, I got a phone call one night & was offered a job with a competitor, Varian Ltd, as UK sales manager for spectroscopy. This opened up a wider opportunity for me as I was becoming very specialised. After 2 years, I went down to

Melbourne, the Australian factory, for 2 weeks to help them with a new ICP-AES product for a new product line. At the end of the 2 weeks, I had to give a one & a half-hour presentation to 40 of the key people in the factory on what I had observed about the status of the project with software, hardware, marketing requirements & sales training, requirements for the present AAS salespeople to sell the new product, what I had recommended & why. At the end of the lecture, to my surprise, I was summoned to the vice president's office, where he said, " I want you to stay." "Oh! How long?" I said. "I want you to live here & head up the project as a world-wide ICP product manager." Gobsmacked, I was given the opportunity to phone to UK to speak to Lyn, my wife (we will call her ex-wife Number 1). She told me that she cried when we finished with joy.

On my return to the UK, I gave the three children & the wife the opportunity to make a "For & Against" table for each. Consequently, we moved in 1990 & settled down in a rental place for the first year & then got a mortgage for a house. After the house in Macclesfield was eventually sold after 2 ½ years, I was able to buy the Australian house (bungalow in English) outright.

Australia 1989

It was arranged that to speed up a permanent resident's visa, they would need to advertise the job throughout Australia via the national & local newspapers & also in the factory. When several people, including Brian Frary, whom I knew from SSI days, applied & found I was the competition, they pulled out so they did not waste people's time with their application. I went down again for 6 weeks, & Phil Thomas the vice president agreed to pay for Lyn to come out for 3 weeks to make sure she wanted to move across the globe.

Arrangements were made, & Lyn & I went down to Melbourne, & again, we stayed at the Mulgrave Hotel. We met Paul Thompson, an American service specialist who was also, by chance, spending 6 weeks training on AAS updates. We spent time together & then I heard that there was a local major league athletic competition each Tuesday night at Olympic Park, where the Melbourne Olympics were held in 1956. I asked Paul whether he could take Lyn out for dinner that night while I investigated the local athletics scene.

I used my Varian loan car to get into Melbourne & watch the discus. I met a certain Peter Young whose son Scott was throwing in the competition we were watching. I made a note of his address & contact details & said I would be moving "down under" sometime in the next 6 months. He was keen that I coach Scott, as he had no coach & knew that Scott had potential at the time; he was throwing about 43m.

Lyn has an affair with Paul

Meanwhile, that night was VERY eventful for Lyn. Paul took her to a restaurant & then, apparently, things went well at dinner, so he suggested going down to Frankston Beach. The story I gathered over a period of weeks & months, as Lyn could not stop talking about what went on, giving different snippets of information to various audiences. "We had a wonderful amorous evening on the beach", "his body is so manly", "we had fun on the beach", "we kissed a bit". One night, we had an assembly of maybe 12 colleagues, and Lyn quickly sat next to Paul. During the evening, it was obvious he was fondling her & she him under the table. I could see she was breathing so hard, her chest was heaving, that she may have been having an orgasm. It was embarrassing to watch because most on the table could also see what was going on with certain glances my way as to say, "do you see what is going on?"

Lyn went after her allotted 3 weeks & then Paul & I were left for the remaining 3 weeks. Paul alluded to certain other activities, & I said to him, "I have guessed what happened on the Frankston Beach." He was not sure what I was going to do. Hit him? Strangle him? "No", I said, "any action would be futile. By doing nothing, you will feel justifiably ashamed & would not want to do it again." He then said, "I admire you for that you could have put me in hospital & yet you want to let me feel ashamed to stop me doing it again. I agree, I will not touch Lyn again." He was true to his word, & my approach left an indelible mark on him. From then on, he confided in me on personal matters as well as business matters.

Life is quite interesting in Australia. People are very friendly most hardworking, and BBQ is made at the drop of a hat. However, all were always claiming "poverty," even my manager, who one day said to me, "Roll on Friday, payday." The vice president told me that his American boss in California was getting a pay rise more than his salary! Even though I was paid enough to be in the top 2.5% of wage earners in Australia, I had a decent life but was not able to save or make investments for the future as I did in the UK. A major reason for this is the % stoppages on one's salary. This is something I would find also when I moved to France later.

Introducing a new product & a new technique to a company & personnel, that did not understand the subject properly, was problematic & caused much extra work to convince people they were wrong. Imagine work done by R & D for some 6 months & then I came along with a few pertinent questions & when they answered, then said to them, "Throw the data away; it is meaningless!" They were not happy or believed me to start with, so I had to explain the differences between ICP-AES, a multi-element high-temperature plasma approx. 10,000 C technique & AAS, a single element low-temperature flame technique.

The work involved making everything from scratch: Software specification, hardware, accessories that some did not think important but were crucial, production testing schedule, specialist training programme, salespeople training, brochure, publicity & helping my service colleagues with the service manual. Without PowerPoint at the time, it meant collecting technical papers, competitive brochures & notes & literally "cutting & pasting in a presentation & training manual, then photocopying for marketing & salespeople throughout the world. Late nights were always required; my record was start at 9 am and finish at 01:15 am the next day in the office before I left for home.

Although PowerPoint had been invented by then, no commercially available PC was available at the time with enough RAM to run it! At the time, PowerPoint needed 16MB to run. The inventing software writer was convinced by "Moore's law" (that chips would double in power every year) & predicted that PCs would be able to run it several years later. He was correct, & eventually, he sold out to Microsoft.

Family & athletics had taken a back seat, so I made efforts each weekend to go out to the Dandenongs, usually with the kids only. Lyn was not interested in being with us even though we lived close to FernTree Gully near the Dandenongs. The Dandenongs are a beautiful range of temperate rain forests and were only a few kilometres from our house. Appreciation of the forest, the beautiful birds & getting away from work were important, as were athletics to retain my sanity & release stress due to the problems with my wife at the time. This would serve me well as my stress would be just as bad later in France but in a different way.

During the first 2 years, 1990-1992, I did not compete in athletics; just threw discus/shot in training & coached on a Sunday. Slowly, I built up my fitness while coaching athletes in the Melbourne area. I would eventually compete & break the UK & Australian M45Vets record in Sydney 1994 (Australian record still standing in 2025) and also accept a coaching position for "Little Aths." The first time I saw a Little Aths meeting, I was appalled by the attitude of the parents who run the association from the age of 5 to 15 years before they are required to join the full athletics association. One example exemplified my feelings when I went to one of these meetings. During a 100-metre race of about 8 years old girls, this father was running the whole length on the other side of the rail, and when the girl came "only" second, he shouted & castigated her for failing to win. I soon found out that Little Aths was an association for failed parents to make an achievement through their children. Another example was a failed parent who pushed his 8-year-old boy with maybe 6 different events over a 3-hour period. The poor lad was there before my throws squad arrived & was still there after we left! I said to the father he was pushing the lad too much too early and to wait until he was 15-16 years old. Those comments from me were treated with, "Ok, Peter, just beat this Victorian record & then we will go ....". Official Victorian Athletics Association figures showed that only 7% of Little Aths kids joined the Victoria Athletic Association at the age of 15 when Little Aths finished. That is a 93% drop-out rate at 15+!

When invited to coach the Victorian state elite Little Aths throwers, I had a choice: either refuse out of principle or accept & try to change various parents' attitudes. I decided on the latter option & proceeded to run the Victorian Little Aths elite squad for discus & shot putt.

One of my throwing squad members, Scott, was 19 years old & said he was stale because he had been doing competitive athletics for 15 years. I said, "You cannot have done; you are only 19 years old", but he said he started at 4 years old. I made a gentle programme of light weights, no more than 30 minutes of training, to gradually frustrate him to WANT to train harder. I encouraged him to come for social reasons & he found the training easy, so within 9 months, he was keen enough to want to do full training. Many athletes in Europe & America can be doing various sports & then gradually specialise in the late teen years with a real keenness to train harder to achieve their goals. Athletics or any sport should be fun, not a chore or being bullied by parents. My kids came to watch & occasionally do some training, but it was always up to them. Keeping generally fit is good for their health, but not to be taken seriously at such a young age to fulfil parents failed sports life when they were young.

Back in the home, we would have a BBQ either at our house or at various colleague's houses. Like in the UK, Australian colleagues became friends, and this is very different to France, where they leave work & rarely associate with colleagues after work. Houses were generally larger than in England, with larger gardens where anything grew quickly. However, gardening presents certain problems, namely, do not let the grass grow tall; this is a bush fire hazard, and if you do not cut it, the local municipality will give notice and will cut it within 10 days & charge you for the job. Mice are likely to multiply in long grass, wood stacks or any junk left in the garden. Mice attract snakes that like mouse meals, & all Australian snakes have highly toxic poisons. Finally, there are always "redbacks", a common venomous spider in Victoria. In the house, one always checks the toilet before sitting down; redbacks like to hang to the underside of anything, including toilets…not good to get bitten up the bum!

Go to bed and check under the sheets to see if a white tail spider is there. Although not proven, some attribute a gradual flesh-eating poison that can eat a whole arm over, say, 10 years, causing such pain & distress people have committed suicide.

Eventually, we launched the ICP-AES product in 1991. The launch involved my marketing plan to release the product in stages according to the market & our coverage by subsidiaries & agents. I invited 17 AAS specialists in two groups two weeks at a time. They had a theory all morning from me & practical work in the lab that I had devised on the new product in the afternoon.

With a few weeks gap & then off to Chicago, USA, to launch the product at PittCon in late February with the aid of my assistant. Before the exposition, I trained a further 100 salespeople trained at 25 at a time, over 2.5 days each. Flavio Finotelli, my assistant, had never been outside Australia, so when I warned him that Chicago would be VERY cold, I did not understand that for most Aussies, 12C is **very** cold. He showed me some thick material he had purchased & was getting this made into what I can describe as a "great coat" that was worn in the First World War. We arrived in Chicago with temperatures of minus 15C. He "died"; he could not imagine temperatures so low. When he arrived at the exhibition hall the next day, I found he did not have a vest underneath, nor a jacket!

One night, we went to a strip show with a whole group of Varian salespeople from all over America being trained by me. With contributions, we set up Flavio, as it was his birthday. He was shy, so having been paid, the two strip dancers chased him **from** the men's toilet, dragged him out, took off his shirt & sat him on a chair on the stage with explicit instruction: hands behind your back; do not move. Erotic dancing by both all over him, one sitting astride his shoulders, we all cheered as the show progressed, after one even wrote on his back in indelible pen, her phone number!

After four enjoyable but exhaustive weeks, we were off to Zug, Switzerland, & a further 100 salespeople trained at 25 a time over 2.5 days similar programme of training. Zug is not Chicago; other than the beautiful scenery, it is boring. We were glad to return home to Melbourne after some 6 weeks away. A new product line & a new product was thus launched for a steady but successful rise up among the market leaders.

For the next two years, we dramatically increased our ICP-AES market share. I was working on various software GUI (Graphical User Interface) feature definitions for the software engineers to work on, new accessories & ideas for the future. Additionally, I worked with R & D for the next product, an ICP-MS (Inductively Coupled Plasma Mass Spectrometer). This is a technique that, by using a mass spectrometer for detection, is at least 1,000 times more sensitive. Now, instead of measuring down to ppb- parts per billion (or $\mu g/L$ –

microgram/litre), we were detecting down to ppt -parts per trillion or ng/L (nanogram/litre).

Two years later, the ICP-MS (mass spectrometer version) was launched. I had differences in marketing strategy with the vice president for a high-ticket item like ICP-MS. This led to lost orders due to his insistence on a high product release price of US$ 240,000, & when the client decided to buy the competition, he said, "OK, offer him US$ 180,000", I said it was mad & would now be too late & would be an insult to the client. I was right; we lost & the client was not happy with the last offer after the event. Pricing & marketing ideas have to be different for high ticket items of ~ US$ 200,000 compared with low-priced products like AAS at US$ 20-50k. I was frustrated, and this was exacerbated by a meeting with the visiting American president, who wanted to rename a new product ready for launch within weeks.

I had a few job offers, one from the European vice president of the company & another from an ICP accessory company, CETAC, whom I knew well from dealings with the company. This unhappiness ensured I had to move. Which job should I accept?

I knew the president & owner of an ICP accessory company, Cetac, well, and I had a choice of starting up a UK subsidiary company of ICP accessories for this company based in Omaha. He opened up to me about his global expansion plans, with data that, knowing the UK market, I was sceptical and found out later that the "research" was just imagination. So, based on this, I made a detailed business & marketing plan and gave my report to Collin, the president & owner. I felt the worldwide subsidiary start-up target was overstretching the resources with possible cash flow problems if, as I was convinced, his "marketing research" was flawed & thus needed to be scaled back. While the job of being managing director & starting up a company in the UK excited me, I was worried that it could be over-ambitious & maybe fraught with dangers.

At the last moment, I decided to stay with the devil I knew rather than the devil you don't know, whereby I decided to accept an offer from my present company's European vice president to start up a sales & marketing team in Europe, specifically for ICP-MS. Having decided to stay with the present company, we all moved back to northern England. The marriage was on the rocks & within 6 months of returning to England we were divorced. I bought a house in Haslington, a small village outside Crewe, Cheshire, with money left over from my divorce from Lyn. Sophie lived with me & I paid for Steven to live close by to ensure he was independent. Dawn was too young to be a latch-door kid, so unfortunately, I decided she would be best with Lyn against Dawn's wishes & my better retrospective judgement.

I needed to start up a sales & marketing team for the European ICP-MS product. In inheriting one specialist & taking on two more PhD, we had a successful year with sales from one unit before my team started in the first 2 years to 13 units in one year. However, an internal vice president war between USA & Australian VPs meant when the Australians lost, this led to the disbandment of the team. A three-year campaign to remove layers of management resulted in myself & others above me being made redundant by the "empowerment" of those below without pay increases. The company paid for a professional consultant to help me find a job via networking & advice on making a good CV. Using networking, I contacted an old friend, Jim, to see if he knew of anyone looking for someone like me. He said he was looking for someone like me &, knowing my skills, employed me as a marketing manager.

Environmental monitoring

I worked for some 3 months as a marketing manager for an environmental monitoring equipment company owned by a former colleague & friend Jim Mills, based in Cheltenham, which meant I was going down south to the HQ a lot of the time. At the time, I had been going out with one woman, Anne, who liked kinky sex. Once when driving along a quiet M5 motorway, she unzipped my trousers, caressed & started a "blow job," sucking me at 70mph. I could not stop, so I slowed down & moved onto the inside lane. I can assure you having someone sucking you and giving you a wonderful blow job while driving makes it difficult to concentrate, & even worse when one cums! I had to wait until we got to the next service area before I could zip up my trousers. By this time, she was licking her lips with a cheeky smile, she must have swallowed most of my cum, so I did not need to clean up. I arrived at the head office, making sure there were no signs of the journey's events!

Jim had just created three divisions with air monitoring. He had one salesman, but it was mainly **Jim's** expertise & contacts that made this division very profitable, especially at the time when local councils were investing government money in air pollution monitoring. I went out with various salesmen & quickly saw a big problem. Firstly, they had no visual aid to help them make a meaningful presentation in front of the client. The second was that the air pollution salesman was useless as a salesman & was lazy as well. All the orders were due to Jim with his knowledge & contacts, not the salesman. The organisation was lop-sided with air monitoring by far the biggest income & this would soon diminish as government contracts would cease for the surge in air monitoring. Being an old friend, I was able to tell him things about his company & people that others would not dare. I told him his air monitoring salesman was useless.

* He admitted some years later to me in comms with Jim, that was a major problem why his company folded some years later.

***

Jobin Yvon - Longumeau

Within 3 months of working for the company, I had a phone call one night asking me whether I was interested in being ICP-AES product manager for a French company based in Longjumeau, south of Paris. Atomic spectroscopy is in my blood, and I immediately accepted an interview at the company HQ. The interview went well with god 1, 2, 3 present & the old product manager at the interview & subsequent lunch. When the question eventually was posed to me, "…have you any questions?" "Yes," I said, "I cannot speak French!" No problem was the answer; our brochures, marketing & production documents need to be in good English, & all your communications are with the world where they will speak & write in English because it is the "Lingua Franca." The brochures were a laughing stock for anyone speaking English because of the "Franglais" with poorly structured English & spelling mistakes.

I should add, at this stage, I had taken French at grammar school for 5 years, and each of my teachers was abysmal in their own way. One teacher I had for 3 years, was just too weak to control more than 5 pupils, so there was no chance with some 30 of us. Another was an English teacher acting as a French teacher, so we had 6 verbs per week on 3 tenses & then he read "Day of the Triffids", a SciFi novel, the rest of the time. When I refused to do the French homework close to the GCE "O" levels exams, she sent me to the headmaster (probably expecting me to get the cane). I went to the headmaster & immediately said to him that I did not intend to waste my time doing French homework when I could spend time on the other subjects & pass those ones. Dr Cordingley, the headmaster, was shocked at my determination & logic, so he agreed & said, "Ok, I agree with your logic; just do the minimum to keep her happy". I returned to the class, & she was puzzled that I was smiling a victorious smile.

Chapter 2
Paris & internet search for women

I moved to Longjumeau, south of Paris, & a new life. On arriving in France, I brought with me my girlfriend at the time, Anne (see note 2). She could not speak a word of French (at least, I could crudely). She was constantly jealous & paranoid of any other woman I was in contact with, whether neighbours or work colleagues. She was constantly accusing me & hitting me to extract the answer she wanted. She would accuse me of this woman, or that woman at work was after my knickers.

Eventually, I once set up a trap by mentioning one female colleague whom I had not mentioned before, and I spent 3 hours on marketing. The next night, she said she had contacted my work colleagues & that this woman wanted my pants off. I had warned her back in Haslington house in the UK about her attitude & constant hitting me, but each time I had relented. I cannot hit any woman, even if I am tempted to. I am too strong I would do REAL damage to the person. However, the final straw in life with Anne was when she attacked me one too many times. We were sitting on the sofa with the coffee table in front of us. She started again with accusations & was hitting me. I said I have had enough of this and am going to bed. I walked in front of her & the coffee table to get to the door, and she suddenly kicked me with both feet over a coffee table, hitting my head & elbow hard on the floor. I said, "That's it, you're going back to England". I took her back to England & let her stay in my England house rent-free for several months while she found a flat of her own, so that was the end of Anne.

After I broke up with Anne in late 1999 & took her packing back to the UK, I started looking for someone in France. Being alone, I decided to go online to find a woman locally. I chose love@AOL.com & found, to my surprise, very few French women, but mostly American females & a few from Africa. I think the reason for the poor response from French females is that few speak English & AOL is mainly an English-speaking, American internet provider.

After the separation from Anne, I went with many women, including a number of Africans. I did find that their culture was of being subservient to African males. They saw white men as possible sources of money, property & power by using one major advantage….sex. While African men were susceptible to their sex, it was with white men that they could trap their prey more easily. A close friend once said to me that if their lives in Africa are so poor & that, sex is a way to rise out of the gutter. They would use it & even in Europe, they still do not forget their sexual skills. The difference between them, I found, was the amount of patience they could exhibit. Some would ask for money very quickly, often on the first night together, while others were more long-game patient.

Internet Search AOL begins.

In early 2000, the company had given us all an AOL business & private e-mail account. AOL was an American English language internet provide quite popular in the late 1990s & early 2000, even in France.

I was now single & would "shop around". In searching, I met on the internet "AOL at Love", I met numerous women over the course of a few years, some one-night stands, others a short relationship. I was up late each night, having up to 3 chats (instant messages) at the same time.

Exchange news with some, & some would come to Paris as part of a European tour, & we would meet outside a fountain, Fontaine St Michel, depicting the liberation of Paris in 1944 in St Michel, by the river Seine. This was close to an area with Rue de la Huchette, full of restaurants of all nationalities. It was my "normal" meeting place because I could park easily underneath street level & the fountain was small enough to easily enable me to identify the woman & she me.

Felicia Bodnarscu was a white Romanian living on Ave Versailles and working in a solicitor's office. We went out maybe 5 times; sex was not memorable, & she was more like a friend, so when she was in cash flow problems, I lent her several thousand Euros, which she gradually paid me back.

Kalina, nickname Kabby, was from Sierra Leone and living in south Paris. We met & went out a few times, but she was not what I wanted.

Nathalie originally came from Guinea & lived in Port Villette, west Paris. She worked in the French government. Nathalie was very overweight & not my type, but I met her a couple of times because she was an interesting woman, & I went back to her nice flat. I found the sight of a naked, overweight person, albeit lost much weight, still not appetising. However, she did tell me something that shocked me about French employment laws regarding women having a baby. While in industry, woman could come back to their old job within 3 years, but in the French government, it was for life. So one woman in her office was a supervisor & after having the baby and seeing him grow up, she decided to ask for her old job back after…..20 YEARS! She had to spend nearly a year being retrained on everything: administration, computers, etc.

Bridgetta was Nigerian, average height, solidly built & a lot up top. I met her at our rendezvous in a café in Nanterre. We went back to her small flat in Nanterre, west of Paris, and she made me a cup of tea & said she was having a shower. After a few minutes in the shower & drying herself, she reappeared with a towel around her. I was in the cramped kitchen washing up my cup. She embraced me; we kissed; she looked down at her ample breasts, that I could only see the cleavage…..

at the time. She then said, "You like?" in her Nigerian accent. Teasing her, I said, "Using my imagination, they may look nice." She smiled & undid the towel knot & lowered the towel to reveal a big pair of breasts. I was looking intently at them "Now you like?" she said. Lifting one boob into my hand, I said, "Yes, I like". She put her arms around my neck, we kissed, & I felt the soft sound of the towel dropping on the floor. By now, she was massaging my penis & could feel my trousers getting tight as it grew. She proceeded to undo the belt & then undo my trouser zip to reveal a very tight pair of pants. She now put her hand inside to hold my penis. I could not move as I still had my shoes on, & my trousers were now around my ankles. Noting me look at my feet, she bent down, took off my shoes, pulled off my trousers & then, rising slightly, pulled down my pants & off they came. While in the low position, she decided to give my penis a kiss & a gentle suck. She suddenly asked, "Do you have a condom?" "Yes", I said, & with that, I went to my jacket & pulled out a packet. She pulled me into the bedroom, took out a condom & pulled it on my penis. "Do you want to enter me front or back?" Things were happening so fast for a first meeting in a café, I could only think to say front before she pulled me onto her & onto the bed & legs apart to guide. "James" my name for my penis into her vagina. "James" was happy & over a period of time & gradual increase in intensity I came. The intensity of hip drives coincided with the floppy motion of her boobs. After the action, we had another cup of tea & chat. As I was leaving, she said, "I don't have much money, can you give me €50?" I was to learn that many African women would ask for money afterwards.

Diane Villiers le Morhier was a nice white English woman living in a small village near Chartreux. Well built & above average height for a woman, about 5 years younger than me. She was a widower & had a large house with a disused swimming pool & an adult son living with her. We met in Paris one time when she was in Paris. Afterwards, she invited me down to her house for the weekend. We spent a nice relaxing weekend & went for a walk around the small village. The walk was only about 3 miles (5km), but she was having difficulty, after we returned to her house, she was totally knackered. She said, seeing my fitness, if we stayed together, she would have to get fitter. Being good in bed is not enough for me; I want to be able to do things that meant women have to be reasonably fit to be able to walk, dance, etc. I could not imagine Diane dancing more than 10 minutes in a night —pity, a really nice woman.

Celia came from Cameroon, average height & reasonably thin, but with the typical African bum & boobs, she was quite attractive. She lived in Melun, about 60km southeast of Paris & took me about 30 minutes for me to Longjumeau. We went to a local resto, & afterwards, she invited me back to her flat. What is it with these Africans? No sooner than we had finished our cup of tea, she was fingering her breasts & with….maybe…some body language from me. She was all over me, within minutes, our clothes were off, & I was shagging her. I barely had time to put the condom on. She was so eager, not that I was not slow either. Doggy style & boobs swaying to the rhythm was lovely. Afterwards, I thought maybe I would like to see her again, but then… she asked for money. That was a complete turnoff, and I felt like I was paying for a prostitute. Pity, I did like her.

Patricia was from Benin, a petite lady, she lived in Passy, west of Paris. Dinner in a resto was nice, good conversation, albeit with sometimes finding the words in French for what I wanted to say. She invited me back to her flat & was not as fast as some, but not slow in coming forward with knowing what she wanted. Rubbing my trousers around an aroused "James", my penis made them tight, so she suggested they come off. Unbuckling my belt, undoing my zip revealed her goal & her warm, small hand went inside my pants/culottes to feel "James". He was happy, Patricia was happy, & she did an excellent blow job on me. Hardly any cum was lost from her mouth, just a little that oozed out the side, but that was quickly licked back in her mouth. Perhaps Patricia will be different from other Africans I have met. Well, yes, but with the caveat that she announced she was going back to Benin & was not sure when, if ever, she would return.

Clara was above average height, came from the Central African Republic & lived in Bondy, east of Paris. Although not a raging beauty, she was still reasonably good-looking & conservative. She had one child in her flat, & we met several times going out to restos in Paris. I would pick her up from the car park outside her flat & deposit her at the finish with a kiss & cuddle. She was a bit coy about her flat & the fact her mother would be there looking after the baby, so I never went to her flat. One time, she decided to invite me in & then she found out that her mother, on arrival at the car park, was still there & had not taken the baby as arranged by them beforehand. I could see Clara was disappointed as she confided in me in e-mails that she regretted not inviting me into her flat before because she really wanted to make love to me.

By this time, events were happening on other female fronts, and afterwards, I did not see Clara again, even though we stayed in contact for a while.

Stella Arlette whom I saw a few times, was more a friendship.

Michelle & "son" **Sharif** stayed a few nights in my flat, & we spent some days visiting the Paris area. She came from Los Angeles & claimed some things that did not add up. The "son" Sharif did not seem young enough to be her son, more her partner or toyboy.

I was already seeing Monica at the time, not sure whether it would be serious, so I kept my options open. We reckoned he was with her toy boyfriend because they did not act like mother & son.

Michelle claimed to be an actress in Los Angeles, showing me photos of her in a stretch limousine, but her false eyelashes were enormous, her bum was best described as a "bubble butt" & boobs like coconuts. She stayed with her "son", whom I suspected was her toy boy, so we had sex when he went to sleep & then she would creep back to him in my spare bedroom.

Another woman, **Johanne Leaird,** a white American I met online & met physically in Paris, was blind & a superwoman. Formally an air hostess, she had to resign due to some malady that was making her body gradually disintegrate, including a heart (with a pacemaker), liver problems & making her go blind. Taking a blind woman around was interesting, especially as we could talk about so many interesting things. She was a very keen bedmate. She was a wonderful woman coming from Hawaii & was prepared to pay for many things. She could determine just fuzzy shapes only, so I was surprised when she wanted me to take her to the "Crazy Horse" theatre to see a spectacular show.

She stayed in a nice hotel on the south Paris periphery off the peripherique for a week. During that week, we saw each other nearly every day. I found it odd to be in bed with a blind person, but she was wonderful, appreciative of both oral & normal sex. She liked all positions & was determined to maximise her visit & time with me & maybe life.

We stayed in contact for many years; she told me of her various trips, obviously paid for by her insurance money, including one time in Morocco when the heat got to her & her pacemaker. They had to air ambulance her back to the USA. The specialist told her off for trying to be normal & going to hot countries which were not compatible with her health. Communications were occasional until she "disappeared". I fear that her health eventually caught up with her. Shame, a tragic story of a really nice woman who suddenly, in her prime, was struck down with some unknown malady that destroyed her health, which is why she was determined to enjoy what life she had left.

I met many women online, mostly from America, & we for years became "pen-friends" by online chat. Sometimes, I would chat with three women at a time.

One woman, **Joan Mousa,** from Nappa Valley, California, became so hot & steamy with our online chat that one day I was able to make her cum (she said, "Oh, I have wet my chair"), just by my steamy chat, perhaps I should have been a writer?

Many would be just online chat friends & recently, some 20 years later, in 2023, one American lady, **Joan Meechee Williams,** from New Jersey, said I helped her see the direction that helped her life. I missed an opportunity to meet her in 2019 in New York when **Rachael** did not want to be diverted from our programme in New York, & again, Joan made an unexpected lighting across the English channel from France to London visit in 2022 while I was elsewhere. Maybe in 2025, we will eventually meet. Two other regular American pen friends stated I had helped them with their lives in difficult times.

Catherine Scott, who I called cowgirl from **mid-west** USA, **Viv,** who had a side business of making perfumes, **Susan** in central USA, all were interesting in their own way with diverse interests & careers. **Peggy Alber,** who got married & liked cruise holidays.

I was up late each night, having up to 3 chats (instant messages) at the same time. I got close to one lady, Kay, in Alabama; she was a school teacher and owner of two schools. Due to her divorced husband, Ruel, extracting money from the school company, she had immense problems paying for basic bills like electricity without going bankrupt. I transferred $2,000 to cover the outstanding bills to keep her afloat. I went over to spend a Christmas with Kay in Huntsville, Alabama, met the family & made a visit to Charlottesville. While there, I repaired many things, & we cleared out what was an office, moving things into the attic. After some hard work, she now had an office again. Her house was quite big, with an open lawn all around with 4 bedrooms. As of 2025 she still lives there.

Kay, whom I have called my **"Rainbow".** We started communicating a lot in the year 2000. We became very close, so she came to stay with me in my Longjumeau flat. Being American, she said when she arrived, "Where is the bathroom?" So I directed her down the corridor to the bathroom. She returned rather puzzled & said, "Eeerm, where is the toilet?" "Ah", I said, "it is here", showing her the door to the loo by the entrance, where I was standing. The saying is indeed true: America & Britain are separated by only one thing….language!

Within the two weeks we were together, we went over to England via the Cherbourg- Portsmouth ferry overnight & that gave us to dance together & win a Toblerone prize for best dancing. A visit to the north of England & then London where over the full day we saw most of the sights on walking. I forgot to realise that Kay was not used to walking (except from the car to the shopping mall & back) and that she was completely knackered. I started looking for a pub, but the area of the mainly offices was, by this time, dead, & as we rounded St Paul Cathedral, we found a pub to eat, & I realised she was close to tears as her legs were aching so much. I wanted to show her around as much as possible & give Kay a day to remember, and I succeeded!

I got close to Kay in Alabama. She was a school teacher and owner of two schools. Due to her divorced husband Ruel extracting money from the school company, she had immense financial problems paying for basic bills like electricity without going bankrupt. I transferred £2,000 to cover the outstanding bills to keep her afloat.

I went over to spend the 2001 Christmas with Kay in Huntsville, Alabama, met the family & made a visit to Charlottesville. While there in Huntsville, I repaired many things, & we cleared out what was an office, moving things into the attic. After some hard work, she now had an office again. Her house was quite big, with an open lawn all around.

Having got close in 2000 & 2001 with Kay, I was in constant contact remotely, but further visits seemed far away. I had a job as an ICP product manager. I loved my job-based in Paris & investigated a move to the New Jersey office, but I could not anticipate getting a similar job in the USA. The alternative for Kay was to move to France. This would have been especially difficult due to being the owner of two Montessori nursery schools. Kay suggested she sell the schools & come over to France to live & get a job. I mentioned the problems of getting a job if one is not able to speak French. My job was an exception because more than 80-90% of Jobin Yvon spoke English, & all whom I needed to speak in detail could. Much of my work was conversing & writing to people around the work where English was the lingua franca.

By 2002-2003, the problems of living so far apart from Kay were being shown up by never-ending school teaching & financial problems. There seemed to be no end to her problems to try to sort out. Meanwhile, I was keeping my options open by seeing Monica a lot; she was living in Melun, 70km SE of Paris.

Any plans for Kay to live in France seemed impossible due to Kay having no knowledge of the French language & to get a job in France without French or specialist knowledge would be extremely difficult. In addition, of course, she also had the schools to run & closing those would be problematic as she WAS the schools. These schools were a millstone around her neck due to the amount of work involved & the work required to improve pupil numbers to make them financially viable. Some 20+ years later, there are still plans to finally sell the last school in 2020 & 2023. Kay is finally deciding to retire & sell the last school. In 2025, Kay is still trying to sort out the enormous amount of kids' furniture & paperwork.

It was a difficult decision, but I wanted Kay more than Monica (chapter 3). I loved Kay so much that I did not want Kay to be unhappy, regretting a traumatic move to a country where she could not speak the language & could not get a job, plus, she had the schools back in Huntsville. I had a deep love for Kay, & because of that love, I did not want her to be unhappy, making such a dramatic change in life & finding so many problems to make her unhappy. I felt it would always just be beyond the horizon (rainbow) & never get closer.

I had to send a regrettable letter to my "rainbow" to say that I had chosen Monica rather than her. In subsequent comms over the years, she has never agreed & said it could have worked. I still stick to my conviction because without spoken French the chances of a job are minimal. Being able to start a school in France with all it's incredibly difficult bureaucracy & of course, who could fund the enterprise if the schools back in Huntsville are barely making a profit & cannot be sold?

I was an exception due to Jobin Yvon being a company mainly exporting ICP-AES. They could not find anyone in France, hence why they searched throughout Europe, I was the most qualified & experienced.

3 rue Leontine Sohier
Longjumeau 91160
France
Tel: (33)-1-69-34-33-63
Mobile: (33)-6-85-57-21-79

Dear Jane

Dear Kay (my Rainbow)

    As you have summised, things have progressed with me & Monica, since we last met. I asked her to marry me on bended knee on the balcony one night & we bought the engagement ring the next day.

    It is difficult for me to write this letter, as I am sure it will be even more difficult for you to read it. You are a wonderful person & I would still have been a happy person if things had gone differently & it were you that I had asked. As Peggy said of her Stuart, she does not regret one single moment they were together & cherishes the times, but life goes on & now she has found someone new (a Jeff would you believe it) to whom she is very happy. She is hopeful of coming to Paris sometime next year & she would be a welcome visitor. I hope you don't regret a single moment we were together, we had fun & I wanted to show you so much of England that I think I have made you shorter still with all the walking & traveling. Each day was action packed to ensure I did fulfill your dreams. I want to be your friend for life & Monica is happy with that arrangement, as you & I now move into a new different relationship of eternal friends (I hope).

    As I mentioned to you & all my female friends, I was keeping my options open & since we first met you were always my no: 1. Monica knew this when we first met & she knew as you did, I was seeing other women to see what was available & a comparison with the women I knew. The same was true for you & for Monica as I encouraged her to start a Love at AOL site (maybe it is still there....
"Sophisticated lady in Paris"). I saw Monica from time to time & tried to help her with any problems she had in her traumatic period when she first arrived in France. In fact due to the Xmas we spent together in Alabama, Monica decided that as there was no prospects of her & me together, so she said to her old ex-boy-friend in Cote d'Ivoire that she would marry him if he wanted her still. That meant complications when he came to Europe from time to time, but my aims were always clear at the time that "somehow" we (you & I) would work out how you,

my No: 1 & I would get together for life. As I said so often if you cannot speak French it is nearly impossible to get a job (a bit easier if you are from a EU country). That was why there were always sound reasons why you would not have been able to come to France on a permanent basis. I had plans to come to USA for a post in JY at Edison, the chances were always going to be dependent on many factors, some outside my control. Monica constantly said, ".... you love Kay & I have to make plans with that in mind, I want you, but your heart is elsewhere....". At the time it was true.

When you & I were first in contact with each other we immediately got on well with each other, so that I believe neither of us had any worries about our first physical meeting when you came over to Paris back in July 2000. We then departed for England to attend the BNAAS conference in Sheffield. I wanted to show you as much as possible of the "green & pleasant land of England", the countryside, the people, the history, the Roman cities, the pubs & its beer & pub meals etc. I hope you have a different perspective of England & why it was the mother country to America.

The long gap of 9 months with the cancelled holiday was a killer. I said to Caz I was not sure you would come & when you said at last you had bought your ticket, I really got excited that at last it would be on. As with you, I was soooo disappointed & that holiday although Caz & I had a good time I felt... flat. I think maybe a period before & certainly after there was a distinct lack on e-mails, so much so I analysed the number of contacts & the type (I am a scientist) over 5 months & decided you were less interested in me (maybe someone else) as well as worried about the whole chapter 11 mess you were in. I tried to help in advice & money as much as I could & hopefully it helped the darkest days when telephones were going to be cut off & house re-possessed. The two schools are still a problem for you, I so hope you are able to sell them off to finally get that burden off your shoulders. Starting the new job as head teacher at the new school will at least give you money to stave off the "wolves" until they are finally sold. Remember, I said it would be at least 4 months before you are able to sell them?

Only when you are financially more sound & it will not cause you headaches to pay back the money, should you send me back the money I loaned you.

At Xmas 2001/2, I wanted to give you a good time & show you London & see what the position was with us. I was determined you would see London, hence the reason I pushed you so hard that day to see all the sights, would you have missed all the extra sights we crammed in that day? I am sure as long as you live, you will never forget that day, both the experiences & the sights, we probably walked 5 miles that day,....not 20 miles you were convinced. Remember we stopped many times to see the sights & investigate. The 9 month gap & the apparent indifference by lack of communications had taken off the edge, the relationship with Monica was getting closer & now you were only marginally ahead of the race.

In January I saw in Edison more than I had seen before, it started to pose extra questions, I also started to think of Monica at home more than Kay in Huntsville. It was then I realized that maybe the balance was changing & that maybe Monica was now No 1. As time went by it was tru, so that when you asked me a question at the restaurant in New Orleans , "am I still your No 1, I had to be truthful "no", You said during the weekend in Lafayette that for the first time you saw me without an agenda & was just able to meander around without rushing. This was true, because each time you came to Europe I wanted to show you the maximum of the place & surroundings, whether Paris or England. I hope now I have got you used to having holidays & that you continue to have them, whether it is with Kathy & family or with someone else in some other part of the world. Enjoy life, remember you have one, so don't waste time. Remember you can gain an extra 1.5 hours sleep per day for yourself by reducing the "laboratory" to an absolute minimum & taking 5 minutes....... now there's a target for you!

I have in the past been one of your best friends, I hope I can stay one, that means you can still ask me for advice, remember I "bounce ideas" off several people, to see whether the initial advice was sound, you must do the same, I hope I am one of those you bounce ideas off.

Remember: a problem shared is a problem halved.... Absolutely true..... even if the person cannot help you.

You have in the past kept problems to yourself & not shared them (Oh....I did not want to bother them with my problems, they may tire of me...."). I now know that period of time with little communications was such a situation.

I hope I do not just remain a distant memory, buy that you involve me as a friend & keep me updated with the family & your schools & life etc. Now that you are getting freer of financial problems you maybe able to get pout with some man, friends again, You manty find a man of your dreams & be able o marry him. I will keep you updated with my life (if you want me to) I have always tried to be open with you all about my situation of being single & looking around, making comparisons & seeing whether I could spend thee rest of my life with that woman, only two fitted that bill, you & Monica were the only ones that passed all the tests.

We talked much that last weekend together & I hope this personal letter to you conveys some of my feelings as you once said that Sergio your former Italian boy friend has changed to a dear friend. I hope I will always be your dear friend & that we could meet anytime be it in USA or here in Longjumeau. You asked me the other day when I Monica & I are to get married, it will be in February here in Longjumeau (at the time of writing 15th or 22nd) & you are of course invited.

I hope you sure able to recover your life after all these upheavals this last 18 months & make sure you enjoy life e.g. have regular holidays & enjoy Kathy & your grand children (Bo's as well). I hope by re-introducing you to Kathy & making you appreciate her feelings you are happier & more complete person. I have decided on the love for the rest of my life (I hope) & I hope you are able you also find your love. Look after your body & it will look after you remember in times of stress....do exercise & lose yourself in the activity (you cannot worry if you are knackered & cannot think of anything else than the schedule..... This is the most effective way to reduce stress.

A bientot

Love, a big hug & many kisses

Geoff your teddybear   oxoxoxoxoxo

C:\Geoff Kay-Alabama Dear Jane- Kay letter.doc

Chapter 3

Meeting with Monica in southern France on holiday

First meeting with Monica

One internet female contact was from Cote d'Ivoire, and via communications, I found she was Rwandese named Monica. Monica was living in Cote d'Ivoire (Ivory Coast). In communications summer of 2001, she mentioned she & her son, Lennon, would be staying with friends near Montpelier, south of France. She said she was staying with a Rwandese friend, Jeanne & Jean-Marc.' This was at the same time as I would be camping on holiday near Montpelier on the western side with my youngest daughter Dawn, 16 years old, over from England for a 2-week holiday. We decided to meet, and I said it would be easier to meet her where she was staying in the small village Gallargues le Montueux on the eastern side of Montpellier, than in a city like Montpellier. With the address, map (no GPS in those days) and a one-hour drive, we found the village & the house fairly easily. I met Monica for the first time & went out for the day on a beach not far away.

Later, when we returned to Jeanne & Jean-Marc's house, we were invited for dinner. They all suggested we stay over-night at their house. After consultation with Dawn, we accepted & stayed the night at Jeanne & Jean-Marc's house. Jean-Marc had a consultancy job dealing in African affairs & Jeanne owned an African goods gift shop in Aigues Mortes, a picturesque small, completely enclosed walled tourist town not far away. Both Jean-Marc & Jeanne were very nice. Jean-Marc was white French, & Jeanne was a long Rwandan friend of Monica's from their early life in Kigali, the capital of Rwanda.

Jeanne & Jean-Marc's house was new, barely 5 years old, with 4 bedrooms. Dawn slept in a bedroom, and I slept on a couch on a semi-circle landing. In the morning, when I saw Monica, I was surprised that Monica said to me, "Why didn't you come into my bedroom after all had gone to bed?" I said that I have never forced myself on any woman & to do that without an invitation was difficult for me. She said, "you are so English, OK, please come to my bedroom tonight....I assume you will stay another night!" What an invitation; how could I refuse?

Another enjoyable day on the beach & swimming with Monica, her son Lennon and Dawn. I should add that by this time, I had the opportunity to go to the pharmacy to buy some condoms to be prepared for a sexual night. With a condom purchased discretely, what followed was an energetic night-time activity that certainly relieved any sexual frustrations I may have had. Monica could speak English, even if she sometimes made mistakes or was lost for certain words. This helped with a wide variety of conversations. Monica knew how to please a man firstly, a blow job until the pleasure would be close to climax & then gently grabbing hold of my penis & inserting it into her vagina. I barely had time to put the condom on & up my penis, "James" went. We cuddled naked in bed for a while until I crept back to my bed on the landing.

How can I describe Monica? Well, she was (at the time) a bit over weight, good looking & had enormous boobs, more like melons, maybe JJ cup. I was able to kiss her nipples from behind her by lifting up her boobs towards me. I do love large boobs, but these were not just coconuts; they were like melons! They floated by her head when she swam in the sea like floatation collars!

She had an insatiable sexual urge, which suited me fine at the time. Come what may, Monica was "hot" & enjoyed all positions & types of sex. Quite an exhausting time was spent at night time & then, while exhausted, I needed to creep back to my bed on the landing.

We got on well. The four of us, Dawn & Lennon, were of similar age. Monica got on well with Dawn, and so did Dawn with her – that was crucial. Dawn & I returned to the campsite after a few days. Dawn was happy to spend a further couple of days at Jean-Marc & Jeanne's house, allowing Monica & me to get better acquainted. "Skinny dipping" one dark night in the sea is fun & exhilarating, but have you ever tried to put on a condom in the sea? Believe me; it is difficult and, of course, fun trying & succeeding. Sex on the beach is also problematic due to the sand getting on everything & potentially abrasive if in the wrong place during "activity"….ouch! Not inhibited by anything at this stage, Dawn took some photos of us naked on the beach, one with her melons supported by my hands, note, BOTH hands!

With condoms, I was able to safely investigate much more of Monica's pussy & found a puzzle that I would only find out sometime later. I have never had difficulty finding & playing with the female clitoris to excite them to the point of exhilaration, but could I find Monica's clitoris at all? No! I found out later it was FGM (Female Genital Mutilation) when she was a young girl in Rwanda, where it is common for most girls in Rwanda & much of Africa.

More visits to the local area, including Arles, a small but immaculately preserved Roman amphitheatre that they still use for local events. Nimes amphitheatre* was magnificent, I could have stayed longer, but Monica & Dawn, although interested, did not have the same enthusiasm to stay hours & hours.

* Many years later, in 2013, I stayed in Nimes for the French national Masters' athletic championships & spent four hours on my own in Nimes amphitheatre. It was more interesting & better described than the Colosseum in Rome, which in many respects is disappointing with poor information available on the walls.

After the second period of two days, Dawn wanted to get back to the camp site & be alone, just the two of us, so we departed & exchanged all details. It never crossed my mind we would meet again, & certainly not so soon after.

Meeting Monica in Paris

Returning home to my flat in Longjumeau after the holiday, I thought I would not see Monica again since she lived in Cote d'Ivoire. Suddenly, several months later, in September, I got a phone call saying she was in Paris & asked if I could pick her up from the CdG (Charles de Gaule) airport. It was already late at night, so I agreed and, eventually, met her at 4 am on my birthday at a nearby IBIS hotel. I went to the hotel & no one had any idea where she could be; there was no political asylum area as Monica had claimed. Suddenly, after some considerable time of an hour or so, she appeared at the bus station opposite after numerous phone communications. Hours later, she said they had been processing her as a Rwandan refugee in a special quarter of the hotel & let her go from this area. She said that her visa for the UK was still valid but expired in France, so at the Paris stop, she gave her passport to another Rwandese on the plane & then, on landing, got off & claimed refugee status. Although bizarre I accepted the explanation.

I was to find out some years later that the story was a lie. She had arrived some 2 days previously, taken Lennon down to Montpelier by TGV to her friend Jeanne & then returned to Paris to meet me in CdG. The delay was getting transport to CdG at that time of the morning when there were no trains or buses. In reality, the drop-off in Paris was to allow her to go back to Montparnasse TGV station to pick Lennon up from Montpelier, return to Paris & stay in the allocated hotel.

We went back to my flat south of Paris to sleep what remained of the night. We were both too tired for sex, but snuggling up against her was nice before sleep took over me. However, when both of us were refreshed, sexual desire from us both ensured a fun morning. However, I had no difficulty with finding & cuddling her "melons".

She spent 2 days at my Longjumeau flat before she said she needed to be dropped off in St Michel, Paris, so she could go to the hotel allocated to her without the authorities knowing she had spent the weekend with me in Longjumeau.

Within the next 3 months, Monica & Lennon were moved from one poor hotel to another. The second one had a well-worn, bare wooden floor with a toilet at the end of the corridor. These hotels would have a communal toilet at the end of the corridor & well-worn wooden floors that needed shoes to walk; otherwise, you would have splinters in your feet. Paris, at this time, had a terrible reputation for fires in these poor hotels with refugees put in them & suffered a number of deadly fires. Eventually, the third hotel was in Clichy near the peripherique.

Monica, she was VERY patient, and it was her patience that I admired & left me in a state of confidence in her morals & good, true intentions. Other African women I saw were quickly after money within the first or second date. One could see so easily the difference between American women, who immediately would offer the share the cost. While African women, it seemed the thought never crossed their minds & wanted money. Once Monica asked for € 200 money to tie her over, she promised to pay me back, & she did. This was unusual for African women, I fell into her spell of confidence & honesty. We are not talking of weeks or months but years of honesty. She would invite all her Rwandan friends for dinner, lunch or stay over for the night or two.

After one failed marriage, I was determined to be very careful about who I would marry. The woman would need to be much younger than me to ensure they were as energetic as me. In the early years, like all men, I needed sex, beauty, intelligence, the capability to converse on any subject, be sporty, like going out. I found little of that with the other women I met, although I did meet a number of women at dances with singles clubs in England & eventually, when I moved to France, the internet AOL@love.

When I met Monica, she stayed with me in Longjumeau. On Thursday nights, I would visit her hotel, and then we would go out somewhere in Paris. Parking in those days was not a problem in Paris. You could park anywhere without police worrying, so even though all parking spaces were full, one just parked on corners anywhere now they have posts stopping this practice.

Clichy, near the peripherique where the 3rd hotel was situated, was close to a prostitute touting area. On my way home, I once stopped at the traffic lights only for a "woman" to get into the car! "Qu'est ce que vous voulez?" "Nothing! Get out!" as I pushed "her" out of the car before speeding away from the green lights. Close call that, especially as I had a flashback on her looks & realised "she" was probably a "he" in drag!

Monica was getting a government refugee allowance, but Monica always paid up any money I lent her. It was refreshing to see her honesty & that helped me trust her more & more. We went to CdG several weeks after she arrived to pick up her luggage sent separately. She needed something in the luggage, opened it up in the dark & then closed it again. She did not seem too stressed when she said all her jewellery was missing. Several days later, I eventually found a small cloth bag in the boot of my car with all her gold items worth many thousands of Euros. She was so pleased to receive them & wanted me to look after them as it was safer with me than in the small hotel.

Weekends were spent going out & meeting other Rwandese who had arrived before her. They had been allocated different flats around the metropolitan Paris area, called in French "Isle de France".

We would see other Rwandese at the monthly Rwanda "Tontine" meetings as well as visit various friends. Monica managed to learn that due to back problems, she could get a breast reduction on the French social, so she was admitted into a hospital near St Ouen by the Peripherique & came out with much smaller boobs. The "melons" size JJ were gone! Now, she only needed a "C" cup+ that fitted nicely in a man's two hands! From now on, Monica would start losing weight & acquiring a slimmer figure that she was proud of.

No longer conscious of her over-weight & massive boobs, she started wearing sexy clothes that were very pleasing to the eye & yet not expensive. It now became apparent she would spend much time admiring herself in the mirror & making friends with different men she would meet.

Now, 9 months after arrival in France, Monica was transferred to Melun, a town about 70km southeast of Paris. The refugee centre was an old mansion based on large grounds with new male & female building blocks for the refugees.

One man she met was her dentist Pierre in Melun, who lived in a small flat that was VERY basic with very little there and only a small hotplate to cook on a wooden box — surprisingly, basic facilities for a dentist! I was introduced to him & met him several times, while Monica met him many more times, both professionally & as a friend. Over time, I suspected something extra but never had any real tangible evidence.

Now based in Melun, Monica became more part of the Rwandese refugee scene, with many based both within the centre & housed in the Melun area. Rwandese had these "Tontine" meetings once a month held at different friend's homes. For me, it was now normal to accompany Monica to her Rwandese friend's flats & was now a normal programme for the weekend & Thursday nights. I got to know many Rwandese & hear their stories of how they got out of Rwanda when the genocide started. Rwandese are special people, a close-knit community, especially in France & Belgium, with a common cause of a bad history of five rebellions over the previous 20 years. (Note 4)

Monthly Rwandan "Tontine" meetings

In these Rwanda monthly meetings, I was able to speak with a few of the group people who spoke English, even though I could sometimes get by in French. However, most of the group spoke in Kinyarwandan, so I was taught a few keywords like "yego" (yes) & "oya" (no), which is useful when asked whether you want a beer!

Over a period of years, Florence who was a meek older lady would always make the excellent samosa. She was excellent at making these, so much so that whenever we had a group or party at our place, Monica would invite her to make them before the party started, but she would never stay. I never did find out whether this was because she was shy, or whether Monica did not invite her.

I got to know some Rwandese women better as we visited their homes often. One was Claudine, who eventually moved to near Sainte Genevieve des Bois. While her husband, also a Rwandese, got a job, Claudine decided to start up a business importing hair from the USA to act as a supplier to hair & salon shops.

Many men in the group were former managers of various companies & governments, but all had to flee to save their lives with their families. I saw just the successful ones; up to a million never made it, slaughtered in the carnage that went on mainly in the first 100 days after the ex-president was assassinated (Note 4 Rwanda).

In these meetings, I would ask about various subjects & was given assuring noises about Monica's father. Rwandese are a close-knit community, especially when dealing with outsiders like me. Monica claimed her father had a big mansion & a freight business with four large articulated lorries. When I asked various Rwandese in the groups if they knew her father & business, the collective answer was "yes", and that he was a successful businessman. I would find out — maybe 10 years later — it was all lies. (Note 3)

Chapter 4
Historical stories & the truth

Life with an African woman

We would have monthly meetings with Rwandese, and they were all very friendly & welcomed me. Each "Tontine" meeting would rotate at each other's flat, and there was a kitty that all contributed € 50 each month. This would be for helping someone in the circle who needed help. Often, they would help their friends out. They would like all black Africans to refer to each other as "brother" or "sister".

When I returned home, I would find the flat was untidy, except when friends came & stayed. Monica would complain about the work required & explains that "…….When I was in Africa I had a servant to do this……"

She would tell me that her brothers were killed in the genocide. She said her husband & Lennon hid in a hole in the garden for some days before escaping across the border to Uganda at night.

Monica used to tell me that after her father left being a policeman, he started up a transport company & expanded it to have 4 large articulated trucks & a large house in which she did gardening as a hobby. During the genocide, she would tell me harrowing stories of their escape and that all her brothers were slaughtered. She told me that she & her husband dug a hole outside in the garden & hid in it with a cover made with earth on top. Then, they paid money to escape to Uganda & get a plane out of the country to Cote d'Ivoire.

Her mother was saved because her father chose another woman some years beforehand, and she was banished to a small village, where she was still living when Monica & I met. Monica claimed she was a mixture of Tutsi & Hutu & could never return to Rwanda. However, I was to learn she went back to Cote d'Ivoire & maybe Rwanda before our marriage to get false documents easily obtained when money passes hands.

She married a man in Rwanda who made her pregnant with Lennon. Although the story seems maybe otherwise (see Note 3), there seems to be no love lost when he died. He was a forest worker & died of meningitis while up country in Cote d'Ivoire. Apparently, from a Rwandese researcher contact living in Cote d'Ivoire, (Note 3) witnesses told him she wore a mini skirt & seemed happy, smiling most of the day during the funeral & the "wake". Afterwards she was dancing, including what I call the African "bum dancing". How can I explain without video "bum dancing?" Well, the typical large African bum is extended as far back as possible & swung from side to side, forward & backward, which, of course, pushes the breasts forwards. This dancing is quite erotic, especially if you can imagine many women dancing like this with the local African & local pop music being played with a special rhythm. (example on Utube https://www.youtube.com/watch?v=I6SkdEjnLRk)

Later, I would find out from a former Rwanda politician Faustin (Note 4), who did not know her before researching with his many contacts in Rwanda & Cote d'Ivoire. He researched for me in Kigali that the father was indeed a policeman, but then bought a small general stores shop in the capital, Kigali. Also, Monica was known as a known prostitute in Kigali, and her brothers disappeared BEFORE the war of 1994.

One person whom Monica called Uncle Stanley also arrived sometime in 2002-3 in CdG & was placed in a detention camp within the confines of CdG called ZAP 1, 2 or 3. Here, asylum seekers or dubious immigrants are held in new porta-cabins in a secure area until they are either accepted or sent back. I got to know Stanley quite well as he was moved around, and we constantly met him. I found out years later, with my research, that Stanley is not a direct relation. He is the relation of cousin Nick, who is the son of Monica's father with the 2nd wife.

Monica always had affection for Uncle Stanley. Looking at Lennon & Stanley side by side in a photo, one sees many similarities & knowing now that she would have sex with anyone to further her life, Stanley may have been more than just an uncle. Stanley was a former minister in Rwanda, so he had the power & money to have paid a man volunteer to marry Monica & claim he was the father?

Chapter 5

Monica moves in. Geoff gets dad to change will.

Eventually, after 2 years, Monica was given permission to stay indefinitely, and having decided life with Kay in France would not work for reasons given earlier, I decided to marry Monica.

Having money tied up in England as well as France with my Longjumeau flat & with Dad getting worse, in late 2002, I decided to get Dad to change his will from 100% me, to 20% each to Steven, Sophie & Dawn & leave me with 40%. This would be my present to my children to ensure they had money and could have the down payment for the house.

Previously, Sophie wanted money for a project, so I bought her out fairly early around 2005, increasing my holding to 60%

I planned to move back to England when I retire in late 2013. I decided, in 2012, to get two Chelmsford estate agents to estimate the value of the Great Baddow house, take the mean value and ask Steven & Dawn if they agreed to be bought out at that value. They both agreed in writing, and I transferred the money to their accounts. Steven bought his Stoke on Trent house outright & Dawn was to keep it in a UK account.

In 2013, however, her partner Al had other plans for her money & persuaded her to keep extracting money from the UK to Australia for his pet projects over a period of time, so in the end, there was only £5,000 left. The repercussions were that Dawn in 2021 was unable to get the type of house she needed. Mid-2021, however after considerable saving Dawn a single mum, at last, was able to buy a 2-bedroom house.

Monica & Lennon moved in with me in Longjumeau

Monica & Lennon moved into my flat, and we made plans to marry in March 2003. The wedding list included many Rwandese & an African friend called Andre, who also worked for ADB in Abidjan, Cote d'Ivoire.

One thing with Monica was she normally thought for a long term, so she looked for a job & was prepared to work for a forestry agency in Paris with training & possible job at the end for no salary for 3 months. However, in the end, they just used her & many others as a no-cost way of getting workers on false pretensions. While she learnt things, she was not happy about getting anything at the end except experience.

One day, Monica left her computer open with her e-mails visible & I saw the title "je t'aime" from a man called Andre. Intrigued, I read the e-mail, and he described his love for Monica & that when he had divorced his wife, he would come for her to marry. Looking at her reply, I realised a problem but decided to see what would transpire by monitoring any comms on her e-mail or phone.

During Monica's time in Cote d'Ivoire, she met a colleague, Emmanuel, who proposed to her & was engaged to marry when she suddenly decided to come to France. The ruse given to him was that she would create a French bank account with money he gave her, and they then would meet together again in France. I stayed in contact with him, & he sent me a letter, "Stitches in Time", via a mutual friend Bibianne of Monica & Emmanuel, when he heard of our marriage plans. It was a private & secret letter to me not to be shown to Monica, whereby he said Monica was given money to start up a joint account in France & that he would follow later. He then heard that she had intended to marry an Englishman. His letter outlined the promises & what Monica was like & warned me.

TO: Mr. Geoffrey TYLER
   26 Residence Berlioz
   3 Rue Leontine Sohier Longjumeau 91160
   France

FROM: Emmanuel SAMAH
   African Development Bank BPV 316
   Abidjan, Cote d'Ivoire

SUBJECT: "A Stitch in Time Saves Nine"

You should surely be surprised to receive this letter from me because we have never met. I have, however, deemed it expedient to drop you these few lines in order to put you on your guard within the context of whatever relationship you might be having with our common friend Monica xxxxxxxxx.

I first heard about you from Damien at the RUSHEMEZAS in Abidjan. The above-mentioned family had invited us to dinner and I was in the company of Monica. By then Monica and myself had agreed on the plan concerning her relocation to Paris. We were therefore looking for an address to which I was to airfreight her personal effects, as the circumstances under which she was travelling could not permit her to have a suitcase. Damien was very willing to come to our rescue by providing your address. That's how I was able to airfreight those things to you on 22 September 2000.

I have given you this background because Monica has been a girl friend of mine since 1995. The relationship did not progress much by then because I had a woman at home, with whom I was not very pleased. I was therefore on the verge of separating from her. Monica had to go to France because her chances of getting a permanent job with the ADB were quite slim. She was not also sure whether I really wanted her for marriage and therefore left for Paris in September 2000. This was of course with my blessing as I gave her all the support I could muster.

It was when I visited her in Paris in December 2001 that we formally decided to subsequently live together as husband and wife when she would have got her papers. At the same time I was supposed to sort out my life and get rid of any impediment on my side that could frustrate our plans. The lady that was with me at home left in October 2000, so that problem was solved. It was during that same visit in December that we decided to open a common account in Societe Generale in Paris (One of the statements of Account is hereby enclosed for reference). She said nothing about you apart from the fact that her luggage arrived intact and that you delivered it promptly. We decided that she would return to Abidjan after getting the refugee status and that Christian would be sent to a boarding school with the possibility of travelling to Abidjan every vacation. My own son, Junior, currently attending school in Abidjan would go to join Christian in Paris. The accommodation she would be provided upon obtaining her refugee status was to serve as a holiday resort for us any time we took time off to fly to Paris from Abidjan. This was our plan and I fell flat for it. Thus, as far as I was concerned, I had a wife-to-be in Paris for whom I had to cater at all cost. I started running two homes, i.e. Abidjan and Paris.

My December 2000 visit was full of bliss, with no suspicions at all. We did all the errands together and I had no reason to doubt anything.

I came again to Paris again in June 2001 after a mission to Spain. The stay passed off somehow smoothly. Things were however a little different when I paid another visit in 2 July. This was during my annual leave and I was to stay for a longer period. Maybe the length of the stay did the trick. I found her to be uneasy most of the times. She panicked each time she received a phone call, especially when we were in Brussels. She would complain that the line is not clear. (We had the enclosed photo in September 2000 in Brussels. The date behind it can confirm it). Things came to a head in Paris and for the first time, I accused her of living a double life. Your case finally came up and she confessed that you had proposed to her but that she refused because of our on-going relationship. According to her, your intention too was marriage and you had even brought your children to her so that she could meet with them and know them. I was shocked and to say the least, I had my misgivings. Notwithstanding, she has continued to reassure me about her faithfulness and her deep love for me. I am enclosing two of such missives for ease of reference.

I was on mission to Stockholm in December and passed through Paris where I spent three days. She even accompanied me to Brussels to pick up my flight. But we are now at the verge of separation because I cannot tell any longer when Monica is telling the truth. She has become paranoid and suspicious of my slightest gestures. She does not want me to call some of her compatriots at their Centre because they do not like her and could tell me evil things about her.

I have taken the pains to relate all this to you in order to put you on your guard, in case you want to have a more serious relationship with her. If she becomes more focused, sincere and less materialistic, then she can be a good woman to have in the home. The decision is yours but don't say that you were never warned. Don't be a victim like me. I am still leaking my wounds and counting my losses.

You can transmit all these details to her if you don't mind. I have no intention of remaining anonymous. These are my contact numbers and address:

Telephone: (Office)   (225) 20 20 42 41

(Home)   (225) 22 52 5090

(Cellular) (225) 05 04 90 52

(Fax)   (225) 20 20 49 59

E-mail   e.samah@afdb.org

NB

I am not even sure whether you will receive this letter because she had told me, during my last visit that you had left for the United States where you were going to assume other functions.

As the date indicates, I write this letter on April 8 but only decided to mail it on the 22nd when I was absolutely convinced that you should better know the person you might be with the now i.e. Monica. You do not deserve what I have.

He warned me of her devious planning schemes & the true story of their plans together. I ignored the warning & its undertones because I felt "all was fair in love & war".

Later, I also found from other sources, including Emmanuel in Cote d'Ivoire, that the secretary job she had in ADB (African Development Bank) based in Abidjan Cote d'Ivoire at the time was, in fact, a limited contract job. She worked for a manager, Charles. I was to meet him with his lover some years later in Paris. I could see the eye contact that was not just a manager secretary look, especially when the girlfriend went to the loo & we were just three together. Knowing now what Monica was like, I am convinced they had an affair, especially as he is also a person who obviously like female company other than his wife!

Jan 2003   Discovery of Monica in bed with Andre

A couple of weeks before the wedding, Monica advised me not to go training because it was cold & said I was tired. Then the phone rang. She took a phone call from someone & immediately disappeared into the bedroom, rather than just speak where she was in the lounge near me. I followed, eavesdropped & heard a few things about meeting at some time to be arranged. Coupled with this knowledge, I decided to leave my notepad with secretly marked pages & hard pencil by my bedside next to the phone. All was ready for Monica to make notes when the follow-up phone call was made. Sure enough, some days later, the phone call was made & I could tell a page was missing. With a soft pencil, I was able to do some rubbings to reveal Monica's message. "Andre Mercredi (Wednesday) IBIS hotel Bercy (Paris) après midi (afternoon) salle (room) 606."

Monica mentioned that on Tuesday night, she would be late next day as she was going to a meeting with female friends at the flat & then meet other female friends outside to discuss last-minute things for the wedding 3 days hence. I worked at the office in Longjumeau, with the meeting continually on my mind. I did not know the time of the intended meeting with Andre, so I phoned Monica at the flat every 30 minutes in the afternoon with some excuse or other about wedding plans. Eventually, at about 3 pm, she was just about to leave. The time of action had arrived. I estimated she would need about an hour to get to the hotel by getting the bus, train & metro to arrive at Bercy Village. I decided that I would take less time than Monica, but I needed to park the car & find a car parking near the hotel.

I left work early & found the hotel ahead of schedule, parked & surveyed the large foyer. I sat down on one of the comfortable seats & then waited while reading one of the large newspapers in one of those metal things that prevents the newspaper disappearing and keeping an eye open for Monica to pass by the large glass windows. I also looked out for someone who would be waiting for her to arrive. Eventually, Monica walked past the window before entering the foyer. I kept the newspaper high & peered out to see who she was with. Monica smiled, embraced & kissed Andre on the lips, and immediately, they went around the corner to the lift to his room. I wanted to catch them in the act of an affair, so I went back to the car to rest & waited long enough for some action between them. I waited about 30 minutes & then went back to the hotel to go into the lift & found it needed a room key to activate the lift. After a quick survey, I realised the stairs were also blocked needing a hotel room key, so I sat on the side of the entrance to the lift, waiting for an opportunity. A well-dressed hotel staff man walked past me, but luckily, I was always dressed in a shirt & tie with a jacket, so no particular notice was made of me reading. After some 10 minutes, I saw my opportunity. A group of Japanese tourists made their way to the lift, I walked & then ran across 15 meters to just get in the lift just before it closed shut. Fumbling with my imaginary room key, one of them put theirs in & I pressed the 6th floor.

Now, I was on the 6th floor & looking for room 606. I listened outside the room & did not hear anything. Should I knock on the door now or wait longer? A cleaner comes down the corridor, so I walked on & when she has gone, I returned. I knocked on the door of 606 & Andre opens the door with a towel around his waist. I burst in, walking past Andre, whose towel drops onto the floor & walking further into the bedroom, I find Monica lying naked on the bed with her legs bent slightly on her side & her boobs hanging over one side.

"Geoff, what are you doing here? "she exclaimed, " I could ask the same," I said. "We haven't done anything", I move to the bedside cabinet & pick up a heap of wet tissues & put them to my nose. "Oh, really, that looks like a heap of wet, sticky tissues that ….(sniff) smell of sex fluids ".I said.

Monica tried to find something to cover herself & tried to pull the bed sheet over her, but because she was on it, she was failing to cover herself. "Why are you trying to cover yourself? Both of us have shagged you and we know every inch of your body. You might as well stay naked so we can both admire your body." I turned to him, "Don't you agree, Andre?" Andre starts to realise that I am not going to put him in the hospital.

"Errrr, yes," he responded, not wanting to disagree with me. "I forgot to introduce myself. I am Geoff, you must be Andre". I reached out my hand, and he shook it with a look of relief. I sat down on the bed next to Monica, who was still looking for something to cover herself. "You know, I love looking at your body, so please stay like that, Andre & I want to see you like this," as I caressed her leg & tummy.

Now that the atmosphere was more relaxed, Monica sat up as I continued caressing her leg & lifting her boob nearest to me. Andre eventually said, "We only planned to meet after so long & we eerrr got carried away. Before we could think, we started taking each other's clothes off." "Oh," I said, "what do you plan now? You know we are supposed to be married Saturday. You were invited to come to see me & Monica for the marriage, not shag her". "I think I can say for Andre, we did not plan this & we will never do it again," said Monica. "Ok, but can I trust you again? Can I trust Andre or any other man you may meet? I love you & now I am in a quandary as to what to do. Do I cancel the marriage or carry on?"

Taking my hand from her ample breast, she looked into my eyes lovingly & placed my hand near her crutch, "This is yours. I want you," & with her other hand, she started stroking my swollen penis. "& this … it looks as if he is excited. Do I excite you?" I started melting as she started undoing my belt, unzipping my trousers & holding my excited penis. She then caressed it before moving down to swallow it & giving me oral sex. She continued with ever more excitation until I ejaculated with a fountain of cum over her face & on my leg. I had succumbed to her charm. Meanwhile, Andre had started putting some clothes on after the "sex show" & while I was recovering from my efforts. Monica showed a face of satisfaction, still with cum dripping from her face & continued to caress my body.

"We will be Ok together. There will be no change to our wedding plans, promise?" she said, kissing the fast-shrinking penis. "OK….but I do not want you to have sex with Andre again, promise?" Monica looked at Andre & back to me & nodded. "We hadn't seen each other for a long time since we were in Cote d'Ivoire & meeting here in the hotel seemed the easiest meeting place, aaaand we just became, well, just, overcome with joy at seeing each other aaaand events just happened without planning."

I knew they had planned today for many weeks. I did not tell them I had been monitoring their communications for some months & increasing traffic in the last days & weeks for today's meeting. It was hard for me not to spill the beans. I needed to keep control of my methods, perhaps for the future!

I broke the silence it by asking Andre how was things in Abidjan & work he was doing in the forestry division. We continued talking for some while until Monica mentioned perhaps we should go home & at that, we left for Longjumeau. The journey home was uneventful, with small talk & not about what had happened in room 606.

What to do?

What do I do? Can I REALLY trust Monica not to meet Andre again & have sex? What about the promises she had made to Emmanuel to marry him & ignore the arrangement & the money in their joint account she had opened? Would there be other men? The wedding is so near, just days away, my family & friends have booked flights & hotels for the wedding, my brain is buzzing & completely fuddled. Should I cancel? Should I continue as if nothing has happened?

At work, I was thinking maybe I should cancel, but when I get home, Monica's charm is like I am completely under her control, like a puppet or an obedient dog looking for love & attention. Boy, did she lay on the charm & seduction during the days leading up to the wedding? Wearing the sexiest clothes when I got home, cuddles & affection & of course the most amazing sex you can imagine. She loved sucking "James" to show me her mouth with my cum oozing out & then sharing it with me as we kissed after (a rather salty taste), other times she knew I loved seeing her boobs swinging, so doggy sex in front of a mirror gave me sexual satisfaction of a good shag & seeing her boobs swing in rhythm & all this time she herself was in ecstasy, that I love to give women equal satisfaction.

Chapter 6
Getting marriage 2003

The previous months to the wedding date included Monica saying she needed to go to Cote d'Ivoire to visit friends. Later in my research in 2010, I found she returned to Rwanda to get some false documents. In France, we both needed various documents that amazed me. I needed the British Embassy to give me an official letter saying that in the UK, we did not have a document called or similar to "certificate de Coutume". Other documents needed were my passport and birth certificate with a date within 3 months of the required document. In the UK, a birth certificate is for life, with no updates, but in France, you can have as many copies as you like because they are only valid for 3 months to prove you are you & not somebody else. So, I have this 3rd document & when we go to the "hotel de ville"*, they want all three documents as well as the British Embassy document. What is the point of the 4th document then?

* A funny story in the newspaper & TV highlighted a difference in language & meaning. The "hotel de ville" or "Marie" is the town hall where the mayor & his administration work. In one French town, an English woman wanted desperately to go to the loo, so seeing a "hotel" near closing time, she asked for the loo. She had a toilet problem, so she took so much time, that when she had finished she found she was locked in & nobody around! She wrote in bad French message on paper & kept banging on the glass door when people walked past. Eventually, someone opened up to free her from her embarrassing situation. Incidentally, "Hotel de police" is the police station.

With a French wedding, the mayor marries you in a municipal building, usually with some grounds for photos. Longjumeau has the old Marie on the edge of the town centre with nice parklands. We had arranged our reception at the municipal "Salle Anne Frank", an entertainment centre. We had invited over 100 guests, including my family & friends from England & Longjumeau athletic club. Several of Monica's relatives and Rwandese friends came, including Andre. I found out later she had also invited a few people (men) she had only met recently.

Saturday, February 15th 2003

The freezing cold **Saturday, February 15th 2003,** wedding day arrived, and I had to have a translator to ensure I understood all that I was promising. The Mayor, with his tricolour sash who married us, was so astonished that an Englishman & Rwandese were getting married in his small town that he gave us a large glass vase in recognition.

In France, the mayor always marries couples and also it seems a French, or maybe an African "tradition" to be late. We went to one wedding of Emmaculet & Robert, Emmaculet a friend of Monica who was marrying Robert, a French butcher. All guests arrive on time, with the mayor ready with his tricolour sash. Robert, the bridegroom, turned up 30 minutes late, and Emmaculet, the bride, was 55 minutes late! The mayor did not seem overly perturbed & when Emmaculet arrived, we all went into the Mairie/town hall for the ceremony. I said to Monica & others that this could never happen in the UK. You are given a 30-minute slot & if you are late, you lose the slot & would need to re-book another time, maybe 6 weeks later!

Another observation I made over the years with African weddings was that no precise directions are given for getting to the reception. One wedding in the Paris periphery had a reception some 30km away along the A4 east of Paris, exiting off the A4 to a small village several kilometres away from the A4 junction & held in the village hall in the middle of "nowhere". We all had to follow the car in front with maybe 10 cars; it was easy to lose the car in front & as I found out later, only a couple of car drivers knew where to go. Why did the bridegroom or organiser not make a map with the address to give to the guests? In the days of the internet & at the time "Mappy", this was so easy to do. I encountered similar poor organisations many times as we went to many African weddings in the following years.

Our wedding photo shoot was held in the Mairie gardens under a winter's freezing blue sky, where many guests froze. When photos were finished, we were off to the reception (to the relief of the freezing guests) down at the municipal Salle Anne Frank hall. The hall was near the sports grounds in Longjumeau just down from my flat on Rue Leontine Sohier. We found the cost of € 400 reasonable, partly because living in Longjumeau gave us a preferential price. Monica had organised for a Rwandese dancing group for traditional Rwandese dancing. Everyone was well in the swing of the dancing, both watching & dancing themselves to the DJ playing a good selection of songs. Dawn & a few others, including Cloe & Pierre, served our provided drinks behind the bar. As one does, Monica & I circulated around the guests to make sure everyone was happy. At one point, I noticed that Monica went outside with Andre following her. I asked a friend to follow & see discretely what was happening. It seems that a conversation took place, plus a kiss, before returning to the celebrations. Andre was sad about losing the woman he wanted to marry; his marriage was finished & a divorce was imminent.

Monday 17th February

I arranged a honeymoon holiday in Rome with Monica's friends staying at our place to look after Lennon. In Rome, Monica had friends Justin & Agatha who lived in Rome. Justin was working for a UN agency based there, and he would normally work for about 3 years before moving around to another location of the same agency. His previous assignment was in Cote d'Ivoire, where Monica met them both in ADB Abidjan & his next assignment, several years later, was in Canada & still there in 2025. We spent time with them & looked around his office & had coffee on the tall building canteen roof space. The Canteen had chairs & tables & one could see a wonderful view of Rome. That evening, at their home, when asked where I would like to go on Saturday, Justin, by chance, mentioned Pompei first & without giving him a chance to suggest anything else, my immediate answer was Pompei. I said it was always a dream of mine to go there.

Pompei, what a place! So amazing to walk around buildings that were approximately 2000 years old to see the frescos, the ancient graffiti & shop signs. Justin & I walked around for 5 hours, marvelling at the road, buildings, amphitheatre, frescos, shop fronts artefacts & of course, the plaster casts of the entombed dying people, etc. Meanwhile, Monica & Agatha, bored with old buildings, just sat on a wall & chatted most of the time & were impatient to leave as they had no feeling for history & their surroundings. I cannot say Africans in general are not interested in history because Justin was African, but he was very educated, so maybe there lies the answer, maybe not just for Africans, but people in general, white or black.

We returned to our hotel, exhausted, but Monica was not happy. Justin & I had left her & Agatha alone for such a long period! I pleaded that Pompei had been my dream, so please don't be angry; while to start with, she was having none of that, gradually she succumbed to my advances & I was able to feel her body. Sex is a nice way to make up; doggy style following a mouth prelude was our favourite & all the effort makes one tired enough to sleep immediately.

The next day, we went around Rome and, of course, the Coliseum. I must admit I was a bit disappointed it was not as well preserved as Nimes amphitheatre, not giving much information; however, the sheer size & the brilliant design to be able to evacuate people quickly has been the inspiration of modern stadiums around the world.

I read an e-mail from Monica to Andre

18th March 2003   17;10 hrs

"Hi, Andre,

How are you? Are you in Tunisia or on a mission? I am in Benin, it's hot.

I am not well and maybe "health problems", or woman problems when they are waiting for a period ***

I hope things are Ok!

I miss my husband, he is going back to France.

Bis Monica

24th March 2003 02;39hrs

Andre, at last, replies

Hi Monica, thank you for your mail. I am sure you will be OK. I was getting worried, you know what I mean. Mais, it was a sweetest small small.

I spoke to your husband in Paris before I left. He was with Cloe and Jeanne, so when I spoke with him. I am on a mission in Gambia and off to Sierra Leone on Friday.

Enjoy yourself in Benin. I miss you

Love, Andre.

"Small, small" is Andre's words for a shag. He uses the term often when communicating with Monica.

Monica was obviously worried for a while that Andre had made her pregnant (Monica & I used a condom to avoid her being pregnant, so it could not be me).

When I questioned her some weeks later, so as not to arouse her suspicions I had seen the e-mails, she claimed that "Andre only put his penis between her legs for about 10 minutes, so I could play with it to make him cum & not up my pussy" for a shag. How pathetic was that explanation?

The e-mail clearly showed both were worried that she may be pregnant. Especially if she were to have a baby, it would have been totally black & not mixed race if from me.

Chapter 7
2003: Monica starts work

When we returned, Monica, now married with an English surname, started to look for a job. She visited many people she knew & was always willing to talk to people with only a casual meeting. She mentioned one day, she had gone to a government agency. On April 10th, Monica got an SMS to ask her to send her CV for a job. She was offered a job on April 29th in an office at a local chemical factory. She started work near Massy & went by bus from Longjumeau. Monica was happy working there & sometimes, if I planned to be in the area, I would arrange to pick her up from work. Her hours, while normally standard, would often be later due to working on something that would take more time. I got used to her late arrival due to being a conscientious worker. Having been distrustful of Andre, I checked her mobile phone periodically in case of problems & on 25th May, I saw ten SMS messages of no particular significance from 8 am to 7:20 pm to a person "Gris".

One night, we were chatting about various things as usual, including sex & desires, when she came out with a joke that she has sometimes dreamt of getting off with a manager for a job. In some dream, I said, "Sorry, I cannot offer you a job, you do not know anything about chemistry," ha, ha, we laughed. Again, later talking about colleagues, she said she gets on well with a male colleague from Wissous, about 5km away where the laboratory & some offices were also located.

I saw an e-mail from George-Taylor Lewis, a colleague & boss at ADB in Abidjan, Cote d'Ivoire. The tone of the e-mail was not of a boss & secretary but a more sexual relationship. One does not address a person working for you as "Cherie" & "bissous mon amour", interesting. ADB seemed a hotbed of sexual relationships & marriage promises!

One day in June 2003, I had an athletic meeting in Les Ulis, about 10km from Longjumeau & only about 5km from Massy. The meeting was cancelled due to rain, so I tried phoning Monica at about 6:50 pm so that I could pick her up if she were working late. However, there was no reply, so I drove off leaving a message & still on the way, I stopped again 10 minutes later & tried again on the way back. This time, Monica answered, "Oh, I read your message & was about to phone you". I offered to pick her up in 10-15 minutes, "OK, so pick me up at the Massy station". My estimation was way out & I arrived after only 5 minutes, so I rang again, "I am at the moment walking to the bus/train station at Massy-Palaiseau. I did not want to wait for you while you went to the office". Now as I have said, being a scientist, one becomes a good detective & when walking on a road, you hear traffic, birds, walking & breathing noises. However, her voice was not one of walking; also, I could hear background people's noise & her voice echoed as if she were indoors in a big hall. I was already parked & looked carefully for her at Massy station from the bridge that separated Massy from the Palaiseau side of the train station. Eventually, after some 10-15 minutes, I saw her arriving from the opposite direction from Massy TGV direction at 7:15-7:20pm. When I queried her about arriving from the opposite direction than normal, she brushed the inconsistency off saying that she had gone over the other far bridge at the other end of the platform. I said nothing else, but it was not logical to go so far out of your way to cross the lines & also, the echoing voice & lying that she was walking concerned me. She obviously had lied, so now the question was, why? What, or who was she lying for? I made later some notes that read:

1) She lied about walking (in which case, it would have taken her 5-10 minutes to meet me). Clearly, she was NOT in the office, but she was in a big interior enclosure or hall.

2) Why did she come from the far bridge to cross the railway lines? Monica did not like walking much.

3) She must have heard the 1st call but only replied when I phoned the 2nd time 10 minutes later. It takes 15 minutes from the office to Massy station, plus leaving time of, say, 5 minutes to clear up her work at the office. Monica arrived in 10-15 minutes after I arrived at 7:05 pm.

My notes stated there were two possible answers:

1) She was doing something in the office & did not want to be disturbed

2) Maybe we have another man.

She had already said a few weeks previous that she wanted to invite two colleagues home, including a lady (therefore, the other must be a man?). She constantly complained of carrying heavy walking shoes & yet one night, she was not wearing them and was wearing high-heeled shoes, so she must have had a lift in a car. Who from?

I started noticing an increasing frequency of Monica arriving home with her office high-heeled shoes on. Like the Andre affair, by lying, she had focussed my attention on her activities. Now, I would be investigating ANYTHING that did not seem logical or suspicious.

Another affaire - "Gris"

I decided to stake out her arrival firstly by phoning her at 6:30 pm & then wait by the bus stop at Longjumeau centre. No sign of her, so I returned home at about 7:15 pm to find her at the flat. I did not mention I was looking for her near the bus stop in Longjumeau, but I said I went to the supermarket for something. She made herself more comfortable by going into the bedroom to change her more formal office dress for another. Remembering I wanted to say something, I followed her a bit afterwards & happened to see as she was facing the mirror to put her other dress on, that she had no nickers (pants/culottes) on! Where were they? I disappeared quickly without her knowing & decided to quickly search her handbag. No, they were not there! Where were they? I waited while she started cooking to check her coat & VOILA, they were there! Mmmmmm, imagine my thoughts! I have a problem, and she is probably seeing another man & letting him at least finger her pussy or even more! Who is he? From now, I was in overdrive to investigate everything she did or said.

One day, I took her to the office early, and she remembered she had lost the code to get into the office on a piece of yellow "post-it" with also telephone number. She was just about to phone a person & then decided, as I was there next to her, that she would not make the phone call & pretended she did not have the phone number. Later that night, I checked her address book & the piece of paper was gone. I had started to look at her phone calls & noticed several calls from "Gris" ("grey" in French). I looked up her contact list & Gris was there. Who is Gris & where do they meet?

I needed to set traps to see what was happening, so I left her some clean nickers/culottes on the bed each night, as I knew she liked to go to bed with clean culottes on.

Wednesday, 18 June:

There was a leaving party in the office that night for a colleague, and Monica phoned Lennon to buy a pizza for himself. He did not have any money, so he came to the office after school to ask me to give him some money for his pizza. I had already arranged a RASP (**R**eal **A**le **S**ociety in **P**aris I had formed in JY) meeting with colleagues at our Paris local of the "Bombardier" pub near the Pantheon. I would be out Friday night until maybe after 9-10 pm because we usually found a nearby "resto" (slang for restaurant in French). Lennon mentioned that a big boss came that night and had a few beers while Lennon ate his pizza in the bedroom to be out of the way. Interesting, because I had tried to phone Monica on her mobile twice ~ 7:30 & 8:20 pm with no reply. I checked the waste bin & found 2 Leffe beer bottles. I did not buy Leffe, so they had brought the beer from somewhere back to the house. Mmmmmm, more intrigue. Monica started chatting in bed that night that the office party for a retiring person was getting boring, so "Paul", the boss, gave her a lift home, so she invited him into the house for a drink, & she was surprised when he accepted!

While normal in England & Australia, in France, it is not normal to meet outside work & especially your boss, nor for that matter Monica. It is also not normal to call your boss a top director whom you may meet occasionally in France by first name. My company HJY was an exception being a very international company depending mainly on exports, foreign contacts & English speaking people.

I asked a few pleasantries about what he did & what he looked like without arousing suspicion. She opened up & said Paul was a big boss in charge of the region for the chemical company & that he was about 55 years old with grey hair. Voila! We have "Gris" — he is Paul, & she is closer to Paul than she wanted to admit.

Saturday, 21 June 2003:

Monica & I went shopping in CORA, a big supermarket in Massy, when she got a phone call. She told me afterwards that the call was from a male acquaintance, who had invited her for a drink in his flat. She told him she was with her husband in CORA Massy & could not come, but maybe another time. My French was improving by listening & reading the various snippets of information. Why would an "acquaintance" give his mobile number to Monica & why Monica to him? What a load of bullshit, was I supposed to believe that?

Monday, 23 June:

After work, I went down the road to the local stadium & did some weight lifting in the weights gym. I was about halfway through my intended session when Lennon arrived & said that we had a guest at the flat & would I come home! We walked back together & he told me the big boss took Monica home & was at the flat & that Monica wanted me to meet him. When we enter the flat <u>Monica was sitting next to Paul</u> on the settee. She had her nice smart work dress on & high heels shoes still on. Monica introduced us to each other & I noticed the coffee table had 3 bottles of Leffe. We chatted in French about various subjects with each other & Monica looked on with a look of satisfaction that I got on well with Paul & he with me. I could sense a feeling of relief that her gamble of introducing me to Paul had paid off. She could feel safer to mention his name more often.

Sunday, 29th June:

Monica received a call that she did not answer when she saw the caller on her mobile phone screen while we were visiting Rwandese friends in Augin les Bains. Later, when we got home, I investigated Monica's mobile phone & saw 2 SMS messages from Gris (Paul).

12:09 "Je t'aime, que fait tu aujourd'hui" (I love you, what are you doing today).

12:53 "aussi je suis avec toi" (also, I am with you)

I also saw he phoned her at 21:06 when they chatted quickly for 53 seconds.

Monica nearly caught me with her phone & with suspicion, she took her phone. When I was able to inspect her phone again some 30 minutes later, the messages had been deleted!

Anyway, I had the evidence: Paul has fallen in love with Monica, has she fallen in love with him?

Tuesday, 1st July 2003:

I went training after work & returned home at 7.30. I tried phoning Monica & after 3 attempts in 10 minutes, she said she was at Carrefour (a big supermarket), however, I could hear outside noises, so I kept her talking so I could learn more about her situation & then heard a man's voice "poulet" (chicken). She said she was exchanging a bag. I asked, "Are you with Annie?" "No, I am with another person". Monica then said, "We" will arrive back soon & was obviously speaking from a car park. I decided I would check how she would get home & with whom. I went up the road to the T junction, which I believe would be a good drop-off position without being outside the flat. I took a position that would not be seen by the driver or passenger & waited. Eventually, I saw a Renault Espace & noted the registration number & the occupants. Paul was driving; he stopped & let out Monica to walk the last bit down the road. Monica used to walk slowly due to fibroids, so I was able to run another way back to the flat & beat her without her knowing I was out. She said to me when I returned that she had a lift to Carrefour & then got a lift back.

Top executives do not give lifts to a supermarket, go around with them & then drop them off at home! But, of course, Monica did not know I had investigated & seen her being dropped off by Paul. Monica gave no other information then or in the evening. I quizzed her about the bag that night & she became very defensive about why I was asking so many questions. At bedtime, I noticed she was not wearing nickers/culottes again. I got up in the night & looked for these missing nickers/culottes. I eventually found them in her handbag, they were by now stiff! Basically, her nickers/culottes could only have become stiff when she had an orgasm. So, with Paul, she had had an orgasm that night. Do they do it in the car or somewhere else? I remember back some months ago, she said she had fantasies that she was having an affair with a boss.

Now, I had increasing evidence of the extent of this real affair with Paul. First Andre, & now Paul. She always claimed she was not complicated. I had gradually noticed that she was becoming increasingly cool to me. Was this because of her love for Paul? I needed to know where they were "playing". Was Paul & Monica just having sex in the car? This was unlikely; they would need to be alone & that would be difficult, especially in daylight!

I was to find out, many years later, that Paul had a friend who gave him a key to his often vacant house not far from Massy.

What shall I do? I know Monica is having sex with Paul.

Seeing Monica that night, I took off her clothes slowly & removed my clothes, but even though I was excited at her body & her touch, James's erection was not full. When I inserted it, the customary full pressure was not there, & after 10 minutes, we gave up. I felt terrible about failure. I wanted a shag & yet it did not happen. Monica had a mixture of disappointment & pity on her face. Later, she suggested I try Viagra & that I would require me to go to the doctor for the prescription.

Chapter 8

Showdown on discovering affair with Paul

Wednesday, 2nd July 2003

I started fiddling with Monica's phone in the morning while she had a shower, with dramatic consequences. I had accidentally put her phone on divert to Paul due to my French not being that good to know what the function was.

I tried to phone Monica at lunchtime & was immediately put through to Paul's phone answerphone message: "Paul je suis indisponible, laissez votre message…".

Does Monica know she has put her phone directly through to his phone? In the evening after work, I took my colleague & Aussie colleague friend, Dick Palin, back to Paris & went to our favourite pub, the Bombardier, to have some real English ale. I tried phoning Monica & again got Paul's phone message.

When I got home, Monica immediately asked me whether I had tampered with her phone. I admitted to her I had. She explained the situation & the problem created. I said I had found out about her affair with Paul and that I had watched her from viewing at the traffic lights when she dropped off the day before. She tried to say she knew because she saw me outside the Marie (town hall near the flat). That's interesting, I thought, I was nowhere near the Marie. By keeping calm & cool while dissecting her lies, she eventually came clean and admitted that they were indeed having an affair & that she loved Paul

Paul loved her. "Is Paul married?" Monica replied, "Yes, but he is very unhappy with his marriage & is having a very difficult time due to his wife being close to a nervous breakdown & is causing mayhem in the house with damage to household things…..sometimes, he is worried about her state of mind & sometimes, for his health. He is suffering so much & needs to speak to someone,& I am good at that, as you know. I am good for him & his well-being."

I told her I loved her, but since November 2002, when I first saw some comms with Andre, I had been worried & the episodes with Andre in the hotel bedroom, the information Emmanuel gave me & now Paul were stressing me, so I could not sleep properly. She looked at me with some pity & then cuddled me & kissed me, said she loved me & she loved Paul. "I love you both," she said. "I want to make you both happy," with her hand stroking my leg "you must believe me, don't you?" smiling at me, her hand moved as she gradually caressed my crutch. I was melting once again! I looked into her eyes & started to put my hand down her dress & under her bra. She started to undo my belt & then unzipped my trousers to feel my penis, James. I was spellbound & unzipped her dress, undid her bra to feel her lovely breasts. She bent down & took down my trousers & pants & immediately started sucking my penis. "Let's go to bed". We moved into the bedroom while she shed her clothes on the way & had wonderful sex doggy style. With us facing the mirror, I could see her boobs swinging back & forth with the rhythm of my pelvic thrusts. I could see in the mirror her face of satisfaction; she was winning.

I would have to accept her indiscretions — that was my destiny. After the effort & laying back on the bed, we snuggled. She smiled again lovingly & placed my hand on her breast & softly said, "You love me, don't you?" "Yes, of course", "Please, I need Paul as well. Can you accept that? I love you & Paul. I need you to understand & love me". I was so meek & helpless, so many things flashed through my head and nothing made sense except so slowly. I nodded my head in acceptance, which resulted in a wonderful smile & hug kissing me all over "Oh, I so love you for your strength & acceptance, thank you, Geoff".

Thursday, 3rd July:

Monica woke up & caressed me with one of those wonderful smiles. We chatted in bed. "You know you need not be threatened by Paul, he is very gentle & nice. He gave me my job, so you should be very happy to know him." I said I was happy that Paul was "Gris" & that she was focused on him to forward her career as she "played him," & maybe also good for me as well in understanding you more. "I think you need to be open with me & that we three should meet to chat over the situation". The need to get up for work curtailed our conversation. All day at work, I was mulling over what we spoke about the previous day & this morning. Sport is my release, so I decided to do a hard weights session to help me get rid of any stress. I worked hard at the weights & returned home knackered but stress-free. The evening went uneventfully, other than a lot of loving by Monica towards me & another good shagging session before sleep.

Friday, 4th July

We both went to work that morning. In the late afternoon, Monica phoned me & said that she was with Paul in a bar. She was fulfilling my wish to be more open with me. After some 15 minutes, she phoned me again & said Paul agreed with my suggestion to meet. They were in the corner bar in the middle of Longjumeau. I agreed & immediately tidied up my desk & left for the Place de Steber, a marketplace on Saturday & Wednesday mornings, but a car park any other time. I entered the bar & saw Monica & Paul at a table in the corner. I approached & both stood up & Monica introduced me to Paul & him to me. I asked whether they wanted another drink, and I could see Paul relax a bit by saying, "oui, une Leffe, s'il vous plait." Monica asked for a brandy & a few minutes later, I returned with the three drinks. Paul nervously said in French that Monica had said I had found out about their liaison. Monica had warned me Paul spoke virtually no English, so we spoke only in French, except when I asked Monica for a translation when I did not understand. I replied in bad

French; yes, being a scientist, I was a good detective & being rather educated, I could detect mostly truth, possibility from bull shit. I said to him Monica had told me she loved you & if I tried to stop it now, Monica would hate me for it & our marriage would suffer. I would have to let it run its full course until it faded & went to just friendship. I wanted to keep her affection & I accepted Paul. He looked so relieved that he said he admired me & was pleased I understood & accepted the situation. Deja vue Paul Thompson with Lyn.

I have one condition. They both looked at me, worried. Again in bad French "I want both of you to be open with me. No secrets. If you meet, I want to know & if you do not mind, we can meet, all three of us. If you want to be alone together, again, I want to know, so I do not have to worry about who you are with or where you are. I have to accept you made love together, but you can tell me afterwards." I looked at Paul, and he nodded & agreed. I then turned to Monica, who looked at Paul, then back to me, nodded & agreed. "Good, let's make a toast," lifting my glass. They lifted their glasses, and we said in unison "sante".

We chatted about various subjects, including the subject of his wife, who was having a mental breakdown & had attempted suicide. She did not want to mix with people, wanted to be alone and spent all day tidying the house as she did not work. While he doted on her, he did everything. He loved her, the kids & his job & my discovery was putting all that in jeopardy; until now, he could relax with the knowledge it was a secret between the three of us. However, he needed help with his stress, unfulfilled & insatiable sexual drive. Monica was a good listener, good advisor &, of course, a good lover — he needed all three. As the conversation went on, I realised he confided in Monica everything & she was able to advise on everything he needed. I knew exactly what he meant; that was one of her qualities that I loved.

He always needed to be home by 8 pm, so finally, at about 7 pm, we went our separate ways. Dinner went uneventfully & we retired to bed early. Monica wanted to reward me for my strength & understanding, but she decided tonight would be cum-in-mouth night. Wow, she knows how to play a man. I wanted to keep back, so I waited & waited as long as I could until the volcano erupted over her face & in her mouth as she carried on sucking & deep-throating, swallowing my penis, James, until it was just a limp-shrivelled excuse of a manly shaft. She lifted her face full of satisfaction & smiled a smile that could launch a thousand ships. She was happy, I was happy that I had preserved my love, my wife. Sharing with another man now did not matter; it was Paul, & now I was to know him more & accept him more.

It was about 15 mins by car to the factory, so I used to take Monica in the morning & someone would bring her home, if it was not Paul.

Chapter 9

Lady with two mutual lovers

Saturday 5th July 2003:

We got up early & picked up Virginie, a friend of Monica from Benin, at about 9.30 am from another friend whom she was staying with. We went to Belle Epine, a shopping mall between Longjumeau & Paris. Parking is OK early but virtually impossible later in the morning & rest of the day hence never go late! After about an hour of meandering around the shops, Monica gets a call from Paul. He seemed desperate & wanted to see Monica, so we arranged to see him at a bar in the Pallaiseau.

Paul was already there when we arrived some 30 minutes later. After pleasantries of introduction, Monica indicated they wanted to be alone, so I took Lennon & Virginie away to look around the shops in Palaiseau town centre. We returned to the bar some 45 minutes later & then I offered all for a drink. Paul came to the bar with me & offered to pay for all the drinks. He said to me softly thank you for bringing Monica & apologised for interrupting Saturday, especially with a guest present. However, as Monica will tell you, I was desperate to talk to her about Christine, his wife.

As director he was expected to come with his wife to a big social client meeting on a boat on the river Seine in Paris. Christine had had the "screaming habdabs" that morning, breaking plates & smashing various household things. She was impossible to control, embarrassing his kids; given the importance of that day, what to do about the important meeting later that day? He was totally stressed & needed to chat with Monica for her advice. He seemed more relaxed when he left compared with when we saw him originally in the bar.

Tuesday 8th July

Paul gave a lift to Monica back home & came up to our flat to have a beer or two. He recovered the situation he mentioned to me at the bar & we discussed his predicament with Christine, who is stressing not only him but also the two children who had to see their "mother go mad". He said he went to the important client meeting on the boat by himself with trepidation, worried about what she might do in his absence. The river boat client meeting went well, and he returned home to very upset children as their mother had had another bout of madness earlier that day during his absence. She was in her bedroom, calm. By the time he went to the bedroom, where she was lying down, with him there, she went to sleep. I understood Paul's mental state in such a domestic situation & realised more about why he needed Monica. She was his strength, mentor &, of course, relief from his sexual desires. He left on-cue at 7:30 pm for home to ensure arrival before 8 pm.

Wednesday 9th July

I had an athletic meeting at Chelles for a 5:30 pm start, so to ensure I arrived in time, I needed to leave at about 4 pm from work. Lennon came to my work to come with me. As I had mentioned, there was a roller skate park next door to the track. We got home at about 9 pm & found Monica in her sexy silver negligee. When Lennon went to his bedroom, she asked me to take some photos of her in her negligee. Now, this was interesting because she was always reluctant towards taking photos of her in sexy clothes. Paul had been there that evening, so I guessed she had changed for him. Did they have sex? I wanted to test her openness without asking. She said nothing but was very keen for the photo. I said I would show Paul the photo the next time I saw him, and she said, "No, no, I do not want to encourage him… He was reluctant to come a 2nd time in a row, but he felt an irresistible urge to come when she said I would be away with Lennon at the athletic meeting". "Well," I said, "Did you have sex tonight?" She would not tell me — so much for the openness I asked for. Her reluctance to admit or deny they had a shag, just reinforced the probability it happened. When she started making dinner, I checked the bedroom, and it certainly looked a bit different with her clothes all over the place, including her nickers/culottes.

After dinner, Lennon retired to his bedroom, and Monica & I sat down on the settee. I looked at her inquisitively, waiting for her to say something. "You know, I am playing Paul. I want a permanent job at the office; Paul can get that job. Of course, I love him as well but do not rush me. I do not want Paul to affect us two or for you to feel threatened." I looked straight into her face "I do not feel threatened. Paul has so much to lose at home & work. Remember, I have accepted you can have sex with Paul, but I just want to know so that I do not worry about you lying to me. Think of you having two husbands."

She objected to that comment, but my comment made her quiet & thoughtful. "Do you really think of it like that?" "Why not? Muslims have up to four wives & can have sex with any at any time, while the other wives must not feel jealous," I said. Monica, full of thought, said, "Mmmmm, I see what you mean, but you are married to me, and Paul has Christine. Don't you feel jealous of me & Paul?" I looked into her eyes, "I suppose I would if you did not love me & had sex with him & not me." "You do not need to worry then because I do love you, and I always want to please you," still looking into my eyes.

She then put her hand on my trousers & slowly rubbed my leg, inching ever closer to my crutch. I felt the urge to feel her pussy, and as she relaxed more, I undid my belt and removed my trousers so she could feel my shaft. He (we used to call him "James") responded, she dropped down onto her knees and pulled down my pants to give me a deep-throat massage. Oh, how can I (or anyone) resist her when she is so amorous? I think she must have been tired from previous excursions (with Paul), so she kept her mouth massaging James until I came. Her laughing eyes looked at me all the time with a big smile, and gradually, sperm oozed out from her mouth. "What does it taste like?" I asked. She got up, sat next to me, wrapped her arms around me and gave me a long mouth-to-mouth kiss whereby much of my own sperm transferred to me. We kept together kissing for maybe a few minutes until both our mouths had swallowed everything. "… well do you like your own sperm?" "Mmm, it is different!"

Thursday 10th July

Paul & I arranged to meet together in a bar in CORA at lunchtime, not far, maybe 2-3 km from both our offices. We chatted about our respective situations & roles. He told me that Monica loved me & he did not think Monica loved him. I sensed this was an agreed storyline, but I shrugged my shoulders, that it may or may not be true. I showed him a copy of Monica's photo in her negligee I took last night. She liked it very much. While I offered the printout to him, he said he dared not keep it in case Christine saw it. He enquired how I felt about Monica with him & what they do. I said to him that I anticipate the liaison will rise further, stabilise, plateau and decline slowly to a level where, eventually, they will be just friends. I said I am sure their love will increase more until they reach this stabilisation plateau state.

He nodded slowly in thought & said he felt I would be a good friend to him. I said to him that I asked one thing of him that he should tell me whenever they meet & whenever they have sex. "Did you have sex with Monica last night?" Rather coy, he admitted to having sex last night & that she tried on her silver negligee for him (hence the reason for the photo request by Monica last night). While lunchtime for us is flexible, we parted ways after maybe an hour.

Paul dropped Monica off at home early from work & returned about an hour later for a drink before I arrived with a black colleague, Roger Soumah, to take some clients out for dinner. Monica had already changed into something nice for the evening. Monica saw Paul to the door & gave him a passionate kiss, out of sight of Roger, but not myself. She waited until he entered the lift, gave a little smile and waved goodbye. True love signs if ever I saw them.

Quickly, she did last-minute things to ready herself. During dinner, Monica received two SMS messages from Paul. One said, "ne blague pas le black" (do not joke with the black), referring to Roger. Jealousy? Monica showed me later this; the 2nd message "tu dors bien avec Geoff et je t'aime" (sleep well with Geoff, & I love you). I felt content that I have Monica's confidence now with their liaison so that she can tell me & that Paul is looking after my interests with her as well. Paul will be on holiday soon. How will the liaison carry on afterwards? That was a question inside me as I reflected on them together at the lift.

Friday 11th July

I arranged with Dick, my Australian colleague friend, to have a RASP meeting. Dick has a flat in Paris near Montparnasse. He was employed as a consultant on GDS (Glow Discharge Spectrometers), working for 3 months in the factory or on trips & 3 months back in Australia. He did not qualify for a company car, so he normally arrived by train or bus. Supping our ale, I taught him that English ale had only natural fermentation gas, so one could transfer a half pint into the half-empty pint glass without it frothing all over the place. This is not possible with keg beers that are pushed up to the tap by CO_2 gas.

As a friend & confidant, I needed to garner his views on my story of Monica & Paul. He said that you have to understand the life Monica has been through with the Rwandan genocide, where you have to survive any way you can. If that means you stay alive by having sex, so be it, even if it is with reluctance. Similarly, to get a job or something or succeed in something by a liaison with someone will feel normal, although not normal to others in a non-violent society. It was good to chat with another man and get alternative views to my own. He felt I was doing right to treat the situation. After our beers, I dropped Dick off on the way home at Montparnasse.

Saturday 12th July

We were to meet her "uncle" Stanley, who was in ZAP2, having arrived from Africa at CdG airport. The ZAP compounds are for arrivals where their status is being questioned, either due to being illegal or where paperwork needs to be done to approve entry into France. We were early for visiting time, so we had something to eat at "Flunch", a canteen type resto. We chatted, of course, about Paul. She said she felt sorry for him. His marriage is a mess due to Christine's illness, with indeterminate chances of improvement. She would not admit she had sex with him Wednesday night but then gazed in the distance "Imagine going to bed & having sex with him, he is grey hair, & also I have my fibroids."

How that was supposed to affect her sex life when it did not affect ours, I was not sure of the logic. I said, "You know, I have plenty of condoms in my bedside cabinet in case he forgets to bring some." Ignoring my statement, while moving her head to look at me, she said, "He needs someone to talk to and have a confidant to share his problems & get possible answers."

The time arrived to see Stanley in the ZAP 2 compound. They were new porta-cabins with all facilities with a secure fence around them. Here, they could walk around while their papers were processed. We chatted in the small refectory for a while & then left for home.

Monica received several SMS messages that evening "je suis avec toi pendant 2 semaines" (I am with you for 2 weeks). He was having a walking holiday in Switzerland with Christine & the two kids. In the evening, another SMS near bed time "bon nuit mon amour a demain. Je t'aime" (good night, my love' until tomorrow, I love you).

Monica took a copy of my diary from my case Saturday evening when Lennon & I went to the airport for Joseph, a friend of Monica's & family, who were staying one night with us before staying with other friends.

Sunday 13 July

Paul couldn't get Monica out of his mind & sent an SMS, "Tu est dans mon Coeur" (you are in my heart). She later erased all her SMS messages & said that she admired & respected him, but there was nothing sexual. Who is she trying to kid? She more or less admitted the other day, & did she not know Paul was more honest with me & has admitted he had sex with her? A little later, she, out of the blue, said again, "…if you look at Paul, his age & looks, would you think I would go to bed with him? I admire him I feel sorry for him."

I am trying to work out why Monica does not want to admit to a sexual relationship, as well as all the reasons she said. Is she feeling remorse for having a relationship within months of being discovered having sex with another man & at the same region of time getting married to me? Is it just the embarrassment of being sex mad, or that she is willing to sell her body for favours? If so, then she maybe feeling like a prostitute or less insulting … an Escort.

I started thinking about Sandra, a cousin of hers in Benin, who was living as a girlfriend & lover with the president. She visited Paris once, and I must admit she was a stunner, especially with the clothes she wore. Mini skirt, tight-fitting and low plunging top with ample breasts giving a deep cleavage. With such attire, I could see not only the president melting in her presence but others doing whatever she wanted & giving favours. I could see Monica admired her & felt that what her cousin had achieved, she maybe able to do by dressing nicely & flirting & maybe more to get what she wanted.

Tuesday 15th July 2003

Paul sent another SMS, "Tu suis mon conseil je suis gentil avec Christine mais je suis tristesse est au fond de moi repond a mon message je suis soulage que tu prends mieu mon amour." (You are my advice I am nice with Christine, but I have sadness deep inside me answer my message I am relieved that you take my love better). When I got home Monica was having a shower. However, Monica saw me reading her phone SMS message from Paul & making notes. I pleaded with her that we had agreed that she & Paul should be open about their liaison. I did not mind; I had accepted their liaison & love, but I wanted to know. Not knowing was stressing me & therefore, she could help me by showing me all her SMS & e-mails from Paul.

She looked at me with doleful eyes of pity & removed the towel covering her. She then smiled, took my hand and placed it on her breast. I started fondling her breasts & she fondled me down below. My blood pressure started rising with its inevitable consequences. She then took my hand & led me to the bedroom, closed it & then started undoing my belt and trousers. Here we go again, I cannot control myself when I am with her. She knew exactly how to play me. Tonight was the doggy position. Oh! I do love seeing her boobs swing in rhythm with my pelvic thrusts; it excited me so much I could cum too early if I am not careful.

I never know if Monica had an orgasm because she was always quiet, unlike some women who make a lot of noise even before they reach a climax. Maybe it was because she has had her genitals mutilated. It took me some time when I first met her to find her clitoris. Then, one day, she explained that it was custom in Rwanda & much of Africa to have a little girl's genitals cut to pieces. Her clitoris was cut into three pieces, and maybe she found it hard to get an orgasm, I am not sure. Maybe without the normal female feelings, women who had their genitals mutilated have less shame to have sex with multiple men. If so, this is the opposite of what was intended by its proponents.

Wednesday 16 July 2003

In playing with Monica's phone, which was in French, I made another mistake, so I sent an SMS to Paul in my bad French: "whoops je fais un faux je suis desole, Geoff," & then I followed up with "nous avons descute hier soir, cet affaire elle dit elle t'aime mais je suis premier J'ai accepte vos amours et plus. Pas de secrets de moi est tres important". (we have discussed last night this affaire, & she said she loves you, but I am her first love. No secrets from me are very important).

Thursday 17th July 2003

I worry less now - I share Monica

Since the day I learnt that GRIS was Paul, I was very happy with that fact:

1. Paul has a family, and a family life he does not want to lose.
2. He has a good job & position that, again, he would not want to compromise.
3. Monica is his love, but it must not interfere with either of the above 2 points.
4. Paul would not want to take Monica permanently, nor does Monica want Paul permanently.
5. Paul is not a danger to me, in fact, he can help me with my relationship with Monica. He understands some of my needs & thoughts better than Monica, so he can influence her to help me.
6. My intense stress, which was affecting my health, disappeared.

At last, I have been able to sleep at night without worrying about the unknown dangers of a young lover. I have been able to work at JY without worrying all day about what would happen that evening with some unknown person or persons. I don't worry about all the problems, the lies & the previous deceptions when doing athletics; it was affecting my athletics due to lack of concentration on the event. Since the 4th of July, I now sleep well. Our relationship has dramatically improved, my athletics has improved, my work load at JY has improved…..In fact, I feel generally happier, more relaxed, more forgiving & less stressed………. Thank you, Paul.

I must be patient & very flexible in my views, and I need to be willing to share Monica with Paul at any time. I must do no actions that would alienate either Monica (or Paul). If I upset Paul, then Monica would be upset & then she would turn against me. I need to ensure a stable relationship between Monica & Paul that eventually, in time, turn to maybe just friendship.

Another point is that while Monica has Paul as a lover (especially if they have an active sex relationship), Monica is less likely to want another (3rd) man who really maybe a danger to me because he maybe younger, more eligible and, therefore, pose a possibility of Monica leaving me.

I love Monica & like any man all I need is: love, constant affection (like a dog or cat) & sex. With those things, I am putty in her hands, whereby I will do virtually anything.

<u>I made notes as follows in my diary:</u>

Paul loves Monica and, at present, he can think very little of anything or anyone else. Monica loves Paul, but she has problems reconciling her love and at present says it is mainly admiration for him, pity for him and wanting to ensure a good chance of a permanent job if a vacancy should arrive in time for the finish of her contract in October. Although she says otherwise, after some delay and thought,

I don't think she would refuse him the chance of shagging her should the opportunity arise. The reasons maybe three-fold:

- i) *He could help considerably with getting her a permanent good job,*
- ii) *She feels pity for him with his present family situation,*
- iii) *She may want to experiment with sex with him. Her reasoning for letting Andre shag her was pity for him and I think the case of pity for Paul is stronger, although he may not be so attractive.*

*I cannot accept the scenario of her leaving me for another man; the thought would make me distraught. I must, therefore, **encourage** both Monica and Paul with their relationship to make it as enjoyable as possible for them, as stable as possible for them and as free of inhibitions with me around as possible. If they cannot behave as they want with me around then I must make excuses to be absent to enable them to do whatever they want together. By helping to make their bond of love stronger, I help myself to a better and happier life with Monica.*

*Paul is my **guarantee** of a stable married life and stability against other potential partners of Monica and a less stressful married life. I am a co-husband (like the many wives of a Muslim man) of Monica. I can live with that so long as our relationship is less stressful, full of love, affectionate and <u>desiring</u> sex with me (rather than just a duty…as I sometimes feel it is for her….). If I have all that, then sharing Monica with Paul (with or without sex) is a small price to pay for the happiness and low stress that would be obtained.*

Monica's happiness with the status and my reaction of the affaire with Paul, since it came out in the open that wonderful Friday, has helped us be less stressed and happy. If she is happy then we all benefit. Long live the affaire, long live our happy marriage.

Saturday 19th July

I kept notes about things & my mental state at the time before I started work in the office &, sometimes, brought them home to add anything that happened that needed immediate notes.

We had good discussions on Saturday, Sunday & Monday nights (where she referred to the diary contents without mentioning she had taken it & photocopied it).

Sunday 20th July 2003

After training, I returned to the flat & at last, I realised I had convinced Monica to be open. She showed me a SMS from Paul "bonjour ma beau amour, donnes moi de la nouvelles," & later, "Aujourd'hui pas un bon weekend je suis tout le temps avec toi je t'aime mon amour" (Today not a good weekend I'm all the time with you I love you my love). "tu es passe une bonne soirée ce soir, Geoff est-il la?" Did he want to chat to Monica? "heureusement que tu es dans mes pensée tout le temps car ces vacances sont interminables tes messages me son d'un grand réconfort. Quelle solution? " ("Happily you are in my thoughts all the time because these holidays are interminable your messages me it's a great comfort" "What solution?").

After I had read his messages, Monica said that she was thinking of stopping this affaire because it was getting too serious. She was even contemplating leaving the company. Are these just words, could she really stop the affair? Could she leave the company? Getting this job was good for her. I said she should keep things as they are because I am sure things will stabilise & then, eventually, just become friends. She needed Paul to get a permanent job.

In France, it is not easy to get a permanent job. The socialist rules mean it is difficult to take on a person in permanent position & then get rid of them. Socialist rules make it very difficult, so they take people on for 9 months, then upon good performance, extend the contract for a further 9 months. However, at the end of the 18 months, they then have to either: take on the person full-time on a permanent contract or say thank you & goodbye. Unemployment in France is stubbornly high, typically > 10% over a decade. The socialist government in the late 1990s brought in the 35-hour week to try to reduce it by "forcing" companies to take on more people. Of course, nothing changed; companies just paid overtime. In fact, unemployment INCREASED. The socialists (now in opposition at the time) were dumfounded & could not explain this phenomenon.

Later, I saw Monica's reply SMS, "Quelle solution tu trouves tes messages patient mon amour" (What solution do you find your messages patient, my love). She later erased this message she sent, in case I realised what she had said earlier was bullshit. She still loved him but did not want to put too much pressure on me & wanted Monica to suggest her what she really wanted anyway. I think she is trying to think what to do maybe. Does she love me? If she does, why does she continually confuse me?

Monday 21 July 2003

I went to work as usual after making my normal notes on events in my private diary kept at work. I sent three SMS that she must not dump Paul & that she also needed the job that she liked.

I was occupied with an impending visit to the UK on 28-31 July.

My father was getting gradually worse from lung damage he incurred with getting Tuberculosis (TB) when he was young. He married a woman called Violet as a death pact. She died, but before he was to die, the doctor said there was a new experimental idea and if he wanted to try it. Having said that, there was nothing to lose in being a guinea pig. They proceeded to collapse one lung while getting help with the other & then vice versa every day. The idea was that by resting the lung for some time, it would aid recovery.

It worked, & he survived & met my mother during World War II. Of course, after having beaten death, he could not do strenuous hard work, so he was exempted from serving in the war. He tried various jobs moving around London & Gosport near Portsmouth & south Essex. He always told me the story of being shot at by a fighter plane, so he ran & burst into a doorway, startling the woman inside who had not gone down to the shelter.

Eventually, after working for BATA on the Thames side making shoes, he left to start up his own little shop in Laindon, Essex, where he met my mother, Ellen. After the war, they moved to East London & started to think about starting a family when things had settled down in 1947-48 from the war & also because my mother was now close to 40 years old. I was born in what was called the "baby boom," & because there was no room in the local hospital, I was born in a nun's hospital. She was so gassed (nitrous oxide gas) that when she woke up after my birth, she thought she was in heaven because the nun nurses wore big white winged hats. Within a year of my birth, my father saw a shop advertised in Chelmsford, a small market town "in the middle of nowhere" as his family claimed (45 miles north of London!). The shoe repairer's shop in Chelmsford was started with borrowed money & even an agreed delayed rent to the landlord to ensure he was able to buy stock to start up the business! We moved in the Autumn of 1949, so my informative years were in Chelmsford & I grew up with a Chelmsford, Essex accent. These days, you would never guess because, gradually, Londoners moved out to bring their accent with them.

As it was school holiday time, I was taking Lennon with me to visit various friends & relatives while I was in Essex. I needed to book the ferry & make visit arrangements this week before we left on Sunday 27th afternoon. I spoke with Monica twice that day & she was very loving in her voice & wanted to work until 7 pm. Was it the same person who wanted nothing more with Paul & wanted to leave? No! I thought she was playing tactics with me to get me to plead for her to stay with Paul & the chemical factory. It's what we both wanted because I felt secure with him that would exclude any other male possibilities.

In the evening, we chatted more about Paul, & she then said again she wanted to finish with Paul. However, I pointed out Paul was too much affected by her & too much in love, that being so affected by home life & a break-up now, he could be so fragile he may try suicide. She must continue until the affair peters out. She sent him an SMS in front of me reassuring him of her love, saying 'I miss you'.

Monica was now fully open with me & showed me all her SMS messages for example "bonjour mon amour comment va tu?" "Ta solution va t'elle nous faire souffrir? Dit le moi", "Je t'aime tant que même si je souffre je ne veux pas ta perdue", "comment s'est passe la journée tu me manques a ma être désespère j'essaie d'être gentil avec Christine mais mon cœur est vers toi a répond mon amour." (Hello my love how are you?" "Will your solution make us suffer? Tell me" "I love you so much that even if I give it, I do not want to lose you" "how did the day go, I miss you to me to know I try to be nice to Christine but my heart is to you, reply my love"). Monica sent a reassuring reply that she showed me.

I felt she loved me now that she was open with me. And now, after Lennon went to his bedroom, she started arousing me on the settee. "Do you like my boobs? she asked. "Of course, I do. I love everything about your body." She started unbuttoning the shirt she had worn for work. I started to help her & then reached around her to undo her C/D-cup bra. She smiled & played with me down below. After some initial play & undressing, I was on my back & Monica was on top of me, riding me like a horse. She grimaced a bit to start with due to her fibroids, but sexual pleasure took over, and she rode me like a real cowboy. Oh, how my athletic hip strength helped with good sex when underneath!

Relaxing on our backs after the exertion, we chatted about little nothings until she joked that other men in the chemical company admire her & make comments that she was beautiful & dressed well. "So what do you say to them?" I said. "Oh, I just look at them & smile." "Mmmm," I thought. She originally said little snippets like that before I found out about Paul. I hope, between Paul & me, we can keep her occupied! Paul could keep her happy when I was not there & augment any sexual desires she may have. I was sure she did not want to complicate her life more! A famous English saying is "Many a word said in jest", I suppose it is a case of "watch this space".

Feeling we had enough energy to retire to bed, we lied down. She reflected (probably thinking of the week ahead when I would be in England with Lennon), "Can you imagine Paul & myself in bed together?" "Yes," I said, "I can imagine you will both have a good time."

She saw a couple of SMS before trying to sleep. Paul has sent two messages; one was significant. "…bonjour nous allons aujourd'hui au montagne et promener, la nature ma rappelle toujours notre journee de Fontainebleau" (Hello we go today to the mountain and walk, nature reminds me always our day at Fontainebleau). Oh, I said I did not know you went to Fontainebleau. Oh, didn't I tell you? I must have forgotten; it was some weeks ago when we left work early to walk through the forest. "I don't have a problem with that, but remember, you have both agreed to tell me everything to stoop me worry about what you are doing.

I told her the analogy of worrying about being late & missing the plane back to Australia & when it finally happens that you HAVE missed the plane, then you, after the initial panic, start calming down & then thinking & planning about WHAT you need to do to resolve the problem & get to your destination. I have been in that situation several times in business with missing flights & having to sort out where & what to do. One example was when I was due to go home from Switzerland to Australia via Abu Dhabi & Colombo. The flight was delayed in Abu Dhabi, so when we arrived at Colombo, my twice-a-week flight departed. The Sri Lankan airways manager said not to worry. I would be staying at the hotel at their expense & then introduced me to a taxi driver & said he could take me anywhere. When

I asked "how much", he said 15 American dollars for the whole day! I could not refuse such an offer!

The next day, he was there waiting in his taxi, & we went to Kandy, the old capital. The journey was amazing & REALLY tested one's heart! I thought in the first 30 minutes that I would be killed in a car crash. He would start over-taking when there was only space for two vehicles on the two-way bumpy roads, meeting an oncoming car head-on. The other cars on both sides moved over, and — hey presto — we have a middle lane (a suicide lane). Remembering India & Sri Lanka are on the left-hand side of the road like the UK, so imagine over-taking on a left bend with the mountain on your left & deep drop on the right. He started over-taking when he could see nothing. I had visions of dropping over the side in a crash, but no, the oncoming car moved close to the drop & the car being overtaken moved as close as possible to the mountain side, & voila, we passed.

I went around various stops like a textile factory, a gem factory, an elephant orphanage for lunch & rode an elephant that performed the various instructions given to it afterwards by its owner. Amazing animals, maybe 22 words, the elephants recognise what to do. We went to the Kandy itself & saw the largest lying Budda in the world & the surrounding temple. After a full day we returned to the hotel in pitch black, through small villages with just a few light bulbs illuminating the small shops.

Missing the flight or worrying about what Monica was doing without being told gave me stress, so I needed to know, even if I did not do anything about what they did together.

I remember reading the book **Women Who Stay, with Men who Stray" by Dr Debbie Then** gave an example that was the exact situation of myself. I just wanted to know, even if I did nothing. The book says there are two types of women who know their husband in cheating but do not want to leave of divorce

1) Women who turn a blind eye & do NOT want to know what is going on

2) Women (read Geoff) who, while accepting the affairs, WANT to know everything, so they do not worry.

Paul understood, but Monica? Sometimes she did, and sometimes, she was still secretive. At the moment, she was open, I must keep it that way.

Tuesday 22 July

Monica showed me in the evening, Paul's SMS "…impossible de t'appeler au telephone malgré mon desire. Dis moi comment tu vas? Comment sont les relations avec Geoff" ("… impossible to call you on the telephone despite my desire. Tell me how you are doing? How are relations with Geoff?) She told me that Paul phoned her about 6 pm and said he would be promoted to be the big director of the whole region. Monica also told him I would be away for a week with Lennon in England from Sunday afternoon until the following Saturday night. Being good at reading body language, I saw she had a look on her face of excitement & reflection of a week together with Paul without me or Lennon about. Maybe feeling guilty or just wanting a shag, she enticed me inside the bedroom, took her clothes off & offered her ample breasts for me to suck. Caressing them with my hands as I sucked them, she fell back on the bed & hurriedly took my clothes off. I resumed sucking her breasts, and she held my expanded & excited shaft, "James". She smiled, put her lips on him & then swallowed him "James" was happy. He became happier & happier as the pressure built up to a volcanic crescendo, and all my anxiety that Monica caused was gone. Happy James, happy Geoff.

Wednesday 23 July 2003

Diary notes written at home now moved to office.

I was taking Monica to work, as we went to the car from the apartment block & in the discussion she complained about the diary I was keeping that she saw four days ago.

She had used it for intimating she would finish her liaison with Paul. She did not like things to be open, but I said these notes were for me & not others. She got to know my views by reading those notes, and she was passing this onto Paul by taking my diary & showing him. I had already seen my diary in her handbag on Monday morning before she returned it to my hiding place. It was from this event that I decided to move the diary to my office & write notes before starting work. I thought to myself these hurt feelings were false.

Paul phoned Monica at about 6:30 pm, and they chatted for about 5-10 minutes. While having a shower, I read a couple of his SMS & as well as the normal amorous comments, asking whether she still loved him… with that came an interesting comment. He mentioned that her request for a couple of RTT* days off next week had been approved. I wonder whether she would tell me about that?

* The socialist govt at the time, made a law that all organisations must give all employees a paid one day off per month, to improve the unemployment in France, it could be accumulated, it did not decrease unemployment as intended.

Monica suggested I go to the doctor the other week. After a quiet evening, tonight, she suggested having more fun. She suggested me to take a Viagra pill that the doctor had prescribed for me. I found Viagra last about 8-9 hours, while Cialis last 4-5 DAYS! Sometimes, when she was wearing something sexy, I would be walking around like a tripod! I was always worried the zip on my trousers would burst! I could not wait for Lennon to go to his bedroom. She unbuttoned her blouse, and once I saw those wonderful breasts ample & barely contained within her bra, I was already straining my trouser zip. She smiled at seeing my anticipation & looked down with immense satisfaction & then started unzipping me. Woooooh, slow down, wait, James is there, he is stuck & the zip will not undo properly! Slowly does it, yes, trousers down & off. She realised the pressure needed a more careful extraction of my clothes. She decided I should ride her doggy style this time. I felt James was so big, he might go right through her! Cor! I should have been a cowboy, yee haa. What a feeling & what an event, what a release! Shag over, cum oozing out of her pussy. Monica was happy, I was happy. I literally had no energy for anything else. I was knackered, so satisfying! Zzzzzzzzzz.

Thursday 24 July

I hear Monica's phone "bling" an SMS message & because she was in the loo. I quickly read Paul's SMS. "bonjour mon amour, as tu profiter du Viagra hier? Moi rien tout sera pour toi". I quickly put the phone back, but I was upset, & yet I dared not show it. I wanted Monica to tell me whether she told such private things to him because she was passing on information about myself that I needed Viagra & later, she suggested Cialis. It was hypocritical of her to complain about me making a diary of events & yet she was telling very intimate details to him. That is a sign of her love for him. She would not do that unless she REALLY did love him so much — so much for all those crocodile tears of being offended. She was also making a joke of my sexual prowess to Paul. I was not happy with that knowledge. What were they talking about me? Am I an idiot accepting him? Or I cannot get an erection without Viagra? I felt very insecure again.

I decided during the day to send Paul an SMS to make sure he was open with me & asked him to keep me informed on any developments. I told him something he already knew that I would be away with Lennon next week.

Paul phoned Monica in the evening while I was at the club doing weights. She informed me that he had briefly phoned & asked after me. Yes, I could imagine they discussed that I needed Viagra & he did not. I could not admit I knew about what I had seen.

Friday 25 July

I sent an SMS to Paul to say have a good time next week with Monica & remember you have both agreed to tell me. He replied that I was a gentleman & that he admired me & wanted always to be my friend. In the evening, Monica was in a funny mood, maybe in anticipation of the oncoming week of fun. Even though I was fully occupied with arranging the trip to England, I hoped to have a good shag before I went, but I failed to perform that evening, hoping that I did not require medication help. If I am not 100% concentrated, I now know I cannot perform to both our satisfaction.

Saturday 26 July

Paul sent an SMS in the early evening, which Monica showed me. "Le retourne (from their holiday) es difficile avec, Christine. Nous avons disputons sans arrete dit moi mots pour ne remonter vivement Lundi" (our return is difficult with Christine we had a dispute non-stop & said not return <when I finish work> Monday). Monica & I discussed the nightmare situation Paul was in with Christine's erratic manner & state of mind. He really needed Monica to lean on for advice because women, in general, & Monica, in particular, was good at it. I also imagined, with such a psychologically erratic person, sex would be impossible. Monica fulfilled a vital function for both his sanity & sexual desires. I also felt I could help maybe in the future because he was not a man who would easily meet people outside work. Christine had ensured this with her mental state; she was embarrassing. Monica was happy with my reaction to that SMS & that Paul needed help from her.

At night time, Monica suggested I should take some "medication". That night in the bedroom, I had no problems whatsoever to get James fully erected and hard; God, James was like a rock. I wanted to try and hold back without losing it easily. I succeeded because I maintained the pelvic thrusts for ages & really think I made her cum. It was always difficult to find out whether she had an orgasm or was just pretending and trying to satisfy me that she had cum. During the recovery period, she said to me that she would never mention to anyone I took Viagra. What a lie! I had seen an SMS from her telling Paul I needed it to ensure good sex.

Chapter 10

When the cat is away, the mice will play (Monica alone with Paul)

Sunday 27 July 2003

Visit to England with Lennon

I went to training early & returned to have a shower & get ready for the drive to England. Lennon was ready, and we packed the car & then we were off to circumnavigate Paris via the Peripherique, the A3 & then the A1 to northern France & finally to Calais, a time of approximately three & half hours. Pre-booked, we waited the customary 1 hour in the waiting car park on the quayside, before driving onboard the ferry. Lennon wanted to look around the ship before settling down on a comfortable seat with drinks & food for the two hours+ sea crossing. For me, routine, but for Lennon, a 14-years-old, it was exciting to be on a big ship crossing the English Channel. As we got closer to the white cliffs of Dover, he was mesmerised by looking out on deck as we approached England for his first time. I must admit I feel "English" when I see those white cliffs of Dover. Having docked & driven off the ferry for a further 2 hours, we arrived in Chelmsford to stay with my father.

Monday 28 July

I had some business visits locally within Essex including a visit to E2V (former English Electric Valve) to describe the type of CCD (Charged Coupled Device) we wanted with deep UV detection down to below 170nm. The E2V product manager said they had no data below about 220nm, so we had to research ourselves to see whether the special back-thinned CCD would do the job. CCD is a detector chip that has a layer of silicon, therefore limiting the wavelength to about 220nm. However, if one etches away the silicon layer with HF hydrofluoric acid, it is then free to accept & detect light down to 120nm.

I gave Lennon some money to enable him to go to Chelmsford town centre & return home afterwards. My father was getting more ill from TB he got when he was in his twenties, there was nothing they could do, other than give a small oxygen tank to help his breathing.

My father was basically housebound because over the latter years, although he managed to recover from TB, he was having more difficulty to breath & coughing up blood & bits of skin. The doctor said to him, "I am sorry, I can do nothing. You should have been dead a long time ago. You are evidence of the marvels of modern medicine." My father increasingly needed that small oxygen tank near him to help him, so Lennon needed to explore Chelmsford alone until he came back home.

Meanwhile, Paul took Monica home that evening early from work & took two large boxes of 12 bottles of white wine, one assumed to cover the week together. He told me they went to bed, made love, drank and made love again before he left to be home by 8 pm, which for him was the "Cinderella time". Monica was more shy about the details, but Paul was obliged by his promise to tell me. He was not so much into kinky sex; he was more of a traditionist & preferred doggy style, especially when he realised he would be able to see themselves in the cupboard mirror having fun & both seeing her breasts swinging back & forwards with the rhythm of his hip thrusts. He sent me SMS on a daily basis with basic details & elaborated later when we met together alone in the bar.

Tuesday 29 July

After fulfilling my business in Essex, Lennon & I left for Stoke on Trent to visit my son Steven. Having arrived in Tunstall, a part of

Stoke on Trent, we settled in & then went out for a meal in a local pub & of course, tasted the local real ale. Steven liked to go for a ride into the northern countryside & I like driving on country roads with their small windy course & wonderful views that are found in the Pennines just 15 minutes away. The Lake District & the Welsh mountains, both within 2 hours of Stoke. We planned what we would do the next day & decided to go to Wakefield for the national coal mine exhibition.

Wednesday 30 July

Down a coal mine

We left early to cross over the Pennines & arrived at the Wakefield coal mine at about 9:30. We had an explanation by a local Yorkshire ex-miner of what went on when it was an active mine & what to expect. Lennon could speak English well, but he said to us afterwards that he understood <u>nothing</u> of the chap's broad Yorkshire accent. There was a limit of 16 people for each tour because the visit meant we all went down in the miner's cages. We were to experience the journey down to the bowels of the earth, where coal was mined until the mine shut down in the late 1980's. Strict rules were explained & adhered to by those because there could still be methane seepage, which is a natural product of rotting vegetation like coal & peat. The visit was memorable & made an indelible impression on all three of us to appreciate what miners did to extract coal. After water power from the steep valleys in the north of England & South Wales, coal was the fuel that helped make & accelerate the Industrial Revolution. I have been in a gold mine in Johannesburg, South Africa, that was interesting, but the depth of the mine was nothing like the UK deep coal mines. An interesting fact from my gold mine visit near Jo'burg was they invited & employed Cornish tin miners due to their knowledge of mining seams, equipment and techniques.

Thursday 31, & Friday 1st, August

Steven, Lennon & myself toured the Welsh mountains, the Lake District & other areas of the northwest Pennines. All three regions of England are beautiful in their unique way & just a small walk is so restful, especially when one has at the back of one's mind what is probably going on in France. Paul was sending me e-mails about his activities with Monica, as he had promised.

Saturday 2nd August 2003

After some local things to do, Lennon & I started our journey down south. By coincidence, when we stopped for a "pee-break" at a service area, Monica phoned me & when I broached the subject of Paul, she said nothing had happened & she had not seen him. Her denial angered me, and she constantly kept saying the same thing even though I knew the truth. When she put the phone down, I was still angry, so I blurted out what Lennon's mother was like. She was having an affair with Paul, and I found her in bed with Andre; she did things for money or favours. He seemed quite philosophical & seemed keen to know more, so with my anger diminishing, I explained all the things that had gone on with Paul & Andre, the lies & the deceit. Being intelligent, I think he had suspected the goings on with Paul, so nothing seemed to surprise him. He just intently listened as I drove.

We stayed the night at my father's & then the next day, made our way to Dover to catch the ferry back to France.

Sunday 3rd August

We arrived home without incident & Monica welcomed us at the door with a big cuddle for us both. Lennon, after the initial ½ hour, went up to his bedroom & then while together in the kitchen, Monica said she had bought some Champagne & wanted to celebrate us coming home. We cracked open the bottle & sat together, drinking on the sofa. "I have missed you," she said as she slowly edged up her dress, revealing more of her leg with a mischievous smile on her face as she looked into my eyes & then took hold of my hand to feel her leg up high close to her groin. My pulse raced as sexual desire took over & un-aided, I caressed her pussy through her pants. She started enjoying the sensation, so the pants came off quickly for me to access her pussy unimpeded.

Normally, she would take some time to really start breathing heavily with breasts heaving up & down, but now she was already at this point. My trousers & pants came off quickly, revealing a very solid-looking penis that was only too keen to enter her as I manoeuvred Monica to a more comfortable position. Wow, what a shag! Monica really tested my fitness; she has a way of slowly increasing the tempo, so it was easier for us both to climax together. At the conclusion of events, we both relaxed back, exhausted; perhaps, I need to do more cardio workouts? I still wanted to feel her breasts & with just her dress & no bra on, it was easy to access her ample boobs. She was still keen for more & unzipped her dress so both boobs were exposed as she lifted herself up so that I could suck them alternatively. Oh, I do love those breasts.

Eventually, after a recovery period, we resumed drinking the Champagne & then she gradually started unwinding by telling me about her week with Paul. She did not go into the details that Paul had told me, but by prompting her she gradually filled in the details that she initially was reluctant to give, especially on the phone in England. I said, "Why didn't you say when I was on the phone in England? I had already been told by Paul as part of our collective agreement". "I'm sorry," she said, "I feel embarrassed to tell you, my husband, that I had sex with another man, even though it is Paul & we had agreed to tell all. I do not want to upset you." Having already melted, I said I would always want to know to stop worrying or imagining things.

Monday 4 August

Monica's period had arrived, & as often happens with women, it caused pain. She was in a bad mood, and I could do nothing right. Paul tried to help by being caring through SMS, "ça me fait mal de savour que tu souffres, Tu ne peux pas rester comme ça" (It hurts me to know that you suffer. You cannot stay like that).

He sent a number of SMSs that day showing concern & wanting dearly to be with her to help her through the day. He popped around after work & was still there when I arrived home after work. Although, he did not stay long because it was about 7:30 pm & he always needed to be home by 8 pm to Christine, his wife.

Monica had a shower & while I was reading today's SMSs, Paul sent another, and it did not make its usual message ring. Hopefully, she did not realise later that she did not hear the ring for a message.

When Monica finished, she was in just a short silver satin negligee, mmmm, blood pressure showing down below. I try to give her a cuddle & feel her boobs, but she made the excuse she needed to cook dinner. Moving to the kitchen, another opportunity arrived when she was facing the worktop & my hand slipped down her breasts from behind. "I am not a sex object!" she said without resistance. "Don't you know I love you? I love our conversations & life together & your body is part & parcel of that love," I said. "I know, I am not the only one that loves you; you also have Paul, Emmanuel & Andre." "Why do you mention Emmanuel as well as Paul?" "Well, for a start, you promised to marry Emmanuel & your move to France was part of the plan, as was setting up a joint bank account." "Why do you say that? Where did you learn that?" She denied it.

Whoops, I should not have divulged all that information I know. I had learnt from the letter "Stitches in Time" he sent me via Bibianne, a mutual friend of both. Emmanuel, working for ADB (African Development Bank), met Monica there in Abidjan, Cote d'Ivoire

(Ivory Coast) & eventually, they promised to get married. Their plan was to leave Cote d'Ivoire for Kenya & then leave Africa. Firstly, she would go to France to set up a French bank account & then Monica would move first (her ADB job was just a temporary job), & he would follow later. He learnt from mutual contacts that she had sent her baggage to my address & then said that she was staying at my place for a few days. He stayed in contact, then he learnt she was seeing me several times per week & that we were lovers. The letter "Stitches in Time" outlined their plans, the broken promises and a warning to me about what Monica was like.

I quickly moved on by saying, "Paul loves you. We both love you for what you are & why not also your beautiful body?" She seemed pleased with that comment. She relented & relaxed. and I could caress her breasts & play with her nipples to enlarge them. A saucepan boiling over interrupted our fun.

I made copious notes every day in my diary when I was at work, but sometimes at home, about my state of mind. In reading this book, you can see my state of mind….100% in love & willing to accept unusual situations & many affairs, as long as I knew & Monica was honest with me.

Wednesday 6 August 2003

Monica, Paul & I met for lunch at a local Novotel. Monica dropped a bombshell by saying she was thinking of leaving Chimique de France because of the liaison with Paul & its effect on our marriage. I immediately said not to do that, asking why she thought her liaison with Paul was affecting our marriage. She said that she felt she was under pressure from both Paul & me. It must also be undesired pressure on me as the husband to see Monica's lover most days. Paul was still in a state of shock & was trying to think of something to say to dissuade her. I explained in my best French that Paul was helping to RELIEVE pressure on me. While Paul was her lover, I knew Paul.

I trusted him, & he informed me as per our agreement, so I was happy with Paul as her lover.

However, if he was not there as her lover, she could have another man, whereby I would be more worried & suspicious of any man & what she was doing basically I could not trust her. With Paul as a constant lover, she would not have time for other men, especially when I am not there on business trips!

As it turned out, later, my words were actually prophetic in that she would have other men, many of them! My French must have been good enough because Paul understood, and Monica gave me a loving smile. We finished lunch time, all happy the status quo would be maintained. Outside the hotel, I cuddled & kissed Monica & looked at Paul; he also gave her a cuddle & kiss. I realised I needed to ask fewer questions about their relationship so that she did not feel under pressure.

I phoned at 6:15 pm to ask whether she wanted a lift from work, and she said she was waiting for Paul. She said, "Are you happy?" "Yes, of course & you?" "I am so happy that I can stay with Paul. Let's celebrate with Champagne when you get back home." I was surprised she arrived home at about 8 pm, having gone to a bar with Paul earlier for a drink & a chat. She said Paul now understood her & would not allow any salesman from Chimique de France to take her out & would protect her. I did not understand this comment about a salesman, but I let it ride. This is why I want a happy threesome to avoid unforeseen problems. Better the devil you know than the devil you do not know.

At home, while waiting for Monica to arrive home, Lennon & I chatted about the developments & what happened at the lunchtime meeting. He was keen to know what happened & confided to me (even though he had promised not to tell me) that Monica had mentioned that " …it was almost impossible to not have an affair with other men!" Oh, wow, then I have to accept she will have affairs with other men? My thoughts were even stronger that I needed Paul to be her full-time lover so that she does not have time to seek other men! Even, with Paul, I need to be on my guard for other men.

Over the bottle of Champagne, she told me that night that their relationship was more than just sex; he needed Monica because Christine was constantly having mental problems & he needed Monica to discuss & help him get over his problems. Lennon also had a glass with us & was happy that we were both pleased with the day's events & discussion with Paul. He liked Paul, probably influenced by the little gifts he brought sometimes at home. Seeing Monica & myself happy was music to his ears with a happy home. I think Lennon had European thoughts & ideas of stability while remembering African ideas of what is often normal in any relationship. As a friend once said to me, if an African woman is used to having to use her wile & body to raise yourself above poverty or to achieve a position of power in African life, that is not usual or accepted in European life. As I discovered with the initial meeting with Paul, her relationship was initially designed to get her a job in Paul's company. I was to find time & time again this would be repeated with various liaisons to get various favours, jobs, contracts, car repairs & the like.

Thursday 7 August

I meet Paul at lunchtime at "Flunch," a chain restaurant in Massy & give him some nice photos of Monica. He sent me an e-mail later to thank me not only for the photos but also my information regarding Emmanuel's promise of marriage, Andre's previous affair in Africa and sexual encounters prior to our marriage.

Friday 8 August 2003

Paul picked up Monica from home early at 6:45 as arranged so that I can sleep more. I read Emmanuel's letter "Stitches in Time" again, thinking more about what he said. Paul also arranged to take Monica to Vincennes Hospital for 4 pm to see the doctor regarding her fibrosis problem that is causing her pain so often. Monica's period had finished, so I thought they might make some arrangements to find somewhere to have a shag. She phoned twice to say they were only having a beer in a Paris pub. Why does she keep this charade about being in a pub with Paul? She said on her return at about 7:30 pm that she couldn't have sex with Paul since she still had her period. I didn't press the point because I knew she had finished, evidenced by no pads in the bin & the fact she did not have pants on in bed last night. Being a scientist, one is a very good detective. Why is Monica still reluctant to tell me when she has sex with Paul? I worry if another man appeared on the scene, I would have more problems finding out. If Paul was true to his word, he would tell me. Sure enough, when I asked him on SMS, he answered, "Oui j'ai passe un très bonne après-midi avec Monica". I was to find out later they sometimes went to a sex club called "2+2" in Montparnasse, Paris.

As we chatted that evening about my increasingly difficult capability to raise it, Monica had advised me a few months ago to take "Viagra" or "Cialis" to ensure a good enjoyable shag for both of us. By having sex with Paul, Monica was always feeling more amorous, whether of guilt or just desire for me. Either way, Lennon nearly caught us in the act on the sofa. As it was, he "only" caught us completely naked recovering! He is good at ignoring us & went straight to the kitchen. I sent an SMS that night thanking Paul for "warming up Monica for me".

Sunday 10 August

We had two visitors, Cloe, Monica's best friend & Stanley, her uncle (at present staying in a nearby town's hostel, he had been released from the CdG ZAP compound for the day. We chatted & had a little walk around the town. Later in the day, I was about to take both Cloe & Stanley back to their respective places, and I told Monica she did not need to come as I knew she had much to do around the house as Lennon was still doing the washing up. Monica took me aside & into the bedroom & asked why I did not want either Monica or Lennon. She was basically accusing me of wanting private time with either or both of them. I blew up & was angry about her accusation. I left abruptly with our two visitors & took them back to their respective places, which were within 5 km.

Monday 11 August 2003

That morning, we both went to our respective work, with the preparation & breakfast time hardly speaking. When I said, "What is your problem?" She replied that my reaction yesterday was guilt! I cannot believe the woman. She had double standards! Is it jealousy because I can chat with anyone about any subject?

Camping holiday in South of France 2003 Grau de Roi

Tuesday 12 August

I went to CdG airport to collect my youngest daughter, Dawn, who was arriving from Manchester. Previously, when she was younger, she travelled alone with a big identity tag on her neck & was constantly monitored & handed over by staff to the young person office to be collected by myself at CdG airport at a special office#2. Sometimes, I would joke, "nah, I do not want that package!"

The journey back home was uneventful because the Peripherique was not so busy being outside peak hours. Dawn was over here in France to come with me & Lennon to go down south to the Grau de Roi on the Mediterranean coast for a holiday. Monica could not come because having only recently joined Chimique de France, she did not have any holiday accrued, so she would need to stay behind. Frankly, I did not see much resistance to staying at home. It gave her ample opportunities with Paul without having to make excuses to me & Lennon. We made all the preparations with the trailer tent in the apartment car park to make sure everything was ready to make an early start. The car park had a gate accessed only by a code, so it was safe to prevent somebody from driving away with my trailer tent. We sorted out other things in the suitcases that evening for our holiday.

Wednesday 13 August

I took Lennon & Dawn camping with me in the south of France. Monica could not come due to the fact she did not have any holiday with new temporary job at the chemical factory.

Dawn, Lennon & I got up early & departed for the south of France via the A6 & onto Clement Ferrand A75 via a bottleneck that sometimes can be jammed for hours at Millau. This is now totally bypassed by the famous & beautiful Millau suspension bridge. Once past the Millau area, it was a relatively easy ride to Grau de Roi.

I sent Paul an SMS informing him that we would be away from Wednesday, so he had opportunities with Monica, starting today, Wednesday until our return. Paul replied that he was very thankful & would tell me afterwards of any sexual fun they had together. I have told him that because of the last 9 months, I have difficulty in "raising it", he is able to satisfy Monica & I have noticed she is frustrated. By Paul satisfying her sexual needs, I know she would not wander to other men. Without fail, he sent me an SMS "J'ai passé une bonne soirée avec Monica." Seems like they had fun.

I like Paul; he is a man of honour & for this reason, I have stayed friends with him for more than 20 years after his affair with Monica finished.

The three of us arrived very tired at the campsite & erected the trailer tent in a record time of an hour. This gave us time to look around the camp, have something to eat in the camp café & have a few beers & wine in the evening twilight. Sleep for all occurred very quickly!

Thursday 14 August 2003

We had a quick drive around the area which is near Aigues Mortes & Le Grande Motte, to get our bearings. Aigues Mortes is a lovely, small, totally walled medieval town with little streets & car park on the outside of the town walls. We were to visit in more detail later. However, this trip was just about getting our bearings, so we returned to the campsite to have lunch in a nearby "resto" to eat & drink. Soft drinks were not available where we went, (joke) only alcohol, usually a beer or cold rose wine! French usually refer to restaurants as a "resto", Coca-Cola as "Coca" and MacDonalds as "MacDo". Do not get confused with MacDoanlds in the rest of the world, where it is a "fast food chain". There is nothing fast about French MacDonalds; you wait for ages in the queue to get anything & I have several times given up (after 15 minutes) & left to go somewhere else.

After a lazy lunch & rest in the tent area, we walked down to the beach & made camp on the sand with an intermittent swim to cool off. Swimming makes you hungry & thirsty, so we again found a resto that only served food & alcoholic drinks….. funny that.

Friday 15 August

By a unanimous decision, we had wonderful local French croissants & pain au chocolate breakfast by the tent, time on the beach & swimming, followed by lunch at a resto, repose on the beach with intermittent swimming & later retired to the tent for a well-earned rest.

In the late evening, we went to Montpellier TGV station to pick up Monica. She had left work early to get the TGV high-speed train (300kph / 187mph) from Massy-Palaiseau TGV station that is local to us in Longjumeau. 4 hours later, she was here to spend the weekend with us. Although she was tired, we all had dinner at a local resto to us by the campsite; tiredness, food & alcohol made us all sleep again quickly.

Saturday 16 August

After our traditional French breakfast, we rested on the beach & went swimming. I gave further swimming lessons to Monica, who by this time had had an operation to reduce her JJ boobs to a more manageable C/D cup size. Without her "frontal floatation collars", she found it more difficult to stay afloat. Once she got the knack of it, she was happy swimming around the calm sea. Funny thing that always occurred on the beach, she would cover herself completely. When asked why, she said, "I do not want to be more black." "Who cares?" I said, "You are black, just accept it & enjoy the sun."

After lunch in a local resto, we went to Aigues Mortes, where Monica's friend, Jeanne, whom Dawn & I first met Monica & had stayed at Jeanne's house 2 years earlier in 2001. She had a small shop in Aigues Mortes selling African goods, including large items like wooden seats, masks, tablecloths, nick-nacks & other various African goods. Asked what she had taken so far that day (mid-afternoon) she had sold just €100 of goods & needed close to €200 to break even. I suggested she also sold much smaller items of maybe €1, €2 or €5 each that would entice people to enter & THEN maybe see something more expensive. She had nothing less than €10 & most started at €20. Offer something that kids might like & buy with their pocket money for friends & relatives would also get the parents to enter. Looking at shops & businesses, I often find it amazing how naïve & lacking marketing skills some are with regard to business. These days, with websites, it is easier to make yourself known to the world, & yet some still depend on using Facebook & say that "likes" means their message is good. One acquaintance of Steven has many friends ticking "like" even though they have not been in his shop! The fact that a Google search for his specialist shop is on page 64 or whatever escapes them.

We wandered around the small, confined town (probably no more than 800 x 800 m square within the walls) & then we waited until Jeanne closed shop & followed her back to her house. We had dinner at their place & then were invited to stay the night. Deja Vue, would Monica feel as sexy tonight as she was 2 years back? Monica wanted me to take some Cialis to ensure I performed. With a rock-hard, fully extended James & an inviting pussy, I must have expended a similar energy as a 10km run. Wow, she can be so sexy, caressing me, her pussy & inviting me to caress her boobs & gentle nipple massage alternatively. When she does that, it is difficult to hold back until James cums; I dearly want that Monica cums as well. Perhaps the fact she has been Genital Mutilated when she was not even a teenager has an effect. Certainly, feeling shredded parts of skin rather than a normal clitoris is weird & until I was told, I was puzzled why I could not find it. It was my naïve Western culture and I had not even heard about this barbaric practice done in Africa.

Sunday 17 August

We accompanied Jeanne to the local Boulangerie to buy the customary croissants & pain au chocolate for breakfast eaten on the patio. Jeanne had to open the shop as normal, a Sunday usually being her best day for sales. We said au revoir & we departed for Pont de Gard. This magnificent Roman three-tier bridge has survived the robbing of materials until Napoleon stopped it. In more recent times, there was a flash flood that rose to the second tier, while modern bridges were swept away in that same flash flood. It is hard to imagine on a quiet sunny summer's day with the river below what height these flash floods of some 20 metres (approx. 33 feet) can rise to. When you see Roman buildings like Pont de Gare, the Coliseum or Nimes amphitheatre, you realise how brilliant the Roman engineers & designers were more than 2,000 years ago.

We spent the day wandering around the surrounding area with the aqueduct for miles still clearly visible that transported water from the hills many tens of miles away to the city of Nimes. We sat on the small sandy beach below the bridge & spent some time swimming in the river. It was so refreshing that Dawn & Lennon came in as well, but

Monica was not so confident & had forgotten to bring her swimming costume, leaving it in her suitcase in the car, so she stayed sitting down, forgetting time to cover up.

Mid-afternoon, we started to make our way to Montpellier so that Monica could get her TGV train back to Paris.

Later that evening, Paul sent me an SMS that he had picked up Monica from the Massy-Palaiseau TGV station to take her home. He was able to do this because Christine was visiting relatives, so he was able to stay longer than the normal 7:30 pm. I think Monica would have been tired from the long day because no mention of sex was made & Paul would have told me if he had had a shag.

Monday 18–Tuesday 26 Aug

South of France holiday

We had a good time, although it would have been better had Monica been able to come, but she had no holiday so she couldn't come except for those couple of days over the weekend. She was working at the chemical factory on a 5-month contract, but we were hopeful that she would get a permanent contract.

We were joined by a friend's boy called Joel. The three of us (Dawn, Lennon & Joel) went to various places & at one venue, the three went Go-Kart racing. Dawn & Lennon became intense rivals & while Lennon was clearly in the lead against Dawn, who was being more careful, Lennon crashed & by the time he was back racing, he had let Dawn through to "win". You can imagine the banter that day afterwards!

Monica sent various SMS messages at night times & Paul had nothing special to say either.

Apparently, Paul had few opportunities during the period 18 to 26 August due to a constant flow of Monica's friends visiting & staying to take advantage of spare beds while we were away.

Wednesday 27 August 2003

Monica phoned Lennon several times while I was driving home from the south of France to find out where we were to gauge what time we would arrive home. She did not want us all to arrive home & find Paul & her in bed together! As it was, we did not arrive home until closer to midnight, totally exhausted. We all quickly brought our luggage into the flat, had a quick drink, ate the filled baguettes Monica had made for us &, after a quick chat, retired to bed.

Although we had a good time & the kids really enjoyed it, I was missing Monica.

During the day, the last of Monica's friends had gone because we were back late that night, so Paul picked up Monica from work & was able to experience his 4th shag of the holiday with Monica. With so many "missed" days lost due to visiting friends, he was so pleased to relieve his sexual frustration because Christine was constantly having bouts of shouting, throwing things and frightening Paul & the two teenage children.

Christine's mental health was a major factor in why Paul needed a friend to confide in &, of course, have the shag he could not get at home. Monica is a very good listener & often is able to give very sound advice to both me & others. Paul needed her to advise & help him through his difficult times. While he loved Christine, he could not cope with her bouts of insanity when she "flipped". He told me much later that he would arrive home & the place would be a mess with broken plates & children hiding in the bedrooms for fear of what she may do.

Christine was intelligent & intellectual, and later, we went several times to visit their large house within large gardens. She was most cordial, friendly & could talk about many subjects. They met at university & one could see why Paul loved her. When out of her gaze, I could also see Monica was jealous of the lovely house & surroundings & pined for something similar. While my job was pretty well paid, I was not in the same salary league as Paul being director of a large corporation. On our visits, he was keen to let the "girls" talk, and we would go into the garden to look at the bees in his tree hives & stroll around his garden. I was sure he was hoping that Monica could chat & help Christine over her problems without giving any hint of their relationship.

Thursday 28 August

During lunchtime, I phoned my dad. He was not there, but nan said he was in hospital with bronchitis. I got the phone number so that I can phone him in the evening.

Most of the day was spent relaxing & taking both Lennon & Dawn walking around Longjumeau town while Monica was at work. Paul & Monica arrived about 6 pm & had bought some beer on the way back. Monica was wearing a silver short dress with a low plunging neckline. Both Paul & myself were constantly glancing at her half-covered breasts. It occurred to me that the sight would send her male colleagues' hearts racing if she was there all day. We all began drinking the Leffe with him while Monica looked pleased at the harmonious gathering. When it was his customary time to depart now at about 7:45pm, Monica wanted me to accompany him to his car parked on the road outside the apartment block. We chatted, and he informed me of the good sex they had last night before we arrived home. While Monica could not bring herself to say she went to bed with him last night, by wanting me to go down in the lift with Paul to the car, she wanted him to tell me. Proxy messenger!

When the opportunity arose without Dawn or Lennon within earshot, I mentioned to Monica I was pleased she had a good time in bed last night with Paul. She hugged me, kissed me & caressed my crutch & said she had got something for me later. I had a sudden rush of blood pressure in my pants & hoped that the kids wouldn't arrive that moment with my trousers bulging out & putting a strain on the zip!

When no one was looking, she gave me a packet of Viagra, which I slipped into my pocket & went to our bedroom to take the little blue pill. Dinner & the kids going to bed could not happen quick enough! We tidied up the things, got breakfast things out ready for the next day & then, with a glint in her eye, Monica led me to the bedroom. "Do you like how I look?" she said as an invitation to say & do much more. "Yes, I think you look gorgeous & I cannot wait to feel you." She smiled & started undoing my trousers zip while I started simultaneously unzipping her dress at the back. Monica's dress fell to the floor about the same time as my trousers fell. I pulled off my T-shirt while she went inside my pants, pulled my fully erect penis James and then pulled down my pants with the other hand.

My eyes were glazing at the lovely feeling & yet I was not distracted enough to stop me from undoing her bra. They call bras "Souten gorge" in French for a good reason: It "supports the gorge" of the breasts together. She slipped off her nickers & then said to me, "Sit on the bed." I duly obeyed, and she then went on her knees, kissed & swallowed James. You have to remember he was fully erect & yet my shaft fully disappeared down her throat. God she can swallow a penis so easily deeply!

I tried to reach her boobs as they were swinging nicely to the rhythm of her mouth movements, but I was losing them every time she made those recovery retractions between deep throat movements to breathe. I wanted her to stop & yet I wanted so much for it to never stop. I could not move for the ecstasy. Now a feeling was starting to well up inside me. Oooooh, I am going to cum. All the time, Monica was looking into my eyes, reading me like a book, until POW, an explosion of cum ejected all over her as she was taking one of her breaths for the next deep throat. Within a nano-second (0.000,000,001 seconds, yep, very fast), she deep-throated me again to reduce the amount of cum over her face. Some eventually oozed out of her mouth, still with that enigmatic smile of satisfaction & splattered cum face.

She continued sucking away until the "mountain" reduced to a molehill & then a walnut. Only then, feeling the event was over, did Monica wipe her face with her hand & lick her lips to make sure she had swallowed all the available cum. I was knackered, but I knew there would be no rest; it was my turn to please. She moved onto the bed & now it was me that had my head between her legs. As I have said, exciting a woman without a full clitoris is immensely difficult; however, I always wanted to try & please her. After what seemed an eternity of playing & help from herself, she finally came. I was pleased I had been able to please her as well as she had pleased me.

We lay together, both exhausted. I was fondling her breasts, trying to get her nipples to react when …..what's this? Viagra & her gorgeous black body was making a second bout seem imminent. Yes, round-2 was coming. She looked at the growing mountain & that smile reappeared. This time, she went on all fours on the bed facing the mirrored wardrobe so that I could mount & ride her. I had no problem finding her pussy; it was as large as an open gate. In it went, James was happy, hips thrusting away with all my reserve energy would allow. Seeing her boobs swinging to the rhythm of my thrusts raised my tempo even more until, at last, a 2nd climax. There were some after-thrusts, then a relaxing time on top of her before sliding off & onto the bed, totally exhausted. Oh wow, twice in one night, straight after each other.

We lay together facing each other & with her smile, she said, "Welcome home, I have missed you," "I have missed you, too." We lay there motionless for ages with many thoughts still buzzing around, when suddenly she said, "You know, I love you. I only have sex with Paul because he needs me at the moment, but once Christine, his wife, gets better, he will not need me." "It does not matter; he satisfies you when I cannot, & he is a good friend & has given you a good job. So long as I know about your affair, then it is alright. What I do not like is when you hide the fact you have met & had sex. He is a gentleman & informs me." "I know," she said, "that is why I wanted you to go with Paul to the car last night so that he could tell you. I always feel embarrassed that I should tell you I am having sex with another man."

Friday 29 August

I took the kids to Fontainebleau town & surrounding hills & forest before returning home in time for Monica to arrive. Paul arrived with Monica at the normal time. When I had the opportunity alone, I told him of the wonderful night of sex I had had with Monica. I thanked him for warming her up for me. Paul was helping me understand Monica on various things & his advice has minimised our disputes. She now caressed me more. He left as usual about 7:45 pm with the arrangement that I would meet him for lunch in Palaiseau CORA café.

However, he sent Monica an SMS at about 10 pm saying he had returned to his "prison". He informed Monica that he was not allowed to be with other friends, and she complained all the time when they went shopping. She couldn't drive due to her mental condition & stayed at home, did no housework & waited for Paul, the kids or a twice-weekly house cleaner to tidy up. After their holiday, she complained about a small mark on the car that needed to be cleaned, then left a mess & then went to bed. He was a nice man & deserved better. She had several times tried to commit suicide by slashing her wrists or taking an overdose of sleeping tablets.

When Monica told me this, I immediately thought of my ex-wife Lyn. She would do nothing & expect the kids to do all the work. She once said to friends, "I want kids, so I do not need to do anything; they can become my little slaves". Little did she realise, so many years later, her attitude would alienate her from her daughters, so much so Sophie never invited her to her wedding! Lyn did not find out for some 5-7 years afterwards!

Saturday 30 August 2003

End of Dawn's visit

Dawn's holiday in France was over, so we took a scenic route back to CdG airport & said, Au Revoir. Monica suggested we pop into her friend Cloe, who has a flat in Chilly Mazerin, a small town next to Longjumeau. We stayed for a coffee, & I did a bit of a repair job on her wardrobe. When we returned home, I suggested we went for a walk around the park area of Longjumeau, this passed several hours in the nice sunshine.

Sunday 31 August

Sunday was my traditional training & coaching day, so I went throwing. It was nice to get rid of the cobwebs & just see the discus fly out. Once a discus goes a fair distance, the flight is a wonderful experience that is similar to watching Concorde. The stadiums & training grounds in France are much more numerous than in the UK, plus free entrance, which aids training frequency & time to train. Within approximately 5km radius of Longjumeau there are three other all-weather stadiums. On the wall of a Longjumeau estate agent, they have a giant reproduction of a local map showing three stadiums.

Athletics clubs, in fact, ANY sports club, have no problems with finance. The central government pumps BILLIONS of Euros into sport & the departmental "Conseil Generale", hands out money to the local municipalities who, in turn, to the clubs. Essonne AC was a conglomerate of 6 other clubs at the time, & Longjumeau was one of these. I was invited to many of the constituent clubs because I coached as well, so these AGMs had Champagne, "petit-fours", whiskey, whatever you wanted at the finish. No wonder the club officials were not interested in ideas to raise money, as one official eventually explained, "Geoff, you do not understand, do you? We have so much money; we do not know what to do with it!" This is similar to local Mayor meetings, where after the boring 45 minutes speech, Champagne & whiskey flowed with 15 attendant servers & entertainment live band, all at the municipality's expense & taxpayers. Now I understood why my tax was so high.

I took Monica for a driving lesson in my company car in a supermarket car park on Sunday when shops & supermarkets were shut in France. She was totally clueless, yet she had a "valid" Cote d'Ivoire driving licence. When, how did she get the full licence? (see precis at finish)

Monday 1st September 2003

I met Paul for lunch & explained to him that he was helping me get closer to Monica by not only giving her the sex she desired, where I often cannot perform, but also helping Monica to understand me more through a man's eyes. He was providing the interface of understanding, much like she was doing for his problems at home. He sent an SMS later, "J'étais un mari en or." I was a husband of gold.

Tuesday 2nd September 2003

Due to my car being a company car, no one else except employees of HJY (Horiba Jobin Yvon) are allowed to drive my car on the road. Monica said she could drive & had for a while kept asking me to buy her a car. Eventually, we saw a friend who offered a light green Renault Clio for € 5,000. It was in good condition, so I agreed to buy it for her. Monica paid for the insurance & road tax. I bought the car for her, so she could start driving to work. I was scared when I took her for a quick drive in her new car in the local supermarket car park, mainly empty of cars.

Monica then said we should go for a ride, mmmm I wasn't sure of confident, but she insisted. We went around the local roads, I was shaken & needed a drink when we got back....yes, that bad!! She did not panic because she didn't realise the danger at the time, her reactions were so slow; it confirmed all I had predicted when she was constantly "back-seat driving" with me or anyone else. I was amazed at how little control she had & I did not believe she drove in Cote d'Ivoire. She could not change gear or have any control, plus reversing was an impossible task for her. Rwandese / Cote d'Ivoire driving tests cannot be of the standard of European ones!!!

Wednesday 3rd September 2003

Monica hand-cuffed at Driving licence office.

She was determined to go to work by herself in her new car, so that's what she did...no accidents so far...I keep my fingers crossed for the future. Monica decided she wanted to get her Cote d'Ivoire driving licence transferred to a French one. She went early from work to the driving licence dept of Conseil General in Evry. After waiting for some while, suddenly, she saw two police officers who handcuffed her & took her back to the police station. They claimed the official at the driving licence dept said her Cote d'Ivoire licence was forged or not correct. After some 4 hours, when she was not allowed to phone me at work, they returned the licence, let her go without charge & said she needed to take a French driving test.

Having inspected this licence later, it did indeed look "fishy". It stated with a stamp over it, "valid ONLY OUTSIDE Cote d'Ivoire". If she paid for corrupt forgery, Cote d'Ivoire officials would know, but other countries perhaps not. I remember that in Africa, most things can be bought & you can just learn by experience how to drive, but this would be lethal on European roads.

Monica started a driving course firstly with CD's to take the written exam & after that it was 20 driving lessons costing over € 700.

After her 20 lessons, the driving instructor said she was ready, & when she took it, she failed. He tried to get her to take another 20 lessons. Monica rightly claimed if she was ready after 20 lessons (another € 700) why does she need another 20 lessons? They compromised at four more lessons before the 2nd test, which she passed.

During the period of learning to drive, I took her out in her Clio & taught her basic things that driving schools would not teach because they teach you how to pass your test & not necessarily how to be a good complete driver. One thing she was taught was to put two hands together when turning! I said in the UK, you would fail, if you turned with one hand over the other, or two hands together. In UK, you had to have a 10 o'clock - 2 o'clock hand position & use push-pull technique to ensure that basic position when turning, also let the steering wheel slide between the hands when straightening up. Monica always thanked me for the tips & advice on driving.

Thursday 4 September

Monica went to work by bus & gets back home from her Palaiseau office, & at about 5:30 Paul arrived from the Rungis office & labs. He brought a bag & said to us that there was a permanent job at a German subsidiary of Chimique de France to be announced. The job involved logistics of requirements & shipments for the chemicals required by the chemical company & because the Germans cannot speak French & the French, not German, the post is for an English speaker as this is a common language. Paul was sure Monica would get the job because she was the only English speaker among 200 employees at the Palaiseau office & works, plus he had recommended to the Germans: Monica was the person for the job. He then opened the bag, & there was a bottle of Champagne. Monica loves Champagne, so within a micro-second (0.000,001 seconds), the bottle was cracked open, and a toast was made. Everyone was happy. Paul was good for us, especially Monica.

I gave Monica a printout of something I had written, "Why I love you more," which included the relationship with Paul. I let them read my notes while I went into the garage to do some weights. On my return to the flat, Paul was still there & Monica hugged & kissed me in the kitchen. Monica sat down on the couch next to Paul, opened up & said what I already knew that she had been to bed with Paul a number of times. She said she had been reluctant to tell me herself because she thought I did not want to know all the details of their sex together. I said that I just wanted her to tell me when & where they had sex. She was happy & promised to tell me the next time. However, she said she was still embarrassed to kiss or cuddle him in front of me. I said I did not mind. In fact, by kissing & cuddling with me there showed they were not hiding anything. Monica looked at Paul, & with an approving look from me, she moved closer to him & cuddled him &, eventually, with arms around, they kissed. When they parted, I said, "That was not so difficult to kiss & cuddle together in front of me, was it?" They both smiled, and Monica, most of all, she had what she wanted: a loving husband & a loving boyfriend that she could openly kiss & cuddle when she wanted. What else could she want…..maybe "menage a trois"?

It was now close to the 7:45 pm witching hour, so Paul eventually left with Monica accompanying him to the lift. She went in with him &, with a nod from me, cuddled & kissed him as the lift doors closed. Once down in the public domain, she stayed not so intimately close to him; we had many neighbourly eyes that would be able to see them.

When Monica returned, we sat down on the couch, & she started to explain how they first met. She said that she went to a supermarket in Palaiseau one day on the way back from Paris & next in line was this man with grey hair, hence the phone entry "gris". Both made eye contact & he asked her whether she needed help with her shopping bag. She said yes & on asking where she lived, he offered to take her home. During the chat, he said he was a big boss, & she asked whether there were any jobs available. They arranged to meet again while he investigated possible temporary jobs she could do. I helped her with a CV & she had an interview & was given a post based in Palaiseau.

Sunday 7th - Friday 12th September

Granada Conference, Spain

I was in Spain from Sept 7-12 2003, for a conference in Granada. I was able to visit the famous Moorish occupation Alhambra; some days, it was 39C. After the conference finished, we visited a JY ICP customer at Huelva University in the west of Seville near the Portuguese border. After seeing their work on analysing the Rio Tinto River pollution, I asked whether I could use their work in lectures & give them publicity at worldwide conferences. They were very keen & sent me the data subsequent to my visit. Using that data, I was able to make a 30 minutes PowerPoint presentation with acknowledgment on the start page & the references & acknowledgments at the finish. They were able to use the presentation at their university & environmental conferences as well.

When I was away in Spain, Monica decided (I must admit she is very determined to be independent) to go to work on her own again. I told her we would need to go around driving lessons so I could help her still on what she was doing wrong, but she said that I made HER nervous!!! What about ME? I am a nervous wreck!! But I do need to do it; she NEEDED some help, or she could kill herself & others on the road.

Paul apparently was very busy most of the week & did not have much opportunity to do anything other than a quick rendezvous at a bar until Thursday the 11th. Lennon used to come home from school at about 5 pm. Paul needed to find somewhere else to be sure of a place where they would be uninterrupted. He asked whether Lennon could go roller skating, but Monica was not too sure of that possible arrangement. Paul found a friend who owned a vacant house, so Paul procured the keys to allow a venue for sex whenever the occasion was opportune. Information from Paul & Monica confirmed they left work early & spent a number of hours having sex with Paul, excelling himself twice.

Paul informed me via SMS that they had a good time. When I spoke from my hotel that night, I asked Monica whether she was keeping Paul, my friend, happy. She said that they had had little opportunity. So, I corrected her, EXCEPT last night at his friend's house? "Ah, yes, it is a nice house. I wish we had a house like that". "Did he satisfy you? It is important for me that Paul satisfies you," I said, "When you go to bed with Paul, you want me more, so I want you with Paul to make me happy when I return". "Yes, my dear, Paul made me very happy & I am looking forward to your return."

Thursday 11th September

A medical examination for Monica regarding her fibroids has resulted in an appointment for an operation at Clinique d'Ivette.

Friday 12 September

I read her phone in the morning with a message timed at 03:45 am, "je ne dors pas et je pense a toi. Si j'avais ta cle je voudrais te voir." He could not sleep & was thinking of Monica & would have liked our door key to see her. I could imagine Christine was having one of her "screaming ab-dabs", no wonder, he said the other day, he felt like he was returning to prison every time he returned home. Could she return to normal one day? Maybe this type of mental illness continues for life. What causes mental illnesses like that in a seemingly normal, intelligent woman?

I returned home from Spain early evening &, after dinner, we all sat down in the lounge & chatted about the week's events while I was away. Finally, after Lennon went to his bedroom, I stroked Monica's leg & then further up her leg as she looked into my eyes expectantly, eventually I reached her pussy, "Can you shag me without Viagra?" I replied, "I hope so, I want you so much." I led her to our bedroom & slowly took off her clothes. She felt me down below....mmmm, not too encouraging. She tried her best stroking, kissing & sucking, but James was not hard enough for penetration. I did my best to satisfy her by kissing & sucking her pussy & "maybe" she came & maybe she did not. I tried to fake a climax, but I was as dry as a bone when I retracted. Women are famed for pretending to cum, but for men, there is a lack of evidence showing afterwards. What is wrong with me? I cannot satisfy my wife & depend on a friend & lover to do the job for me. If she got tired of Paul at any time, she could turn to another man, with whom I would not have the same agreement.

I read books that said some women know their husband's infidelity but do not want to know anything else & keep quiet. While others still accept the infidelity but want to know everything. I am the latter in reverse, and I need to know, even if I cannot do anything about it. Not knowing is torture for me.

Saturday 13 September

We have Stanley & a friend, Madeleine, staying with us for the day. Madeleine has a problem with her new husband regarding money. Monica, as ever, was the "agony aunt" who listened & fixed people's problems. Taking Madeleine back to Massy station, Monica was criticising me on all different things. What is wrong with her? She demanded to leave her by the bus stop, as she could take a bus home. I left her there & returned 5 minutes later to the bus stop when she had cooled off.

Sunday 14th September

We went to the chemical company fete west of Paris. Wanting to dance with Monica, she only danced to two songs & then wandered off to dance with a male colleague. While I chatted with one of her colleagues, she danced for a long time with another male colleague. However, when I arrived, she wanted to immediately stop. At the finish, her colleagues effectively forced her to dance with me. For 4 minutes, she did not look at me for one moment, even though I was looking at her all the time. Does she love me? Why behave like that?

She criticised me for giving my visiting card which contained a photo of me, to one man whom we chatted for some while. "Why did you give him that visiting card?" When I was dancing, she did not like the fact several people said I danced well. Monica cannot dance well in western style, but was superb in African style, especially what I call bum dancing. Lastly, she did not like the fact that I was talking with so many people on all sorts of subjects & she could not. She would approach when we were talking, interrupt to try & destroy the conversation. Monica is intelligent, but NOT intellectual, hence cannot talk about a broad range of subjects.

When we got home, however, she talked to Lennon that I did not care about her fibrons (fibroids) that were causing her pain. I suggested she postpone the operation date of 25 September to ensure she gets the chemical company, German subsidiary full-time job. Lennon was not happy with me with that suggestion because he was told it was an emergency. I told him it was NOT an emergency, "Who told you it was an emergency?" "Mum told me." I was angry; Monica was trying to alienate me from Lennon.

I was not happy with her criticisms & tactics. We started a discussion about a programme on the TV & then when I proposed a different view, she would walk off. I was angry because this used to happen so often, and she did not want to listen to an alternative view. I tried to cuddle her, no effect. She shied away from me & went to the bedroom, so I decided to continue watching TV. She came in complaining about the noise, and the row escalated, whereby she opened the door to the apartment corridor to the lift. I gently persuaded her to come back into the flat. We returned to the sofa, & I said I was not happy about the lack of affection. She then said the reason that she did not kiss me was because of my beard. Would shaving it off help? She said that I did not understand she was ill & with her very low pain threshold it made the slightest pain much worse. I do not know what to do.

I went to bed early & ignored her. I did not like the games she was playing.

Tuesday 15 September 2003

After work, I met Paul & Monica in the Novotel in Massy. We discussed our problems & Paul was very helpful for us. Paul asked me whether the relationship with Monica was affecting my relationship with Monica. I said emphatically, "No, you are helping our marriage!" While we were sitting in the lounge area, they constantly held hands & as we left, they held hands all the way to the car. At the car, she cuddled him & they kissed.

When we got home, I later showed her my SMS to Paul "merci pour ce soir, tu aides moi et Monica avec ton mots et aussi quand tu fais amour avec elle, parce que je ne peux pas fait une érection". (Thank you for this evening; you help me & Monica with your words & also when you made love to her because I am not able to get an erection). My French is not good, but he understood what I mean. Monica was so happy that she immediately went to the bedside cabinet to get me a little blue pill. I crushed it with my teeth & washed it down with water — it acts quicker that way.

Monica was immediately affectionate & kissed me & pulled me to the bedroom. She did a small striptease while I was de-robing myself. Oh, the power of Viagra, James has come out to play. She was happy & wanted me to mount her doggy style. I like doggy style, better penetration, more down to basics & also, I could see her boobs swing to the rhythm in the mirror. I love swinging boobs. As per normal, I was not sure she came, but she seemed satisfied & maybe wanted me satisfied; she liked to please me.

What a difference a chat with Paul makes. My SMS to Paul made Monica happy not only that night but the next morning she was singing before work. She said she was extra happy because I was open with Paul that I could not perform without his help or the help of a little blue pill. The previous episode last week proved I cannot raise it without one. Now she knows she has my full approval to go to bed with him anytime. What sort of husband am I to say that? One that is desperate to keep her; I love her, to love me & help me in any way with my sexual problems. Paul is a lynchpin to our relationship. If that should ever fall, I feared for the worse for our relationship.

Thursday 18th September

Monica saw a specialist. He examined her & poked around, took a sample, which aggravated the fibroids. Monica had been having pains for more than 3 years due to fibroids. As it was getting worse & worse, she saw the specialist to have the operation for a hysterectomy due to many massive fibroids. The fibroids operation was planned for next Friday, but the stomach was so swollen that she looked 6 months pregnant & kept joking about it....but inside, I know she was sad due to the fact she would not be able to have the baby that she wanted with me after the operation to remove the uterus. They needed the stomach to reduce before they could operate. However, by Thursday evening, Monica was in so much pain we called the doctor out & he arrived at about 11:30 pm. He immediately arranged for her to go to hospital, so we went there. We arrived at about 1:00 am Friday morning at Clinique Yvette where she stayed for the operation. The fibroids operation was planned for this coming Friday but was moved as an emergency.

Friday 19th September 2003

Fibroid operation

Monica was put in a maternity ward; however, a small room with two new babies did not help either. They changed the room, and she was improving with the pain although the stomach was still big. If it is wind, there will be a gale at some time!!! She went down to the operating theatre at about 14:30 hours & I went back to work.

During the operation, the anaesthetist didn't give Monica enough anaesthesia, so she could hear ALL that was said & FEEL all that was being done, but she was paralysed with her eyes shut, so she couldn't tell them. Only after about 30 minutes of the operation did the doctor said there was something wrong due to tense muscles & asked for more anaesthesia. He saved her life because she was, at the time and some time after, traumatised. At the time, she wanted to die as the organs were being cut & removed. When she told the nurse past midnight of what had happened some 8 hours earlier, she was shocked. The doctor came the next morning on his rounds to see Monica & was also shocked by what he heard. The next day, he had a discussion with the anaesthetist about the nightmare.

The next day (Saturday), he had a discussion with the anaesthetist about the nightmare. Physically, she was progressing fine, but mentally, she was destroyed. She needed counselling. I made an official complaint when she came home & to get some lawyers involved. A procedure has to be made to avoid this from happening again; another person could easily have died with such trauma.

Monday 22nd September 2003 (4 days after operation)

I told my boss that if need be, I would work at home for sometime during the 3-week convalescence. From different women's experience, she would not be able to lift anything, even a kettle. During the next 3 weeks, I, sometimes, worked from home when I had urgent deadlines & I didn't want the disturbance of the office, so I could get a lot done that is difficult in the office with constant interruptions with colleagues wanting things or advice and phone calls from our agents.

4 days after the operation (Monday), the anaesthetist came round the ward & spent 2+ hours trying to convince us it was normal!! I inspected the operation record, it is useful being a scientist & started

asking awkward questions about the Systolic pressure & pulse rate trends before & after the extra morphine was given.

I visited her during each lunchtime & in the evenings. By the time I got home to cook dinner for Lennon & myself & do some other things, I would be ready for bed & crash out immediately.

Steven moved at last into his own house on Monday 22nd Sept & was now a proud house owner in Tunstall, Stoke on Trent. He was close to his main shop where he was the CoOp supervisor. He was especially pleased as he would not need to spend so much time staying at his mum's due to work nearby. He was close enough to go when he WANTED to, & far enough away to get on with his life when he wanted to.

Tuesday 23rd (5 days after operation)

Monica was now walking by herself slowly down the corridor. She was due home this Friday 8 days after the operation. I can imagine it will be many, many weeks before she can think about work or doing many of the things in a normal life. We have friends of Monica's staying with us in the next few weeks, so the house would be full of beds & probably people falling over each other to help her. I said I would get her a crown so she could dish out the orders….she had to smile at that one.

Wed 24th September 2003 (6 days)

Monica stayed in the hospital for her fibroids (fibrons) at Clinique Yvette, Longjumeau. During the operation, the anaesthetist did not give a strong enough dose, so while immobilised, she could hear the chatting of the surgeons while they operated and feel some of the pain. I made notes & made an official complaint. Eventually, I met all the big bosses at the hospital with the operating team. The female anaesthetist was so nervous that I could hear her sigh with relief when I said I wanted the hospital to learn not to punish them.

Friday 26th September 2003 (8 days)

Monica was progressing well & on schedule, I was able to take her home & have the day off. I drove slow & as careful as possible, to our flat just a kilometre away. Careful walking with my aid when required, we went in the lift. When it arrived at our floor it jolted to a stop & I noticed a grimace of pain on Monica's face. Carefully she sat down in the armchair & I made a cup of tea.
During the day, she became more sprightly & more adventurous, each time she was going to do something like lift something, I said "no!", wait for me to do it.

Saturday 27th September (9 days after operation)

Marina another friend who is a medical doctor in Nantes arrives for a visit from Nantes. She is nice, good looking, educated & likes to have fun with us. A number of Rwandan friends came to us for a welcome home party, & the girls dressed up. With so many Rwandan women in sexy dresses having fun, it was hard to take group photos without ogling at them afterwards. While, we, British make only glancing looks at women that we wish we could ogle, some other nationalities make a habit of ogling & smiling to seduce from afar. However, it was difficult when getting drinks or something from the kitchen, a sexy Rwandan made smiling seductive looks. Of course, I would chat, but no more. Anyway, Rwandans "never" take somebody else's white man. This, as we will see later, was broken by Monica to get Gisele's white man with a big house & money, but more of that much later.

Sunday 28th September (10 days)

The next day Sunday, Agatha (still living in Rome with her husband. Justin) arrived as well, so it was rather cosy with us all there. By this time Monica was well enough to travel, so we went out with other Rwandans to Versailles chateau gardens & had a picnic on the grass overlooking one of the fountains. Agatha stayed one more day, but Marina had to leave for Nantes to start work again on Monday at her hospital. She worked as a doctor in a Nantes hospital. One time we went for the weekend there. It was not too far to get to the coast from Nantes.

Rush to England; Dad ill

When my dad got Bronchitis about 5 weeks ago in August, it really pulled him down & with coughing. He was coughing up blood* all the time & not getting any sleep. Nan said she needed to go to Bournemouth for 3 days. I phoned him on Sunday, the 28th of September night, just before we were sitting down for dinner with seven guests. He seemed so poor & with the neighbour Bea saying he couldn't be left alone. I decided to go instantly to England. I packed and said to everyone that I apologise but had to go to England immediately. Within 20 mins of the phone call, I was in the car on my way to Calais.

I got to Dad in Chelmsford at 3:30 am Monday, 29th September morning & Dad was coughing all the time. He was sleeping nearly all the time & couldn't chat for more than a few minutes at a time without closing his eyes. I got the doctor in for lunchtime, he gave him some more antibiotics. This seemed to work by the Tuesday he had a more restful sleep. Nan arrived back Tuesday night & we said no way Dad could climb the stairs, so I would moved the single bed downstairs into the lounge in an alcove area, where we could put up a curtain to hide the bed in the daytime. By Wednesday 1st October, he seemed to improve & was able to chat more normally. I left at lunchtime for France, returning home at 9 pm that night.

* Dad got TB tuberculosis when he was about 24 years old & would have died if a doctor said to him that an experimental idea of collapsing one lung a day after the other to rest it may work, dad said I have nothing to lose & he recovered, but with 2 half diseased lungs.

In later life his breathing became worse as the remains of his lungs slowly started to break up, hence coughing up blood.

Saturday 4th Oct 2003

We went to Evry-2, a large shopping mall in Evry, which is a concrete town with nothing of interest & a shopping mall. Everything is relatively new but devoid of taste. Monica said she wanted to buy Paul a nice coat to thank her for the one-year job contract. In passing, he had said he wanted to buy one.

That night, we had a big row. I had made a document in English about our complaint to the hospital about the botched anaesthetic application during the operation & having made a basic translation, I wanted her to proof read it & correct my bad French. For days running into weeks, she said she did not have time to read & correct. I said she had no sense of duty, probably the difference between the British & Rwandese. I said someone else might die unless they were aware of the problem. Monica exploded & started on, "My friends were amazed that you complained to her friends about cold food at Rwandese parties. How can you have my friends cooking on Saturday with that attitude? You have no friends in France except my Rwandese friends." I retorted, saying that she was the biggest hypocrite, second only to the pope!" She criticised me all the time & yet when I criticise her, I was shouting, even if I was talking in a normal voice. I think maybe it is my tone that makes the difference! Then, she shed the crocodile tears.

Knowing Monica, she would send information & then explained our row to Paul. I sent basic details of MY story to Paul in an SMS. I saw she sent an SMS to Paul. Paul replies with the question: "Do you want to leave, Geoff?" "non, mais la situation familiale et mon travail me perturbé", she wasn't happy with me or her job situation….Huh? That did not make sense unless there was more pressure on Paul to give her a permanent job. Paul answered: that we are a family & is Geoff happy with Paul & Monica's liaison.

Monday 6th October 2003

Monica was progressing slowly from the operation. She was supposed to be going to work on Tuesday 7th, but both Paul & I said, "No way." She got tired at the slightest amount of work. This was natural; I know so many women who have had this operation, so why do they think she would be able to work so quickly? I thought she would get a week or 10-day extension of the sick note. In France, you lose some money as the state pays most of the money for you & not the company whom you work for & it was therefore not on full pay.

We have so many friends coming for either the day or a few days or a week that the house was permanently like a hotel, with Lennon usually sleeping in the lounge on the "canopy lit" bed settee I had bought for such occasions. She went driving in her car one day to get a few things at a supermarket about 2 km away. She was knackered for most of the day afterwards.

Monica got the job for 5 months as cover for someone having a baby in the chemical company. The job would be extended further as the lady stayed away longer. We lived in hope that Monica would get the job on a permanent basis. Although Monica hoped that it would be in a different dept, the sales dept was very pressurised due to the number of quotes that have to be done each day for product. Before the operation, she was often starting at 8 am & finishing at 7 pm. As she wanted the job & to create a good impression, the extra hours were not paid.

Chapter 11

Question marks on our marriage

Analysis of Monica

During this period when she was in hospital, I was able to collect my thoughts & write down the ideas I had as to why we had all these rows. I always have a notepad, pencil & pen by my bedside, so if I cannot sleep thinking about something, I can make notes on the subject so I can rest mentally to sleep, & in the morning, I can expand the basic words. I started assembling my ideas to make a theory of what my problems with Monica are.

The key problem for Monica & our marriage is this: She is intelligent; however, she is not educated enough & not intellectual. Her attention span on listening to information is low, ADHD? With a lack of general knowledge, she cannot hold an intelligent more diverse conversation with more educated people. For this reason, she would try to interrupt any conversation I have with others or change the subject to one that is simple. When people have an inferiority complex, then they try what Australians call "tall poppy syndrome." They would, instead of working to RISE to the higher standard, they would try to PULL DOWN the other person to their lower level. She would try to be-little me in front of others. This was evident that Monica was criticising me all the time to pull me down to her level. It even applies to the fact she does not want me to teach her anything she does not know e.g. PowerPoint. An example: it took her 3.5 hours to do five simple pages that should have taken her no longer than 5-10 minutes. I could see her mouse hand wavering about various icons, looking for something because she did not know how to use PowerPoint. She does not want to listen to anything that educates her & especially from me;

this caused friction between us — especially when she does not want to admit any blame.

When I was talking to her about anything more than basic, it was like talking to a brick wall. She did not understand or did not WANT to understand.

There was another problem for Monica not being intellectual; she would lie to hide her extra-marriage activities & not realise her lies were not credible. I saw this before, for example, her meeting with Andre in the hotel before our marriage & I would see this increase as she started to expand her sexual activities.

Being a scientist where one has thoughts & theories, then one tries to fit all the evidence together and experiments to prove or disprove the theory, we make really good detectives. When Monica told me something that did not seem credible, I would investigate & often, I would travel to places to prove or disprove my theory. My thoughts on small things she said were added to my database of information. I started to make comparison notes to compare with other titbits of information & gradually, many things came together. Sometimes, days, weeks, months & even years after. Many things about the initial liaison with Paul were like this. For example, when I phoned her one time after work to pick her up, she said she was walking & yet I could hear an echo & no traffic, nor walking steps. Paul told me years later, they were in Massy TGV station, hence the echo.

All the lies & deceit were playing on my mind, trying to work out things so that even during my athletic training, I would be thinking of Monica & what she was up to with regards to the latest information that did not make sense. It was stressing me & did not want to lose her. One divorce (with Lyn) was enough. When we were not arguing, we would be best friends & confide in many things that Lennon would have no idea of. What do I do?

Like a witch doctor, she has me under her spell. Even years after and all the heartache she caused me, that attraction caused by her spell was unnerving.

She often would send an SMS to Paul saying, "I do not think you love me." He, of course, would try to reassure her. It was a game Monica played well with Paul and me & I am sure many others. Another reason was she wanted Paul to give her a permanent job. However, due to a possible takeover of the company, any permanent jobs were postponed, so she was given a one-year contract in the sales department & the possibility of a transfer. He had to be careful not to show obvious favouritism & also ensure people did not see him giving lifts all the time to Longjumeau.

Tues 5th Oct 2003: the three of us in Palaiseau bar with Monica showing affection with Paul

Monica invited me to meet her & Paul in a Rocker bike bar on the high street in Palaiseau. I found the address & met them. It was run by a chap who loved everything about bikes & rock & roll, including hard rock & Elvis Presley. I found them sitting close to each other with her hand on his knee. She smiled when I arrived & Paul got up to buy me a drink. I indicated I would get this round of drinks & asked him whether he was drinking Leffe. When I returned, I indicated he should resume sitting next to Monica. She was happy at that & resumed her hand on his knee.

We discussed the rows & what was causing them. She cannot understand my helping nature & I did not understand her selfishness & other men. Why does she want other men as well as Paul? He looked at her, & she said, "I make "friends" with these other men to improve us both & our marriage. I am happy to be married to you & I have Paul as well". She looked into his eyes & rubbed his crutch. He held her hand gently as if to move it, but she had other ideas & moved his hand to her leg, exposed by her mini skirt riding up as she sat down. It was not exactly what he intended, but he did not retract, & she smiled a satisfied smile at him & then at me as if to get my approval.

"You know I would you rather do that in front of me than tell lies & hide things from me. Is it not good for a marriage to not be open with me?" I eventually said. Paul agreed that Monica must be more open with me. Monica responded by making his hand rub up & down her leg, looking to see my reaction. "Yes, you see, I WANT you to be open with me, no secrets." Being in the dark corner of the bar hidden from the other main part by a partition, she leaned further over him & embraced him with her free arm & kissed him. Using her other hand, still holding his hand, she pulled his hand up to her fanny. Paul was helpless as his sexual urges took control of his own hand & rubbed & fingered her fanny. Slowly, her breasts started heaving while still joined together, kissing passionately. Eventually, after a time that seemed ages, they parted. Monica turned to me & said, "Do you mean like that? Are you happy now?" "Yes, no secrets," I said. The rest of the time in the pub was less passionate, while still, his hand was holding her leg up high as we chatted about less controversial subjects. As usual Paul broke to leave about 7:45 pm because his house was only just up the road, to get home by 8 pm.

Saturday 8 October:

The phone rang, & when Monica picked up the phone, her body language was similar to when she was talking to Paul. However, this was a blast from the past; it was Pierre, the dentist in Melun. She met Pierre when she was in the refugee centre & I think she had some sort of liaison. Even though we met a number of times, if he did have something with Monica, it would have been accepted it was "on the side". Having been to his flat, I was amazed that, for a dentist, he had such a basic kitchen with a camping hob on boxes & very little else there. Surely, dentists make a lot of money? Surely, he could have made his kitchen facilities better with just a little expense? People like that amaze me by having no imagination or desire to improve their lot.

Sunday 9th October 2003

Paul sent an SMS wanting to know whether he could visit in the morning or afternoon. He came around in the morning while I was training down the road at the stadium. He had left before I arrived home, but I could see the evidence by the two Leffe bottles in the waste bin & the remainder of the pack in the fridge. "Oh, Paul popped round for a few minutes while you were training". Funny few minutes, I thought later, when I saw the beer bottles. Probably nothing more than conversation because Lennon was at home, but why does she lie?

That evening, we had another row before going to bed. I finished with, "You had better marry Paul if you want to. Or maybe you want Andre. I notice you were shit scared that he had made you pregnant last March & because he goes with so many women, we may have AIDS." That hit a nerve because she still loved Andre, even though I am sure she told him to be careful not to contact her because of me. Monica swung around, hit me in the mouth and again on my left cheek. I looked at her & said, "See that mark on the coffee table? That was a mark made when Anne* hit me & I went flying over the coffee table & hit my head & elbow on the floor. You can push me so far until I say that is enough, then she was history as I took her back to England. I will tell you now, you are pushing me close to that point."

We look at each other, eye to eye, for a long time. She could see my look of hurt & determination and I could sense her brain cogs wheeling around in her head (married to a white British man, with a good secure job, apartment, secure home for Lennon, the chance of getting more of his money, the chance of being British passport holder, Geoff got rid of Anne*……."). Still eye to eye, slowly, ever so slowly, as the possible situation dawned on her, she started to change her expression to one of remorse with eyes dipping downwards and the tears started, followed by a big hug, saying, "Darling, I am sorry, I got carried away, I did not mean it, I want to make up with you." Monica knew how to say sorry, first the hug, then the kissing & caressing of my lower parts and then, when the time was judged right, leading me to the bedroom for a good blow job followed by a long noisy shag. I do not remember anything else. I was out for the count, totally knackered.

The next few days, I was on holiday, remembering that I often accused her of talking to a brick wall & that often, with Lennon, I was like a fly on the wall, to be ignored. Monica was as nice as pie with me & started to involve me more in conversations with Lennon, which were normally between the two of them in French. While my French was improving, every time I said help me with French, she was too tired & it was "demain, demain" tomorrow. When I asked what was being said, "Oh, I will explain later."

Wednesday 12th Oct

Paul phoned Monica, asking her if she was evading him. Monica assured him she wasn't, but I wondered whether she was applying subtle pressure to get a permanent job contract. In her comms, she was constantly asking, do you love me? I said, he needs to show sincerity from you. When he was here alone chatting with you she changed from her work dress, skirt or trouser suit to something else nice & sexy. I said he needed a sign that you were comfortable with him & cared about him & not just using him. "Tu est malade". He phoned again & this time, after she had finished the phone call, she started mentioning that maybe she needed to show him more positive signs. However, she was embarrassed to show Paul affection in front of me. "OK, tell me in advance while I am at work & I can arrive late. I can ring the doorbell at the building entrance before I enter the building & the lift to the 6th floor. Lennon has basketball practice 5:30-8:30 pm."

Why am I doing this? Why am I making it easier for Paul & Monica to make love? Because I love Monica & do not want her wandering with other men. I know Paul & he is honourable —better the devil you know than the devil you do not know.

Friday 7 November 2003:

I arranged to meet Paul at the Cora shopping centre in Palaiseau. We had a beer & I showed him some nice, sexy photos of Monica. He did not want to take them in case Christine saw them. We chatted about Monica's embarrassment to show him affection in front of me the other day in the Palaiseau bar was an exception.

Saturday 8 Nov:

I mentioned to Monica that I met Paul yesterday and showed him some sexy photos & then showed her the photos. I said he loved the photos & that you should not feel afraid or embarrassed changing at home in front of him. She looked at me unconcerned & smiled a contented smile, indicating she was happy that he had seen the sexy photos.

Wednesday, 19 Nov:

Paul brought Monica home after work & they had an "ageable" time. I worked late as arranged & when I arrived home at about 7:45 pm, I saw Paul moving off in his car to get home by 8 pm. Monica was in the kitchen in her silver satin night dress; she looked gorgeous. I hugged her & smiled "Did you have a good time?" She smiled & nodded affirmatively. "Good, remember, no secrets, it is so much easier, eh?" she nodded. Although I searched, I never found any evidence of a condom, not that Paul would have any transmitted disease, but she was young & he was fertile. Then I remembered she had her fibrons removed with no chance of a baby in future.

Various communications between Paul & Monica centred on how to get Monica & me closer to his family so that the meeting would not be so suspicious. Paul did not want to lose Christine, she went to university where they met & she was intelligent. However, during the past few years, she had been going off the rails with bouts of smashing plates & looking for an argument. I found that you could have a good, intelligent conversation with her. This pleased Paul because we were one of only a few outside people she had been in contact with in the past few years. Paul mentioned that the big boss of CMR was retiring in the next year or so, so there was a possibility of promotion to an even higher position. Monica wanted to get closer obviously to Paul's family, however, she said that she would be a hypocrite to get closer to Christine to influence Paul. I said there was no chance of her stealing Paul away, but anyway, how could she be a hypocrite? Paul was the 2nd affaire, Andre the first.

Sunday, Nov 23rd

I opened up the 2nd delivery of a desk for € 610. Monica goes bananas because she had ordered one for € 200 which I sent back. I said what was the point of an unstained, un-polished desk that needed money (at least €50) & time spent on it, being below €500, it carried a €50 delivery charge, so the total charge would have been at least €300, plus much work & possibly not looking so good. The row escalated, & suddenly, she threw a large, heavy "La Redoubt" catalogue of hers in my face. Monica tested my patience & cool. Finally, she went out, I said to her, "I love you", & she played the game "I'm not sure", so I responded "I do not think you love me", she replied "Can't you see", "No" I responded. No fun tonight, I think!

I started to write notes to myself on the situation.

- ➢ Monica is jealous of me because I can talk with anyone about anything
- ➢ To cope with that jealousy, she has the "Tall Poppy Syndrome" (instead of aspiring to RISE to a higher level, you try to bring everyone DOWN to your level). Monica criticises me all the time, including in front of others

- She does not accept she is a hypocrite... having an affair with Paul & still wants to get closer to Christine, his wife, to have more access to him
- Monica often cannot answer my questions, so she gets violent
- Monica wants me to be her "puppy dog" to do as she wants all the time & does not like to realise I am independent & can help others & attract other females. I ask, what if a female was attracted to me? THEN she would have cause to worry!
- Monica has no long-term determination to carry things through. Athletics & my work experience has shown you need patience, determination & hard work.
- Monica can't be bothered helping others, e.g. giving a lift home to Stanley & Cloe.
- Monica doesn't want to admit she cannot do certain things without help. PowerPoint episode is an example.

Mon 24th Nov 2003

Monica passed the final internal interview with the top German bosses of the German subsidiary company of the chemical company that supplied chemicals for making the final product. The interview was totally in English as the Germans could not speak French & the French office people could not speak German, so they needed a common lingua franca language for the person at the French end in Palaiseau to communicate with the Germans. Paul made a quick memo to the factory people, informing them that Monica would be working for the Germans while still in the Palaiseau office but would have her own office & work for Jerome Marchant.

Monica phoned me while at work & said she was with Paul in the car, but I did not hear any engine noise & when at home, she arrived at 7:45.

Tues 25th November

Early that morning, Paul phoned her while we were still in bed, her left leg started moving away & up with now the right leg moving sideways as if to ready for sex, while she was softly chatting. The body language was very clear & when she looked at me, she had a contented smile. I was to find out much later that Paul had found a friend who had an unoccupied house to which he had access to the keys for intimate times with Monica. Later that day, Jeanne another friend living in Evry, the concrete town south of Longjumeau, who also came from Cote d'Ivoire arrived. I entertained her until Monica arrived with Paul. On the settee, Monica talked to Paul mainly with her back to Jeanne, the body language was clear for us both to see as Monica moved her legs constantly in her skirt that started to ride up. When Paul left around 7:45 pm, Monica then paid attention to Jeanne before she left around 9 pm

Monica was late home again with Paul, and they had been in the rocker bar on Palaiseau Grande Rue (high street). Paul was starting to get a bit guilty due to Christine getting a bit better, and he was in a dilemma as to what to do. Monica said he has to decide & she would go with the flow; however, I said to Monica I think the relationship was too deep at the moment to break off just like that. Monica said it was not just sex; she loved him & he her. I said, "I know, but sex is part of the love & she did enjoy going to bed with him." Monica did not respond to that.

Wed 26th November: my dad is getting worse

At work, I received a phone call on my mobile from the sister nurse at Broomfield hospital, where dad was since he was getting worse. She said to me he did not have long to go. She said he was concerned about Nan, who lived with him in his house. I thanked her & told her to tell dad that I was coming the next day. I fixed a ferry for late evening Thursday 27th, after work to see dad, maybe for the last time.

Monica & Paul had lunch together, apparently, they discussed the shifting sands as Christine was improving & guilt was entering both parties. She said on the phone they had discussed things & he would not be coming around "chez nous" tonight, or like before. I could not see how they could break it off just like that when they both loved each other.

After work, I met Monica & Paul in the Palaiseau rocker bar, which played some really good hard rock music & had Harley Davidson & various motorbike memorabilia on the walls & bar.

We went into a corner area & Paul said to us that he wanted to stop the affaire. Monica started crying heartbroken & snuggled up to him, holding his hand. He explained that he loved Christine & when he looked in the mirror, he felt guilty loving both Christine & Monica. She pleaded with him not to stop as she needed him. They both openly admitted to me together they had had repeated sex. I asked whether he would change his mind because life is a "roller coaster". He indicated that, maybe, but probably not, unless Christine went back to her mental problems again. While Monica said she always wanted to stop when she met Christine — that is false — she loved Paul so that in the bar that night, it was far deeper than I had imagined.

All the body language was she was truly broken hearted. Later that night, she admitted it might take a few months to get over it. She tried to explain to me that she loved him deeply, but it was a different love for me, her husband. I had said to her many times she loved Paul more than me; this was proof. I saw how when he phoned, her voice & toned change whenever she chatted with him. She would chat with him for maybe 10 minutes even if they had been together that night! Monica admitted they share all feelings together with no secrets between them. When we got home, she blew up at Lennon for something small &

went to bed crying with me left to explain as much as I dared what had happened. During the night, she murmured & started talking in her sleep.

Thursday 27th November 2003: Frantic rush to England, dad dies before I arrive.

While at work, I received a phone call from the nurse again at Broomfield Hospital that dad was worrying about what would happen. I instructed her to tell dad that he should not worry. Nan, who also lived with dad, could stay as long as she liked at the house. I finished up work quickly & left early to drive up to Calais & the ferry back to England. Whilst I am waiting at the Calais dockside, ready to board the ferry, I received a phone call from the sister nurse again at 10 pm France time (9 UK) that dad had passed away. The journey back to Chelmsford was uneventful as I arrived at 3 am. Nan was asleep, so I crept into the house & slept downstairs on dad's bed that I had installed in the alcove area.

Friday 28/Saturday 29/Sunday 30/Monday 31: England death arrangements

I am mainly with cousin Don as things need to be done, including registering dad's death while I am in England. Don was great, taking charge as I was sad & "not with it". Monica showed sympathy on the phone, she liked my dad.

Wed 3 Dec 2003

Paul came around our flat at night while I was training & coaching in the local stadium, but now Lennon told me the relationship would be "just friends". It seemed that maybe the sexual relationship is over?.

I would be on a small foreign trip for a few days in the Czech Republic to return on Saturday morning. Lennon stayed at home Friday, 5 December & apparently, he told me Monica took, Pierre, the dentist from Melun, out to the Bistro de Boucher restaurant for dinner south of Longjumeau on the N20. When they returned, Lennon made them coffee & then he went into his bedroom, closed the door with headphones, listening to music & fell asleep. Lennon told me he did not know what time Pierre went because he did not wake up until the morning.

Early Saturday morning, I arrived home & saw Monica in the kitchen. Almost as an afterthought, she said hello & rushed back into the bedroom almost in a panic. I followed slowly & found her gathering up toilet paper that was somewhere in the bedroom, put it in a plastic bag & put it by the outside door to go downstairs the next time we go to the bins. The speed & the specific visit to the bedroom when she was already going to the kitchen, before she saw me arriving at the door, aroused my curiosity, especially as remains of the toilet roll were left on the loo cistern. I knew Monica used loo paper when she had sex to clean herself up, so this needed investigating. In the middle of the night, I got up as if to go to the loo & took the plastic bag somewhere where the rustle would not be heard & investigated. The crumpled loo paper was quite wet & had a pussy smell. Being a chemist, one is used to remembering the identification of different smells, and this was a very familiar smell. I had no conclusive evidence, but after chatting privately with Lennon, I was certain if Paul was history for sex, Pierre was contacted to have sex. Blimey! She worked quickly to replace Paul. This confirmed some nagging thoughts of when she was in the Melun refugee centre with Pierre. The thought struck me regarding his poor flat, WAS he really a dentist?

Sunday 7th December 2003

In the morning, as we were in bed, I tried saying, as a test, that it did not matter if she had sex with Pierre, so long as she told me. She got upset that I could accuse her of jumping into bed with any other man. This was a claim I had made before referencing Andre & Paul, each time with similar reaction & words. She was in a bad mood all morning, but after I returned from training, she was totally different, nice as pie, affectionate, loving & promising to have nice sex later. She wanted me to promise that I did not believe she went to bed with Pierre. I promised, but I still believed the evidence & the fact that Monica was a convincing liar. She did not know my evidence; what she does not know of my investigations will help me for the future, and she will not think of covering up the evidence.

I predicted that the liaison with Paul would now be friendship & that she would now try for another man, Pierre or perhaps Jerome, a colleague in Germany. I kept hearing his name often.

Monica often feigned innocence, but guilt was only 5 minutes long until reference to Andre just before marriage & voila, 3 weeks after marriage. Monica wanted to stay friends with Pierre as a friend maybe, just maybe, she would resist going to bed again with him. Much depended on opportunities, but then she often planned things ahead. She was good at organising! Monica claimed that the sexual relationship with Paul was now finished; remember, she claimed the relationship was NOT sexual. So why get so upset when Paul said he wanted to finish the affair? She could still chat with him ANYTIME. It would be interesting to see what happens if Christine has another relapse with her mental health. If he came back for a repeat sexual relationship, how accommodating would she be?

In the afternoon, we relaxed in the lounge & she said she wanted to be married to me for the rest of her life & was not happy that she hit me from time to time. She knew about Anne & Lyn, knew that I never hit women, no matter what the provocation, however, I would have no hesitation in leaving her if she "put the hair that broke the camel's back". She said she was sad & remorseful. I think she realises she needs to change or eventually lose me.

Monday 8th Dec 2003

Monica got up singing & was very happy. She went to work, & we met in the Victoria pub/resto near the N20 Chilly Mazerin/Longjumeau border. No sex, but a nice evening.

Tuesday 9th Dec 2003

I discovered hidden in the bedroom, notes Monica wrote for a letter given to Paul. In it, she described her love for him & was heartbroken when he said the love affair was finished & then tried to mind games to using her wiles by accusing him of using her…really? I think it was a mutual thing. I saw the number of phone calls she made to him in those initial 2 months. She did not think I would look at the itemised telephone bill. She tried to change it by deception of being me, but I changed it back again. She was trying all the female tools at her disposal to win Paul back. There was a small nagging doubt that the letter was not given to Paul, so I wanted to meet Paul with or without Monica to see if he had received or read the letter. If he saw the letter in front of me & Monica, I wanted to see BOTH their reactions & body language.

I had a business lunch with colleagues at the local Italian resto, so I phoned Monica, "Did you phone me for something urgent? "No, just a quick chat," I replied, "OK then, we can chat this evening, I have a lot of work this afternoon". Funny, the difference of her reaction between me phoning her for a few minutes & Paul, whom she would chat for 10 minutes, within a short period of him arriving home after being with her for hours. What am I, a carpet?

That night, I told her I felt like a carpet & in her eyes, I was unimportant. That night, she brought some work home. It was to make a simple PowerPoint presentation of 5 pages. It was something simple that should have taken 10 minutes maximum. I could see the mouse hovering over the various icons & that she did not know what to do. I offered to help her many times because it was obvious she had no idea what to do. However, she refused & carried on; it was painful to watch. Eventually, it took her three & half HOURS!

Sunday 14 December: Big Row after Jeanne Habyarimana's visit

We went to Jeanne in Courcouronnes, near Evry, they lived in a double house, it was two semi-detached houses, with the lounge knocked through to make one large house. Within the house lived the whole family with the mother, wife of former Rwandan president Juvénal Habyarimana, & all the adult children. Everywhere was memorabilia of her husband, pictures of stately events; it was like a mausoleum.

In chatting with Jeanne's mother, who was cold & I mentioned she needed a string vest. This type of vest has holes & traps the body heat to be worn under her top. Monica arrived on the other side of the room, leaving a conversation with others & interrupted me by saying that she already had one. I said, "I hardly think so, as I have not seen the type of string vest with holes in France. It is the holes that trap the heat from one's body like a woollen pullover does the same. I promised to buy one the next time I went to England & give the mother one."

On the way back home, Monica exploded, "Why are you trying to help that woman? Why do you try to help everyone? You should not do it." I said, "It was my nature to help people, just as I tried to help you last night with your PowerPoint, instead of wasting all night trying to do a 10-minute job. Just ask! You obviously do not know anything about PowerPoint." She then hit me around the head while I was driving through Longjumeau! She was wearing a mini skirt, so I smacked her right leg, obviously not hard, while driving. She hit me again around the head & threw Lennon's drink all over me & the car, "You're a nutcase! You ought to be locked up," I said.

I drove past the entrance to the apartment car park. She screamed to stop the car as we passed the police station & proceeded up to the

Grande Rue. She then opened her door & left it open while I passed a bin that was knocked over by the open door. I turned from the Grande Rue & drove a little into Place de Steber in the centre of town. At very low speed, she pulled up the handbrake, leaned over, took the ignition keys, got out & went to another driver behind me to call the police. I snatched the keys from her & drove home with Lennon in the back. Monica walked home & I refused to let her in. With a mood like that, she could be dangerous. She got in the apartment block & went to our neighbour, Michelle & Raymond, immediately below us. They arrived with Monica to chat about the situation. I explained with difficulty because Monica kept interrupting me all the time. I said I was a carpet for her & that she used me only when she needed me. I said I must be mad to accept all her male friends & what is going on. I did not elaborate in front of Monica, but I had mentioned to Michelle & Raymond the affairs & the sex Monica had had with various men. After some time, with the atmosphere more relaxed, they left. Monica said that she was going to bed. I decided to sleep in the salon.

Monday 15 December

Monica was cold as ice with me all day & evening. I slept in the salon for another night, thinking of the situation.

No love for me. She did not listen to me. She did not want to learn from me. She did not want to talk to me or have me involved in a discussion with friends. She had no respect for me. Rarely wanted sex, except when after a session with Paulo, yet Paul, in the same period, had had sex about five times or many more with her. She criticised me all the time, trying to bring me down to her level. No affection yet again, plenty for Paul. Not only did she not want me to help, she did not want me to help others. I feared I was close to a total marriage breakdown & yet she accepted zero per cent blame for the situation.

Monica would not accept when she started an argument & in this case, what triggered the BIG argument was when she hit me, especially when I was driving, a stupid & dangerous act.

Tuesday 16 December 2003

I ask Monica whether she has spoken with Mr Villiers, her immediate boss, about the fact she was working full time plus ½ day in the sales dept. She had said it was a priority she wanted to ask him. However, she replied curtly, "Haven't you got anything else to say other than work?"

I was so pissed off, I made more notes I had started writing on the 12th on what I saw as the situation with us. Final notes below.

Problems with Monica   Dec 2003

16/12/03

Monica is an independent women who wants things & is determined to get those things even at the expense of others. She is selfish in trying to achieve what she wants.

1. I don't think Monica loves me & probably not since late 2002

2. We used to talk about anything & everything (I read the other day some notes I wrote in early 2002)...now nothing. I try to start a conversation & she walks away or why are you always talking about work (the fact that it was a topical subject of cause of stress for Monica e.g. chat with Mr Villiers about the dual role....too much work & stress)

3. Monica will not listen to me even when it is her interest to listen & learn.

   a. e.g. didn't want to lean PowerPoint from early September (when the new job was a possibility) to now, when it is even more important to learn. Why not ask when she doesn't know how to use PP & spends 3 hours doing 10 minutes work on just 5 slides !!

4. Monica has no respect for me...treats me like a carpet/tapis

5. Monica never wants to involve me in anything

6. Rarely wants to make love & then wants to get it over quickly

   a. Paul had sex more often than I did with Monica, during the same period

7. No affection towards me for over a year Oct 2002 was the change. Again she had more affection for Paul

8. Monica never wants me to help her & doesn't want me to help others. When I have offered to help people she doesn't want me to... why? E.g. Stanley, Chantal

9. Monica tries to be-little me, making me seem incompetent controlling me. E.g. with Paul: Alosi take-over would take months if it was to happen. Monica interrupts, but Paul agreed. E.g. with Jeanne's mother ref. vest for warmth. She agreed after she wanted one. I will buy in England.

10. She will interrupt me in a good discussion of subjects she doesn't know little or anything about, so she wants to change the conversation to her desires. E.g. Justin, Joseph, Roger, Toura, Paul.....

11. The problem for her: is that she knows very little, because she never wants to listen & learn. oh, I haven't got time, not interested etc. etc.

    I can understand Paul wanting to keep Christine, because she is intelligent, knows a lot can talk about many subjects. (At the dinner on the boat Monica could not talk about many subjects & just sulked without chatting to the person next to her)

12. Monica is selfish

13. Monica never wants to admit that in our disputes she is partly to blame. If she didn't do these things & didn't hit me...there would be no dispute.

Future:

Where do we go from here? I feel that Monica has totally rejected me & that we now have nothing in common. If I want to talk to a wall, I have many in the house. Monica sees this on Mon 22nd says she is sad, the doesn't like the comparison with Christine, Maybe, now I learn from Paul that Christine liked talking to me, I can see. This passage really hit a nerve, she is jealous (maybe why she interrupts conversations!)

Monday 22 December

Looking for some documents in my case, she found my notes "problems with Monica Dec 2003". Monica saw this note that I had written for myself on the 12th & printed out on Monday 22nd December. She said that she was sad. She didn't like the comparison with Christine. I learnt from Paul that Christine liked talking to me, which was confirmed after I wrote these footnotes. I saw this passage from my notes really hit a nerve with Monica. She was jealous which was why she interrupted me in conversations.

Time & time again over the Christmas period, she referred to these notes, by saying "....oh,, I know l am not intelligent...." Or "...I know I do not know much...."

Tuesday 23 December 2003: Paul suggests to try other women just for sex

I met Paul in the pub, alone because Monica was stuck in a bouchon (traffic jam). When we chatted about sex & the fact that Monica did little or no foreplay & just a quick insertion. He said that he used to insert & retract, which made Monica plead to re-insert. He also said to look for other females for sex. We continued about other women & sexual techniques by Africans. He also said he had a Cameroonian girl just for sex who was great at foreplay. He repeated several times for me to find another woman just for sex to satisfy me & be happier afterwards with Monica & her escapades. This suggested he had done this before & that having affairs was not new for him. How many has he had? However, maybe he did not fall in love with these women like he had for Monica. He said that Monica was authoritarian, perhaps due to her upbringing as a wealthy Tutsi woman. (see Note #3)

I would learn some time later from Paul that it was one of these casual meetings in a supermarket that he chatted with Monica, who liked her looks & demeanour. They chatted, & she mentioned that she was looking for a job & being a big manager in a chemical factory, he was able to offer a job. Paul said he was so messed up with Christine's mental health & state she considered suicide. He found a Senegalese woman before Monica, although she was satisfactory in bed. However, she was not the answer to his need to chat & get advice on his marital problems.

Paul mentioned to me that my French had improved as I understood him more & he could understand my poor vocabulary & accent. He asked me whether he was the source of the conflict. I quickly assured him "no", he had helped us because our problems had been there since we got married! We chatted about Monica not wanting to learn from me, the "tall poppy syndrome". Eventually, we had to leave as Paul needed to pick up his son at 7 pm. He said to me that Christine liked talking to me because I knew a lot & was a pleasure to talk about different things, like himself. This was at variance with what Monica had said to me that they found me boring! He also mentioned that they liked intellectual conversation because Christine was an information freak & could "speed read" text.

Saturday 27 Dec

Monica & I were listening to the TV about the USA warning Gadaffi in Libya that they would attack if he did not stop his nuclear programme & stop funding terrorists. She did not listen properly & said something different than what they said on the TV. I tried to correct her, but she would have nothing to do with what I said. It was interesting that she had a low attention span & listened to maybe 80-90% of what was said, but missed the crucial 10-20% that could change the whole meaning of what was said. ADHD? (Attention Deficit Hyperactivity Disorder)

Sunday 28 December 2003: beard shaved off

In bed that night, Monica wanted to chat & said Lennon needed to do his homework & asked if I could help him. I said that he was pig-headed & probably would not accept my help like his mum! All affection ceased, & she turned over & went to sleep.

Early in the morning, about 5 am, I was awoken by a hand feeling & stroking my legs. As I woke up properly, I saw Monica was smiling at me & started to remove the bedclothes. Next, she moved my hand to her breasts. How can one resist feeling her breasts, then she started playing with herself. Oh wow, she started to heave, I helped her massage with her mutilated clitoris. Should I shag her on top or doggy style? She smiled, read my face & she turned over for a doggy-style shag. She has wonderful "love handles" & when one sees her boobs swing to the rhythm that makes it a wonderful experience.

Had she thought more of what I said earlier? Had Paul had a word with her about her attitude to me trying to help her & her poor affection for me? Later, before I went training down at the stadium, she said, "Will you shave your beard off? You will look much younger". I reflected on what she said during training. When I got back home, I shaved my full beard off & appeared in the kitchen beardless. Monica looked around, & when she saw me, she cried with joy, kissing me & rubbing my lower parts. The temptation to remove my tracksuit bottoms was tempered by the fact Lennon was in the lounge. Escorted to the bedroom, off came my athletic clothes, off came all her clothes & she turned her back on me on the bed on all fours. I hoped I could make without the Cialis, her pussy looked so inviting. Surprisingly, almost immediately, James was ready to go, and we were off, riding Monica like a true cowboy! Love handles for better grip, the mirror to get a better view of the action, which included her smile of sexual pleasure.

6-10th January 2004: Plasma Winter Conference - Fort Lauderdale, Florida

Leaving Paris CdG airport on Sunday 4th, I was off with several colleagues to Fort Lauderdale, USA, via Atlanta for the Plasma Winter

Conference. I was due to give several lectures on ICP-AES. The conference, as usual, has a small exhibition area for instrument manufacturers to exhibit their products. A colleague made me laugh, & several minutes later, I saw Dr Stan Smith, a quite brilliant scientist who was the research manager of IL (Instrumentation Laboratory) in the 1980s. He recognised my laugh from over the other side of the exhibition area & came looking for me. He had retired & moved from the Boston area to Florida.

We reminisced about our times together, including the time in about 1982 when he & his wife, Barbara, took me to their golf club for dinner. After he said to me, "Would you like to go to the Concorde club?" I said, "I did not know what that was & would leave it up to him." All the while, Barbara was saying, "NO!" by shaking her head. He was keen to take us there, so off we went & we arrived in a wooded area with a large old wooden building surrounded by a car park & a forest. We went inside, Stan paid one dollar for us each to get in. We found a small table near a semi-circle stage area & ordered drinks. After a time, the lights dimmed a bit & on came a lovely-looking girl & with music. Suddenly, I realised she was a stripper! After some minutes with clothes slowly coming off, Stan Smith, this quiet unassuming brilliant scientist, was standing on our table whooping it up and cheering. I looked at Barbara, who had a resigned look of "Here we go again". I could not believe the change in him. The next day, in the IL factory, we saw that normal quiet Dr Stan Smith. When I recalled the story, he laughed.

Together with some American colleagues, we were all staying at the Bon Adventure Hotel. During time off, several of us have a round of golf & I also played American racket ball (the racket ball never stops bouncing, unlike a squash ball, I couldn't "kill" the ball as I am able to do in Squash), with a female customer. She was a very good-looking woman & if single, I might have been attracted to get closer, but I was married & also always wary of getting too close to customers. At the weekend, with one of my ex-colleagues, Dr Stuart Georgitis, we drove down to the Florida Keys, a series of sand bars extending out into the Gulf of Mexico. After some time motoring down the keys, we decided to stop & taste the local beer. On the way back, we stopped on a Miami Beach & watched something quite different to anything in Europe: weight lifters on the promenade, bikini girls rollerblading up & down, almost parading their figures & young men trying to catch their eyes. Meanwhile, on the beach, several beach volleyball games were being informally played.

Sunday 11th January 2004

After returning home, I found that Monica had gone to Melun to meet a friend. I looked into her e-mails & found she had emptied her inbox, but forgot the outbox that had the history of the IN messages she had sent out. She was communicating with a certain Paul Mpayimana, who lived just south of Melun. The name seemed vaguely familiar & I remember he was with Jeanne of Montpelier & Cloe one night when I was with Monica in the Melun area. Monica stayed the night with Ann-Law in Malesherbes south of Melun last weekend, or did she? The text was open to interpretation by enjoying each other's company & a "bonne soiree" & the fact that they exchanged five e-mails within a few days makes me suspicious. Is he a one-night stand?

All these extramarital activities by Monica were getting to me. I want her, but so do all the men & she was responding to their advances. What can I do? I was in a trap & I did not want her to leave, I loved her. I would have to work closely with Paul to ensure he has no competition. I trusted Paul, with others who knew what they would do or what they might give. Giving in to Monica was often her goal, but with other men, the chances of getting some sexual disease were increased.

Tuesday 13 January 2004

I saw she received an SMS arranging lunch with Paul. It seemed he still loved her, but not to the same intensity as before. This was what I predicted in the initial meeting with Paul & Monica in the Longjumeau café back in July last year. She never mentioned the SMS that night, she had lunch with him. I believed we were now at the good friend stage of this relationship. Will it stay like that, or will there be a few passionate interludes or maybe rise again if Christine has a relapse?

Friday 30 January

I also noticed Monica was now often erasing her SMS messages to & from him. What was the secret between them that I cannot or should not know? However, I saw a significant SMS from Paul "bonjour mon amie j'ai soufre pour le dos". I noticed significantly "mon amie" rather than "ma Cherie" or "mon amour", it seemed that the sexual relationship was truly over. If this was so, what next? Who next? That was my worry; if it's WHO next, this was driving me bonkers.

No time to think, but I realised I needed to move. I was to pick up Monica's friend Marina, the doctor from Nantes, from the TGV station in Massy-Palaiseau. Marina was nice, good-looking & educated in Europe before the genocide, so she had not seen Rwanda for many years. She stayed for the weekend & we met various Rwandan friends at a party Saturday night. Both dressed up, looking sexy. When we arrived, there was a surplus of beautiful Rwandan females. I was spoilt, except a few speak English & all speak French or Kinyarwanda, the language of all Rwandans. In my time with Monica & the monthly Rwandan "Tontin" meetings, I have learnt a few words in this language, otherwise, it is English or French for me.

Tuesday 10 Feb 2004

George-Taylor Lewis sent an e-mail from Abidjan. The tone, like back in April last year, was amorous & made me think he had a sexual relationship with Monica when she was working for ADB.

I found out before I got married from Emmanuel, her intended husband, in Cote d'Ivoire. Emmanuel had opened up a French bank account & transferred money to it as a start for Monica to live on until he got his divorce & would then join Monica in France to live a new life. Monica, of course, met me on holiday & reneged on that agreement. He found out by his contacts what Monica was doing in France. He sent me a long cautionary letter, "stitch in time" & sent it to Bibianne, a mutual friend of both Emmanel & Monica, to give to me by hand to ensure I received it & read it without Monica seeing it. Monica only had a temporary job at ADB, so she needed to "influence" the boss's attitude to give her a permanent job. Sex can be powerful when used & given into the right "hands".

I was increasingly aware Monica would use any method to get what she wanted & if it meant having sex with a man, so be it — just enjoy the same as the man.

It was obvious that although now just friends, they were close. One thing to be admired was, Monica kept her relationships quiet & confidential, sparing the wife any distress. Bosses like that, need a bit of nooky on the side to keep their penis happy & relieve any marital frustrations with a good listener. Oh yes, Monica is a good listener.

Lennon told me another day that George-Taylor Lewis was her boss at ADB in Abidjan & they were often invited around his big rented mansion on the edge of town. ADB moved some of their bosses around to get experience & help sort out other offices around the globe. I reckoned he rented this by ADB paying his rent until he found something of his own, which he did some months later by buying a flat near the centre of Abidjan. As well as Monica & Lennon going around his place, he used to come around their house often after work. Lennon was usually told to go out & play with his friends accompanied by the housemaid. Even at this age, 9-10 years old, Lennon suspected something but said nothing that would endanger his mum's job or lifestyle. Unbeknown to me at the time, he had seen this, so many times in Kigali, Rwanda.

Saturday 14 February

Paul sent Monica a Valentine's message by SMS & she showed me that evening.

Chapter 12

Monday 19th February 2004: Monica at starts Alosi (part of the chemical company)

Monica started her new job for Alosi, another subsidiary like the French chemical company she didn't have to move except down the corridor. She was a happy bunny & went next week to Germany where this subsidiary factory (that makes the chemicals that go into some chemicals) was based. I found out later she had a "good time" with one salesman Andreas.

Tuesday 17 February 2004: Germany training

The new job with Alosi required factory training in Germany, so she drove to Germany & spent 2 days & nights in Hamburg & talked about several men. Arend Hoss was one that was making peculiar statements & situations. Being taken out to a restaurant is normal when alone invited by head office. Being escorted back to your hotel room & having a drink from the room fridge is maybe OK under normal circumstances, but now I was suspicious about EVERY man.

Oh, this was ridiculous! She couldn't be flirting with all the men to get something from having sex with them. **It was me, I was getting paranoid.** As a scientist, I MUST have evidence before I really started jumping to some conclusions & then TEST those conclusions BEFORE making any accusations. Meanwhile, I must go mad trying to gather the information!

Sunday 29th Feb 2004

I discovered condoms in Lennon's bedroom while looking for something. I suggested he come with me to the garage to find something. Then, I mentioned what I know and found & told him that he MUST be careful. He said that I was different to other dads as they would just blow up. It is better to educate them than just blow up.

Monday, March 1ˢᵗ

Pierre sent an e-mail & the message showed there was something going on between them. What now? I couldn't get my head around all this activity.

Lennon went on holiday with the school & I saw he had packed 12 packs of condoms. When he returned some days later, just two were left — seemed like he had similar sexual urges, just like his mum!

Saturday, March 13ᵗʰ

Paul & Christine came around the flat for drinks & "petit fours". Afterwards, I noticed SMS activity from Paul was high again. He had further problems with Christine.

Friday, April 2ⁿᵈ

Monica arrived home at about 7:30 pm in a good mood. When I asked out how her day was, she answered that it was good with a smile that indicated more than just a good day at the office. "Well," I asked, "What happened?" "I met Paul after lunch & we went out for the afternoon, we had a good time", "Ah, may I ask what?" "I am embarrassed, ask Paul, you are best mates". I sent an SMS to Paul later & found she had rented a room at "Formule 1" hotel in Chilly Mazerin next to a "pub" for the afternoon, where they had a "nice afternoon". He told me another day that SHE booked the hotel, & when he arrived, she let him in the hotel & onto the room she was lying on the bed completely naked, waiting for him. All his frustration caused by Christine & work led to a most energetic sex session with Monica for some considerable time.

It was my turn that evening & Monica was ready to experiment with me. Experimenting with sex is nice & I felt good afterwards. With these strings of beads going in & out of her pussy, she came ready for me to finish off the play with a doggy-style finish & those swinging boobs.

Thursday, April 22nd 2004

I read a series of SMS on Monica's phone from Paul dated Wednesday 21st, which puzzled me "STP .... Tu ne va pas au club sans moi", "...je t'aime", ".....mon amour". (S'il te plait- please, you do not go to the club without me ..my love) There was obviously a sudden re-kindling of the love affair with both Monica & Paul. He hasn't used "je t'aime" since November last year 2003. Why, what's different? Probably Christine again, when she goes bananas & throws things, he gets unhappy, he turns to Monica to talk over his problems & sex, which is a good comfort. However, what was this "club" he referred to? He had never used the word "club" before*, so this was something different to a pub or hotel.

*   see later September 30th

Friday 23rd April

Paul brought Monica home & stayed for a couple of Leffe beers he brought. I arrived late & only saw him leaving, with Monica holding his hand as the two walked to the lift. She escorted him down the lift before he departed on the steps of the building. Looking down, I could see them embrace one last time. I said to her when she arrived back that things seemed to be back to normal & that they were both in love with each other again. I said it does not matter so long as we are all three happy. She dismissed what I said, but later on reflection, she cuddled me & I reiterated that we are three, do not exclude me. She smiled & put her arm around my neck & kissed me that turns into a passionate snog. My hands wandered, & soon, I was holding a boob out in the open.

Looking to see if Lennon was around, she guided me to the bedroom & then we played the slow game of stripping each other. I liked stripping her & now fully naked, she pushed me down on the bed, kissed my penis James & sucked him. I couldn't reach her boobs, but the pleasure stopped me from trying more. I was clay in her hands, & when I felt the enormous urge, she continued until she had a mouthful of cum still moving her mouth up & down my shaft. She must have swallowed much before retracting & showing a mouthful of my cum. With a smile, she took a gulp & swallowed the rest. We had not had dinner yet, we had have already had the hors d'oeuvre. I have no energy for getting up for a while & Monica was happy to lie beside me & rest.

Monday 26th April

Monica was ill at work & went home early, with Paul bringing her home. When I arrived early due to her SMS, Paul was sitting on the bed. After a while, we left her there in bed while we chatted over a few beers before he left. Returning to Monica in bed, I noticed her night dress was still on the chair & covertly cuddling her, I realised she had nothing on. Did she undress completely in front of Paul before getting in bed? Thinking about it, who cares? He has shagged her, so he has seen her naked.

Wednesday 28th April 2004

Society Generale bank statement arrived that showed Monica paid €27.50 for the Formule1 hotel on 2nd April, confirming their sex session together that afternoon. Initially puzzled that Paul did not pay, I thought more & realised he could not have a hotel in his name, so that meant he would have paid her the money in cash.

Saturday 1st May: Paul shags Monica in front of me at home

Paul came around about 10:30 pm while his teenage kids were asleep & Christine was on holiday in Morrocco with a friend. We drank & chatted, & Monica was so happy for him to be with us. Lennon was asleep, so they felt less inhibited. They sat together on the settee & me in the armchair & with looks of whether I approved. I smiled & said, "Paul, I think Monica wants a cuddle from you". Gently, he put his hand on her leg, and she looked lovingly into his eyes & he swapped hands to enable him to embrace her. All the time they kissed, his hand slowly moved up her leg & closer to the target area. They broke off, looking at me & with my nodding approval, they continued. This time, Paul was able to feel her pussy in her culottes / panties. Monica's breasts started heaving with emotion, & her legs spread further apart. She reached out & felt his now bulging trousers. Monica looked anxiously at me, but each time, I smiled & nodded for them to continue. She got bolder, undoing his belt & unzipping his trousers to be able to hold his fully erect penis. Suddenly, Monica broke off the entanglement & pulled off her top, undid her bra leaving only her culottes & skirt. Paul started sucking her nipples one by one while she had a firm grip on his penis. It was not long before all thoughts of me being present were lost as Paul pulled down her culottes & mounted Monica with her legs wide open. After a lengthy period of thrusting, he finally hit his zenith & shagged her with all his might. I was transfixed in my armchair by the activity; it was like watching a sex movie, except this was real & with my (now) friend shagging my wife. I was reflecting on how, since they had renewed their love affair on 13th March, Monica had been nice to me & our relationship had been so nice. After the normal exhausted bodies recovered enough, Paul got up, looked at me and said, "merci Geoffrey, you are a gentleman". Good "Franglais" I thought, his English is improving! I replied in French, "Remember I have no problems with you & Monica together as long as I am told. I want no secrets". Time goes quickly when you are enjoying yourself. Thirty minutes past midnight, a contented & exhausted Paul left for home.

Monday 24th May: First mention of a new housing estate on Longjumeau hill

Lennon, who went to a school up the hill, came home & told Monica they were building a lot of new homes on land next to his school. Monica told me that night & wanted me to try to get an extended mortgage. I said that as her job was on a temporary contract, it could only be possible on my salary. Monica said she would investigate about how to buy & finance a new house. They were selling the first batch of houses within a time-line with a €20,000 discount for €320,000 instead of €340,000.

Wednesday 26th May 2004: first visit to Kauffmann Broad

Monica & I went to the Kauffman Broad porta-cabin sales office to obtain information and brochures & we put our name down as interested. With our name down, we are possibly eligible for the €20,000 discount if we could get a mortgage approval & sign papers within 2 months. I said she needed to save up money like myself for the house.

Later, when the opportunity arose, I discovered on Monica's phone a disturbing message in English, "I am sorry for lunch today. I will call you in the afternoon. Kisses Auber 0615372467" Who is Auber? He gives kisses as a sign off.

Thursday, 27th May

I met Paul alone at lunchtime in Cora shopping centre, we chatted about Monica. Like me he was unhappy about Monica lying to him, as well as to me. At some point, he said if she did not stop lying, he would stop the relationship. He said to me that she was a compulsive liar and would lie over the slightest thing, e.g. with a friend who came over to our flat. Paul said he thought it was an "African thing".

He told me again about how they met, that it was one of these casual meetings in a supermarket that he chatted with Monica, who liked her looks & demeanour. They chatted & she mentioned she was looking for a job & being a big manager in a chemical factory he was able to offer a job. Paul said he was so messed up with Christine's mental health & state, she considered suicide. He found a Senegalese woman before Monica, but Monica was special, he could talk to her & she would listen & make good advice.

He liked affection like me & had said to Monica to give me affection as well. He told me about April 2nd, where they had a rendez-vous at the Pizza pub in Chilly Mazerin & said she phoned him to say she was the nearby Formula-1 hotel waiting for him, "come to me!" She gave him the code to get in. When he entered the room, she was lying naked on the bed. It was the only time he did not like the idea of meeting Monica in a hotel, he felt as if he was seeing a prostitute. We talked about the secrets, the lies & Monica hiding her affection for Paul while I was there with them. I said I wanted them to be open, no lies, for all of us & I wanted affection & them to not hide their affection for each other. We now knew that after dinner "chez-nous" at our flat on March 13th, they got closer together, but Monica planned the total assimilation of the relationship by seducing him in the hotel. He was happy to be with me & of course, Monica, better to be with all of us all together, including his wife Christine.

He wanted to talk, have meetings with Christine to help her be happy & be with all of us, spending time more feasible together. I told him Monica would totally ignore me. For example, she put on "her" TV programme while we were talking about something important. I was annoyed & turned the TV off to continue on the subject & insisted she wanted to watch the programme. Paul then told me the same thing happened one night when he went around our flat to talk about finance & a house that she put the TV on & started watching the TV, so after 20 minutes he said to her he was leaving, "why are you leaving, you have only just come? He was being ignored & yet she did not understand...amazing! Paul understood perfectly my problems & was a good friend to help resolve our problems. If Monica & I were happy together, then he would have easy access to Monica who was helping him so much with his problems with Christine & her volatile temperament & of course, relieving his sexual desires.

That evening while Monica had a shower, I read more disturbing SMS messages. "Hello Monica, how are you this morning? Had you sweet dreams last night? Today, I am on RTT * if you want to call me, no problem." This indicates something happened maybe in the afternoon or evening? Why would he say sweet dreams? We have now another man in the lover frame! He was not a native English speaker, probably a second language that was not French, therefore probably not African because he would be a good English or French speaker. He used English & due to lunch appointment on Wednesday 26th, he must be working in the Palaiseau area. Did he live nearby?

From past experience, he must be 40 plus, managerial level job with something to offer Monica that she wanted. Was he in Monica's factory or Alosi? Watch this space. Oh, why did Monica complicate both our lives & then say I was complicated?

* RTT was a typical idealistic socialist idea, where everyone is given one day per month holiday off. When introduced by the socialist government in the late 1990's, it was supposed to reduce unemployment, by enticing companies to employ more people, because the present employees have more holiday! The socialists were surprised when unemployment INCREASED. Once you have an extra 12 days holiday, it is impossible to change back, the unions would not accept & there would be protests, so it is cemented into work contracts.

Sunday 30th May 2004

I did my daily inspection of Monica's phone messages when she was having a shower. I saw something really puzzling, "Pourquoi n'as-tu pas téléphoné, tu n'es pas Christine ". I then remembered a phone call yesterday while we were in the Carrefour supermarket. The phone time & reference corresponded to Auber. What had Monica said to Auber to enable him to accuse Monica of not phoning him & that she was being like Christine Paul's wife? Why did she complicate her life with all these men? She was not a nympho, so she must always be looking for men that can enhance her lifestyle.

I could not dwell on the subject because we had guests that day. Stanley, her uncle & Cloe, a close friend, were spending the day with us at the flat, arriving at 9:20 am. That night the phone rang at about 8:15 pm. Since Monica had her hands full with a casserole of hot food, I quickly took the phone & opened it for her. It was Paul; I said hello and was about to speak with him, but Monica was able to take the phone call. She then moved to the bedroom & afterwards, when she returned to us in the lounge, she said to Stanley that it was Jeanne, another friend. Why lie? She did not need to say anything, I knew it was Paul & as for Stanley & Cloe, it was just another phone call.

Later after dinner, I offered & took our guests home, dropping off Cloe at her flat in Chilly Mazerin & then Stanley to his digs near Rungis, not far from Orly airport.

When I returned, Monica complained about why I offered to take them home & then took them both home when they could get a taxi. "Are you real? Of course, I should take them both home; it is 30 minutes of my time with no cost to me" Monica responded with, "I do not know what you are doing, what you say to them, I do not trust you". I was gobsmacked by her hypocrisy. She did not know what I was doing, what you say & trust? To avoid a row, I just let it ride & made myself a cup of tea & offered Monica one to diffuse the situation. Nothing was said that night, but it rankled with me her hypocrisy and allegations. Is this a game to accuse me of hiding HER activities?

Sunday 1st -6th June 2004: Annual summer sales conference in the south of France

I left by taxi to rendez-vous with colleagues in Orly airport. We were off to Biarritz, SW France, to our annual HJY international sales conference. When we arrived at the airport, we met various agents & subsidiary colleagues from around the world & we all got the same plane. When we arrived in the local airport, we all got into a pre-arranged coach to the hotel. The venue was a golf club just north of Biarritz. We settled in & I arranged all my things for the Monday morning start of the conference. As normal, the ICP sessions were dominated by yours truly, with many lectures on various ICP-AES* subjects.

After the last lecture of the first day, I quickly changed & met colleagues from around the world. We walked about 800m down to the nearby beach. Still warm it was good to swim, although the waves & the under-toe was dangerous. The following day, I went again quickly, this time, alone & went a bit further down the beach than the previous day. I sat down on the sand & realised I was the only person with swimming trunks on. Oh, well, when in Rome, do as the Romans do, so I pulled off my trunks off & lay down in the warm sand. After some minutes, I heard two German colleagues "Ah, Geoff, you have no clothes on. We will join you," & with that, they also took off their swimming trunks. Three of us lying naked on the beach, then soon a South African & a Spanish joined us, now we are 5 naked male bodies. We chatted & then I went down to swim, I passed our shocked female secretary Benita Alonso, who was walking along the beach in her bikini, as I was near the sea. It was so nice to skinny-dip in the sea, one feels free. Later that week, I was shown a photo a Japanese colleague took of us, a long way off, luckily, he did not have a good zoom lens!

* Inductively Coupled Plasma Atomic Emission Spectroscopy a technique using an Argon plasma at 10,000K for analysing & determining elements at ppm & ppb levels (parts per million & parts per billion) in basically anything e.g. steels, water, petroleum, plastics, pharmaceutical products, food etc.

Friday, 6 June

I arrived home in a taxi that evening & was greeted by Monica with a big hug. She said things were progressing with the possible purchase of a new house. She told me that both Monica & Lennon went to Philipe & Christine's house during the week to discuss a mortgage offer from my bank, Caisse d'Epagne. They were offering a mortgage with a 4-6% interest rate. Monica kept saying she had a job & salary, but I countered that the job was not a guaranteed job, it was contract only.

I read that evening an SMS from Paul "Es tu contente d'etre venue. Essay encore en 01 60147xxxx."

Saturday 7th June 2004: discussion with Kauffmann Broad for the new house

Monica & I went back to Kauffman Broad's sales office to discuss further a possible purchase & look at designs. It was at this time the sales person said Kauffman Broad had an arrangement to get mortgages at 2% with Credit Agricole bank. This was very interesting because the mortgage repayments were foremost in my mind to not stretch my resources too much, especially if Hope did not get that permanent job contract.

Tuesday, 10 June

I left the office early to get to Credit Agricole bank before it closed at 12.15 hrs. I made an appointment with the Credit Agricole bank to discuss a possible mortgage for later in the week.

That evening I read a SMS from Auber "comment va ma petite panthere?" (How is my little panther). Interesting, he was calling her that. I suppose she did look like a panther when she was lying down naked, so has Auber seen Monica lying down naked? Maybe he was also black, because if he was white, he might have said Black Panther.

Wednesday, 11 June

Tucked under Monica's bedside cabinet, I noticed a piece of paper with Auber written twice & "amour" crossed out. She must have sent it to him some days ago. At the next opportunity, I inspected Monica's phone & saw two SMS messages from Auber "tu peux te liberer eventuallement demain midi, biz Auber" (can you free yourself eventually tomorrow noon, kisses Auber?), why did Auber write in French this time? Later that day, he sent another "Your answers are like an iceberg". I could not find any record of Monica sending a message to him that day. Did she delete it, or is Auber getting frustrated at no response?

I opened the mail that night & got the usual fixed telephone bill & found a call on April 21st from Tunis. I knew that ADB had temporarily moved their HQ from Abidjan Cote d'Ivoire to Tunisia due to riots & a possible civil war. Who is this? Andre, Emmanuel, George-Taylor Lewis or someone else?

Friday 13 June 2004: we see the CA bank manager the first time

Monica & I saw the Credit Agricole bank manager about a Kauffman Broad house special arrangement mortgage. With my present flat & salary records, he mentioned that it should be OK because I already owned an apartment & that he believed the head office would approve quickly.

Tuesday, 17 June 2004

After work, I trained in the weightlifting club as usual, & on my return, I saw the SMS from Auber on Monica's mobile. "Gare de Massy Verriers centre 17:15 to 17:30 biz Auber". Monica lied about something, & eventually, with the continued lies, I got so annoyed that I spilt the beans about what I knew about Auber. She tried to continue lying by saying it was "Martin" & a contact of some 6 months ago & that she re-contacted regarding a friend in Society Generale bank. Of course, I know it is a lie. Maybe Jean-Michel from Caisse d'Epagne?

However, I first saw comms from Auber 26th May. She said Auber was not African and that he was a white Frenchman, so I said his French was worse than mine & English was a second language. She then tried to tell me that she was teaching him English. I said sarcastically, "Try French as well". She was not amused. I continued, "Both Paul & I do not like your lies. He said to me that he would stop with you if you continued lying to us both". She did not believe that.

However, when I showed her a SMS from Paul to me, she was gobsmacked. "So, you see, you may lie to us both, but we both see through you. You are a poor liar; try telling the truth — it is easier. Remember, nothing can shock me these days. I have lived through sexual affairs since we have been married also other men you are meeting like Auber. All you have said are; lies, lies, lies, who really is Auber". She said nothing, so I took her phone & left a SMS message for him on her phone. I called in Lennon & told him in front of Monica about Andre, Paul & now Auber, she was distraught that Lennon now knew about her mother's sex life & men other than her husband, me. "OK, are you going to tell us? Remember, Lennon was there still, who Auber is?"

Reluctantly she started slowly looking sheepish, that Auber had a car & lived near Massy train station & his real name was Martin & she met him on the Metro & gave him her phone number. "How can you give a strange man on the Metro your phone number just like that? That's insane. Lennon, do you think it is normal or right for your mum to have affairs with different men?" I had placed him in an impossible position, but at that very moment, I didn't care. He needed to know what she was like & maybe privately influence her ways.

Mon 21 – Friday 25 June 2004: Japan trip

I was in Japan on business, which included both Horiba, our parent company & a secret visit to Yokogawa, part of HP (Hewlett Packard), to try to negotiate a partnership of selling their ICP-MS* & they sell our ICP-AES. In the end the solid state detector ICP-AES project, I started was delayed by some three years & by that time, HP lost interest. HP scientific, a division of HP was spun off as "Agilent", later they would buy Varian & inherit their ICP-MS as well as their ICP-AES. Without the shackles of a parent company HP who understood little of scientific instruments, they expanded & have become a major player in the Chromatography & spectroscopy world. Seeing the HP ICP-MS factory on our factory tour was an enlightening experience of the differences between production methods of HP & JY.

One evening, Dider, my immediate boss & I went looking for a bar. We went into a building & up to the 7th floor. We went to order a drink & quickly, two Japanese ladies came scantily dressed to take our order & then sat down next to us. All very nice, but a bit worrying about what could happen next. We chatted & they were keen that we should have more drinks as their hands wandered over our trouser legs. They tried to guide our hands over their exposed legs. Both of us thought this could get out of hand (sic) & also cost a bomb. Didier said, you pay & I will sign your expenses, so when we finished our drinks, I paid $70 for two beers! It was a good job we escaped with just two beers!

* ICP-MS: Inductively Coupled Plasma Mass Spectroscopy, another technique using plasma as the heat source for analysing & determining elements down to & below PPT levels (parts per trillion) using a mass spectrometer as the detector. Basically, again analysing anything e.g., steel, water, petroleum, plastics, pharmaceutical products, food etc., for trace elements

Friday, 25th June

I arrived home from my trip using our usual company taxi driver, Rodrigues & found Paul there & Monica, who decided to go running at about 6:30 pm. Lennon was staying with a friend overnight. Paul & I chatted about various things & he told me they had had a shag before I got home. We discussed whether Monica would admit to me privately later. He reiterated he wanted Monica to admit to me when they had a shag & stop lying to me as well as to him. He did not understand why she lied all the time, he wondered whether it was an African thing to continually lie. He said that because many Africans he had met were not intellectual, they did not realise that with superior knowledge, many of their lies were not believable, I agreed wholeheartedly. He then told me about a Cameroon lady & a Sierra Leon lady he had for a lover some time previously. He said both she & Monica had a lovely sex smell when aroused from their pussy.

Monica returned later. With some prodding from Paul, while constant looking at me, she admitted about Auber. Afterwards he said, she should NEVER give her phone number to a complete stranger on the Metro, especially when she admitted SHE phoned HIM first to make a meeting.

Sunday 26ᵗʰ June 2005

I noticed Monica was wearing a new ring of gold with blue & white stones. She claimed it was only €5 in Auchan supermarket; however, when she went to take it off that night, I noticed it was hallmarked on the inside, so it was REAL gold. Who bought it? Paul, Auber or someone else? If she had bought it why lie about it?

Paul sent me an SMS to say they had had another shag while I was training yesterday (Saturday 26ᵗʰ). I had recorded that in my records that was number 8 shag together? I just hope that Monica was satisfied with sex with Paul & not with more men.

Monday 12ᵗʰ July (13-18ᵗʰ (UK family & business trip)

While I was on a trip to UK, I got an SMS from Paul and they were together somewhere, having just finished having sex together, and number 9+ shag. He thanked me for being so much of a gentleman & allowing him to enjoy Monica. I replied I was happy he had confidence & that he was telling me after each shag. I just wished Monica had the same openness when she has sex with Paul, or for that matter, with anyone else.

Tuesday, 13ᵗʰ July

While I was in Plymouth, I found out later on my return that Monica had phoned Auber (Martin) for 40 seconds. A quick message?

Saturday & Sunday, 11 & 12ᵗʰ July 2004 Monica in Germany at ALOSI party

Monica was invited to the annual ALOSI dinner dance. She drove by car to Germany on the Saturday morning. The dinner disco was in the evening & she returned back to the hotel at about 3 am. She phoned a German number 49-172-237-676-xx, for 4 mins at 4 am and sent an SMS at 9:30 am. The entry in her mobile phone is under

"Saltzkotten", so I think he lived locally & maybe did not stay in the hotel. I later found a number 49-151-125-**xxx-xx** entered under H. Arend.

Monica obviously made an impression with several men. The second was Arend Hoss, a salesman for ALOSI, and he covered southern German living at Rheinkaistrasse xxx Mannheim 68159. I found all this by researching later. She sent two SMS messages on Friday 16th at 22.34 & 23.04 hrs & again at 20.01 hrs on Saturday 17th. All this information I gleaned from the monthly telephone bill. One has to remember she had a shag with Paul earlier that day. What's going on? What DID go on in Germany? Does Arend have two mobile phones? Maybe one private, the other business?

Monday, 19th July: Arend confirms affair with Monica

I met Paul at the Palaiseau pub while Monica went to Switzerland to see some friends for a few days. He told me he shagged Monica on Saturday the 10th as well as Monday the 12th, so a total of 11+ shags. He said he felt embarrassed, making love with Monica in our bed in the flat. I said it was not a problem & I gave him a friendly slap on the back. I started a long e-mail later in the evening which I finished Wednesday.

When Monica was in bed, I read an e-mail to her from Arend sent on Sunday night. "I am back from Bonn, Germany, tired because the night from Saturday till Sunday was very short. I love everything about you & you please me a lot. You are a very beautiful lover. With pleasure to see you again. I know that you have to get organised every time. Call me how you want to make arrangements. Soft kisses, Arend".

OK that confirmed Arend shagged Monica while she was at the ALOSI party. While I accepted Paul shagging Monica, I am NOT happy with all these other men.

Wednesday 21st July 2004

I sent an e-mail to Paul thanking him for being a friend who is helping both Monica & myself.

Reproduced here in my very bad French:

Bonjour Paul,

Merci pour le soiree au pub, j'ai pas de l'ocassion parle avec un ami debout toutes les chose en France. Tu est mon mieux ami en France, tu me comprends & je suis contente parle avec toi pour les suject tres personnale. Tu es bienvenue al'appartement et notre chambre, c'est bon, c'est confortable, pas de probleme, quand d'habitude SMS moi...... c'est bon. Quand tu fait amour avec Monica, elle est tres contente et tres gentille avec moi. Le plus amour avec Monica tu fait, le plus contente & gentille Monica est avec moi. Aussi quelque fois je ne fais pas amour, tu es mon ami et fait Monica heureuse pour moi. Je reprose, tu / vous voudrez amour, SMS moi, et je travail tard pour nous et je reste au bureau tard pour vous ou fait exercise / entrainment direct de travail. Lennon a connus pour beaucoup de mois, it dit l'annee dernier, si il est OK avec moi, c'est bon pour lui, il est tres intelligent et il regard les signes apres quelques mois et discute avec moi. J'aime Monica, je suis je ne lui done pas l'amour elle a besion, merci a donner l'amour elle desire. Je pense elle aime quand je bissous sa pussy (chat) et quand elle bisous mon penis. L'annee dernier elle n'aime pas, maintenant elle est contente, je pense memo exercise avec toi change lui cerveua, le difference est toi, merci.

Je dis, je suis different peut etre unique, mais j'aime Monica et j'espere elle connu mon amour pour elle. Tu es tres important pour moi et Monica.

Je suis contenet avec toi, pas de concourant pour mon marriage et elle ecoute a toi. J'espere elle presente ta amour pour toi (bisous, ambrasse etc) devant moi, puis je sais pas des secrets, elle est ouverte. Je ne voudrais pas les autres hommes, elle est pour nous seulement.

Peute etre dans le futur, tu voudrais une nuit avec Monica dans une hotel pour un stage ou weekend (quand l'ocassion ce present).

Depuis tu rentre a Monica hier Avril, elle progresse etre gentille avec moi, la vie progresse, la vie est bon. Je voudrais avec Monica: heireusement, ouverture, affection, conversation et amour, tu es le cle. Cles, si tu veux, je tu donne les cles de l'appartement encore? Si tu es avant Monica, tu entre et fait du the ou biere. Rappel, Lennon est contente parce que je suis contente, pour lui est tres important, il est tres jolie, il sorts si tu veux pour une temps seule" pour une conversation tres personale...". J'ai discute avec Lennon avant, l'annee dernier.

J'aime notre conversation au pub ou l'appartement seule, mais avec Monica aussi les autre fois. Il y a temps quand seule est mieux et les autres fois avec Monica est mieux.

Merci mon ami et bon vacance et quand tu rentre un autre l'ocassion pour une biere.

A bientot

Geoff

In English, what I wanted to say;

Hello Paul,

Thank you for the evening at the pub, I have no occasion to speak with a friend conversing all things in France. You are my best friend in France, you understand me & I'm happy talking with you for subjects very personal. You're welcome to the apartment and our bedroom is available & comfortable, no problem, as usual SMS me ...... then it's good. When you make love with Monica, she is very happy and very kind to me. The more love with Monica you make, a happier & kinder Monica is with me. Also, sometimes I can not make love, you are my friend and make Monica happy for me. I approve when you will want love, SMS me, and I work late for you and I can stay at the office late for you , or go direct to training. Lennon has known for many months, he said last year, if it is OK with me, it's good for him, he is very intelligent and he looks at the signs after a few months and discusses with me.

I love Monica, I am not able to give what sex life she needs, thank you to give the sex she desires. I think she likes it when I kiss her pussy and when she kisses my penis. Last year she did not like it, now she is happy, I think more sex exercises with you, have changed her mind, the difference is you, thank you.

I said I am different maybe unique, but I love Monica and I Monica she knows my love for her. You are very important to me and Monica.

I am content with you, no competitor for my marriage and she listens to you. I hope she presents her love for you (kisses, hugs etc.) in front of me, then I do know there are no secrets, then I know she is open. I would not want other men, it is for us only.

Maybe in the future, you would like a night with Monica in a hotel for an night or weekend (when occasion presents itself).

Since you returned to Monica that day in April, she progresses to be nice to me, life progresses, life is good. I want with Monica: happiness, openness, affection, conversation and love, you are the key. Keys, if you want, I give you the keys of the apartment again? If you're before Monica, you come in and make tea or have a beer. Reminder, Lennon is happy because I'm happy, for him it is very important, he is very nice, he tells me if you want for a time alone "for a very personal conversation ..." I talked with Lennon before, last year.

I like our conversation at the pub or the apartment alone, but with Monica also the other times. There is time when alone is better and other times with Monica is better.

Thank you my friend and good holiday and when you enter another occasion for a beer.

Friday & Saturday, 6th & 7th August 2004

I discovered e-mails to & from Monica & Andre. They were discussing possible ways to meet after November in Tunis, where

ADB are presently based during the troubles in Abidjan, Cote d'Ivoire. No doubt, Monica will want to make some excuse to go to Tunis if she still wanted to meet him. Maybe she would say, she was somewhere else, like Switzerland or Rome, just for a shag with Andre? I really did not understand Monica; she was so complicated & yet her communications to Andre said, I AM complicated!

I might have made a mistake in replying to Monica's request to have a week off in October. She might say what about the house situation? I assumed she would be staying abroad. A mistake, did she notice?

I tried to phone the German numbers, but no reply & no answer. Monica said to Andre that she had changed the password to her e-mail (she hasn't) & I could not access her e-mails, but she said she would set up a new e-mail address for sending details of a rendez-vous in the future. She started up a new e-mail address. **mxxxxxxce2000@** with password: ALOSI1

Monday, Aug 9th: Geoff ill, Paul & Monica have sex on my bed in front of me

Paul came around our flat while I was ill in bed. They both sat on the bed & we talked together. Monica was wearing a skirt & top, rubbed her leg against Paul, who responded by holding her leg above her knee. Monica looked at me & with a smile, she cuddled & kissed him. Within a short time, they were having a long passionate kiss together. I smiled & said in French "I am glad you are not hiding your affections in front of me. Remember I want you to be open". Monica nodded in agreement & cuddled & kissed encore. Their hands started to wander, I could see Paul wanted to hold her boobs "tes seins sont magnifiques" & quickly he put his hand down her bra "Oui, tres magnifiques". Monica loved it; her eyes glazed a bit & she looked at me. I smiled.

What were they going to do? Monica was in a quandary; she wanted him to shag her, but felt guilty. I was ill & Lennon was at sport.

Monica decided to make things easier by taking off her top. I was ill, but I did love seeing Monica's body & boobs bulging out of her bra. Paul was not slow to undo her bra. He caressed her boobs much better while they kissed passionately & she caressed his bulging lower parts. Soon, it was apparent that if she didn't undo his trousers zip, it would burst, so she undid his belt & zip. She put her hand down into his pants & pulled his penis out.

I had never seen him in this state, but I could see why she enjoyed it so much; it was like a solid rock & of course, needed sucking. She dropped down on her knees on the floor to give him a blow job and deep throated it in & out. Paul eyes glazed half closed, all inhibitions gone until a volcano of cum spurted out of Monica's mouth not able to contain the volume, cum was all over her face and boobs, some rebounded on the side of the bed and dripped on the floor. By Jupiter, what a volume, what a performance! I was shocked by such a spectacle I was full of admiration, if ONLY I could perform like that! Smiles were on all three of our faces. Monica splattered with cum as she tried to lick what was around her mouth & then used her hand to try to wipe her face & boobs.

After a while, Paul was apologetic for getting cum on the bed & floor, but both Monica & I told him not to worry as it could easily be cleaned up. I started feeling a bit less ill after that entertainment! Monica gave Paul one last chance to fondle her boobs before she put on her top & left her bra on the bed to go to the bathroom and get a towel to wipe down any evidence on Paul's trousers & herself. She then got a damp sponge to make sure there was no evidence on his trousers, otherwise, Christine might see when he got home or when Christine washed them. Both now presentable, standing up at our bed, Paul took Monica's hand & with a look of agreement, said in French "Merci, Geoff, for allowing us to have fun just now; we both appreciate it". Monica agreed, "Thank you, Geoff. I love you." I felt great & happy. We chatted a bit more before the "witching hour" arrived for Paul to go. Monica saw him down to his car. Monica returned some 20 minutes later & came to me & thanked me profusely with a cuddle & a passionate kiss.

Tuesday Aug 10th: 2nd meeting with CA bank manager for house mortgage + more shags

Paul came around again after Monica & I had another meeting with the bank manager at Credit Agricole to discuss the mortgage for the new house. Paul sat next to Monica, as usual, on the settee. After a chat about the house mortgage & things, Monica, feeling more open in front of me, cuddled Paul & kissed him. He responds with a long, passionate kiss. After breaking off, they held hands & looked at each other often. I asked what they chatted about that took so long when they left last night. They looked at each other, hugged & kissed again even more passionately. Monica said, "We did not feel it was fair to have sex in the lounge while you were ill in bed." "You know I would not have minded," I said. "Yes, but then you seemed to encourage Paul to hold my boobs & with your encouragement I to hold his penis, we could not help it." "That's fine. With Paul, I have no problems; with other men, I do have problems."

Paul looked into Monica's eyes & said he agreed with me. Monica looked remorseful & kissed him again while holding his crutch. It took so little time for his trousers to start bulging. He started caressing her upper body but dearly wanted to feel her boobs. Monica loosened his belt & trouser zip to fondle his penis. With Lennon in his bedroom, I thought it would be better if they went into our bedroom. "Paul, take Monica to our bedroom. It is more private, in case Lennon comes to the lounge." They looked at each other & zipping up his trousers & belt, and they went into our bedroom. Some 30 minutes later, they both emerged happy with smiles & both said thank you. After a chat again on the settee, Paul went at his usual time.

Later, Monica gave me a blue pill & said, "I want to reward you for allowing Paul & me to have sex together in our bed". Viagra does have a wonderful effect & James was very happy with Monica this time, playing cowgirl, riding me hard on my back. I was still recovering from illness, so her pelvic thrusts were needed more than normal.

A great day with much achieved, house mortgage, Paul keeping Monica happy with a shag & then Monica getting us to have a good shag.

Thursday 12th Aug 2004

I read an SMS from Arend re-sent, due to the previous "gobbledegook" "Dear Monica, I am sure you don't make mistakes because you very responsible. Cheers, Arend" What was this referring to? What mistake? What decision?

I tried the German numbers again & with the xxxx646 number a young teenager girl replied. However, when I tried many times later, no reply or response.....mmmm puzzling, maybe his daughter?

Saturday 14th Aug

When I was out to the local shops before they close, she tried to phone Arend, but no reply.

Thursday 26th August 2004

Arend sent another intelligible SMS. I used her phone on the 31st to re-send the message because I (Monica) couldn't understand the message. He did not reply nor did I did see her reply. If she deleted it, then I wouldn't know.

Credit Agricole Bank agreed to the mortgage & we saw the bank manager start up various bank accounts, both single & joint accounts, for mortgage payments. The house design we chose would not be ready until approximately April / May 2005. Our house would be one of the first to be completed in the first of four stages of development of the present green agricultural field. Having now got an approximate date, I needed to start planning for selling the flat.

Now we could sign the Kauffmann Broad contract. All the contracts were made up in conjunction with Credit Agricole Bank & we were given an appointment to sign at the KB office. We found out we were one of the first to sign & have a choice of plots. We decided on the first plot which was where, at the time, the KB porta-cabin office was situated.

Tuesday 7th Sept: another shag in the afternoon with Paul

I arrived home from work, & Paul was at our flat drinking his usual Leffe beer next to Monica. We chatted together & then while Monica went to the toilet, he bent over to me & told me they had a shag in the afternoon before both Lennon & myself came home (#12 or 13 now?). When Monica returned back to her previous position, I asked whether they had a good afternoon together. Monica realised I knew, so she looked at Paul & then at me while bending closer to him, she said, still getting closer & facing him with a smile, "Yes, we had a wonderful afternoon" & with that, they embraced & kissed. The two held hands for the rest of the time we talked & then Monica escorted Paul to the lift & downstairs & again didn't return for some 10-15 minutes.

That night, Monica gave me a Cialis pill, she was very amorous (that's why I was happy with Paul shagging Monica) & played with me, giving me a wonderful blow job. Before I was to cum, we switched to doggy style in front of the bedroom mirror, boobs gently swinging until they flopped all over the place when the rhythm increased to a crescendo. Monica always feels amorous with me & wants a shag after she has a shag with Paul.

Thursday, 16th Sept: More Arend comms

Arend sent an SMS "Dear Monica sorry in the morning, I was not concentrating. I am now on the way to ReadyMix Munchen. I think of you, Viele liek Grusse (many greeting), Arend." Monica saw me reading her SMS messages on her phone. I said nothing, nor her. It's best she started to explain "everything". She said that she could not just go to bed with a person she has just met that first day. She promised there were no other men except Paul. I mentioned Pierre, Martin (Auber) Arend, Andre...who else? I was very upset, close to tears, she cuddled me & tried to reassure me both then & the next morning. She told me she confided to Paul, that I would find out some time. I said, I do not understand her. She was not respecting me or Paul. I was totally in her spell, I love her so much & yet she was abusing my trust & love for her. I have accepted Paul to shag her with or without me present, but I do not accept other men.

Monday, 27th Sept

Monica mentioned that there was going to be a take-over of the UK parent company that owned the chemical company. She said she was often contacting Arend for details & wanted him to phone her at home. Why would a salesman know more about the take-over than Paul who is a big boss & would be privy to inside confidential information ....does she think I am stupid?

Thursday, 30th Sept

Monica forgot her mobile at home, & I saw it before I went to work. Arend sent an SMS at 07.58hrs, "Dear Monica you are the rose in my life. Have a nice Thursday. Cheers, Arend". What will Monica say, will she say anything? Watch this space for news. If she was open, she would tell me & tell me not to worry? Maybe she was correct that Arend had family problems with his wife leaving him & wanted to talk to someone sympathetic & females are more sympathetic & good listeners, especially Monica. As I expected, she said she had an SMS from Paul & erased the SMS message from Arend. However, she left other SMS messages, so by reading these I knew what was said.

I also saw something in her e-mail from another man, Mensah Asare, with more than friendly comments "You look wonderful. I wish I could see more of you". Who is he? When did she see him?

Friday 1st October 2004: Geoff's birthday surprise 2+2 club- open sex!

It was my birthday, and both Monica & Paul had fixed up something, a special treat in Paris for my birthday this afternoon / evening. I was to leave early from work & be back at the flat by about 4 pm so that Paul could take us both in his car. Monica was dressed in a sexy dress, sitting in the back, as he drove into Paris & parked the car in the Montparnasse area within 500 metres of the train station. We met Cloe there. She had got a train there direct from her work, & we went & entered a large elaborate club door of 2+2 club on Boulevard Edgar Quinet. I noticed that Cloe was also wearing a nice dress. I was told the rules of the club were women had to wear dresses or skirts & only men with women were allowed in, hence why Cloe was with us well. Paul paid the entrance fee for us all & we proceeded to the bar & ordered some drinks. Chatting with Cloe, we agreed that both Monica & Paul looked as though they were familiar with the club; they knew their way around & explained the look of the place downstairs.

There was dance area & semi-circular booths around the dance area. The number of people present was sparse & then Monica was keen to show me upstairs. How did she know what was upstairs? Both Cloe & I were intrigued as to what we would see upstairs as we ascended. Monica explained that I should go into an anti-room & undress. Paul led the way & we undressed. There were plenty of free condoms provided & then we went into the main upstairs area. I observed a giant bed with naked men & women playing & shagging each other. As we progressed further, there were sofas & more giant beds, all occupied by naked men & women in various stages of sex. Monica arrived & started playing with Paul, she said to me "Happy birthday, dear, you can play with anyone you like here, it is for your enjoyment".

I noticed Cloe was not there & found out later she saw what was going on upstairs & decided she did not want to participate & went back downstairs. She said to me that although she was not in any relationship, having sex with any man she did not know was not what she wanted; she needed to know the person fairly well & respect him.

I sat down on a giant bed as Paul played with Monica facing me & then proceeded to mount her with Monica facing me smiling all the time. Monica's facial expression changed to a glazed look as the pleasure increased & her boobs started to swing to the rhythm of Paul's thrusts. It was a funny sort of feeling to have pleasure seeing Monica's boobs swing to a shagging by another man, but peculiar to experience someone else mounting my wife. While I had seen Monica do a blowjob the other week in our bedroom & shag her in our flat knew they had sex numerous times, I had never seen him actually shag her publicly. What does being married mean? I was totally confused in my mind when a woman started playing with my member, with a smile, put a condom in my hand, proceeded to put it on me & then said, "OK?" She sat on me & guided James inside her. Her sexual movements up & down soon had an effect on me & within a short period of time, I had shagged her. She had a huge smile on her face & said, "merci" as she got off me. What have I just done? I have shagged another woman while still married & my wife is there as well!

Wow, this was like nothing I had ever experienced before. Recovering, I looked around to see where Monica & Paul were. Monica was occupied with another woman who was fingering her pussy & Monica was caressing her boobs. I looked on, bemused. I did not know Monica was bisexual, but there was no hiding the fact she loved every moment with this woman. Once she had finished, Monica looked a bit tired, but the thought of another shag was beckoning. Another really good woman with a nice big pair of a firm-looking boobs, probably "E" cup, wanted to "play" with Monica.

Another show ensued with me on the front row watching with several others. Both women performed well & then Monica got up to rest & sought out Paul, who was recovering so well that once she found him, he was ready for her a second time. God, he is fit. Monica positioned the condom expertly & away they went doggy style again. I was observing a side view this time but still had a good view of the action. They were well into the action when a nice-looking woman with big firm boobs approached me, took my hand and proceeded to manipulate my hands over her ample boobs. I love boobs & the temptation of feeling those was too much to stop me from caressing them unaided. Her nipples were erect & full of anticipation. She proceeded to manipulate my penis, which was still in the process of recovery. After a while of failing to raise it to full erection, she smiled & said, "Je reviendrai plus tard, OK?" This was a bit embarrassing, but will I be able to raise it again? I usually need Viagra or Cialis

Monica was in a period of interlude & saw me with my problem & disappeared & reappeared with a blue triangular pill. "I thought you may want this, so I brought some." Wow, Monica thought of everything for my surprise. . Let me take one. I took the pill, now nothing would stop me now! I watched Monica in action again with yet another lovely-looking woman, both really put on a show for the small crowd of onlookers. They heaved & panted with sexual pleasure until both came at the same time.

Monica really was knackered this time and was watching me. As she smiled a satisfied smile as I looked at the previous ample-breasted woman again, who noticed I had a small erection. She returned & caressed my member, which became fully erect quickly. Not wanting to miss an opportunity again, she quickly placed a condom on the fully erect member & invited me to shag her & turned around for a doggy. Her pussy was so wet it slid up in position with the minimum of effort & then it was a slow rhythm in & out to prevent me from coming too early. I could not see her boobs swing directly, but I could see the mirror image of the large boobs swinging to my rhythm as the pressure was increasing, I had to increase the frequency, boobs now flopping too quickly to go in unison. They were swinging & flopping independently, until climax & squeals of ecstasy from the woman. When we had both collapsed on the bed, she said "merci monsieur vous etes vraiment manifique". That compliment was just what I needed. After some minutes, we both sat up & moved off to leave it vacant for another couple. What is going on with me? I have just shagged two women with Monica looking on with approval!

I noticed, by this time, Monica was ready for another third shag by Paul. Where does he get the energy from? I need to ask him whether he uses Viagra or Cialis. This time, Monica sat on top of a prostrated Paul with his member sticking up for fine weather. Monica rode him like a horse, some horse, back & forth for many minutes until she sensed his closeness to climax & increased the frequency of her pelvic thrusts across his lower parts until both came & were sweating profusely. This time, both collapsed after the event onto the bed & were motionless for some minutes except for the smiles, cuddles & kisses. The two made nods to me & head direction to indicate we should shower, dress & return downstairs. I came downstairs first & chatted with Cloe. She said both Paul & Monica had definitely been here before & I agreed. Monica & Paul eventually came downstairs hand-in-hand. We chatted for a few minutes & Paul indicated he needed to get back home, so we all returned home to my flat.

Having dropped the three of us off, Paul departed, & I took Cloe home to nearby Chilly Mazerin. I took her up to her flat, & we chatted for a while. She was shocked at seeing Monica & Paul together so close. I opened up to her that to the fact she had had several men, & if I accepted Paul, there was less chance of other men whom I did not know about. It was driving me crazy with all of Monica's sexual activities with other men. Cloe was not able to offer much help in the time I had with her, because I did not want Monica to suspect Cloe was giving advice against her, or we were close.

However, before I left, Cloe said to me as she fixed her eyes on me, "I did not want to have sex with men I did not know today. Maybe one day, I will give you a surprise & we can make love!" I was surprised at her comment & said, "I will wait but with impatience." A conversation between Paul & myself a few weeks ago was about whether we thought Cloe was a virgin. I said maybe, maybe not, however, maybe he was right?

Returning home in time for the meal Monica had prepared, she smiled & said, "Did you like your birthday present & surprise?" "Yes, it was the most surprising & most different birthday I have ever had," I said. "I could not imagine Paul was so sexually fit. You must have been very happy he was able to shag you so many times." Monica smiled a satisfied smile & went back to the kitchen. We both went to bed early & quickly succumbed to sleep.

Saturday, 2nd Oct 2004

Monica went down the road to the high street (re-named Rue President Francois Mitterand) to get some odd little things. I saw on her computer a message from a friend, Elodie, in Switzerland, forwarded from her business address. Maybe this was the reason I had not been able to see any comms from Andre? If this was true, I would not see their comms & if they meet again secretly without me knowing. If he does not use a condom, I may be in danger. He seemed the sort of person who would have sex with multiple people & AIDS is endemic in Africa. I have had one HIV blood test with the doctor to make sure, but it worried me with Monica & her possible future male "friends".

Monday 4th Oct 2004: Lies about Andre, his wife & his whereabouts

Cloe was now working for a software company whereby she was visiting HJY often. I spoke with Cloe a lot when possible, in work about Monica & the situation. She confirmed my views that Monica had an inferiority complex which was why she continually tried to diminish, pull me down and criticise me. If she is happy, why does she have so many men? She confirmed something I had said to Paul: Monica is intelligent, but not intellectual. She is intelligent but knows little, which is another reason why, when in the presence of a group, she tries to change the conversation when she knows nothing about the subject, or accuses me of being boring people around me. We chatted about my need to talk to another female who knows Monica to get an alternative angle or view. One can be blinkered with one's own view.

Having realised Monica was communicating with Andre secretly from her CMR e-mail address I decided to set a trap. I sent an e-mail to Andre asking him where he was and what he was doing; Monica was interested? In bed that night, Monica suddenly, without any conversational link, told me that Andre was in England somewhere with his wife & kids. However, Monica did not know due to my comms with Andre directly, I knew he was divorced after being separated with his wife 4 years previously. She said I had told him about the Monica's fibroids operation, not true & that she had only communicated for about a week or so...again a lie. Why tell me he is with his wife & kids when he is single & available? They joked together that she would be his 2nd wife. These were obviously lies, but I was worried that they were planning another meeting or more. I knew from his comms that he would be at Lancaster University & that was only 1.5 hrs from Stoke-on-Trent where Steven, my son, lived in England. Would Monica start making arrangements to send Lennon with Steven, if she could meet Andre again? Next day, Andre sent me an e-mail saying he would be in Lancaster University for 12 months.

Friday 8th October

In bed, we chatted about her men, & Monica told me she had discussed the subject with Paul. She mentioned for the first time that Arend loved Monica, & she had told Paul of Arends. However, I was not sure she mentioned it to him that she probably had a shag with him at the ALOSI weekend party. Whether she did or not, Paul made it plain she should not involve herself with other men. She promised nothing would happen with other men, even though I was sure she did not mention Andre to Paul. Monica briefly mentioned again that

Andre would be in Lancaster for a year. She did not realise that Lancaster was only 1.5 hours from Stoke-on-Trent, & I did not inform her of this fact.

Sunday 10th Oct

Cloe was invited around for the day, & they made samosa together. Paul came around mid-afternoon for a couple of hours supposedly working at his Rungis office. The four of us chatted, & later, after Paul left, I took Cloe back to her flat in Chilly Mazerin. In the car, we discussed Monica's desires for things she couldn't afford but bought anyway & worried about the bill later. It was all to do with "*image*" in front of friends & relations. She mentioned when she was learning to drive, she wanted to buy another PC just to read better her driving CD, rather than the old computer I already had. I really need to discuss further Cloe's views on Monica, but we agreed it should be another time.

Thursday 14th Oct

I met Paul after work in the Palaiseau rocker pub on the high street. We chatted about Monica, Arend & Auber, the latter of whom Monica told me his real name was "Martin", but to Paul, he was "Jacques". Which name was correct? Or, are they both lies? I was sure Monica was getting many e-mails now to her CMR office e-mail address, which I had no access to.

Thursday 21st Oct 2004: A close thing to a liaison with Cloe

I had previously arranged & picked up Cloe from Chilly Mazerin station after work & took her to her flat. I needed to chat with her about Monica & many things that only friends & Rwandans would know. She confirmed what Paul told me about Monica, & Paul's first meeting was some weeks before the first "interview". This explained the puzzling SMS I read long before Monica said she had a job interview. Cloe also mentioned that Monica had met a man with a big silver Mercedes in June/July 2004 time. Was this Auber?

We also discussed the 2+2 club afternoon for my birthday. She said she did not feel right to have sex with anyone she did not know. She would want an intimate place for any relationship or moment with someone she knew & desired; she only knew me, but was not comfortable with other men around. She looked at me, & I had a feeling that if I wanted to pursue the subject more, I would be drawn into something with Cloe. My scruples said no, don't pursue, and she was a close friend of Monica. However, she is beautiful & maybe receptive to me, remembering what she said to me the day I dropped her off at home after the 2+2 club afternoon. I must admit I was so tempted to flirt more than I did. Being English, I have to have clear morals; I have never forced myself on anyone. I think Cloe was in two minds also, whether to fulfil her promise to me. I changed the subject, remembering to do a little job of changing the position of some furniture for her & the intimate possibility disappeared.

On leaving, I gave her a big hug & kiss that became passionate. My hands were wandering, but there was no resistance from Cloe; I wanted more. Did she want more? Oh, I was fighting my conscience; I was continuing to feel her all over & she me, while we stood & kissed. Did she have a boyfriend? I was not sure, she never mentioned one, so no worries there, but I was married, is a shag with a stranger in 2+2 different to a friend? If I shag Cloe, what would happen then, an affair?

My brain was racing, my blood pressure rising, my trousers became tight & her breasts were heaving. I wanted Cloe; she wanted me & yet I was holding back; why? I was feeling her breasts over her top, why was I not moving my hands as she wanted? What was wrong with me? I started to make a start with undoing her top button slowly on her blouse as she keenly watched me, then the second button. Her breasts were more exposed as I now saw & felt her breasts over her bra. Oh, I was not going to stop, I sensed. Suddenly, there was a loud bang from down the corridor & loud shouting outside Cloe's door, then a loud thump against the door & banging on the door. Looking through the door spy hole, I saw a man slumped against the opposite door, trying to get up, banging on the door. It was best to not open the door & just wait to see what happens. The drunk kept on shouting & banging against the door while the woman opposite shouted at him to go away. He stayed & staggered to our door as she slammed the door; he carried on shouting & banging for minutes on end with more of Cloe's neighbours opening their doors & shouting at the man to go away. Eventually, he decided to go away, however, this interrupted our concentration, & the moment had passed. Looking at each other, we both thought anything now was not possible. Now, or maybe another time? She looked at me as if to say c'est la vie. I held both her hands & said "bon soir" kissed & departed.

Oh, that was so close to a shag with Cloe. Do I regret no pursuing more? Only time will tell.

Saturday 23rd Oct: mysterious money in Monica's account

We went shopping at Auchan in Villebon, & with a trolley full of things, I added a pack of beer & then Monica complained loudly, with people around looking at us, saying we could not afford it! "You are joking" I said & left the beer in place. She was not happy.

Later that night, I was able to inspect Monica's bank statements & she had €8,000 in the savings account with €200 in the current account. Where did all this money suddenly come from? She was not earning that amount each month with CdF & ALOSI. I started looking in detail at my bank accounts & wondered if she was getting money from someone else, but for what? Sex? Maybe Auber?

Tuesday 26th Oct: Celebration, boss is going to give Monica a permanent contract

Monica phoned me to come home early as Paul would be there & she had some news. I arrived home early & found Paul drinking his Leffe, and Monica was bubbling with news from work. Jerome, her boss, had said he was preparing a permanent contract for Monica to work for ALOSI. She had bought a bottle of Champagne & was already well on the way to half empty. She said he had made the draught & would tidy it up for signing in Germany by his bosses. Although ALOSI was a subsidiary of CdF & CMR, it was the German ALOSI HR dept. & Jerome's boss who had to approve & sign-off. Monica was so happy she hugged me & then hugged Paul & kissed him & then again passionately with her arms around him. Paul stayed until his customary 7.45pm to ensure he was home by 8 pm.

Wednesday 27th Oct. 2004: Discovery of the plan to buy a new car

I discovered in her Hollywood bag a draft unsigned copy of my will, where she put 1/5th instead of 1/8th that I had drafted. I then discovered, in her e-mails, disturbing details of Renault Modus new car specs & hire purchase for 5 years at €225/month over 5 years. At 5% to pay a total of €13,500 or €12,800 cash. She was planning to use her nest-egg to pay for a car instead of the new house. I needed to ensure that money does NOT go to the new car but to the house project. She did not need a new car. The present Renault Clio I bought her was fine and had no problems. She had it serviced only the other day at the local Renault garage which was just down the road from Rue du Canal where the JY factory is situated. When I had my Renault car serviced, I dropped it off at the garage with the owner Pierre & walked back to the factory. I needed to prevent the loss of the car cash to pay for the new house.

I sent an e-mail to Paul the next morning from work outlining what I had seen.

Friday 29 Oct 2004

Paul came round chez-nous. I have an RTT day off & Monica was ill with influenza. Monica informed me that she did not know I had already found out by investigating her plans that she planned to buy a Renault Modus for a 3-year contract at €150/ month (3 or 5 years ? was my question). Paul already knew from Monica & myself, but he agreed that Monica should have discussed the project with me. What will we pay per month extra for the house & accessories & what will Monica's payments impact our capacity to stay afloat in debt?

From time to time, we went to the building site to watch the progress of the development; just foundations at present being dug, but all very exciting.

Monday 15th Nov

Monica had not mentioned Paul for a while. As far as I knew, she had not seen him & e-mails & SMS traffic seemed to have dwindled. What was happening? Was something wrong with their liaison? Was she contacting other men using the RMS office e-mail address? When I saw much SMS traffic with Paul, I was happy that other men were not in the fray.

Friday 19th Nov: Geoff to arrive late for an arranged shag with Paul

Monica sent me an SMS in the afternoon asking me to stay working late at the office, "Paul will be coming home." I answered, "OK, have a good time with Paul", knowing what that meant. I worked & was thinking of what was happening in our bedroom. I arrived home at about 7:45 pm and was greeted by a very happy Monica, who hugged me at the door & said, "Thank you". Lennon was still in his bedroom

& on hearing me talking with Monica, came out of his bedroom & started talking with us about what he had done at school.

I felt for Lennon, probably hearing his mum in our bedroom being shagged by another man. Lennon was not stupid, if Paul was there alone with Monica & he heard the bedroom door shut, it could only mean one thing: mum was being shagged by Paul.

In bed, Monica & I chatted about the night's activities. Monica thanked me for my understanding & then reached out to a little blue tablet already taken out if it's foil rapper. Would you like to wash it down with some water? I confirmed & washed it down after crunching the pill in my teeth for quicker effectiveness. I started feeling & playing with her boobs & she felt & caressed my member. Kissing passionately, she then started kissing my penis & stroked it with her hand, & all I could do was lie back on the bed & take the good feeling. Now Monica could feel the stiffness getting harder, she came up to me & indicated I should mount her. Like a cowboy mounting a stallion, I put my right leg over her, mindful not to hurt myself in the process & found her wet pussy easily. Grabbing hold of her "love handles", a good shagging ensued, with her boobs swinging nicely to the rhythm in front of the mirror.

It is funny how with a slow rhythm, the boobs swing in a nice pelvic thrust motion, but as the thrusts before faster, the boobs swing faster until then flop wildly independently; there must be some physics to explain it.

Exhausted afterwards, we both slumped flat on the bed. As we reposed, I thought all this time of the time Paul must have had beforehand, & now I was reaping the reward of his efforts. Thank you, Paul.

Saturday 20th November

Paul sent me an SMS about the previous night at our flat. "j'ai passe une bonne soiree, j'ai envie de toi". Why does he envy me, or perhaps it was that I was married to Monica?

At some time during the day, when we were alone, I asked Lennon whether he was alright. Was last night's activities of Paul & his mum in our bedroom upsetting? He said candidly, "It is not my business, & I can do nothing about it, anyway".

Wednesday24th November

I left work early & met Monica at the local Maitre (notaire) Julian Baptiste in Longjumeau to sign the documents for the new house being built at the top of the hill in Longjumeau. We were the first to sign-up, & we got a €20,000 discount. We had the choice of what house, & we chose the one on the corner close to the entrance of the new road, Rue des Amandiers, to the old access road, rue Jules Ferry, that had the secondary school on it some 100 metres away from our new house.

Thursday 25th Nov 2004

Monica came home in a foul mood & had a real go at Lennon for something I heard about later. She then phoned me at the office at about 6:30 pm because she knew I was going to Paris to entertain a Czech client & started angrily with me for going out to Paris, hey that's a business client. After parking in my usual underground car park near the St Michel Metro station, I took the client to my usual Greek restaurant for dinner in Rue de la Huchette in the St Michel area, where I often entertained clients & previously met women.

After our meals & a quick tour of the resto area, I took him around my usual guest route to show: the river seine, through the Louvre, stopping at the arc de Triomphe de Carrousel to see through it & straight up the Jardins de Tulleries, Place de la Concorde & up to the

Arc de Triomphe. I then drove around again to Rue to Rivoli, onto Place de la Concorde, then Avenue Champs Elysees & around the Arc de Triomphe. This has 8 offshoots, so I then chose the lead-off to the Trocadero. I normally stopped for my guests to get out to take photos of the Eiffel Tower from this height, while I stayed in the car. My route was then descend down to the fountains below the Trocadero via Ave du President Wilson, turn right down Rue de Magdebourg & finally Ave des Nations Unie for another photo session of the Eiffel Tower at the bottom. After more photos, I would drive across the bridge by the Eiffel tour & then via Quai de Grenelle, the Peripherique, A6 autoroute back to their hotel. In this particular case, I had the Czech client put into the Relais des Chartreux hotel, instead of the hotel du lac near the HJY factory.

I returned home at about 1:30 am, and although I was quiet, I woke up Monica, who was still in a bad mood, shouting at me for no reason. I decided to sleep in the lounge on the sofa. Why was she in bad mood?

Friday 26th Nov

I saw Monica got a new e-mail from Mensah Asare. He had not been in contact for some while, but signed off with "gross bisous" big kisses. Suspecting I might be accessing her e-mails, she gave him a new e-mail address Mxxxxxxx2000@yahoo.fr. Why the secrecy by making & providing a new e-mail address? Was something else cooking? |

Saturday 27th Nov 2004: Quai-17 club – public sex again

Lennon had gone away for the weekend, so Monica & Paul had arranged a night at Quai-17 club near Bassin de la Villette. Paul picked us both up at about 5 pm, & we went into Paris & parked the car in an underground car park usually in crowded Paris centre. Monica was wearing a short skirt & blouse with buttons down the front.

We entered the club, which, to start with, was rather empty. It had a dance floor & a series of semi-circular bench seats & some leading off for more privacy. We ordered some drinks & drank together, looking around. Gradually, it started to fill up. It was a dance place as well as we discovered something else. Monica & I started dancing, but as usual, she was embarrassed. She could not dance Western Occidental dancing and pulled away pretty quickly, so she did not show herself up. She moved over to Paul, who had been looking around the place as he did not dance. He motioned to move the ensemble to another area that is more secluded.

However, a lovely woman had seen us dancing & wanted to dance with me, so we danced for some time. I was really enjoying myself as I love dancing. The woman called herself Marie, and I said my name was Geoff. We spoke to each other in French above the music. She was dancing quite sensually with me, with some dancing rubbing her legs between mine, I could see Monica glancing over to me more & more as she chatted with Paul. Marie could see the glances & decided to lead me to Monica, she said, "Merci" and looked intently, eyeing up & down at Monica before walking off with sideways glances as she walked away, as if to say, "come back, or I will see you later." "

Monica & Paul had now found a more secluded seat, & they felt a better atmosphere with couples playing with each other, conducive to close contact & lovemaking. Monica embraced Paul as soon we sat down, with Paul on one side & myself on the other side of Monica. Soon, they were kissing & as things got more heated, he started unpicking her front buttons, displaying her breasts in her bra. Soon, he moved her bra down, exposing & playing with her bare breasts. I was getting excited just watching them. She looked at me, smiling & took my hand & placed it on her leg, inviting me to caress her leg & play elsewhere.

Monica loved the attention of two men playing with her, a few men & women gathered by us, not knowing we were not strangers. I could see one man look at me as if to say "When you are finished, I want to take your place". Monica re-focussed my attention as she directed my hand down her culottes. Now, I was playing with her fanny while Paul was fondling with her boobs. Soon, she was moist that she took off her culottes to make access easier. Two fingers, three fingers, and soon, all my fingers up there. She heaved & groaned as Paul was caressing. Meanwhile, Monica & Paul were kissing passionately. Eventually, she came with a groan & indicated she needed to rest.

After some while, the beer was starting to go through me so I needed to go to the loo. I got up & went to the loo, but when I returned, the previous chap was sitting where I was & was playing with Monica's boobs while Paul played with her pussy. I was one of a group of people watching. I waited & then realised she was happy & fully occupied with him playing & was now fondling Paul's penis out of his trousers. I watched the show & sensed both men would not be moving.

I decided to walk around to see what else was going on in this place. The quick answer was plenty. Men with women, women with women & even a couple of men together. I had never seen lesbians or gay men together. Watching them in action was interesting & had me mesmerised. I had always wondered what women would do to each other, now I would see together with another small group watching the show. Like others, I watched for a while & then moved on to see the next show, two men. Trousers down, they were fondling each other's penis, both sticking up like termite mountains, until one spouted like a volcano making the other man smile with satisfaction. Soon, the termite hill of the man withered to a collapsed volcano, & he leaned back with exhaustion.

Having watched two different shows, I returned to see what Monica was up to. I could see the original man was replaced with another who again only had her boobs & Paul was looking at me to take over his spot to ensure Monica did not have two strange men with her. I replaced Paul. Monica smiled, & before I had a chance to put my hand to her pussy, the other man, quick as a flash, was there! Straight into & up Monica's pussy, she did not object as she had a glazed face of satisfaction, & I contented myself with caressing her boobs. Why am I allowing this man to caress my wife's pussy? She seemed happy, am I happy? I do not know how I feel, a mixture of intrigue & not wanting to be the spoilsport to her fun & her love that I am accepting it all. I must be mad that I love her so much. Monica had so much capacity for lovemaking that he made her eventually cum again. Paul & I looked at each other & decided we should try to get Monica to move before the next "shift" moved in. I took her culottes & put them in my pocket while I tried to help Monica with my hand outstretched off the curved bench seat.

I sat down further away & then Marie reappeared from nowhere, "Oh! re-bonjour," she smiled, & I thought, Oohhhh as her hand was already caressing my leg; she was lovely, but I wasn't ready for this! Her hand wandered further & further up & now my trousers were bulging. She looked at me all the time with a mischievous smile, oh wow, she has TWO hands; the other was undoing my belt & then unzipping me, quickly feeling between trousers & pants until out it came! James was in the fresh air & smiling at her! I instinctively raised my bum, & she moved everything down so she could fondle James further, then she dropped to her knees & sucked him. Oh, James was happy, so happy within a short time he exploded. Marie could hardly contain what came out, with cum coming out of her mouth & dripping down. Monica had seen this & did not seem happy. Marie wiped her mouth area & said "merci". I reciprocated, & she moved off.

The three of us moved slowly around & watched the various "shows". At a lesbian show, Monica watched with the rest of the group watching, mesmerised. Even though Paul wanted to move, she was oblivious, or ignoring his motions to move on.

There was now a woman playing Marie, all the while they were playing. I could see a look of envy on Monica's face, & it did not need much encouragement for one of the women to invite Monica to sit between them so they both could play. Sitting on both sides, the women used their hands to keep both the other woman & Monica happy. Gradually, the 2nd woman gave up to the usurper (Monica) & all the attention was to Monica, kissing, & playing with each other's pussy. Monica wanted occasional attention to her boobs that she had exposed them by unbuttoning her blouse again & moving her bra down to let her boobs hang out to the woman. The passion of both women with their sexual play was evident to all & attracted a large group of perhaps 20 men & women. We were all mesmerised by their sex show & then I noticed that Paul had disappeared, he obviously was not happy with Monica being bi-sexual. When both had cum & were exhausted, one felt that the audience was going to clap! If they could, they all would have cried "encore, encore". Monica chatted with the woman & made some notes & later said that she had exchanged details with "Marie".

The group dispersed when both women got up & Monica looked for me & Paul. She could not see Paul, but looked at me & said, "What do you think?" I was flummoxed by the question & did not know how to answer, "Erm, it was interesting to see you having sex with a woman; you both made each other happy." I eventually responded. "Yes, we did, didn't we. I feel exhausted now!" We eventually found Paul who was looking keenly at a black girl in her twenties, I think he would have made a move for her, but on seeing both Monica & myself, he moved away & towards us. With buttons still undone, Monica said, "I feel tired now. Can we go?" & with that, the three of us walked slowly through the club, with many now dancing. Monica hesitated from time to time at something interesting until we collected our coats & were out and on our way to the car. In the car, Paul was quiet, was he upset? Did he not approve of the men or the women or both? Monica looked too tired to hold a conversation, & I was uncertain as to what to talk about; & eventually, I said the club was very different from the 2+2 club. The statement did not invoke any response, so I then gave up. The rest of the quick journey against the large flow of traffic going into Paris was quiet & after Paul dropped us off, Monica went to bed immediately & was soon asleep.

Sunday 28th Nov: jealous Monica about Marie from Quay17

Monica was in the lounge ironing some clothes when Marie from last night phoned Monica & said that she really enjoyed her night with both herself & Geoff, she really enjoyed BOTH of us. I could hear both sides of the conversation & until they had finished. Monica then exploded, "Marie knows your name, & she is keen on you, & I can't have friends on my own without YOU around me." A big argument ensued, and she started hitting me, then scratching me. She even threatened to push the hot iron in my face but retracted the threat quickly. She then stormed off in her car for a few hours, obviously to speak with a friend, unload & unwind.

She returned sometime in the evening, & we have a quiet night. I wanted to avoid her temper, she was dangerous.

Why do some women like Monica & Anne think I am a punchbag? I dare not retaliate, but I can argue with effective logic, perhaps that is the problem? They have no logical answer, so resort to violence.

Friday 3rd Dec: Monica loses ALOSI job

I phoned Claudine, another Rwandan friend, at lunchtime to advise her to chat with Monica & suggested we meet at a resto Saturday night. Either she did not phone Monica, or Monica never mentioned it.

I tried to contact Monica to see if she wanted to go shopping. "I am with Paul at Pizza pub. Come". When I arrived, I found her crying & being consoled by Paul. She then told me that ALOSI contract had not been renewed! She would be out of work from the end of the month. After all the promises & abortive permanent contract signing in March, we got this! Jerome, her boss, said it was his decision, this is bullshit. It was Jerome that was saying to Monica she had the job & was trying to get the contract signed by the Germans. So, what has happened in such a short time? Paul was shocked also, because although not directly responsible, Jerome had informed Paul that he was giving Monica a permanent contract. Nobody else in CdF could speak French & English fluently. No doubt we would hear more about who would get the job & why.

We learned later that Jerome went to CdF Rungis office & met a secretary there whom they got on well, especially as she went with him to Germany. The attitude toward giving Monica a permanent contract changed during that trip because, afterwards, the job was given to this secretary. Monica would finish end of the month. This now put pressure on me for paying the increase in mortgage as the various tranches of money were released for the stages of the new house building. Monica must find a new job quickly.

From time to time, as usual, we went to the building site to watch the progress of the development, now progressing with foundations completed & a solid base in evidence.

Saturday 18th Dec: Lennon has his mobile stolen, but the SIM card is given back!

We were invited to a party with Emmaculet, another Rwandan friend, & Robert, a butcher in Le Raincy, an east Paris banlieue (suburb), with their son Olivier. The party was being held at a room near Claudine. As usual, I was told nothing except to be presentable for a party, so the news & journey were a surprise to me. I found that Lennon had known & had gone in the morning to see Olivier & while on the Metro has his mobile phone stolen by three youths. He said to them, "OK, there are three of you. I will not fight, but please give me my chip back inside the phone; you will only throw it away anyway." Amazingly, they agreed as he was so non-combative.

When we arrived, Monica criticised me for my appearance because I had my bum bag* & the clothes I was wearing. When I looked around the room, I realised I was the best-dressed person there with a green suit, because most of the men I saw were in jeans & open shirts. We said hello & did the customary thing in France with kissing on both cheeks to women & with men, I know the Rwandan thing is to touch foreheads as a greeting. I was a bit puzzled by several elderly couples who greeted Monica with the normal kisses & then rubbed her legs. Was that because she was wearing a short skirt & top & making some sort of point....approval? Monica liked this fuss & said to me some people, reference to me, make a fuss over her.

While much of the conversation was in Kinyarwanda, however there were a number of French present there, so I was able to converse in French. These groups I was attracted to, so I could listen & contribute. Time progressed in conversation until Monica did her normal thing when she saw me speaking with people. She left her conversation & started saying to the group, "Is Geoff boring you?" She really pisses me off with this.

We returned home with Lennon late & went to bed. In bed, I wanted to talk about why she interfered in a conversation she was not interested in joining, but just to disrupt. We proceeded to have a row, she got out of bed & I followed. She then turned around & hit me, "Don't you like what I say", she then punched me again in the mouth & cheek, drawing blood & giving me a bruise that I consequently have difficulty explaining in the office Monday. What was it with women? First Anne, & now Monica also thought I was a punch bag. They knew, I dared not hit back, I was too strong & may do BIG damage. I realised she could escalate this whereby I may do something I regret, so I returned to bed, & she stayed in the lounge & slept on the sofa.

* Americans call them fanny packs, I suppose because they tend to be more security conscious & wear it on the front where the "fanny" is.

Sunday 19th Dec

Monica stayed on the sofa & got up after I went training down the road to the track throwing area. When I returned, she had gone to Arpajon to get her hair done by another Rwandan friend. I did not see Monica all day, so Lennon & I chatted about the situation. I asked for help in understanding why Monica treated me like she did with constant criticism & insatiable need for men. He was understanding & made some comments to help. He found it embarrassing to have a mum who wanted men so much & was prepared to do many things to achieve what she wanted.

Tues 21 Dec 2004

I received a telephone bill from 22/11/04 & saw mobile phone calls & SMS messages sent & received. I started seeing a new number reoccurring, & when I looked up Monica's mobile phone contacts, I found the new number under Marie17. It was her new friend, Marie. A code for the new man? If it were a female she would have put her real name? Eventually, a few days later, I found it **was** "Marie" from the Quai-17 club she had sex with.

Another interesting thing I discovered, when I inspected the bill in detail was an omission. No SMS messages from Paul! This was obviously a sign of less interest. I thought maybe he was shocked by Monica being bi-sexual at the Quai 17 club.

Chapter 13

January 2005

From time to time, as usual, we went to the building site to watch the progress of the development, with now the walls going up quickly every few days. Interestingly, they were using large hollow terracotta blocks the size of UK breeze blocks rather than traditional bricks.

Monica was now out of work & started thinking of possible projects of work. Her first idea was a dating agency online AMM (Afro Match Makers). I started helping her with ideas. At work, I started to make the basis of a business plan. She needed to find a job soon because whenever we take possession of the new house, the monthly mortgage payments would vastly increase. We needed an extra income to ensure no cash flow problems.

Sunday 8th Jan

I went training, & on my return, Monica was angry when I mentioned that I had phoned Marie, her Quai 17 club female friend, on Saturday & proceeded to hit me & scratch my face with her nails. She was not happy at all that I was in contact with her lesbian friend, whom I had met FIRST.

Monday 9th Jan

Monica was nice as pie when I got home from work. When the opportunity arose as Lennon went to his bedroom, she led me by the hand to the bedroom. On closing it, she started undoing my belt, unzipping my work trousers & exposing my penis. She smiled & went down on her knees to suck it. Oh, what she does to me! I was putty in her hands. She, bit by bit, took off various garments until she was naked, and I was only in my shirt and a loosened tie. I played with her fanny & boobs & could only imagine her face due to the darkness in the room, especially when I heard her breathing heavily. Why the turn-around in mood? Maybe the scar on my face was making her feel guilty? Or maybe she wanted to be open about Marie to me? What the hell, I have seen her have sex together.

James was so happy with Monica's mouth deep-throating him that before I could think about moving to another sexual position, a volcanic eruption took place., Monica was not expecting such a fast reaction, so cum spurted all over her face as she retracted to take a breath. She carried on regardless, up & down until James was just a walnut, & Monica had a cum covered smiling face of satisfaction. She licked her lips to take much around her mouth, but there was so much on the rest of her face, eye sockets & cum dripping from her nose. If I were a dog, I would lick her clean; the thought crossed my mind.... Maybe another time!

After she cleaned her face in the bathroom, she proceeded to cook the dinner.... Wow, what a Hors d'Oeuvre!

Friday 14th January: Geoff in hospital – cannot see Dawn before she goes to Australia

I was due to go to the UK to see Dawn for the last time before she departed for Australia for permanent emigration with her Aussie boyfriend, Al. My plan was to work at JY up to lunchtime, then leave for Calais in the afternoon & get the evening ferry. However, at about 10:30-11 am, I started to get intense right leg pain above the quadricep. The pain got worse & worse, whereby I could not sit or lie down. Within a short time, the company medical nurse at work called the ambulance, & I was admitted to the intensive care ward of Longjumeau hospital. The doctor asked about the level of pain, & I said it was 8/10 with no respite. They took an MRI scan & staying still for 2 minutes with such intense pain needed all my concentration & pain resistance. The results concluded that the pain was caused by my prolapsed L4 &

L5 discs in the lumber region. While I have had back problems for donkey's years, some osteopath work usually sorted it out. I was in the emergency ward for 3 days & then a further 2 days in the normal ward before discharge. I was surprised that Monica made only one quick visit to me because she was **so** busy.....mmmm. We lived 600 metres from the Longjumeau hospital & yet she was too busy? Bullshit, she must be seeing men. I then found out much later she **was** seeing men during the evenings, using the time I was in hospital to have free rein on her activities, all the time I was in hospital expecting her to visit me.

Monday 30th January

Monica went to an exposition for Entrepreneurs at the Palais de Congress being run from 28th Jan. I found out she had met many people, including a chap called Claude, whom I would investigate further as things progress with him.

Saturday 4th February 2005

As usual, we went to the building site to watch the progress of the development. Now that all the walls were done & roof constructed, tiles would be added during early February.

Tuesday 9th February

Using some free football tickets given to Robert the butcher, Lennon & I drove to Robert & Emaculet's place & then, with Olivier, we went together to park the car at a place a couple of train stops away from Stade de France. There it was easier to park in a side street near the station. France were playing Sweden, & it ended as a 2-2 draw.

Meanwhile, I find out later Monica spent all day & night with Antoine regarding a possible project to start (Afro Match Makers) AMM. I had been privately working on the business plan (37 pages) with 4 scenarios for 3 years of projected income & costs for a P & L. I also made a detailed website definition (15 pages) to direct exactly what was required to be written by the Web Master & verified by JY software engineers was good, without Monica knowing. I wanted to see what she could do without my help & then be able to present something that would be the basis of the business plan.

Friday 12th Feb: Lennon threatened with expulsion

I visited the headmaster of Lennon's school because he was late, not achieving his potential & was disruptive, with a strong indication he could get thrown out of the school. When I got back home, Monica & I discussed the options, but Monica kept interrupting me four times, not initially wanting to believe things were so bad. I said we need to frighten him for him to realise the consequences of failure.

Saturday 13th Feb

I found the latest "business plan sent by Antoine rev-2. I compared the original text from the training course official template was highlighted; the work done would have taken him about 10 to 30 minutes! However, Monica was with him **ALL day** & evening, so what did they do? The work, or lack of it as it showed:

1) Little work done 2) Both are clueless as to what to do or what was required. I then found out Monica was with Antoine when Lennon & I were at the Sweden vs France football match on Saturday.

Why did Monica keep wanting to see Antoine regarding the AMM business plan when he was useless & was contributing nothing? Maybe he was trying to fix meetings with other people who need business plans. Was he another man in her life?

Thursday 17th Feb

I saw the same entry now for Phber40 Paul in her phone as for her address old book.

Friday 19th Feb

Small row with Monica when she found my notes regarding Antoine & their AMM "business plan". She reads "What to do" & said, "Are you saying I want to bed him?" I said to her that the work must have taken no longer than 10-30 minutes & yet this took all day Wednesday & evening! It did not develop in a bigger row because I think she was seeing that the "work" was rubbish & lacked any professional work by a person who simply did not know what he was doing.

Sunday 21st Feb

Monica's mobile phone screen was broken, & I was able to copy many names & numbers. We went to see Jemma, another African acquaintance who lived in Fontainebleau. We spent some time in her flat drinking & eating with some of her flat neighbours before returning home later in the evening.

Wednesday 24th Feb

I noticed Monica was going online to "Meetic", a personal site for meeting people of the opposite sex. While this was OK to research what the competition was doing, I noticed she was not keeping up to date with e-mails.

Thursday 25th Feb

Monica went online in "Meetic" & started to read 25 male profiles & started to send internal e-mails to some of the men. One was Phber 46 Paul, a journalist living in Paris (75008) arrondissement 8. She started giving a new e-mail address as xxxxxxx40@gmail.com

Friday 26th Feb

Monica could not sleep, & while I was asleep, went online & sent an e-mail, "Hello, I am Monica as an introduction" to Pierre, a Cadre superior (manager). I also saw she met a Jean-Claude during the day. Who is he?

Tuesday 1st March: Opening up to Cloe

After work, I visited Cloe to chat about my worries & disturbance at Monica's activities. While there, I logged-in to Monica's account for Cloe to see her activities, & we saw Monica had promised to send a photo of herself to this Phber40 Paul for a possible rendez-vous. Cloe could not work out why Monica was endangering our marriage for the sake of it or liaisons or possible sex. I explained the night at Quai17 club, & she was not surprised at Monica being bi-sexual. Cloe also divulged that Monica had said she was working on both AMM & a Travel agency project. The latter was news to me.

Cloe made a cup of tea in the kitchen, & as she turned around, our eyes meet. She cuddled me in sympathy for my situation, "Oh Geoff, I want you to be happy with Monica." I said, "I need to be with you to explain more about what I am going through." Her arms were around my shoulder as we embraced & kissed. I could feel her boobs pressing against me, and I wanted more yet, does she? So many questions were buzzing around in my head, I may not be interrupted this time & then what? Suddenly, Cloe's phone rings, she answered, & a friend wanted to chat. As it progressed for some time, I excused myself & left.

Friday 4th March 2005

I discovered an SMS from Claude "Bonjour J'ai un problème avec cet après-midi je te telephone des que possible par SMS, Claude, bis" "I have a problem with this afternoon, I will telephone as soon as possible by SMS. Kisses, Claude". Is Claude the same as Jean-Claude or another man? By indirect means and asking what did you do today & pursuing questions, I abstracted from Monica she had met Claude & tried to explain Claude lived in Marcoussis, west of the N20 from Montlhery, a 20-minutes' drive southwards from Longjumeau.

I told Lennon I was sad about the state of affairs & the ridiculously poor business plan from Antoine & Monica. I showed him theirs & my business plan, & he saw what I meant. Lennon chatted with his mum later, & when Monica approached me, she was a bit apprehensive to try to explain the differences. I was exasperated & tore up my 37 page plan for AMM & 15 pages of the website definition. When she saw all the pages, the detailed financial forecast, the SWOT etc., she was shocked at the difference between this & the puny few pages of their effort & tried to stop me, wanting to keep the Geoff version.

Monica then contacted this Claude that night for help. He said he would get a colleague to do it during their work time Monday or Tuesday latest & would do it in a few hours! This colleague was supposed to have spent some time in Cote d'Ivoire. I was not sure what advantage that would be in making a detailed business plan. It was experience & knowledge of what to ask & make a plan accordingly. Without question & answer session with Monica the business plan would be another poor effort & not relevant to AMM. It was agreed Monica would meet Claude next week to get a copy of the completed business plan. I thought a meeting with Claude would be another excuse to meet another man for lunch — this is so familiar.

What did Monica want out of life? A husband? Someone to provide a British surname, image a nice home? Maybe to tantalise men with her sexual desire for men? She could divorce her mind away her normal life until she desired their attention & sexual desires & finally EXTRACT her wishes, be it a job, favour or whatever. I have been reminded by several people that if it is normal to use your power of being a good looking female, you can work on men's weaknesses to extract many things & use them. She fell in love with Paul, which was unusual for spending a parallel life, but now I think Paul is just a friend. This was something I predicted two years ago that this would happen. However, I did not anticipate the constant desire to look & be with men all the time. Now, with the excuse of the AMM project, she was trying to meet men on Meetic.

Monday 7th March 2005.

I was working late & phoned Monica from the office, she said she was in "Ed" supermarket. However, there was no background shop noise, her voice had an echo as if in an empty office or a stairwell. I left immediately, & she arrived 10-15 minutes later; therefore, she was within a radius of 10-15 minutes from our flat. Monica had a smile on her face that was not a usual face to get home on. What was she up to this time? I think she had a local R.V. Is this with Auber, Claude or someone else? Something else to investigate when more information comes to hand. It was a good job being a former top athlete as I was able to concentrate on subjects like training or work without being too distracted by Monica's antics.

Tuesday 8th March

I arranged a drink with Paul in our favourite Palaiseau rocker pub on the high street. We discussed the new takeover company of CMR, who own CdF because the new company works in a very different manner than the British CMR. They had a hierarchy that prevented any person from being able to embezzle without other sections of the organisation overseeing actions from other branches of the organisation. I can understand this as the new company country is so corrupt.

I took my copy of the AMM business plan as well as the joint Antoine / Monica version, & we discussed the two versions. Paul agreed there was no comparison, theirs was an excuse for a meeting between Monica & Antoine for a couple of days & was worthless as a business plan. Paul said, "Any bank approached for a loan to start a business requires a detailed business plan, & theirs would lead to any loan being rejected immediately." Paul also told me that Monica had asked whether he or somebody he knew could do a business plan for her, knowing the work involved, he said no. I mentioned to Paul about Claude, & he said he had not heard of him, even though during the row, she claimed she had told both Paul & Lennon of the R.V. with Claude.

Wednesday 9th March

I saw various new entries on Monica's phone, including Kidou. Who is he, an innocent person or another male friend? I also saw Claudine, was this Claude under another name? I now saw also Jean-Claude e-mail as jcbenva@wanadoo.fr; maybe Claude was Jean-Claude.....Oh I was going mad working all these conundrums. Looking at the phone number in an old address book thrown out, I now have a correlation with Claude of early February to Jean-Claude. Suddenly, Monica wanted me to take sexy photos of her. She said "It is for a person who may want to put a photo of me in his magazine as a sexy model." She said, "He thinks I am beautiful & will make a good model". I later checked & saw she had sent the photo to Jean-Claude. Yes, Monica was good looking, all my friends say so, but I was not sure at this later stage in her life that a magazine would want to have her photos, even if they were sexy.

Thursday 10th March

I was looking for something & tried looking in Monica's wardrobe when I saw a small booklet. It had some very interesting information that crossed many "dots" & T's regarding Claude (Jean-Claude). I found that he had been in the picture since early January. This was why Monica wanted to have me take sexy photos *"......he wants sexy photos of me in his magazine as a sexy model...."* bullshit, it was for Claude!

Friday 11th March 2005: Gisele stays the night

We have a guest who stayed the night called Gisele, she apparently was a friend of Claudine (lived in Morsang-sur-Orge 5km /4 miles away from Longjumeau), a friend from the Rwandan group who were in Melun. I was puzzled why a friend of a friend would suddenly be invited to stay the night when she did not know her directly & had never met her before. Gisele was puzzled as well. I found out that Claudine had before mentioned her friend was visiting who had a large mansion living with a rich white man. That night at my flat, Gisele mentioned she lived in a very large house with many bedrooms & large amount of land that included 2 horses. David her "husband", actually a partner, owned a Hussiers (Balliff) practice with 5 secretaries to administer the work. Hussiers were invited by advocates & notaries & often, the practice was a money tree. The business had been raised by David's father & was now retiring, leaving David with the whole business.

Monica was REALLY keen to see this house & almost invited herself to stay with Gisele. They made arrangements for Monica to go to Brussels / Bruxelles & stay with them. I took Gisele back to Claudine in Morsang-sur-Orge the next day.

Monday 14th March

Monica went to see Agnes from Cotonou, Benin who was visiting Paris. She was staying at the Evergreen Meridien Hotel with her two children. Her husband was a Scot & in charge of a cement factory as Manging Director in Benin. Agnes had a successful nightclub restaurant that was the highlight of Cotonou's elite life, managed by her elder sister, Virginie. Monica had gone into town by train, so I met them later that evening after work, & we had dinner locally from the hotel. I did not need to take Monica home as she was to stay the night in the hotel with Agnes & the kids.

On returning home that night, I did my customary searches & saw more information about the meeting Monica had with Claude on 28th Jan at the Paris Exposition for Entrepreneurs. She paid for two drinks at the Meridien Hotel bar opposite. If she paid for drinks, then the chap must have bought lunch, so the liaison must have started then. I then found receipts for three gold articles bought at Carrefour with a total of €172 paid on 15th January, the day after I was admitted to hospital with severe leg pain. Monica kept claiming she had no money because her social money had not come through, but when I checked her bank account, there was no record of purchase by Monica. Therefore, the chap Claude paid for it. Monica must be meeting this Claude for a while to get him to pay for gifts of that value. I found credit card purchases of drinks on February 4th at the local Longjumeau Postillion bar. So, I assumed he was entertaining her with dinner/lunch. Dinner would be difficult with me around. However, 5 days in the hospital would have been godsend, or my intended trip to the UK to see Dawn that obviously I could not make.

I searched everywhere, then looked under the bed & found various interesting papers, including the last telephone bill. I normally filed all bills, so this was hidden from me, & the bill showed she phoned Claude constantly. Another man, what is going on? Who was he & what did she plan to get out of him? She always had an ulterior motive, maybe finding another job? I had now found three separate references to Claude in various sources: an old diary, a mobile phone under Lille and a sticker in her new diary with an extra copy of the RV Sat 27 Feb. I was trying to remember what we were doing that Saturday, and it must have been uneventful as I had no record in my diary.

Tuesday 15th March

Monica spent the 2nd day with Agnes at her "Evergreen hotel". She phoned me to pick her up from Massy / Palaiseau "gare"/ train station, & we arrived home at about 8:30 pm. She immediately looked at her e-mail messages & went on Meetic website & message chats with "Bill". I saw later he was asking her about whether she was playing "hide & seek" with him as she chatted with him for some 40 minutes. What did Bill do? Was Monica pursuing with the aim of getting a job? I thought many of these men are to do with that. She got her CdF job due to meeting & being with Paul, so I thought she was trying the same with these other men. The wily ways of African women to get a job are different to Occidentals.

Sat 19 March

I walked up the hill in Longjumeau to see where apparently Aubert lived. I had an address, but I saw no associate name of Jean-Claude Auber or Benouwt at the relevant apartment block, floor 5, flat A2.

I saw later, when Monica was occupied that she had received three phone calls on three consecutive days from the same mystery person. Who was this? I looked up Pages-Jaune (French Yellow pages) to find Aubert was Cedric Aubert. Oh, I was getting confused with all this intrigue & yet espionage is for a scientist's fun, even if it is the fact I do not trust my wife.

I made an update on the AMM business plan that became the last one. I convinced Monica that a major problem for the AMM project was how to access African females who may not have internet. Although females would be free, only men pay; Africa is not Europe, so most suitable females may only have access weekly or even monthly, & this site may not be a priority when you have a rare resource (internet) & pay per minute's access. Monica initially was critical of me not being supportive over the last weeks, but eventually, after some weeks of constant prodding from me, she finally dropped the idea.

Friday 25 March: wild goose chase

Monica & I went for a car meander drive, & I asked where did Claude lived. We went for a while & arrived at Sauvigny sur Orge &

no 27 Ave Charles de Gaule, then said oh, it is in Fontainebleau. I think as she was so vague, she was telling me lies, & this was a wild goose chase.

I found that night, she had been in contact with a new contact, Pierre Mburiro, to whom she had sent sexy photos & wanted photos of him as well. Access to this new xxxxxx2000@ e-mail address has revealed she was in contact with so many men. Are they from Meetic? What for? Some of the messages were "steamy" full of sexual desires, & Monica played up to them. Was she serious or just playing games with them as titillation?

Saturday 26 March

We received Suzanne, a dear friend of Monica's & her husband Jacques from Switzerland. They arrive in the early evening, so no chance to show them around the area, but the flat was very clean & ready for guests.

Sunday 27 March 2005

After breakfast, we took them to Jemma in Fontainebleau, by a large roundabout route de Samois flat E13, 8th floor. Often appartement blocks just have a number e.g. E13 rather than a name, seems very socialist, I saw this in Moscow. Anyway, Jemma's address proved that Jemma -Ave Charles de Gaule was NOT Jemma. It was Claude's address, but what town? Researching the maps & addresses, I realised it must be 27th Ave General de Gaul & that leads to Viry Chatillon.

When we said goodbye, I detected signs of a sexual hug between Monica & Jemma, or am I imagining it? However, as we went to the car, they talked & agreed that Monica would spend the night at Jemma's on Wednesday. Interesting, here are lesbian opportunities for them both because Jemma has no man & 2 young kids. For some reason, Monica suddenly did not want to pursue a sexual liaison with

Marie. I have to be careful because Monica did not like me raising the question of her bisexuality; she was very sensitive about it. Why is it that when I saw her in action, I was am quite willing to accept it?

Saturday 2nd April: ATT - another project

We were invited to a wedding of a Rwandan couple in a church. Afterwards, they were having their reception in a building in part of the park. The park was called ; Porte de Plaisance du port aux Cherises, Dravail, by the river Seine. For some reason, Monica did not want to arrive at the church early, instead, she wanted to go in separate cars. I disagreed, but to save having another row, I let the subject go. It gave me the opportunity to research my theory, so I went to 27th Ave General Charles de Gaule & found Number 27 near the Ice rink. It was a big house with a high wall & no nameplate I could see. Could this be the address finally of Claude? I then seemed to remember recently, we went to the area, & she seemed to know the area well & knew certain things only a regular visit would give her this information. How did she know there was an ice rink & a Pizza restaurant overlooking the lake close by?

Monica said to me that Claude was in charge of a company, ATT, making small RFID detectors for passports, ID cards & important documents to prevent fraud. With government documents like that would need high government officials to approve. The job would involve spending maybe 6 visits a year seeing high government officials in Africa. I said to get any official to approve, it would need the top officials, like a minister, to be convinced & approve. This would mean maybe 2-6 weeks to get permission even to meet these officials for each country & multiple long visits per year. She showed, by her answers to my questions that she had no idea WHO would be clients or about the subject. I said to get contracts like that, they would be ministers in high positions in Africa. It would be a major technical & expensive decision by any government.

It would mean a lot of time away & much communication to organise a good trip. Monica would need to have technical knowledge of the product & have the knowledge of each country's government mechanisms & who pulled the strings to get any order. This sort of product needed patience & time as well as technical knowledge, of which she has no background knowledge & has no idea. I supposed Claude thinks with her persuasion & sexual attractiveness, she could get orders more qualified people could not get. My other worry would be she would use sex to get an order from these high government officials.

Chatting further about the proposal, I came to the conclusion he was spinning a yarn to get sex, because no way could someone with no experience & background knowledge of the subject or education be any good. I know with experience one starts at the lower technical echelons of an organisation & gradually you are introduced to higher & higher bosses until you can reach the REAL decision makers who in this case would be politicians.

Tuesday 5th April

That morning, I took three phone bills to copy at work & on my return home, Monica went mad, & we had a small row. She said she needed the bills to get the account number (why did she not phone me for the account number?) & to get an extension to her credit for while she was in Belgium with Gisele. I asked again who was Jean-Claude on the way to dropping her off at the Massy/Palaiseau gare / train station. She claimed she did not know a Jean-Claude and that it was Claude. She claimed Paul knew about Claude but to not contact him.

Thursday 7th April

I saw an E-mail from Andre to Monica promising to return via Paris when he has finished his 6 month course originally 12 months at Lancaster University. He had mentioned he would finish the course on 30th September. That night, I met Paul at our usual Palaiseau pub on the high street. He said he was getting disillusioned with Monica as she seemed to have changed. We continued to chat about Monica, & neither of us knew what she wanted. Although she mentioned Claude (but not by name), who was apparently helping her with her business plan for AMM. Paul told her my business plan was very good & gave all the required information & subjects required, so why seek others to do what has already been done?

Paul seemed surprised when I said Claude had apparently made Monica a job offer at ATT & would phone her in Belgium to confirm the news to her. I think he had visions of deja-vous with him & Monica 2 years ago & maybe saw more to what I have & haven't told him. When I phoned Monica that night, she proved me correct & a bet with Lennon when she made some excuse to stay in Brussels until Sunday. She wants to go clubbing Friday & Saturday nights with her Rwandan friends. However, she eventually spends the two nights with Gisele & David at David's large house 30km south of Brussels.

UK business trip Mon 11th – Friday 15th April

I went over on the Calais ferry on Sunday the 10th & stay at Dad's house with just Nan there now. I can get the local JY sales people to organise convenient customer visits by visiting Steven in Stoke & Sophie & Roo in High Wycombe. & return Friday night

Thursday April 14th 2005

While in England on business, Monica phoned me to say she would be going to Brussels to see Pierre, a Rwandan friend of Claudine, who could help her with the ATT job, the newly promised job because he has contacts in Congo as well as Rwanda. He picked her up from the TGV station & where she was staying with a friend of Pierre Mburiro Bukavu, a Rwanda number (250) -08313xxx.) I saw his name also on a Brussels number 32-484 92 86 xx & #3419. I must try this number; however, a woman answers, so this is not a hotel, so what is this number #3419? An access code to a hotel. I found out later she had phoned him in a telephone cabin.

All about this visit to Brussels was fishy & somehow I believed something to do with Gisele, but what? Why suddenly all this activity with Brussels? I was sure I would find out; I had to be vigilant & research constantly. I found a lump of sugar from hotel when I saw her bag contents some days later.

Gisele, some years later, said that Monica came to Brussels & stayed with David in a hotel, so that was the start of the affair with David that eventually destroyed David & Gisele's relationship of some 13 years.

Friday 15th April

I thought Monica no longer loved or thought of Paul. When I asked her to look after Paul, she said, "I should be enquiring about Lennon, who had just a cold", & then said that she did not want to see Paul. However, she did see Paul as he had a cheque for €5,400 from CMR part of back-salary & bonus.

Wednesday 20th April 2005: refused French nationality.

I found a letter Monica wrote to French naturalisation dated 14th April in which, she claimed she had not defrauded the social Caisse d'Allocation Familiale (CAF), from their letter dated 21st February 2005 refusing her request. However, she did offer to pay back €6,465 to CAF. This she hoped would help her case for her French nationality request. (see precis at the finish)

Her trying to fiddle the social system postponed their decision on nationality for many years. In an incident in 2010 with Gisele in a shop (see later) in Brussels, it transpired at the police station. She had not then have French nationality but still had refugee status.

Thursday 21ˢᵗ April: Cloe comforts me with a blow job

Cloe phoned me at work about needing €200 loan for a week. I said no problem & suggested her to come to our house that night after work. I went to the bank & got €200 from the ATM in Longjumeau on the way home & arrived at about 6:30 pm. Cloe was already there, chatting with Monica. Cloe was wearing a open button-up blouse & a skirt. She mentioned to Monica she needed to borrow €200 for a week to cover a special expense. Monica said that they did not have any money, so it was not possible. Cloe was a bit shocked & disappointed with her reaction.

After some time chatting, I volunteered to take her home, as usual, much to the annoyance of Monica. When in the car, I told I would give her the money when we arrived at her home. Once outside her flat, I gave her the €200. What was Monica's problem? Cloe often did things for Monica, was she jealous of Cloe in case she took a shine to me?

Outside her apartment, Cloe offered me to come up for a cup of tea, I thought, "what the hell", I would have a problem with Monica when I got home anyway by taking Cloe home. I accepted her offer & up in her flat, I sorted out a faulty door handle. We then sat down together on the single sofa with a drink of coffee. We chatted about how Monica had changed as Paul has also observed. She was becoming selfish. Was she also jealous of Cloe & worried we would have some affaire? I said without thinking, "Monica has all these affairs with men & yet does not want me with you. I do find you attractive, & I must admit I need to be determined not to flirt". She blushed & faced me more, crossing her leg over to my direction.

I am very good at body language, I was now getting aroused. My mind was racing, "Oh, she is beautiful, & I am married, but Monica does not think of me when she goes to bed with other men." My eyes looked into her eyes & then a quick glance at her bosom. Cloe saw that glance, smiled, put her finger at her crevice & close to the top button,

"You are beautiful." She smiled & undid the top button, and now her bosom was more evident, revealing her red lace bra. I smiled & said automatically, "That is my job." She looked as if to say, "OK, then undo my buttons."

One by one, slowly looking into her eyes, I undid her blouse buttons until her blouse was fully flowing open. I placed my left hand into her bra to feel her ample boob. With my right hand around her shoulder, we kissed. She started feeling my trousers with my excited penis. Now my zip was undone & her hand went down my culottes to feel that hard erect penis. Off came her blouse, & I helped her in taking off her red bra. Now I could feel those breasts that I had partially seen for so long. They was so lovely, and I felt I needed to take off my shoes as she was removing my trousers. I lifted up my behind so that my pants could be removed, she did the same as I removed her culottes. My shirt was removed as we were both naked & feeling each other all over. "Oh, I was not expecting this, I do not have a condom" I thought.

She knelt on the floor, took my penis in her mouth & commenced to give me a wonderful blow job until I could hold on no more & filled her mouth full of cum. She did not flinch as she continued to suck up & down my shaft until, eventually, James capsized & shrivelled in size. She retracted her head & smiled with her mouth open showing it was full of cum. She then swallowed all until no sign was evident. We just looked at each other Cloe still on her knees as I was sitting there on the sofa leaning back, exhausted. I could not resist feeling & fondling those wonderful boobs again. I said, "Viens", she came up to the sofa, we embraced & kissed passionately. Eventually, I said, "peut etre j'ai besoin a depart", & with that, we both dressed. With one last embrace & passionate kiss, I left for home.

When I got home, I had the usual frosty reception because I had taken Cloe home as usual & had taken much longer than she would have anticipated. "You took a long time" "Yes, that is correct, I had some things to do, hey, do I go on about all your men? I accepted to go up to her flat, sort out her door handle & have a drink, any problems with that?" Monica may have suspected more, but she could not think of a good thing to say, so she said nothing.

When in bed, I said, "please tell me if you are going to bed with Claude", there was little reaction, resistance or comment. I said, he probably loved her, but she did not deny this, although, with some resistance to start with, she mellowed to accept the fact that I knew about them. She seemed happy when I said I never disagree with her enormous qualities, so I said, "A quality of hers is seeing men & going to bed with them, a bit like an escort, for the benefit of both of us as a family". Monica was happy with what I said & that I understood her motives; she did not object to any of my statements that she used men.

Friday 22nd April: Admits to Claude (ATT project)

She said she had met Claude at lunchtime to go over this ATT job project in Chilly Mazerin. She said it was only the 3rd time they had met, but I said what notes did you make. She said that she did not make any notes as she could remember everything. I asked her again how many times she has REALLY met him because I said that I knew of at least 3 times in Courtepeil restaurant in Massy alone. When I asked her, "Have you gone to bed with him, or would you go to bed with him?" She said, "You would need to see him; he is about 200kg!" I let the subject rest, and she was either convulsed by his body or was hiding what he looked like. Either way, it would not stop going to bed if it resulted in a job.

Saturday 23rd April

I phoned Claudine whom I saw often with Monica to know more about Pierre. We agreed to meet in Epiny Gare train station & chatted for an hour about Monica & Pierre. Apparently, Pierre was a friend of one of Monica's dead brothers, but Monica did not know him. He had a small electromenager (white goods shop,) Claudine said that she did

NOT introduce him to Monica & subsequently was shocked to hear my news. Claudine said that she did not understand what Monica wanted out of life and couldn't understand Monica. Monica told me it wasn't about money, but Monica wanted all the things that money buys.

Wednesday 4th May 2005: Visit to Marina in Nantes

I got home early that night to enable us all to go to Nantes to stay with Monica's Rwandan friend, Marina, who was a doctor in a local hospital there.

Thursday 5th May

We got up, left Marina's flat mid-morning, & she directed us to the local beach less than an hour away. After a while on the beach & a drive around, we returned back to Marina's flat, after a while, we left for Longjumeau.

That night in bed, I raised the question, & we chatted about Pierre. I suggested perhaps she went to bed with him when in Brussels. She denied completely, but when I chatted about Claude, I asked her about him, and she said that if he was using her just to go to bed with her instead of the job (ATT), she would be very angry. This suggested that she had already gone to bed with him with the promise of the ATT job. For reasons I had mentioned to her before, I said that I did not think this job was real & that she should be prepared for the fact he WAS using her for sex. I was to find out this would not be the last time men used her.

Sunday 8th – Frid 15 May 2005: South Africa trip

I went to South Africa to give lectures & make customer visits to boost ICP-AES sales. It is a beautiful country, but areas are dangerous. Vicky, the owner's daughter, who is taking a bigger responsibility as time goes on, had some friends down from England. While Vicky was filling up the car at the garage, the two guests went into the garage shop to buy some sweets (US=candy). Suddenly, she saw them disappear downwards, realising what had happened, she immediately stopped filling the car with petrol, drove off & down the road and phoned the police. They arrived soon after, & luckily, the two guests were very shaken, but safe. In South Africa, there are many simple thefts where assailants shoot the victims. An example: while I was there one time, two fathers were watching their boys playing in a football match in a park, & one was on the phone. A car stopped, 4 men got out, walked across the field to the football field, shot one of the fathers with the phone, took it and then walked back to the car & drove off! A special government commission of some 20 different backgrounds was convened to try to understand why, almost unique to South Africa, assailants murder for a simple theft rather than just steal.

Friday 13th May

I arrived via CdG airport, & my taxi driver, Rodriguez, I always used what was recommended & used by all JY personnel on the trip. I needed to unwind & found three "Middle East" used phone cards at €7.50 each in the bin. These phone cards were used to make cheap phone calls to countries outside using a phone booth at a cyber cafe. I found out she phoned Pierre while he was in Dubai. He phoned home on Tuesday 10th, while Monica was out, so Lennon took a message. I found out in my research, that she had many phone calls inconnu / unknown during the week, a number from outside France, especially on Friday Muslim holy day & start of the weekend for many Muslim countries, especially Dubai. I later saw from the phone bill: the calls were from Dubai, so from Pierre.

Saturday 14th May 2005

Suzanne was a Rwandan friend of Monica living in Paris. She was invited to our wedding, so I know her, & we have visited her in her flat several times, & Suzanne knew from what Monica has told her, I was good at DIY (Do It Yourself). A few weeks previous, on request I had fixed her curtain rail into position, she phoned Monica for a chat. Monica phoned her back later that night.

In bed, Monica started shouting about me talking with HER friends, "find your own friends", she demanded. She was so jealous of me talking with ANYONE & very possessive concerning her female friends. She wanted me to need her all the time, which explained why she never helped me with French. I thought she was worried that her Rwandan friends would steal me from her. She liked the kudos of being married to a white Englishman & having an English name. I think being African, she knew the thoughts & ways of African women! It was so hypocritical of her because of all the men in her life! Monica did not like me helping anyone!

Sunday 15th May

In bed, I started the conversation again about Pierre, she admitted she was in constant contact with him, claiming it was ATT job advice & that she was not sleeping with Pierre in Brussels.

Monday 16- Frid 20th May: Starting of the end of ATT - start of "Moni Clean" idea

During the week, Monica had started to see that the ATT job was just a rainbow & that Claude was just using her. He kept saying the job was there, but he needed to set things up in Africa. All the things she told me that he said to her over the months, I kept saying they were bullshit. Claude was taking advantage of her pride in her good looks, prestige & visiting her home Africa. I kept saying why would a person with: no sales experience, no technical knowledge of RFID* or anything technical & proven ability to liaise with various top country government ministers be able to get contracts. She would still see Claude regarding ATT project with more open eyes.

* She didn't know that RFID was Radio Frequency Identification utilised by a microchip with unique details that can be programmed into it.

Start of Moni Clean idea

She started to think about cleaning houses. I said I did not see this would be a full time occupation, but then we, eventually, started to focus on a business idea to clean offices & business sites. She would start up a company, "Moni Clean." She would find it takes AGES to start up a company in France. The authorities want you to go on a 6 week (useless) course, then go around the various agencies before eventually after some **4-5 months** a company is registered. Monica started research on starting a company. She started to find she needed to go on a 6-week government course in Grigny.

Saturday 21st May 2005

We went & took photos of our house with shutters on. All floors were completed. Looking around the house, it looked good, not long now before we move in.

Friday 27th May

She gets a phone call from Mali (code 233). Who the hell is this?

Saturday 28th May 2005: Monica & Imogen make love at home

Lennon was staying the night with his friend Olivier, son of Emmaculet, to ensure we had the 2nd bedroom for our weekend guests. Imogen, one of Monica's good friends, came with her French husband, Olivier, from the east of France & both stayed the weekend with us in my Longjumeau flat. We had spent the day out in Paris eating in a resto & returned home at about 8 pm. Monica phoned a friend & then Monica & Imogen said they were going out to spend some time with other Rwandese women chatting about home furnishings. They would arrive later and did not wait up for us. Olivier & I chatted for a while, obviously, my French was not so good, so the conversation was difficult, & eventually, at about 11 pm Olivier went to bed. I waited up looking at the TV for a while & then gave up & went to bed.

I left our bedroom door open, so Monica would not make a noise. At about 2 or 3 pm, I heard the front door open, & the hall light put on. There were quiet whispers for a while, and I expected they would both go to bed, especially when the hall light went out, leaving the place in darkness except for the external street lights outside. After some minutes, Monica had still not arrived in bed. After a while, I got up to see what they were doing.

Quietly, I crept to the hall & then looked in the lounge. I saw they were both fully engrossed naked in a lesbian act! I decided to watch & quietly sat down on the sofa opposite at right angles to them. They were so engrossed in love making, both their hands playing with each other fannies & caressing each other's boobs, that they did not notice me for at least 10-15 minutes. For some reason, Imogen opened her eyes & looked right to see me sitting there. Her sudden movement disrupted Monica, & Imogen quickly collected her clothes, & without a word, quickly went to her guest bedroom. Monica then got up, & we both went to bed without a word.

Sunday 29th May

Nothing was said the next morning, especially because Olivier was there. Monica had a quiet conversation in Kinyarwanda, which neither me nor Olivier would understand. Both Imogen & Olivier left in the afternoon back home.

Tuesday 31st May 2005

I made a rendez-vous (RV) with Claudine after work, we met close to Longjumeau & sat in my car to chat. I mentioned the events with

Monica & Imogen. Claudine spilt the beans that Monica phoned her up & arranged for her to contact Pierre Buro & another friend, Jado, to meet Imogen & Monica. They then all met near Longjumeau to go out all together in one car to a night club in Paris. I said maybe it was Quai 17, & Claudine replied, "Yes, that is it". I then mentioned the story when Paul, Monica & I went there last time, & the fun she had with one woman & then followed by another called Marie, the same Marie as before? Claudine was not surprised as she said things got a bit steamy with Monica & Jado & then she found Monica wanted to feel Claudine's boobs as well.

Claudine mentioned she had extremely long nipples & then popped out a good-sized boob to show me. WOW! I have never seen such long nipples. Claudine said she flinched at the club when Monica started caressing her boobs due to these long nipples being so sensitive, so Monica stopped. I asked whether she would have been happy with pursuing things with Monica had her nipples not been so sensitive. She evaded the question by saying she wanted to have an operation on her nipples to make them normal length. She told me that her nipples being so long made them extremely sensitive &, of course, any movement in her bra was similar to "jogger nipple" in pain.

Friday 3rd June

I saw an e-mail from George-Taylor Lewis confirming what I suspected: she had an affair with him, & he had been to bed with Monica when she worked for ADB in Abidjan, Cote d'Ivoire. I now remember that both Andre & George Taylor -Lewis were invited to our wedding, but George could not make it. Also, I remembered Lennon saying George would often come to their place & was enticed to go out playing with his friends.

Sunday 5th -10th June 2005:   Libya trip

written before Gadhafi fall from power

I was asked to train & sort out problems in Libya by our North African agent Hakim, who lived in the Paris area of France. Various people from HJY had been there & had not been able to sort out a problem of lead (Pb) determination in crude naphtha our ICP-AES with an ultrasonic nebuliser (USN) accessory to analyse neat naphtha from the Azzawiya refinery. All business was being blocked unless I could sort out their problem.

It all started with a flight that should have been direct to Tripoli, but it was overbooked, & we (13 people) were directed to Air Swiss to Zurich, then to Rome. When we got there, Air Italia said no agreement was binding with Afriqiya, so we would have to pay for a flight from Rome to Tripoli & claim the money back!!

After starting at 11 am, we arrived at 01:30 in the morning at the Azzawiya refinery west of Tripoli, which had its own small 12-bedroom hotel. The journey should have been a normal 3-hour direct flight!! We got a taxi & arrived at the refinery hotel that was just outside the refinery perimeter.

We went the next morning in the chauffeur-driven refinery company car to go about 600 metres, but it took some 60 minutes of security checks at the gate & reception. Three sets of security guards, first the police look at the passport look at you carefully & if satisfied, passed the passport to the 2nd security guard who is the army, more scrutiny & when satisfied, he passed the passport to the 3rd guard the elite Gadaffi who in being satisfied returned my passport & we were allowed to proceed. This happened EVERY time we went IN & when we went OUT of the refinery. So, although we started early, we did not arrive in the lab until past 10:00 am. Finally, we arrived at the lab, & the lab manager introduced us to the operator, Bashir, of the HJY Ultima ICP spectrometer with its USN accessory.

Bashir, the operator, soon said it was lunchtime & disappeared at 12:00 noon. We then got into the company refinery car & went outside the gates with the three security checks. Then, we had a long lunch taking over 2 hours, followed by the normal three security checks back to the lab at about 2:30pm. I started testing, & suddenly, the operator said we had to finish as it was 4 pm. "What!" The operator said that he must finish at 4 pm. That was the end of the day & other than testing that the spectrometer was OK, I had only about 3 hours of work done!

We went back in the chauffeur-driven company car to the hotel with the usual three security checks. I said to Hakim at dinner that night we needed to have sandwiches to avoid the long lunch & time wasted with the long security checks; otherwise, we would never get the required work done. The hotel manager could not understand, but I insisted he made us a packed lunch & drink we could eat in the lab to avoid the long lunch break.

The next day at 12 noon, Bashir, the operator, said it was lunchtime, so I said no problem. We had a packed lunch that we could eat in the lab to ensure we did not waste time like yesterday. He did not believe it, but when we produced the packed lunch, he said he would join us at the lab bench & eat with us. Suddenly, Bashir's attitude was totally different. He assembled things quicker & said he would try to extend his working hours beyond 4pm. Apparently, if you wanted to work extra hours, the authorities suspected you wanted to stay behind to sabotage the place! I tested the ICP-AES only on the first day, which was fine, then tested with simple aqueous standards the ICP with the USN, which was also fine. So then, I had naphtha solutions with spiked additions of a standard lead organic stand, & all was good. I informed Hakim, who was there, that the system was OK, so it must be the conditions with organics that were the problem.

Bashir then invited us to go to his drinking place after work. He took us in his car to his drinking place, a building on the edge of town with a palm tree leaf roof to shade the outside area where we had tea, & he offered us a Shisha pipe, a bubbling smoke bottle. To be polite, I took a couple of puffs with all of Bashir's friends looking intently.

Bashir took us into the town to find a cyber cafe. I tried to pick up my e-mails, but the baud rate was so slow it took about 2 minutes to be able to read just a simple text e-mail without attachments! I had never experienced such a slow response since the internet was invented. I just picked up what appeared to be most important, & after 30 minutes of just reading a couple of e-mails, I gave up.

He then took us for a ride, & we went to a place where there were perhaps 5 Square MILES of cars, piled one car on top the other 3 cars high scrapped from accidents. I have seen some large car scrap yards, but nothing prepared me for this!! There were millions of $$$ tied up in old cars that had been there for "donkeys years"…..can you imagine miles & miles of crashed defunct cars?

He then took us around the coast, there was rubbish everywhere over the approximately 600m of sand dunes that separated the coast road from the beach. I thought South Africa was full of rubbish, but they are tidy compared with Libyans! All over the place, there were rubbish, plastic bags, soft drink cans, car oil cans etc., dumped all over the place. There was money to be made collecting the rubbish, incinerating the combustible rubbish & smelting the Aluminium can & the steel.

Can you imagine 1900 km of white beaches & no tourists or alcohol in sight?!!! They do not want (at the moment) any tourists… (try getting a visa…..you have to be invited by a company to get a visa), maybe they will try later, but then they would need to provide mixed bathing & alcohol & greater freedom. Perhaps not…that would give the opportunity for rebellion!!

There was no incentive to work; they are over-employed, doing nothing and paid poorly. All the money went to President Gadaffi.

Celebrations of the Gulf War had died down when the people realised President Bush (US president) would not come to Libya to free them; they would have welcomed them with open arms!! The country is so poor & yet billions of dollars are created each day from the oil revenue. This, obviously, goes straight to the Gadaffi family & friends. None of the people have any incentive to work, so they all hang around for business that never comes.

They have toilets without toilet paper, just a hose & a flooded floor, which is normal for Middle East countries. The JY agent Hakim, who was paying for my trip, said in a matter-of-fact manner during the first flight, "….of course, they do not use toilet paper in Libya; they wash them bum with water …...."

What!!! When we stopped at Zurich, I went into a loo & took a whole toilet paper roll, so I was armed with a potential week without toilet paper! I found out that the technique used in Libya & other Arab countries is to do whatever you have to do, then use a small hose to wash your bum, then wade through the water all over the floor & wash your legs & feet….uuuurrrggghhh!!!! Can you imagine at Tripoli airport people with their feet in the basins washing their feet & legs!!! Shit splashed up on their gowns, and the place was flooded with shitty water, so I had to tiptoe in my shoes pulling up my trousers, to avoid the light brown 1cm (½ inch) depth water!!

It was noticeable that so many buildings were half-finished. Wherever we went there were maybe 20% of the buildings that were not finished, e.g. 4 floors with only 2 floors completed. It was amazing all over the place half-finished buildings. I found out that if completed, they had to pay a punitive tax, so they left it unfinished to avoid paying the tax.

Road checks are everywhere, with THREE different forces (police, army & Special Gadaffi Special Forces) at each checkpoint to ensure a rebellion was not universal & perhaps some would fight for the status quo.

Poor people, including my contact, was paid $200 per month as a chemist, & he had to pay 20% income tax on that!!! No credit was available to buy houses or cars.

The driving is something ... (to be missed). Can you imagine doing 170 km/hr on a poor road with a driver who was poor at the best of standards? We told him to slow down and that we were not in a rush and wanted to arrive in one piece. We both had visions of the car grave yard of miles & miles of crashed cars in our minds!!

Some have asked me what are the positive things. Well, the positive things were the people in Libya....they just wanted to be able to live their lives as they could do without the restrictions to keep them in place & poverty. They want to be free. Gadhafi was supposed to be a constitutional head of state, but no salaries were paid while he was on a trip away from Libya. He needed to approve; he controlled EVERYTHING.

I think I can capture the mood as "suppressed people with little hope of salvation", US President Bush in Iraq gave hope for a while, but that hope had subsided with resignation that nothing will change. Gadhafi has many sons (one committed to prison in France for various offences, but kicked out of the country), waiting in the wings to take over when dad goes. Gadhafi has played a clever game ever since the Americans bombed his palace with 6 planes flying from England. He suddenly realised he was vulnerable to England, so he slowly "repented" & gradually paid the various court cases in the UK, USA & France & gave the "culprits" over to the UK for the trial that did the Lockerbie Pan Am bombing.

With an open country one would have many tourists that would bring in money. They have 1900 km of wonderful deserted beaches, more than any other country in Europe. Tourism is what Libya needs, and it has sunshine, good beaches & Libyan people who are friendly (except the checkpoint guards). The lay-back attitude (lay-back to the point of horizontal......) would still be OK for holidays as there is no rush to do things.

The place is rather arid, & there is little water. However, there was a multi-billion dollar scheme that brings water from southern Sudan to some cities.....problem is it is already corroding & causing leaks & then finishes up evaporating!!!! They grow some olives & other vegetables, but very little. The shops are open at all hours at night, but there is nobody in these shops &, of course, not buying anything. Women's dress is reasonably "normal" & nothing like the dress code found in Saudi Arabia, the most fundamentalist Middle East country I have been to, way more than Iran or Libya.

Sunday 12th June 2005

Monica caught me looking at her phone. With Lennon present, I vented all my pent-up frustration with Monica & blurted out, telling her what I knew about her men. I said she needed to decide whether to stop lying to me & looking at Meetic for men. She said nothing, sat in the lounge & then went to bed. I followed much later. Monica now knew I know about Pierre. A few weeks ago, it was Claude in Viry Chatillon. I needed a promise that she would TELL me about RVs (rendez-vous) with boyfriends, at the very least. I think she was incapable of not looking for men. It was in her DNA. What is it with her that always makes her flirt with men? ...And what about me, do I matter to her? Lennon agreed & thought it was natural for her to flirt.

Thursday 16th June

Claude sent an SMS asking what time tomorrow afternoon you will leave. Big kisses. Question: will Monica tell me about this RV with Claude? Will she tell me where it was held, where at a resto or his house?

Friday 17th June: ChromePost excuse to meet Claude

I phoned at about 2:30 pm from work, just after Paul had done the same. She was in the car & said she was going to Chrome Post (Chilly Mazerin) to deliver from work a package that needed to be posted urgently. This was a classic case of ignorance catching her out. Packages from works are collected by Chrome Post or any other delivery service like DHL Fed-Ex, etc. Paul & I went to have a beer together at our normal Palaiseau pub. Although she was invited, she claimed she went to a Pizza pub in Chilly Mazerin by mistake. Of course, she would say that Chilly Mazerin was not far from Viry Chatillon, where she met Claude. I was annoyed that she would not tell me about the RV with Claude.

That night, we have a row. "Neither Paul nor myself believe you these days. You lie all the time", I think it hurt her that she realised Paul did not believe her either with her lies. I said to her that Paul agreed with me that Claude & his ATT project was a non-starter for a person who knew nothing technical, so even basics she would not understand. She was hurt by this trying to minimise the technical nature of the proposed job-selling RFID (Radio Frequency Identification) to African ministries in a few days' visit to various African countries. I said we both think that he was just leading you on some promised good & well-paid job. "You are gullible to believe this, & therefore, accept a liaison & probably sex for a -non-existent job". I would find out she fell for this trick by men many times. RFID was being used more & more in supermarkets to instantly change prices on the shelves from a central computer without floor staff needing to do anything, also passports & ID cards.

Saturday 18 June 2005

Monica claimed to have influenced cousin Nick's new job in ADB, working for George Taylor-Lewis, her manager. I said I could not see how an ex-secretary would have much influence with a manager unless there were something special between them, like a liaison while still married. She got upset, and I had hit a nerve. She claimed he was married, & she was a normal secretary for him. I was sure I was spot-on with my assessment. I had learnt from Lennon that he came around her house in Abidjan often when he was young, & the housemaid would take him for walks & play with him so that they would be alone. Logic tells you that the housemaid knew she needed to get Lennon away from the house to ensure uninterrupted "fun" between them.

Monica said she did not like me being in contact with Imogen. While Imogen said she appreciated having sex with Monica to both of us in separate e-mails. She did not say all because she said to me, maybe next time we can make a three-some "menage a trois. I could not say anything because I know how Monica can be prudish about things like sex in the open.

Tuesday 21st June

Monica & I were on our way to Sainte-Genevieve des Bois to see John & Charlotte when Monica started again that with that how they were HER friends and not mine, "You have no friends." I got on well with both John & Charlotte, & I could see Monica getting jealous when we talked about things Monica knew little, so she tried to change the subject quickly to something she either knew or was comfortable with. Charlotte worked for SOSIP, a large marketing group in Paris, & John was an interesting chap who liked me & wanted to chat about many things. While he said that he worked in an office in Paris, I was not sure with his evasiveness what he did.

We spent a few hours when we all went to a "pub" about a kilometre away with many pool tables, so we all played pool upstairs. After taking them back, we stayed for a chat & coffee at their flat before we went home.

At home, she started again, escalating into a big row, "Charlotte is MY friend, not yours. I don't want you contacting her." Was she afraid I would see Charlotte alone & form a liaison? She continued, "You only see MY friends; you have no friends," then she let out some interesting comments about George Taylor-Lewis, saying that she met him with his daughter & his girlfriend Emily at Belle Epine shopping mall. I was sure she would try to get closer to the 29-year-old daughter Alice, who had a flat in Paris close to the hospital where she was undergoing treatment for breast cancer.

Wednesday 22nd June 2005

I overheard a phone call by Monica to Pierre, the dentist in Melun, about a possible visit to Brussels. I read later her e-mail to Pierre about trying to arrange a long 3-day weekend in Brussels with him. To allay suspicions from me, she would take Lennon with her & deposit him with Gilles, her brother in Holland, whom she would say was the reason for going. I must admit Monica was excellent at planning things in advance.

Saturday 25th June 2005: Claude's (ATT) affair ends in an abrupt irate phone message from his wife

I saw there was a message on Monica's mobile phone, that Monica had not picked up yet. I listened to the message. Claude's wife was absolutely irate & was warning off Monica from her husband. The voice message continued forever, with his wife screaming down the telephone. When I said there was a message on her phone, she listened to the message near me, & I could hear the loud shouting of Claude's wife. Monica tried to dismiss the message, saying that I was misunderstanding the French. Ho, Ho, Ho. No Way! Claude's wife was screaming down the phone with a clear warning. Anyway, Claude became history, another affair to get what Monica thought would be a good position. Will she ever learn?

Although intelligent, Monica was not intellectual; hence, people could easily trick her into getting what THEY want (sex) with promises of money, a job, a position or a contract for Moni Clean.

Well, that is the end of Claude…… next!

Chapter 14

Monday 27th June 2005

Charlotte phones me at work & wants to chat. Could we meet somewhere for lunch? I agree, & we meet at Ville-du-Bois shopping mall just south of Longjumeau on the N20. Charlotte is concerned about Monica's attitude toward me, the way she tries to cut me off & ignore me, but also, she wanted to confide in me about Monica's secret plan to start up a holiday travel agency. Charlotte knows that I did not know about this "hair-brained" scheme. By the way, Monica was secretive about whether I knew about it or approved it. Working for SOSIP, Monica had approached her for information on travel agencies because she knew that SOSIP had one. Charlotte said that due to the use of the internet, SOSIP was closing their travel agency section down since it was not economical to continue. Monica would not listen & had high plans, even though Monica's knowledge was superficial & knew little detail of what was involved. Charlotte was worried I would be sucked into providing funds for the enterprise, which was almost certainly doomed to failure & loss of my money. The expression "forewarned is forearmed" was apt here, & we agreed that I needed to keep my finances away from anything to do with this idea. As Charlotte was sure Monica would keep coming back to her regarding this project, we agreed to keep in contact.

Without going into detail, Charlotte mentioned a few snippets that indicated John was a bit of a maverick explaining his evasiveness on his job. Charlotte was the one with the good job, & it seemed John also would make plans for various projects that never materialised.

Wednesday 29th June

In bed that night, Monica told me that she has been invited to Ann's daughter's wedding in Brussels, so she wants to go & make it a long weekend of 3 days. I said "oh good we can all go as we have not been to Brussels for a while". Monica said nothing. I had scuppered her jaunt with Pierre in one master-stroke. I was inwardly laughing my head off & yet could show no expression. A little information can be so powerful!

Saturday 2nd July: Monica on a 6-week govt training course for company start-ups

We are invited to a fellow attendee to the Government start-up business course at his home for lunch in Chilly Mazerin opposite side of the small river to Longjumeau. We chatted about his truck transport project. He planned to buy several trucks to provide transport for goods to/from different companies. In a general chat about trucks, he mentioned something about drivers & what hours he wanted them to do. This made me mention the tachometer requirement to ensure driver hours are within EU laws. He did not know what a tachometer was, he was intrigued & then shocked that driver hours were regulated! I could not understand how someone having been on a course & explained his project to "experts" in the course for advice had not mentioned or knew about the driver hour's law. We had a nice lunch, & when I got in the car, I said to Monica, "What good was the government course to help people start businesses for 6 weeks with tutorials & advice & then he did not know at the end of the course this important fact!" Monica told me she heard from him some 6 months later, & he still had not started his project. Perhaps I put him off? Perhaps, he realised the enormity of the project without funds or knowledge of the business.

Wednesday 6th July 2005

While Monica was having a shower, I saw an SMS from Claude (under the AIDE project) saying he was leaving the clinic. Was he ill? This sort of information was not something you would tell a future employee, unless you are closer to that person. I think he was leading

Monica with false promises to get free sex. It would not be the first time & as time would tell, not be the last!

Thursday 7th July

John phones me at work to meet & have another game of pool to get his revenge on his defeat the other day. I agreed & met him at their flat & then onto the pub. We played pool & chatted. John said he understood the situation between Monica & me from the times we had all spent together. It was obvious to him that Monica was playing games with me, & he felt sorry for me. As the conversation progressed, I realised that Charlotte had not spoken to John about the situation, so they had both arrived at the same conclusion from their individual observations. I am sure I will learn more from Charlotte because Rwandese women talk to each other in confidence about liaisons & intimate things, especially concerning outsiders like white partners or husbands.

When I get home, Monica says she is going out tomorrow, Friday, at about 9:30 pm, to Paris with Jado & Charlotte. She says Jado lives beyond CdG airport, I knew this was a lie because I found out he lives in St. Genevieve des Bois! So now the question is, who is she meeting? Jado, a female friend, for lesbian sex, Claude or Pierre …. or someone else? Remember, Monica had planned 3 days in Brussels with Pierre, who was now dead. I need to speak with Charlotte tomorrow to find out.

Friday 8th July

At work, I phoned Charlotte early at her SOSIP work & asked her whether Monica was meeting her that night in Paris. She confirmed they were going out to meet a mutual friend Suzanne to go to a night club. Monica had mentioned that she had been there with me. I asked whether Monica had given any details of the club to her. She said "no", but apparently it was fun & would be good for a group of girls together. I thought about making no comment, but the urge overcame me, "I am sure you will have a good time together, & you will learn so much more about each other by the end of the night. Have fun". "What do you mean?" Charlotte said. I responded, "I would like to meet you & chat about various things, & you could tell me how your girlies night out went. Are you working Monday?" She replied, "You could come around our flat early, say 5:30 pm Monday before John comes home, he normally arrives at about 6:30 pm. I know he wants to talk to you about a package he is expecting Monday. But it would be better if he asked you". "OK. 5:30 Monday, see you then".

During all my time with Monica, we often had parties. Florence is always invited to make the samosa as she was good at making these, & they take time to make; Monica never had the patience or the time. I, sometimes, felt sorry for Florence because sometimes she was summoned to come to make the samosa & then when finished, she would be expected to leave before the guests arrived for the party. This did not apply if the guests were Rwandan friends, but would apply for family & other friends. Champagne was never a problem. When I said she did not need to open another bottle as nobody wanted more, she would insist on opening yet another bottle. When I complained of her spending too much money as if I were a "money tree", she replied, "….**It is not me spending too much money, it is you, your fault for not earning enough money by not having a better salary……..**"

Monica always wanted the best, with money no object now that she had a white Pigeon who pays.

Monday 11th July: Monica is angry with me for helping a friend & Charlotte explains girly night out Quai-17

Mid-morning, John phones me at work. Because he does not drive a car, he asks me whether I could collect a package from the ChromPost sorting office in Chilly Mazerin that has been confirmed is ready now for collection. I said, "No problem, I deliver it later tonight at your place".

I left an SMS message with Monica to say I would be picking up a package for John & would be home later after I had given it to John. Monica phones me back & is not happy that I had agreed to pick up & deliver the package to John & starts a row on the phone. Not wanting my colleagues to hear our row, I put the phone down on her.

I arrived as arranged with Charlotte a bit early at 5:15 pm, & Charlotte arrived soon after. We entered their flat as I carried a large parcel for John & started chatting as she made a cup of tea. "Ssoooooo, how was Friday night, eh?" Charlotte looked at me with a grin, "You were right! It WAS interesting, & yes, I did learn something I did not know before!" "Carry on, encore," so I said. "Well, Monica said to wear something that will be attractive & sexy.

We went to this club called Quai-17. When we arrived, we started dancing, then a couple of men wanted to dance. Monica then suddenly decided to stop, and we thought to rest. Instead, Monica wandered over to the side of the club where there were "U" shaped seats & sat next to a young woman in a low-cut top & short skirt. I noticed details because her breasts were nearly popping out, & you could see her fluorescence culottes under her short skirt! Suzanne & I continued dancing but kept a constant eye on Monica. The woman's hand started caressing Monica's leg, & soon, Monica was feeling the woman's breasts, first inside her bra & then pulling them out. Suzanne& I stopped dancing as we wanted to see more of what they were doing. The woman then put her hand down Monica's culottes and, with tacit approval, took them off. Monica was fully engrossed and enjoying the woman's hand half way up her vagina, legs wide apart. Monica was only able to caress her breasts in her present position.

We could not see more for a while as a crowd of maybe 10 people were around them watching. We moved closer to be basically by them on the other side of the U shape seat. By this time, the roles were changed, & Monica's hand was playing with the woman's pussy; by this time, Monica had loosened her top to reveal her boobs for the woman to play with. We were all mesmerised by their display & then when the activity subsided, Monica gestured to Suzanne & me to sit next to them on either side.

We were hesitant, but felt compelled to do as indicated unsure how to refuse. Once seated, both Monica & the woman started caressing our legs. Suzanne said, "I have not had this done to me by a woman, so I was not sure how to react, whether to get up or stay. I started losing eye contact with Suzanne on the other side of the woman. A flush feeling overcame me as Monica slowly caressed closer & closer to my culottes & then under them to touch my pussy. It was a funny feeling. I wanted them to stop, & yet I wanted more. So, my expression must have been pleasurable because, slowly but surely, my feelings wanted to open my legs. I must have lifted my backside up because Monica took down my culottes & then my legs were free to open wide for her hand to go up me.

I can tell you, Geoff, I have never felt like this before. I wanted more, encore, encore, encore, she was taking my hand to her boobs, & it was now just natural for me to caress them. I am a lesbian, I thought. I felt a gush & realised I had cum as I groaned. As I started to recover my composure, Monica's hand guided my hand into her pussy, & I played & played like a little girl. I never thought I could do something like this, & yet, there I was having sex with another woman & a friend as well! I noticed from time to time Suzanne was also initially reluctant, but fully compliant later like me. I now fully understand why Monica said it would be fun & why she said, you will learn a lot about each other by the end of the night! Don't you say anything to John! He would kill me! And nothing to Monica, promise Geoff?" "Yes, of course. Did Monica get the woman's name & phone number?" "Yes, her name was Marianne. She lives & works in Paris somewhere".

We heard a noise indicating John's arrival through the door. John was pleased to see me & the large package I brought. "Let me reward you with a beer at the pub." I looked at Charlotte, "Do you mind, or do you want to come?" "No, I have things to do here. You go with John," she said. We went to the pub, played pool & talked about Monica & her attitude towards me in the presence of other people & her men.

I arrived home at about 9 pm with a furious Monica. "You should have asked me, you only saw John the other day. It is not necessary for you to do errands for MY friends. When you are with my friends, I am sure you tell lies about me." I was not in the mood to have a row, & just sat down in the lounge & let her rant on without any expression or reply on my part. This enraged her even more, hitting me to get a response. I just looked at her & then back to the TV. Eventually like a hurricane, she cooled down. The phone rang, & it was Charlotte, they spoke for some considerable time in Kinyarwandan.

When Monica eventually put the phone down, she went into the kitchen & made us both a cup of tea. Monica was nice as a pie, interesting, I thought, *what did Charlotte say to Monica to change her mood?* Whatever it was, Monica's mood changed. We chatted normally & had some wine together. Lennon was happier to see us "normal" & chatted as well about school & then disappeared into his bedroom. Monica quickly felt that was the signal to start caressing my leg & crutch area. Soon, she undid her blouse, revealing her ample boobs oozing out of her bra. My hands could not resist, especially as she was undoing my belt and zip & pulling down my trousers.

Quickly, my private part was like a banana. While she took off her culottes, she was ready for me to enter her. I turned her over on the sofa, so I could shag her with my favourite doggy style, enabling me to see her swinging boobs to the rhythm of my pelvic thrusts. I so love seeing those boobs swing as I shag Monica. Riding Monica like a cowboy on an unbroken stallion, "yee haa", James was so happy, gradually, the intensity increased to a climax we both enjoyed. WOW, that was a great shag. We both flopped on the settee, satisfied. I volunteered to get some loo paper as cum was oozing out of her pussy. We both slept well, & upon waking up in the morning, the first thing I thought was, *What DID Charlotte say to Monica to change her mood so quickly?*

Tuesday 12th July 2005

Paul sent me an SMS while I was at work, inviting me to meet him & Monica for lunch at the Novotel in Massy at lunchtime. I left work at noon & arrived at about 12.20. Paul was already there, sitting next to Monica at the table. Monica complained about me talking & being with her friends, & I had no confidence in her. The tears ran down, & immediately, Paul consoled her with his arm around her. I complained that I was like a fly on the wall, while she does not look at me & talks always with others ignoring me. He agreed that Monica was ignoring me & suggested her to pay more attention to me while in the company of others. I also said she does not consult with me nor talk much with me. I also said Monica was with so many men that it was stressing me. She said she was only with other men for out sake to improve our financial status & improve our marriage!

"What do you want ME to do? Would you like me to keep going out with other women?" She did not say anything, not approving, more importantly, disapproving! Paul picked up on this & suggested I should find another woman to satisfy my usual sexual requirements & be able to converse with another female person, like he had Monica to help with stresses caused by Christine. Monica said nothing, not objecting, but moving her head very slightly swaying from side to side. Did that mean approval? I pushed the point, "Do you want me to find a woman to prevent me going mad?" Again, she said nothing to start with. When I made a facial asking expression, she murmured, "I do not know, I.....have not thought about it" "You must admit that it would be fair;

you had Paul, & now you have your other numerous men," I said. She replied. "Ah, but I see men for us & our marriage."

I showed a perplexed expression to exhibit my feelings at her logic. Paul took the conversation further by looking at Monica for approval & repeated his suggestion that I look for a woman, and it should be OK by Monica. He looked at Monica for approval, & she said nothing & did not look at either of us. I looked at Paul, & he expressed a facial expression of "I do not know". There was a pregnant pause where the silence was deafening. I broke the silence by addressing Monica, "You know I love you. I want us to be in peace, but you have to know all this secrecy with all these men is stressing me. If you were to at least confide in me with your ideas & who you are with would help me". She looked at me & then Paul, saying that this would be good. She gave me an approving smile. We finished & both of us went back to our respective workplaces.

Wednesday 20-Sat 23 July 2005: moving small items to the new house

Over three days, we had been transferring as much as we could into the new house by car to ease the problem of the final move that we decided would be Saturday & Sunday. The distance from my flat in the centre of Longjumeau to up the hill to rue des Amandiers, a new road off Rue Jules Ferrier was only about 1 km, so we were able to transfer much smaller items more easily than by a removal van.

Saturday 23rd July 2005: Move to the new house rue des Amandiers, Longjumeau

Things were not progressing for the sale of the flat, & yet we needed to move into the new house up on the hill in the new Kauffman-Broad estate. I ordered a van for the weekend & moved everything out of the flat & into the new house. The first dozen houses were now complete & had been handed over to the clients. However, the rest of the road was incomplete, the road swept every day to avoid too much of a mess with all the construction lorries comings & goings.

We were the first ones moving to the new house. The house is about 1 km from the old flat & now just 100 metres from Lennon's school. We were the first to sign contracts on the house project, the first house completed & the first to move in. Part of the price was all fittings inside the house, shrubs, trees & grass for the garden, instant house, unlike many new homes. I took many photos of the house & area as it was at the time. We now have 4 bedrooms plus a very large "family room upstairs, so we are able to accommodate all the visitors that we have without inconvenience.

Once empty, we started cleaning up the flat for sale.

The sale of the flat is not happening, the estate agent says it is because I do not have automatic motorised shutters (I had manual handle wind up/down) & no parquet flooring. I spent money to buy & fit a cheaper version of the parquet flooring that went over the existing hard-wearing carpet. Job done, although fitting it was not as easy as I thought it should be. Eventually, after some months, the estate agents had a few more promising clients, one made an offer which with a little bit of negotiation, we both agreed. In France on agreement, the buyer has to put 10% down as a guarantee of the sale or lose it if they pull out. A good system compared with the poor stressful system in England where buyers can pull out at any time with no penalty. The temporary bank bridging loan could now be cancelled to relieve the extra monthly mortgage payments Credit Agricole Bank wanted. The delayed sale of the flat & the extra bridging loan costs that had been a big worry were now resolved & eliminated.

Monday 8th August: Pierre the garagist

Claudine phones me at work to tell me that she has arrived at our house unannounced after work & found "Pierre" with Monica. He was having coffee & while Claudine was there, she showed him around the house. Claudine describes him as a big, white French man similar in size to me & apparently lives near the Longjumeau hospital with a big Renault car. Claudine said he was a nice man, & she noticed his finger nails were greasy & dirty. I was puzzled why Monica would be making friends with a Frenchman with dirty fingernails who obviously was working with engines or motors of some kind to still have dirty greasy finger nails.

Wednesday 10th August: RV with Claudine explains the garagist

I made a rendez-vous with Claudine near her work in Chilly-Mazerin at lunchtime. She told me more about Monday's meeting with Pierre in our house. Monica had told her when Pierre had gone that he had a nice house & had walked to our flat each time from work & was not happy when Claudine had arrived to interrupt them. Dirty greasy fingernails, well-built, Frenchman, walked from work.....of course, it was the Renault garage owner Pierre in Longjumeau. At that time, JY was using Renault cars, so I used to deposit my Renault car to Pierre & then walk up the road to work. I remembered that Monica would have her Renault Clio that I bought her, serviced there as well. I started to think how Monica used men for jobs, work or favours in exchange for sex. Here we go again, is she shagging Pierre to get free car service? I now understand her character much more.

This explains much, when I said several months ago that she has affairs with men & even go to bed with them for OUR benefit, that she was happy that I understood. Given the opportunity, I saw Pierre was entered twice in her phone contacts with both mobile AND fixed home phone numbers. I knew this because I had the garage number & his mobile number to contact him for my car. This explains when Monica told Claudine he has a large house, she has been to his house.....for what? Obviously to give a sexual favour "service" to pay for servicing her car. This must be her Rwandan barter system.

Monday 15th August 2005: RV at Charlotte's home

Following a dispute regarding her men, all week the atmosphere is frosty between us, so she sleeps with Lennon all week. For weeks now, I have been accusing Monica of being lazy & not packing up things quickly enough for the move. Even when Michel & Raymond from downstairs came up to help, she was not working efficiently or hard enough. In private chats with Michel & Raymond, they agreed she had at the time been doing very little, leaving it all for me to do. I would find a similar situation some 5 years later when we sold the house, she promised to come back to Longjumeau to help me clean up & move things out.

I had to leave work at lunchtime to clean systematically the flat, room by room, lay the low-cost parquet flooring over the old carpet. Each time, I popped in to see Raymond, my retired neighbour on the 5th floor. Michelle, meanwhile, who worked at the local post office a few hundred metres away, was there at lunchtime. They would confirm while she was there, they were helping, but she was so slow that they were doing all the work!

I made a RV after work with Charlotte to discuss the situation with Monica & her laziness with cleaning up the flat for change-over ownership. Charlotte was already home when I arrived & made me a cup of coffee. She was very sympathetic as she knew what Monica was like. She said that Monica was always interested in enjoying the fruits of money, but not exactly wanting to do the dirty work to make the money or anything else. She would do an apparent favour & then make people feel guilty, so they do many things for her.

In talking about Monica & sitting next to Charlotte, she let out some signs that things were not so good between her & John. I hit on this & asked her to open up to me about what the problem was. At first, she was hesitant, but eventually, confided in me that he did criminal things, & she was not happy about this. She started looking tearful, so I consoled her by putting my arms around her.

She seemed to be really comforted & put her hand on my leg, "Monica does not know what she is missing, I wish I had a husband like you". She then started caressing my leg up & down as she talked. This made me realise there was a real problem. I tried to stay focused on the subject of her & John, but her hand was wandering further & further up my leg. She was looking into my eyes, then looked down at her low neckline blouse exposing her cleavage.

Like most Rwandan women, she had a nice pair of boobs, the glance down at them & her cleavage was an invitation to look. *Oh wow*. While I was thinking about what to do, or WHAT not to do, she undid one of her top buttons, still looking into my eyes, periodically glancing down at her breasts as they became more exposed with each button undone. *Oh, my*! She smiled as I started to slowly feel the top of her breast. She continued undoing more buttons, making it easier to put my hand inside her bra, feel her breast & pull one out into the open. She looked down & said, "The other one is getting jealous" "Oh, we cannot have that," as I plucked the other boob out of her bra. She could tell I was nervous that John would arrive anytime. She soothed my anxiety with, "John is working late on a project tonight (probably on "this & that"….) he won't be home until 9 pm."

At that point, she quickly undid the remaining buttons on her blouse then put her hands behind her back, then undid her bra. What a nice pair of breasts; they were a nice handful as I fondled them. She leaned over with her arms around me, kissing me, I fell back onto the rest of the sofa, still holding one breast. My left leg was on the ground, but the right one was now under her with my crutch exposed as she rubbed it lovingly.

God, these Rwandans are sex maniacs, how can I control myself? Cloe is single, but Charlotte is married, that is different, plus I am married....... sort of. My life with Monica has changed my whole perspective of life. I am finding all of Monica's female friends flirting with me & teasing me. My discovery of Monica's affairs left me less than faithful than I would normally be.

All these thoughts rushed through my head as I suddenly realised that I was not holding her breast, my trousers had been removed, & my pants were following fast. Before I could have any feelings of hesitation, resistance or remorse, she was putting my member James in her mouth & giving me a blow job! By this time, I had given up all resistance. She looked up at me with a sort of smile with my penis fully disappeared in her mouth. She took a breath & moved around to put her fanny in my face & then proceeded to continue sucking my penis up & down. Those culottes have to come off, I was thinking.

Charlotte must be psychic, she quickly removed them so I could lick her fanny. I grabbed her African buttocks*, licked & squeezed her pussy lips with my mouth. Who would come first? She was heaving her breasts & buttocks up & down with delight. I felt like a volcano was going to erupt in her mouth any time. Suddenly, I could hold on no longer and came; she was still sucking hard up & down, due to the penetration and must have been swallowing at some point on the up-stroke because when I was finally finished. She had no sign of my cum on her face, nor any sign of it anywhere on me. I carried on pleasing her, rubbing & licking her pussy, and eventually, she came some 5 minutes later.

We both lay there exhausted on that sofa. It suddenly struck me to look at the time. Oh wow, it was past 8 pm, & John could arrive home any time if he was earlier than Charlotte expected. We had both done an efficient job of licking up any fluids, so it was just a case of putting our clothes back on. I helped her with her bra, she looked around, smiled & kissed me again. "I enjoyed that," she said, "Thank you. I needed that to relieve the stress of John & his activities". I thought we both have marital problems, but in a different way.

I bid her farewell with another kiss & embrace, went to my car & drove home. Driving home, I was thinking what is wrong with me, I have been unfaithful twice in about 4 months with two of Monica's Rwandan friends. I was trying to convince myself that Monica does not think of me or has any scruples when she has sex with white men, so why should I have any while shagging her Rwandan friends?

Arriving home, Monica was not happy with me since I arrived home late from work without telling her, so the dinner she had cooked was overdone & left in the cool oven. I promised to phone her the next time I was going to be late. After eating the microwave-re-heated dinner, Monica decided to have a shower. I did my customary search for new men on her phone. I found several phone calls from Paty with a 243-xxxx country code & several calls from "Bosco". Neither seemed like the usual profile of older white managers with money. Maybe they are pseudonyms of white men? Maybe I will find out at some later date.

Lennon:

He managed to scrap by to progress to the 2nd year of BAC at the higher school, called in France "Lycée", it is now about 100 metres from our new home rue des Amandiers. Now, I thought, he will be late all the time, my prediction proved correct.

Lennon has progressed tremendously with the guitar. He has his own group, & they sometimes play at school. Deep Purple even sounds good when he plays, so he is improving!!

Sunday 21st August 2005

Monica receives phone call from Pierre but claims it is Paul. Research later reveals two more calls that day while training at the sports stadium. I also found an SMS from the AID project, "What are you doing today, my love?" Who is this?

I need to make a spreadsheet with all these men, so that I can work out who is who & what they are doing, or promising to do, e.g. job, project help, etc.

Tuesday 23rd August: Roger Soumah for dinner

At work, I had a long meeting with Roger Soumah, who lives in Lyon, about various businesses in the Middle East. Roger is leaving the company to join as sales manager for a company in the nuclear industry. I am due to take over his EMEA (Europe, Middle East & Africa position) from my present ICP product manager position. He explained that Iran was his best Middle East territory, while the rest was just noise-level business. Europe was obviously the best area with emerging former Soviet Union Eastern Europe countries expanding rapidly.

I phoned Monica & told her that had invited Roger around for dinner. She was happy about it when I tell her he is from French Guinea. Monica arrives home early, changes into a sexy dress & starts cooking with an apron on. Roger & I arrive home with Roger following me in his car. That night, we had a nice dinner on the patio, I noticed Monica making eyes at him, at all opportunities, deriding me & trying to belittle me..... as usual.

She likes entertaining in the new house, it increases her image that is so important for her. In company, I try not to rise to the bait. She seems to be extremely interested in where he lives, his family, how often he comes to JY in Longjumeau & what sort of house he has etc.

Friday 26th Aug 2005

Monica & I go into Paris & meet George Taylor-Lewis with Emile, the girlfriend, plus Paul & Christine for dinner. It is obvious the story Monica tells me about George & his wife is not true. Emile is definitely his girlfriend, and they are too amorous to be anything else.

265

Tuesday 30th August

Roger Soumah & I chat more at work, about his old EMEA territory, I invite him & Yuri, a Russian software engineer over from Moscow, to liaise with our software team in Longjumeau. JY has a team of 4 Russian software engineers in the Moscow Horiba office who write most of the GUI (Graphical User Interface) software, while in Longjumeau, they write mainly the low-level platform software.

At home, as I park the car, I see Bekir, my new neighbour, 2 doors away from us, so I invite him for a beer at our place to meet my colleagues. Monica is in her element, acting as host & opens up champagne that she had hidden. Monica is keen to show our guests around the house, flirts more & gets a promise from Roger to phone her the next time he is in the area to visit. Eventually, they depart to have their respective dinners at the hotel & Bekir at home.

After our guests had gone, I checked our joint account, set to pay the mortgage, it was disappearing fast, Monica was spending money on herself & maybe her boyfriends, to influence them for some project. I raise the issue with her that she should not spend that joint account money, I put money into that joint account specifically for the mortgage. Monica says she does not understand why she should stop spending money when I have money stashed away hidden in England.

Wednesday 31st Aug

At work, Roger Soumah & I continue discussions of his EMEA territory, it is a last opportunity before he leaves JY. After work, we go to the only decent bar in Longjumeau opposite Place de Stiber in the centre of Longjumeau. I confide in him about Monica & her affairs & asked him what his reaction was to last week & last night's visit. He initially tried to avoid answering, but then admitted he had noticed a bit of flirting, but he said he did not see the body language she was constantly making.

Friday 2nd Sept

I start searching for a possible name for Monica's new cleaning (nettoyage) company. She starts thinking of using **"Moni Clean"** for the new company.

Tuesday 6th Sept 2005

Being at a new house & new address, we had waited weeks & weeks for the new telephone line & internet to be installed. I have never known such slow service, but then that is France! Eventually, it was done that day, Monica sent 6 e-mails; one in particular to Kadi Doucoure in ADB. She makes a proposition for the two of them to spend time at a friend's house (Agnes & David) alone near St Raphael on the Mediterranean & then rent a studio in St Tropez next year.

I really wonder about her mental state. Does she really want to do this, or is she just fantasizing? It is similar to 3 days in Brussels with Pierre the other month, which fell through at the last moment due to lack of commitment to go through with the deception, & of course, my insistence on coming as well. Did she think I was going to stay here in Longjumeau alone? Does she make these men think she will do these things & just tease them? I cannot make her out. I also find out she has inscribed on "Meetic", it is free for women, so she did not need to pay anything, only men pay.

Thursday 7th Sept

Monica replies to a message on **Meetic** to a new Pierre, who is black and sees her profile on the website. He sends his reply via Meetic messenger rather than e-mail, as she requested.

Wednesday 13th Sept: **Serencontrer** inscribed AOL Sept Oct

I find out she has posted her profile onto another love / rencontre website "Serencontrer.com" as "Africaines3" on Tuesday. She gets 6 enquiries & has already replied to 2 of them using her (Redacted) **xxxx**2000@yahoo.fr address. I also see that she had inscribed with "Netclub" as well with both her e-mail addresses. What has she done that for?

Why does she want to meet men? Does she just want to tease these men with a free drink & then dump them? She again mentions that night in bed maybe she will start going on escort work using a website. She asked me if I minded that. What can I say? She will do it anyway if she wants. I have no say on what she wants or what she does with men. I am just a doormat.

Serencontre AOL Sept Oct

(e-mail addresses & part of phone numbers REDACTED)

01/10 .EMOTIONS48 .J'attends toujour votre e mail: xxxxxxx2000@yahoo.fr ____Phones Contact three times on the same day week 40

___29/09 .EMOTIONS48 .My email address is: xxxxx200 0@yahoo.fr Cheers 30/09 30/09 ___

29/09 .EMOTIONS48 .Bonjour Emotions!! Yes I am interested by you &, I would like to be in contact w 30/09 ___

.19/09 .THEO PARIS .Je viens de me connecter et je suis très occupée. Vous pouvez m'appeler au numér 20/09 ___

.17/09 .TENEBREUX .Bien sure! vous etes en très bon poète et j'atttends votre message en fin de 17/09 ___

.17/09 .PMAKHNO1 .Hi Pierrick, Je suis honorée de ton message et te donne mon adresse e-mail ci 18/09 18/09 ___

.17/09 .TENEBREUX .Bonjour Tenebreux, J e suis désolée pour le retard, je ne savais pas l'existan 17/09 17/09 ___

.17/09 .EMOTIONS48 ."AFIRCAINE3" a aimé votre portrait et nous a chargé de vous le dire. Bravo! 17/09 ___

.17/09 .THEO PARIS .Je suis en ligne en ce moment si vous voulez m'appeler au 06080028xx. J'espère q 18/09 19/09 ___

.17/09 .JOHN O .Hi Johny, C'est sympa de votre part d'avoir répondu à ma candidature. Je suis 17/09 ___

17/09 .THEO PARIS .Bonjour Théo, je suis heureuse de savoiur que ma candidature vous interesse. Je 17/09 17/0

| EMOTIONS48 vous a écrit le 29/09 | Lu le 29/09 | Répondu le 29/09 | Votre réponse à **EMOTIONS48** |

BONJOUR MERCI DE M'AVOIR REPONDU POURRIONS NOUS FAIRE PLUS AMPLE CONNAISSANCE? SI OK JE VOUS DONNERAI MON TEL FIX E DIRECT AU BUREAU J'HABITE ET TRAVAILLE A MARNE LA VALLEE ET VOUS? A BIENTOT JO

| Vous avez écrit le 29/09 à **EMOTIONS48** | Lu le 30/09 | Répondu le | Écrire à nouveau à **EMOTIONS48** |

Bonjour Emotions!! Yes I am interested by you &, I would like to be in contact with you. My mobile number is 06.08.00.28.xx.(I am marred too). Monica

Vous avez écrit le 29/09 à **EMOTIONS48**	Lu le 30/09	épondu le 30/09	crire à nouveau à **EMOTIONS48**

My email address is: xxxxxx2000@yahoo.fr Cheers

Vous avez écrit le 29/09 à **EMOTIONS48**	Lu le 30/09	épondu le 30/09	crire à nouveau à **EMOTIONS48**

J'attends toujours votre e mail: xxxxx2000@yahoo.fr

Monday 19th – Frid 23rd Sept

I went to the UK for the week in business, getting a flight from CdG to Luton, where a UK colleague picked me up. We travel around England seeing potential & present users. I get a fleeting chance to see Steven but no opportunity to see Sophie within the itinerary without a car of my own, I am being driven around.

Wednesday 21st Sept 2005

I find out that Monica meets Jean-Guy during the day for lunch. By his emails, he really has the hots for her, but she teases him, & he asks some very good questions. "What do you want out of a relationship?" He is disillusioned, & she never answers him for 3 days. Although, they had constant comms every day previously. Eventually, she replies that the relationship was up to him!

Friday 23rd September: I return home from the UK

I was picked up from CdG by our normal JY taxi driver, Rodrigues & arrived home late afternoon/early evening. Monica is in a good mood. After relaxing a bit & some food, eventually Lennon goes up to his bedroom. Monica then says to me that she wants sexy photos taken as she has changed into different sexy clothes,s she wants to send one for the escort site. Sounds like she has made up her mind to join this escort site. She contacts them & gets immediate correspondence as below:

Date: *Fri, 23 Sep 2005*   *12:21:58 +0200 (CEST)*
De: *"Dawn Monica" <xxxx2000@yahoo.fr>*
Objet: *Re: avec les photos en attachement: retransmission des photos de Monica*
À: *"Yann Labûche" <yann@club-escort.com>*

Bonjour Jean-François,
Merci d'avoir répondu aussitot à mon e-mail. Concernat
les photos, en fait c'est vous qui voyer par rapport
aux exigences du club, choisissez donc celles qui vous
plaisent en sachant que je pourrai toujour changer mes
photos. Dans tous les cas, je voudrais m'entretenir
avec vous avant de diffuser ma candidature.
Je vous souhaite une bonne journée.

Monica.

Date: *Fri, 23 Sep 2005*   *19:40:27 +0200 (CEST)*
De: *"Dawn Monica" <xxxxx2000@yahoo.fr>*
Objet: *Re: avec les photos en attachement: retransmission des photos de Monica*
À: *"Yann Labûche" <yann@club-escort.com>*

Bonjour Jean-François,
Mon portable et le 06.08.00.28.xx, je suis joignable à tout moment.
Amicalement,
Monica

De: "Yann Labûche" <yann@club-escort.com>
À: "Dawn Monica" <xxxx2000@yahoo.fr>
Objet: Re: avec les photos en attachement: retransmission des photos de Monica
Date: Fri, 23 Sep 2005   12:40:29 +0200

Hello Monica,
comment ça va, ce matin ?
Ok, je mettrai les photos qui me semblent le plus adaptées (avec certainement quand même de légères retouches colorimétriques et un recadrage)

Volontiers pour un "entretien" mais je m'aperçois que je n'ai plus votre téléphone (je sais... c'est pas bien de ma part !)

Voulez-vous me le redonner (j'en avais 2) ou bien vous, sinon, vous pouvez me téléphoner à partir de 15 heures, avant je suis en rendez-vous;
Jean-François Bressy administrateur
Translation in English
Hello Monica,
how is it going, this morning ? Ok, I will put the photos that seem most suitable to me (with certainly still slight colour retouching and a cropping) Willingly ready for an "interview", but I realize that I no longer have your phone (I know... it's not good of me!) Would you like to give it back to me (I had 2) or you, otherwise, you can call me from 3 p.m., before that I have an appointment

Bonjour Jean-François,
Mon portable et le 06.08.00.28.xx, je suis joignable à tout moment.
Amicalement,
Monica

Sun 25th Sept 2005

I get a phone call from John, who is quite upset that Monica is causing problems between Charlotte & him and wants me to go to see them ASAP. I make some excuse after training to go out & go to Charlotte & John's place. Monica has apparently been saying that John is going out with other women to Charlotte & that Charlotte is going out with different men to John. Charlotte pleaded with John who had come home immediately after work. What is Monica playing at?

Maybe Monica is trying to counter the fact that Charlotte knows of her men & has told me, so when Charlotte said to me that Monica was playing with different men, I said, I know, what is different?

Another man:

An E-mail from "**Francois**" says to Monica, "merci pour hier soir", who the hell is Francois? My head hurts. (see 2nd Oct)

Mon 26th Sept 2005: Club Escort web inscription by Monica

Monica inscribes on Club-Escort to become an escort. Monica tells me in bed she is not sure whether to put "bisexual" or "heterosexual", what would be the advantages? She also decides on "intelligent", rather than "intellectual", being an escort is to my mind no different to what she is doing already with men. Instead of a job, a position, or favours, she would now be getting money & maybe positions at the same time. She wanted me to take a number of photos some days beforehand, she wanted more, the reason is now clear, it was to put on her escort web site.

With her inscribed onto an escort website, she tried to encourage me that night to stay longer in South Africa when I went on Friday 14th, October. She says she will get a cheap mobile phone with a separate number specifically for Escort work. She shows me what she has written in the e-mail. For once, Monica is keen to show me her e-mails…. But ONLY for these comms

Bonjour,

ce message est généré par un répondeur automatique (donc, n'y répondez pas) pour vous dire que votre commande est bien arrivée et que je vous souhaite la bienvenue sur **Club Escort***;*

Je vous écrirai "en vrai" dans très peu de temps
Yann

The web site text she decided on was as follows:

"Je m'appel Monica jeune femme d'Afrique a la fois séduisante et raffinée, j'aime la vie car elle acquise q'une seule fois. Je serrai votre escorte et accompagnatrice a Paris ou outilleurs pour agrémenter vos vacances et facilites vos rendez-vous d'affaires. Je vous accompagne pour votre plaisir ou pour vos affaires dans un cadre agréable. Oui pour curieuse et boit"

English translation

"My name is Monica, a young woman from Africa who is both attractive and refined. I love life because it is acquired only once. I will be your escort and companion in Paris or outside to enhance your holidays and facilitate your business meetings. I can accompany you for your pleasure or for your business in a pleasant frame of mind. Yes, for curiosity and drinks." A photo not of Monica, but…..

Tuesday 27th Sept 2005

I managed to read Monica's normal comms for the first time in a week, while I was away in England & saw that Lennon had tried to access her computer & her xxxxx@e-mail address. Why?

One missing comms deleted, but recovered from the deleted directory. It was to Andre, which said, *"Geoff is in UK all week, I can respire now (so, she could play), that life is complicated and easy at the same time. I cannot tell you how stressed I am, Geoff loves me, but he is very complicated, anyway I have to live with it."*

Chapter 15

Wed 28th Sept 2005: Rebecca 2+2 mate

Monica is in communication with Rebecca who has a flat in Paris as well as a home in London, she is meeting Rebecca with George at 2+2 club. I read this e-mail much later & therefore I did not know at the time "Martin" was "George" in the e-mails.

Rebecca
Wonderful Monica - yes it worked. You may now find that I also have another email address, but as you can see the one you used is fine - either will work.
Do you think that George should pick you up from your home, or from another address? Let me know soonest so that I can inform George.
I thought I would not bring my partner, Ernie, but I have had difficulties in finding someone to look after him for the weekend, so he is coming with me. However, he knows that I have to go out Friday evening.
How often do you check your email? Since I am in an office and can also access my email in the evenings in Kew, I do it regularly.
Please let me know what George should do on Friday evening. Also, we will need to sort out some time.
Much love, Rebecca

later that night, Monica replies (spelling mistakes maintained)

Hi Rebecca,
I am verry happy that we can comunucate by e-mail! Good. I think that Gérad could pick me up from another address like "Antony town which is near our both towns. We can talk easly by daytime because that I am alone at home. I chek my e-mail every time, I have internet at home. Don't worry, if you send an e-mail,

I will see it imediately (if I am at home). You will need to give to Gérad my mobile numbe and he could phone me on friday to discribe himself and where I could meet him.

I send you one of my pictures!!!!! Please look on attachement.
Cheers from Paris
Monica

Another man Jean-Guy, who the hell is he?

Did he meet Monica at 2+2 or elsewhere? As he sent this Wednesday 28th morning, the latest 2+2 orgy was last week. Therefore, Monica must have met him THIS week on Monday, Tuesday or today! Could this be an Escort job or another meeting on the MEETIC website? He is obviously crazy about her.

All this was driving me crazy. So much information, so many men, so many women, so many conflicts & me "piggy in the middle".

With Paul I knew where I was, but now?

WHAT does she want? 2+2 & Quay 17 clubs are a shag & play with women games, Escort work is money & perhaps influential men, but these others on MEETIC?

Why am I putting up with all this? It is driving me crazy.

I love her so much & yet……

Wed, 28 Sep 2005   08:07:38 EDT
De   JGA768@aol.com
A   xxxx2000@yahoo.fr
J'insiste à t'apeller Monica tout court, si tu veux bien !
Ce sera ton prénom rien que pour moi ! Et puis je ne suis pas très doué en Anglais mais j'ai tout de même fait 2 ou 3 études et il se trouve que l'anglais figurait au programme, il m'en reste donc quelques mots de vocabulaire (sourire).

Pour l'instant nous en sommes tous les deux à "sentir" nos émotions chacun de notre côté. Nous avons en même temps des craintes et aussi des enthousiasmes. Craindre de souffrir aujourd'hui ne serait ce pas être en mesure de prévoir ce que notre relation donnera et pouvoir prédire en même temps qu'elle devrait inévitablement s'arrêter dramatiquement. Moi je ne suis pas capable de dire ça aujourd'hui. La seule chose que je peux dire c'est que j'ai envie de toi, j'ai envie de te connaître, j'ai envie de te couvrir de caresses, de baisers, de douceurs, de tendresse, j'ai envie que tu sois bien et heureuse si c'est possible avec moi. Je sais que c'est ambitieux mais c'est ce que tu as généré alors tant que tu ne m'auras pas dit qu'il faut que je renonce et bien je crois que je garderai cet espoir là (I hope !).

Je t'embrasse partout, partout, Monica, et je ne te dis pas comment, j'aurai peur de te choquer, et dis moi toi si nous nous reverrons et quand, donne moi même simplement une idée...si tu peux !

Reviens vite..Jean-Guy

I insist on calling you Monica anyway, if you do not mind!
It will be your name just for me! And I'm not very good at English but I still did 2 or 3 studies and it turns out that English was on the programme, so I still have some words of vocabulary (smile).

For now, we are both "feeling" our emotions on our own. At the same time, we have fears and enthusiasm. To fear suffering today would not be able to predict what our relationship will give and be able to predict at the same time as it should inevitably stop dramatically. I'm not able to say that today. The only thing I can say is that I want you, I want to know you, I want to cover you with caresses, kisses, sweets, tenderness, I want you are well and happy if it is possible with me. I know it's ambitious, but that's what you generated so long as you did not tell me I have to give up and I think I'll keep that hope alive (I hope!).

I kiss you everywhere, everywhere, Monica, and I do not tell you how, I'll be afraid to shock you, and tell me if we'll meet again and when, just give me an idea ... if you can!

Come back soon.. .... Jean-Guy

Thursday, 29 Sep 2005: 12:47:10 EDT

Bonjour Monica,

Puisque dans ta belle famille tu es Monica, dans mon amour à moi tu seras Ma Monica ! Je n'ai pas eu de réponse à mon dernier message, je suppose que c'est parce que ça a été difficile pour toi. Je n'ose pas imaginer une autre raison qui me serait défavorable. Et puis je voudrais que tu me parles de toi, de ton histoire si tu veux bien, de ce qui t'as fait du mal comme tu me l'as dit. Ca n'est pas une injonction bien sûr c'est une marque d'intérêt pour toi rien d'autre ! <u>Tu me laisses entendre que tu es reconnaissante à l'égard de ton mari mais pas que tu l'aimes</u>, mais je me trompe peut être ? Tu chercherais l'amour ailleurs, avec moi par exemple ou avec un autre ? Ca serait une bonne idée que ce soit avec moi de préférence, et pas avec un autre ! Sourire. Enfin je ne sais pas, je me pose plein de questions, peut être pourras tu m'aider à y répondre mais seulement si tu le souhaites et lorsque tu le souhaiteras bien sûr. Je ne suis pas en train de te bousculer.

Quand est ce qu'on se reverra ? On se reverra ??   *Jean-Guy*

Hello Monica,

Since in your beautiful family you are Monica, in my love you will be my Monica! I did not get an answer to my last message, I guess it's because it's been difficult for you. I do not dare to imagine another reason that would be unfavourable to me. And then I would like you to tell me about yourself, about your story if you want, about what hurt you, as you told me. It is not an injunction of course it is a mark of interest for you nothing else! You let me know that you are grateful to your husband, but not that you love him, but I may be wrong? You would seek love elsewhere, with me for example, or with another? It would be a good idea whether it is with me preferably, and not with another! Smile. Finally I do not know, I ask myself many questions, maybe you can help me answer, but only if you wish and when you want of course. I'm not harassing you.

When will we see each other again? We'll meet Again?? Jean-Guy

Thursday 29th Sept 2005: Escort agency put Monica's mind at rest

When I returned home, I had a small conversation with our new neighbour. Within that conversation, I mentioned we have guests this coming weekend. Monica happened to come to join us, but afterwards, she was annoyed that I mentioned we have guests this weekend. So, we have a small row. WHAT was her problem? Another question: why was it so important to visit Jemma tomorrow (Friday) night when we have Marina & Gaspar, her husband, coming during the day & staying the weekend? I also ask, why was Friday night so important for her to have another lesbian relationship with Jemma when we have your guests? Jemma was a stunning-looking Rwandese lady, the type you lock eyes on. She had a RAV 4x4 car & always looked ready "to kill". I was to find out later she was not interested at all with men. I could see that she and Monica had that attraction to each other every time I saw Jemma.

I think whether I should contact Rebecca by e-mail or phone her. It would be easier to explain I got her phone number from the telephone bill, or notes Monica made. E-mail would be hard to explain how I got it. I do not want to try and explain HOW I got it, so I decided I must phone Rebecca.

I was to find out later that night, after Lennon had gone to his bedroom, Monica was really meeting "Martin," a new escort client & did not want to tell anyone else of the secret that I shared.

Monica says he wants to meet as a business client & decide later if "more" is required. Monica is wary of police interference with being an escort, speaking with the website boss. He assures her that most men just want to have a girl by their side when out with business clients, that after a few clients, she would feel less inhibited & worried. He puts Monica in contact with another girl, Cleo, who puts her mind at rest.

Friday 30th Sept

Marina & her husband, Gaspar, arrived that afternoon to stay with us for the weekend. Monica takes them to Evry-2 & buys a very sexy bodice. Marina was surprised to see that Monica had bought the sexy bodice for a "business dinner meeting". I was embarrassed to cover for Monica that night, knowing she was meeting a man for sex while her friends had come all the way from Nantes to spend the weekend with us.

Monica phones me at work & says she had received a call from "Martin" on her special "Escort" phone, he not only wants to "meet" her, but says to her that he could introduce her to other big spending clients who would want her "services". Monica asks me what to do on the phone, but I could tell she already has made her mind to cancel her so-called evening with Jemma & go to meet "Martin". The Jemma meeting was just a ruse, or was it real?

When I get home, I am able to see her Escort phone, there are no records of a call (e-mails I read later on Tuesday, explains it was another lie). She says to Marina that she has an important client & needs to go out for the night to meet him & have dinner meeting. She spends a long time making herself up for the meeting & looked nervous, claiming to me it was her first professional escort job.

She says privately to me that she is meeting "Martin", a new escort client in Paris & would go to Antony & get the train into Paris. I look at the mileage & need to read the end mileage when she gets home.

Saturday 1st Oct

She woke me up as she arrived home past 2 am to see if it was Monica's car arriving. I saw she took 3-5 mins with the car interior light. What was she doing in that long time? She only took a small white hand bag. When she got into bed, I asked about her meeting with her first client, "Martin." She forgot the lie & said she went to Bourg la

Reine to save money, even though I know it is a different train zone and more expensive! She then says she met "Martin" in Chatlet with another lady, "Chloe", from another agency. Mmmm, 5 hour meeting? Escort clients pay by ½ hour or per hour & 5 hours was equivalent to overnight for an escort & much money at approx € 200-300 / hr as a going rate, so this would be equivalent to some €800 to 1200!

I do not believe this, she must be lying to me. She tells me an elaborate story that when I asked a week later had changed completely, because she had forgotten her lies. As I was to find out soon, she met with Rebecca & "Martin" was George for an evening at 2+2 club. Imagine she is good friends with Marina, known her for a long time, a very nice, good-looking woman, invites them for the weekend & then leaves them to have a public orgy shag in a club with relatively new people she knew. **What sort of person is she**?

I find Monica's e-mail that made the RV at 7 pm maybe at Antony with George to meet Rebecca in Paris. I had noted the car mileage before & after, & it was a 27 km total difference, enough for Antony & back.... PLUS approximately 10km extra. Where did she go to add an extra 10km? I looked up "Mappy", the best web map at the time, & found out that Longjumeau to Bourg la Reine is 13.7 km. Voila! 27 km round trip.

She wore the new sexy black bodice when she departed but not when she arrived home. Where & when did she take it off & where is it now? I searched all over the house & car for it & could not find it.

Being a scientist makes one a good detective, but working out all the possibilities & worries creates stress I do not need.

Marina, Gaspar, Monica & myself go out for the day in Paris & have dinner in town before returning home in the evening.

Sunday 2nd Oct

I saw on her phone she received a phone call on Sunday, while I was training, from "Francois" thanking her again for the lovely evening together. Who is Francois? Is this another pseudonym? The second time she has seen him (ref 25th Sept).

I am not able to see Monica's e-mails until Tuesday, but then I see e-mails from both Rebecca & George giving their different accounts of the Friday orgy. Rebecca was very upset by being ignored by George while he only wanted to shag Monica. Now, all was explained.

Tuesday 4th Oct

Having read Monica's e-mails to Rebecca, I decided to confront Monica with some of what I know. I said I wanted to share her life & that meant her friends as well. She is reticent but agrees to have a drink together sometime. I e-mailed Rebecca introducing myself & wanted to meet her with Monica if possible.

Had I read this e-mail below on Friday, I would have been able to understand more about what went on Friday night (30th Sept) .

***

Thursday e-mail from Rebecca

Monica,

I am delighted as well that we can now communicate by email. It is so much faster and easier. And thank you for your lovely photos - you look wonderful. I have forwarded them to George and have asked him to send you one of his - I know he has some. He also has your mobile number and will try and call you today. If he has trouble in getting you, here is his email George.xxx@harmonybti.com and his mobile number 06 11 72 70 xx

Still have not yet sorted out with George whether he wants to pick me up from Rue Rambuteau or whether I should come to Montparnasse. I can so easily do that. I know there is a bar at the corner - the same side as 2+2. I usually meet Ian there when we go to the club (I am his passport!). I am afraid my relationship with George goes quite deep. I am hung up on him but should not (be). He is so much an individual person and I am sure does not want any ties. He has been divorced ages ago.

He Lives in a wonderful house with two of his children in a separate flat above him. George occupies the ground floor.

My mobile number again +44 7803 008 xxx. The landline in my Paris flat is

01 48 04 99 xx - No xx Rue Rambuteau, 75004 Paris - entry code 0x xxxx push the button "key" and then push the door open.

Much love and see you tomorrow.

Rebecca

Who took the photos in our house?

Lennon comes to me & says he has discovered on Monica's phone a photo of her in a long silver dress & then on her computer. This is one that was to be used for the escort website & was made on 19th Sept at 22.35 hours*. However, I was in England, & Lennon did not take it!

WHO took the photo in our house at such a late time? Taken from at least 10 pm to nearly 2 am the next morning. I see in writing this book, that a different wig was used in the photos of the same silver dress taken at 01.38hrs. So, what happened in between those hours in our house to necessitate a change of wigs? The 1st photo, with a time stamp of 10.35 pm, looked more professional. it was not done by Monica or any of her friends. Nobody, even Lennon, knows she was to be on an Escort website. Also, she did not inscribe until 25th Sept, I did not take any photos of her in her dresses until I got back from the UK on Friday 23rd September!

* *I still have the photos and looking at the photo properties in writing this book, I noted something I never noticed before. One photo was taken at 10.38 pm on the 19th of September with one larger "fuzzy" wig on; the others were taken in quick succession at 1.38 am later, now the next day with a smaller wig!*

I also see an e-mail from a "Jean-Guy", complaining that Monica had not contacted him for 5 days, i.e. since Tuesday 27th Sept. Oh, so we have another man, she has met Jean-Guy. He seems desperate to see Monica again, and his language seems like he is in love with her....so quickly? Just a dinner meeting or a shag afterwards? What does she want from him? What does she want from these men? I am sure she wants something he does or can do for her.

Why does Monica search relentlessly for men?

I need to make a spreadsheet of all her men & then work out who is who & what interest Monica has in them. Come back to Paul. I would so love if she went back to Paul & forsake these others.

I am going crazy…. Perhaps I should do what Paul suggested & try other women. Monica was reticent to agree at that time, perhaps she will agree now?

Do I want to do that? **My brain hurts, & my heart hurts**.

Sun, 2 Oct 2005   02:44:06 EDT
De   JGA768@aol.com
A   xxxx2000@yahoo.fr
Sujet   Y'a quelqu'un ???

Ca fait déjà 5 jours que je n'ai eu aucune nouvelles de toi ! J'espère que tu vas bien ??? Je constate aussi que c'est depuis que je t'ai demandé si nous nous reverrons que tu t'es murée dans un silence total. Que dois je en conclure ??? Tu ne veux pas essayer de me dire ce que tu as au fond du coeur parce que pour moi c'est un peu dur d'attendre, d'espérer mais sans trop savoir à quoi m'accrocher...

Réponds moi vite, Monica..Jean-Guy

It's been 5 days since I had any news from you! I hope you are well??? I also note that it's since I asked you if we'll see each other again that you walled in total silence. What should I conclude??? You do not want to try to tell me what you have deep in the heart because for me it's a little hard to wait, to hope but without knowing what to hang on to...

Answer me quickly, Monica

Monday 3rd Oct

Monica receives 3 phone calls in the early evening from "Emotions". It is a rencontre / Meeting "Serencontre" website man from using her "Africaine3" name; no RV has been apparently fixed yet.

Tuesday 4th Oct

I phone Rebecca from work at about 6 pm. Rebecca says she met Monica with a man in 2+2 about 3 months ago. The man was rather short. Interesting, Paul is not short, so who was this man? We agreed to exchange e-mails, so I asked her for hers & gave her mine.

In the evening, I ask Monica why she wants to meet all these men who are not escort work. She explains that we need money, if she can meet a man who can give her work or contract, it can lead to money.

Wednesday 5th Oct 2005

That evening, Monica reiterates that she meets many men for money & to enhance her possible business idea of Moni Clean. She says **she is thinking about joining another escort website**, but decides to leave it to just one.....for the moment.

I received an e-mail from Rebecca & read it from work.

Hi Geoff

So, I have just arrived back from Paris and have found your message. I find it difficult to respond. But let me begin. I met Monica two, three, four months ago at 2+2. She was there with a partner and in the bar we exchanged telephone numbers. I am Bisexual - something I only found out during the last couple of years. So clearly Monica and I have a lot in common. I live in London with my partner who is considerbly older than myself, a wonderful man, but sadly Ernie has Parkinsons. We have a lovely house in Kew, I have an office/studio flat in Chelsea and a flat in Paris, hence our frequent trips. Clearly, Ernie because of his age but primarily because of his illness he can't come with me to the clubs. He does not know about them. If only I would have found out about these clubs years ago - I know 2+2, Chris et Manu, Overside - that's it I think. I love Paris - the flat is in Rue Rambuteau - Boulevard Sebastopol. - , Google "Rebecca Sxxxx" Images and there is photo of me.

I was so sad to hear about your situation with Monica. I never had any inclination of your situation. Do you have children, she said she had. How old are they? Monica told me that you recently moved from a flat to a house south of Paris. I would be delighted to meet you, but can only do so near my flat. If I could do something to help you both, I would be delighted. Why is life so complex?

By the way, George is my heartbreak. I should not be so emotionally involved, but am. We have of course a lot in common. He has children, is the breadwinner, we both love opera, music, the arts generally and are emotionally so close, but of course he has other lovers, now Monica - I introduced them !!!!!!!!!!!!!! I must be mad.

Rebecca

***

Saturday 8th – Sat 15th Oct 2005

Before I left, I saw that under the category "women", Monica had received another man's comms from Laurence Guilliume. Message does not seem like an escort client but just another male contact.

South Africa trip Sunday 9th - Friday 14th

I was away in South Africa on business for the week. I ran a seminar & visited customers in Jo'burg, Durban & Cape Town before leaving for home. I arrived home late Friday night, 14th Oct.

Saturday 15th Oct 2005: Irate message on Monica's phone from Jean-Claude's wife

I arrived home last night knackered & slept part of the day & walked around the town as it was market day up to 1:00 pm. I liked to get my horse meat from the Chevaline in the market. The owner knows me as a regular with 5 slices of fillet 200g +/- 5g. He was always very accurate, & we often joked. Sometimes, he would embarrass me by pointing me out to others in the queue that I was "Anglais", everyone would look around at me, I then felt like an alien.

I see there is a voicemail message 888 on Monica's phone from Thursday 13th. It was a VERY irate wife of Jean-Claude; she had found out about Monica's liaison with Jean-Claude. She sounded, by her accent, African French. Boy, was she angry! Who the hell is Jean-Claude?

Monica gets a message late afternoon from "Daniel Nettoyer" – cleaner). She then took the phone call a few minutes later, disappearing into the guest room & chatting with him for some 10 minutes. I overheard (in French) her saying that her husband had been away & now returned home.

When she returns to the bedroom, she says it was from an escort client who will re-contact her regarding an RV later today or tomorrow. I noticed that it was on her normal phone & not the special escort phone. Later, upon inspection, in the new week, it revealed no phone calls on that special phone. Daniel must be a new man she is trying to woo for some reason. There is ALWAYS a reason she says not associated with sex. She uses her looks, manner & sex to obtain things, be it money, work or some advantage to her.

I also notice a lot of phone traffic with Diane. Who is Diane, another sexual friend?

One message, "Je suis déprimé, je suis désolé, je suis désolé pour le moment" ("I'm depressed, I'm sorry, I'm sorry at the moment"). I would find out later Diane was another lady at the orgy with George & Rebecca on 30th September. It was not only Rebecca who was upset with George spending all his attention on Monica. What is it with George that makes him so attractive to women?

Saturday 22nd Oct: First meeting with Rebecca

Monica was going out to meet with one of her Rwandese friends, so I went to Paris to meet Rebecca at her flat near the Pompidou centre. I rang the buzzer for her flat, & she let the lock release so I could enter the small green door & then go into an ancient lift (ascenseur) with double sliding cage doors. I pressed the old button for the xth floor of her flat. The door was open, I entered to be greeted by Rebecca. She was rather small, thin & well-educated with German birth, but after so many years in the UK had acquired a good English accent with just a taint of Germanic. It was a one-bedroom flat with a small kitchen & a small lavish décor lounge. We did the customary kisses on both cheeks & then sat down on the sofa.

I felt I should start the opening gambit, explaining my frustration with Monica, excluding me from her friends once they wanted to see me. I said Paul & I were good friends & had been with Monica & a Rwandese friend to the 2+2 club.

Rebecca now felt at ease to explain she met Monica with a man called Jean-Claude on Thursday June 17th. She could recall that weekend because she normally comes over to Paris from the UK about every 2-3 weeks. They met in 2+2 when she was with George. After a shag with Claude, Monica experienced other men around the club & finally has fun with Rebecca. They exchanged addresses, contact phone numbers & e-mails.

They agreed to meet again & met at Rebecca's flat & had their orgy there. Rebecca always has a rule: whoever comes must provide a bottle of Champagne.

Sunday 23rd Oct: big row over projected Moni Clean profit & I am shoved downstairs.

Lennon returned from a school trip to Spain that afternoon. Soon after, I had arrived with the athletic group that I coach for some English ale; they appreciated the beers after our training.

Jeanne, a friend of Monica, had been invited from St Genevieve des Bois to help with the Moni Clean project but doesn't want me there to input some glaring assumptions & omissions. I said Jeanne knows nothing of business. When Jeanne goes, I go over her figures. She puts in an income immediately of €65k income & €10k expenses for the first year of business (I put in €35k income first year & €28k in expenses), the difference of Monica's guess of €55k profit instead of my € estimate of €7k is enormous. I said the first year would have many expenses that would not be repeated in the 2nd year & also income would rise as reputation & learning on-the-job improved.

We have a big row when I reiterate her poor assumptions, looking at the projected figures with "rose-tinted glasses" & no reality of start-up business difficulties. She hits me & when I repeat that her advisers are always from ignorant friends, she hits me again. I threw her paperwork out the window, at which point, as I started to go downstairs, she pushed me down the stairs to the first level, where there was a bend. She had cracked my ribs. It was only when I cannot move & groan with agony, Monica starts to realise I am badly injured & helps me up, to get down the rest of the stairs to the lounge. I walk around for some time because I cannot straighten my body & need to stay straight & upright, lying down was not good. Monica wants to call the emergency services, but I make her aware they can do nothing for cracked ribs except put a large bandage around my midriff, so it would be a waste of time.

Monday 24th Oct 2005: Moni Clean business plan starts

Driving to work meant travelling along a 200m section of cobbled road by the side of the church, which I knew would be agony, so it proved as I foresaw. This was my daily routine for about three days until the pain slowly receded & healing commenced.

With Monica's input over the weekend, I made copious notes & started to make a business plan for Moni Clean. She finds it takes months (3-5 months involving compulsory courses) to start a company & asks me how long it takes in the UK. I replied it normally takes 24 HOURS. Monica immediately thought of registering Moni Clean in UK, until I said it would not be possible to conduct business in France with a UK registered company, it would need to be a registered French subsidiary, so that idea was eliminated. She inscribes on a government course that lasts 6 weeks.

Tuesday 25 October 2005

Monica arrives home that evening with Alice....... WOW, she is beautiful, a real stunner, a really Rwandan black beauty. I cannot take my eyes away from her. I have to make real efforts not to stare at her. I also notice Monica & Alice have a special look at each other. I get her mobile number & send her an SMS later & she replies interest in meeting me. She sent me her e-mail address, so I sent her one later that night.

Monica shows a peace offering by shopping for cereal, milk, etc., as I cannot really move much with these cracked ribs.

Wednesday 26th October

I met Alice at lunchtime in Villejust, some 5km away from my work, at a small cafe/brassier. She tells me that Monica is infatuated with her & she with Monica. Alice says that she cares little for men, although she does not mind being with men. It became plain to me that they were having a lesbian affair, although she complained that Monica was not paying so much attention to her lately. I said I would try to help as much as I could without letting on that we had met or were in contact with each other.

Thursday 27th October: A real escort contact

I read some of Monica's e-mails, and one set of communications catches my eye. The e-mails are in response to the escort agency website she started in late September. It is from Nicolas Selves from the French Antilles & is obviously making a proposition to Monica to strip in front of a group of men & possibly more "....*depending on the scenario...*". It seems that the group would arrive soon on business in Paris & would like to have some entertainment & asked whether she could strip & maybe, according to the interpretation of "...de pluralité masculine..." have sex. The door was open for more than €2,000 depending on what "entertainment" she provided. Monica seems quite keen to provide them with what they want. The various translated communications over 3 days were as follows:

From:: xxxx2000@yahoo.fr]
To: nselves@france-antilles.pf
Mon, 24 Oct 2005 15:00:08 +0200 (CEST)

Subject: contac
Hello Nicolas,
Could you contact me about this by tel, 06-08-00-28-xx? Of course I have some beautiful pictures of me, which I will send you after our discussion.
Cordially;
Monica
****

From: "Nicolas Selves" <nselves@france-antilles.pf
To: xxxx2000@yahoo.fr
Mon,   24 Oct 2005 01:18: 25

Subject: RE: contact

Hello Monica!
I am looking for an exhibition service that I pay 2000 euros minimum depending on the scenario.
Would you be interested?
Is it possible to join you to discuss it more seriously?
Would you also have some photos of you to send me?
Cordially.
Biz.
Nicolas.
** *******
From:: xxxx2000@yahoo.fr]
Posted: Monday 24 October 2005 03:00
To: nselves@france-antilles.pf
Subject: RE: RE: contact

Hello Nicolas,

Could you contact me about this by tel, 06-08-00-28-xx? Of course I have some beautiful pictures of me, which I will send you after our discussion.
Coodrialement;
Monica
** ************

From: "Nicolas Selves" <nselves@france-antilles.pf
To: xxxx2000@yahoo.fr
Subject: RE: RE:RE: contact
Date : Mon, 24 Oct 2005 20:29:55 -1000

The scenario is that you do an exhibition in front of groups of passive businessmen.
Duration 1h to 1h30. In Paris (travel and accommodation expenses at my expense)
What are your experiences with exhibition and male plurality ?(this when translated could be: male bonding, male organ or male gaze)
Do you have some new pictures of you?
Biz.
** ****

Date: Thu, 27 Oct 2005 11:17:23 +0200 (CEST)
From: xxxx2000@yahoo.fr
Subject: RE: RE: RE:RE: contact
To: nselves@france-antilles.pf

Hello Nicolas,
I was traveling for this reason that I did not respond quickly to your message. As for your question, I have no exhibition experience, my weapon is my natural beauty. I will send you more beautiful pictures of me soon.
Biz Monica

Mon 31st October 2005

Monica has lunch with Paul, discussing the fact she feels things are close to a marriage breakdown. Monica phones me at work to ask me to come home early so Paul, Monica & I could discuss things. I arrive home at about 5:30 pm, & we discuss various problems over a couple of hours. An agreement was made on her two points linked to my four points. If she does not hide things from me, I would not need to investigate her friends to find out what is going on. She did not like me talking to her friends, like Jeanne in Morsang sur Orge when she was at our house last week.

Paul suggests Monica take me to 2+2 tonight, he leaves, so we can immediately go to Paris as tomorrow is a férié /holiday. We both quickly change clothes. Monica in a sexy dress (dresses or skirts are mandatory at the club). I drive us to Montparnasse, & luckily, find a parking spot on the residential duel carriageway Boulevard Edgar Quinet.

On arrival, we have a quick drink at the bar & then go upstairs to the orgy room. When one arrives, first, there is a small changing area where one hangs up one's clothes, copious supply of condoms is available. They provided a shower before entering the orgy room. Monica quickly attracts a man & suitably protected. He shags her, and I am mesmerised by my wife quickly getting into the action. As I was watching her being shagged, a nice white French woman approached me, wanting me to shag her. I agreed & with that, she felt my penis & directed it inside her. Sitting on me on the settee, she bounced up & down on me, with James getting more & more excited until the final hard thrusts were done, gradually subsided activity. She really did enjoy a shag; I could not believe how hot she became & came to orgasm so quickly for a woman. It is not often a woman can cum at the same time as a man, but I climaxed not too soon, it is always satisfying to be able to satisfy a woman.

Afterwards, she thanked me, & we chatted small talk while I glanced several times to see Monica being mounted by a 2nd man. By the time we had finished chatting, I had noticed Monica had moved & looking around was on a giant bed, maybe 3 metres square. She was on her back legs open with a 3rd man shagging her.

I felt inadequate that I would need to recover when another woman looked at me with inviting eyes, she beckoned me to follow her & like a lamb, I followed to a curved sofa where she invited me to play with her pussy. She was about 40-50 years old, good-looking, with big saggy boobs that needed caressing & fondling with one hand as I played with her pussy with the other. She fondled my penis but had difficulty rising to start with. However, she had infinite patience, eventually, I had a hard erection to be able to do what was expected of me. With a fully erect hard penis ready for action, she moved & sat on top of me like the other woman & effectively jumped up & down. Her ample boobs bounced up & down with the rhythm, whereby the friction excited her & me more, until climax & eruption occurred. She was satisfied & got off me. She sat down next to me again, and we kissed & cuddled. She told me her name was Naomi & wanted to chat, that was not difficult. I needed a rest!

I caught sight of Monica had just finished with another man (4th or 5th ?) & was moving off the sofa, looking at a woman. She made moves to move over to her. Quickly, she was now having fun with this other woman on another sofa. The woman was well-built & had boobs enough to keep Monica satisfied while simultaneously playing with each other's pussy. Naomi, my latest woman, seeing my gaze on the two of them in action, beckoned us to go closer to watch the "show". Quickly, there were about 5 of us watching Monica & the woman in action. Naomi was fascinated, & when things were slowing down, she sat down next to Monica on the other side. Monica looked at her, smiled & started sharing her attention with Naomi.

Soon, the other woman thanked Monica & moved on, leaving Monica & Naomi alone to play together. Oh, Naomi was really happy to play with Monica's pussy & get reciprocal pussy attention. Both played & played until both were heaving up & down with excitement, boobs slowly but gently rising & falling, until both almost simultaneous, boobs as high in the air as possible & bum raised. Their climax had been reached, slowly, both sets of bums & chests receded down to a normal position. Both lay back on the seat with all watching almost clapping with approval.

I looked around without too much attention to anyone because I was sure I would not be able to perform a third time that night. Eventually, Monica, now free, saw me, smiled & beckoned that she was satisfied that we should finish & shower to go home. I must say Monica is a performer. I saw her have a shag with at least 5 men & 2 women that night.

Friday 4th November 2005

I discovered after work, looking at Monica's e-mails that she went to the 2+2 club with someone; arrangements made yesterday (Thursday). I despair….. WHO is this?

Objet: RE: Tomorrow - Nov 4

Date: Fri, 4 Nov 2005 02:32:57 -0500

De:"Sxxxx, Rebecca"   Afficher infos contact

A: "caz Monica"

Don't worry Monica. I do remember your partner, very nice indeed. Pity I can't join you in the afternoon at 2+2. But remember, I very much want to on a Friday afternoon. Your partner could take two women, yes? Can we arrange this for December 9? I have a particular reason for being there on a Fri evening, this man Didier I met there but he comes from outside Paris so will probably not be there in the evening.

Anyway your idea of coming back to my flat at say 6 p.m. today sounds great. I do so much want to show the flat to you. Would you have some one with you?

Here is the address   REDACTED

xx Rue Rambuteau, Paris 4. I am on the xx floor, the entry code is 0xxxxx push the button marked "key" and then push the door open. flat is at the right side of the lift.

Basically it is between the Pompideau Centre and Boulevard Sebastopol a burgundy coloured door between a shop called xxxxxxxx and the xxxxxxxxx

Yes we must talk on the phone. At the moment I must get ready

See you later-

R

From: caz Monica [mailto: xxxxxx2000@yahoo.fr]   REDACTED   spelling mistakes kept

Sent: Fri 11/4/2005 2:16 AM

To: xxxxxxx, Rebecca

Subject: RE: Tomorrow Nov 4

Hi Rebecca,

I am sorry that I complicate the programme, the thing is that my partener his marred & canot come by nighttime. Is the one who I was hith last time when I meet you & there is another one who lives in Africa (kind of personne & very intergent, I want to make a surprise to him, he've never been to the club & likes enjoying his life, I hope that he will appreciate my surprise. We can olso make an arrangement like that: I go there in afternoon with them & come back later one to your flat (arraound 6 pm) then see you, mybe go back later night to the club?) My mobile is on now, we can communicate by phone.

I hope that we will find an arrangement.

Cheers

Objet: Tomorrow - Nov 4

Date: Thu, 3 Nov 2005 06:48:08 -0500

De:"Sxxxxxxx, Rebecca" Afficher infos contact

A: "caz Monica"

Sunday 6th November 2005: 2nd escort meeting Client pays well

Monica gets a phone call from a Jurgen, who, she says is from Switzerland on the border with Italy. Is it her first or the 2nd escort job? She dresses up for the night & leaves at about 7 pm for Paris. She returned in the early hours when I was asleep. I am curious how much he gave her; it would have been in cash.

Monday 7th November 2005: Business start-up course starts for 6 weeks

Monica stayed in bed longer because she was very tired from her nights "work" the night before. She did not need to rush because she was starting her business start-up course in Ris Orangis that will last 6 weeks. I looked in her handbag before setting off to work & found 10 x €100 folded notes loose in her bag. When she wakes up, I ask how last night went. She is rather reticent to say much other than she met Jurgen from Switzerland, and he took her out for a meal & then to a nightclub. Later that evening, she tells me that he took her to an expensive Latin bar & then to a nightclub with three levels in Bastille until maybe 2 am. He bought a bottle of Champagne & then paid her well for her services in his hotel. She said that he was very amorous & seemed disappointed that she was married. I could sense she was a bit techy, so I did not pursue my questions, even though I was bursting with questions.

Now, she has started her first escort work. I suppose she will find it easier to go out in the evenings "on business", leaving me at home wondering who & what she is doing.

I wonder when she will see those business men in Paris. It seems all communications will have been by phone since I have not seen any more e-mails. I got the impression they would be arriving soon, maybe while I am away in Iran? I will be away for a week starting Friday morning to travel on Islamic holy day of the week & be ready for work on Saturday, which is the Iranian "Monday". It gets very confusing that Iran & Saudi Arabia* have Thursday/Friday, weekends, while the rest of the Middle East have Friday/Saturday for the weekend. Later, when I organised a 2-week Middle East tour, it would be useful to travel in the middle of Friday, so I work every work day to maximise my tours.

* Saudi Arabia have since changed to Friday/Saturday, leaving only Iran out of sync.

Later that night, when I mentioned I needed to get US dollars for the Iran trip, she handed me €1,000 & $1,000 cash each in 100 notes for when I go to Iran. They only accept cash for everything preferable UK Pounds, US dollars or Euros.

I assume the $1,000 was for the 1st Escort clients show? I hope to find out later.

Friday 11th – Friday 18th Nov 2005: Iran trip

After the invitation, I should have received the visa for my trip to Iran, which should have been simple. However, going to the Middle East is never easy, and we were told a week beforehand that the visa would be issued the week AFTER I was supposed to leave!!! I was told by the HJY Agent Kamal, owner of JamAra in Tehran, that the only way was to go to the embassy. So, I went & arrived at 9 am & was told they could not find my passport as it would not be ready. So, 4 phone calls to/from Tehran at last gave news that it would be ready after 14:00hrs. Finally, at 15:00hrs, I walked out of the embassy with my passport with a valid visa to Iran. More phone calls were made to confirm the flights, & finally, the next day (Thursday 10th), I left for Dubai & then onto Tehran.

I arrived on Friday, an Islamic holy day, as a BIP (Business Important Person) with special attention at a special BIP lounge, where I am all for myself & all security & immigration were done. Outside, a chap with my name on a board, took my luggage, & we got into his old yellow car. I arrived in the hotel in the capital Tehran 05:00 hrs on Friday completely knackered. When I arrived at the hotel in central Tehran, I slept 14:00 in the afternoon!!!. Ready to work on Saturday, the first working day of the week. I have to travel on Thursday/Friday as this is the Iranian weekend, so I could do my lecture for the seminar planned for Saturday morning finishing at 16:00 hrs in the afternoon.

I had an intensive week running an all-day seminar & visiting customers in the Tehran area. Kamal, the owner of JamAra, took me around various customers, some of who were users, & I was able to sort out most of the problems due to my knowledge of ICP-AES. JamAra operated through Dubai where Kamal's son, Robert, ran the SMT company operation.

I went for a walk from my hotel in Tehran, & crossing the roads at Vanak Square was an experience. There are flashing amber lights for the motorists & constant not working lights for the pedestrians, so one has to deliberately walk carefully & PURPOSELY across the road, not hesitating that a car is coming at you; just keep walking as it passes you by, slowing down near you!!! I am still alive!!

The view from my 13th floor of the hotel is wonderful, with snow covered mountains that surrounds the northern edge of Tehran.

My full day of lecturing finished OK, the audience seemed to like my style of audience participation. They all stayed awake even in the afternoon "graveyard shift" straight after lunch. Walking from the platform & up the isle between the audiences talking through my microphone kept them awake, especially if I asked some of the audience a question !

I have found things are more open than 4 years ago. Everyone wants to know HOW the president (Ahmadinejad) got elected, nobody here voted for him, & they all talk about it!!

So long as you have a loose head scarf you are OK, NOBODY wears a burka here!! They are quietly revolting against ANY effort to restrict their life style*. The president is out of touch with the population.

* Things have changed for the worse since my visit in 2005

I read e-mails on my return. These, to & from Jean-Guy. He is in the building trade, & maybe Monica is playing to get some work out of a relationship.

Comment va tu?

Je m'excuse du silence, j'en avais besoin, je ne voulais pas te créér de problème (que tu te fasse appaler par mon mari car il a lu tes messages). Je sais que le silence est parfois douteux mais je n'avais pas le choix. Par contre, j'ai toujour été joignable sur mon portable, tu m'avais lassé un sms mais comme je te l'ai dit, je ne peux pas envoyer les sms car ca laisse les trace. Bref, je ne suis pas mal elevée, je pense à toi, si tu veux, tu peux m'appeler la journée sans problème.

Je t'embrasse très fort et à bientot.
Monica
How are you?

I apologize for the silence, I needed it, I didn't want to create a problem for you (that you get called by my husband because he read your messages). I know silence is sometimes questionable but I had no choice. On the other hand, I have always been reachable on my mobile phone, you sent me a text message but as I told you, I cannot send text messages because it leaves traces. In short, I'm not badly brought up, I'm thinking of you, if you want, you can call me during the day without any problem.

I kiss you very hard and see you soon.
Monica

Monday 14th November 2005

Bonsoir Monica,
Tu sais je ne voulais pas te créer de problème moi non plus et puis j'ai eu l'impression que tu avais besoin de savoir, de réfléchir, à ce que tu voulais faire de ta vie. Ton mari a lu mes messages et alors qu'est ce qui c'est passé ???

Alors j'ai voulu respecter ton silence et aussi te laisser revenir vers moi si tu le souhaitais. Et puis tu m'as envoyé un sms bizarre : "merci, merci beaucoup", le même que tu m'avais envoyé plusieurs semaines plus tôt sauf que là moi je ne t'avais rien écrit. J'ai pensé que ce sms était destiné à quelqu'un d'autre, quelqu'un à qui tu plaisais peut être et qui te plaisait peut être. Voilà ce que j'ai pensé ! Alors j'ai voulu que tu me dises toi ce que tu veux...

Moi je t'embrasse très tendrement et à bientôt...Jean-Guy

Good evening, Monica,

You know I did not want to trouble you either, and then I felt like you needed to know, think, what you wanted to do with your life. Your husband read my messages and so what happened???

So I wanted to respect your silence and also let you come back to me if you wanted. And then you sent me a weird sms: "thank you, thank you very much", the same one you sent me several weeks earlier except that I did not write anything to you there. I thought that this sms was for someone else, someone you may like and who you like. That's what I thought! So I wanted you to tell me what you want...

I kiss you very tenderly and see you soon ... Jean-Guy

Tuesday 15th November 2005

Monica, je n'espérais plus jamais entendre parler de toi. Je voulais attendre que tu me dises ce que tu voulais. Je ne voulais pas te poser de problèmes non plus avec ton mari... Et alors comment il a réagit en lisant mes messages. Il n'a pas pu croire à une erreur ou à un simple admirateur !

Mon téléphone : 06 82 45 51 xx

Tu as l'habitude de rencontrer beaucoup d'hommes ???

xJe t'embrasse et je t'attends..Jean-Guy

Monica,

I never hoped to hear speaking about you. I wanted to wait that you say to me what you wanted. I did not want to make you problems neither with your husband... Well then how has he reacted by reading my messages. Was he not able to believe in an error or in a simple admirer!

My telephone: 06 82 45 51 xx

You are in the habit of meeting many men ???

I kiss{*embrace*} you, and I wait for you.

As I thought, this chap is REALLY intelligent & reads Monica like a book!!! Jean-Guy is very intelligent, as I thought before. He often questions Monica's mentality & lies.

Wednesday 16th November 2005
Comms without spelling or sense corrections

Jean-Guy,

Je suis contente de prendre contacte avec toi à nouveau. Je n'ai pas l'habitude de rencontrer les hommes comme ça, je ne suis pas à la recherche, je cherchais simplement un amour qui pourrait m'apporter l'affection et l'équilibre (j'ai souvent des conflits dans ma vie de couple). quant alors j'ai commencé à contacter les gens (par toi) j'ai eu une mauvaise expérience car mon mari a lu les messages.

En ce moment je peux encore communiquer avec toi car je sais qu'il n'est pas dans les là, il est en déplacement jusqu'à vendredi! J'efface alors mes messages aussitôt lus. J'ai bien noté ton numéro et je t'appellerai demain à partir de mon poste fixe (car le portable laisse des traces). Entre temps je n'avance pas dans mon projet de nettoyage industriel, ça me déstabiliser car je compte les mois passés à la maison sans job, et l'année s'achevé bientôt, cela me fait peur, de penser que je risque d'être encore au chômage en janvier 2006!! Bref la vie continue et elle est belle. Bisous

I am satisfied to get in touch with you again. I am not in the habit of meeting the people like that, I am not in search, I looked simply for a love which could bring me affection and balance (I often have conflicts in my married life). So then I began to contact people (like you) I had a bad experience because my husband read messages.

At the moment, I can again communicate with you because I know that he is not reading them there; he is on business until <u>Friday</u>! I erase, and then my messages immediately read. I noted well your number, and I shall call you tomorrow from my fixed telephone (because the portable leaves track). Meanwhile, I do not advance in my project of industrial cleaning, that has destabilised me because this is the last month at the house with a job, and the year finished soon; it makes me fearful, thinking that I risk to be unemployed in January 2006!! In brief continuous life, and she is beautiful. Kisses

Date: Fri, 18 Nov 2005 23:20:34 +0100 (CET)
De: xxxx2000@yahoo.fr
Objet: Nouvelles
À: jga768@aol.com

How goes you? I was not able to call you because I was in training in the chamber of commerce, in fact I had asked to participate in it but I had no confirmation on behalf of the chambre of business. The portable died today and in the evening I did not know if I could call you (it is not the urge that missed me). How goes your business (work, project of fetes of the end of year)?

Kept silent found your love by the net? If yes, how is she? (Smile)?

Friday 18th November

When I arrive home on Friday, Monica welcomes me with a big grin & says she has stayed at home all week, except with Satar. She said she is working hard on her "Moni Clean" project, inscribing on various French government courses for start-up companies. She said she had been seeing Felician in conjunction with the Moni Clean project.

I read an SMS from a Jacques saying that he loves her & wants to take her on a business trip he has organised to Havana, Cuba.

Sunday 26th November 2005: Businessmen hire Monica as an escort, meeting loads on money

I go training over the local Longjumeau stadium down the road. When I return home, Monica has gone to Paris. Lennon has gone locally to see his friend, so alone I start tidying up & looking for anything interesting. I noticed in her bedside cabinet that part of an envelope was stuffed in the bottom drawer and fell out the back on pulling the drawer out. To ensure I could put it back, I found the envelope was large, A4 size*, hence why it was protruding out from the back from below. I pulled out the drawer completely to access the envelope, oh wow! It was stuffed full of €50 notes. I count them all, & the total comes to €3,000!

* Probably by using an A4 envelope the men could drop their share into it easily from Nicolas who was organising the meeting.

Nicolas Selves & his colleagues must have been happy to see Monica strip. With more money than the offer mentioned in the e-mail, she must have performed very well, providing them with all the requested pleasures. My mind starts working overtime with visions of a businessman's "gang bang". I then recalled the previous month at 2+2 club, where she was quiet at home with 5 men shagging her plus fun with 2 women. I cannot imagine there would have been more than 5 businessmen. They could have hidden €600 each within their business "expenses". I cannot say I have found the money, nor that I saw her e-mails where she was due to meet Nicolas Selves & his colleagues at anytime. I need to find that out with some round-about questions.

Monica tells me on her return from Paris that evening that she met this man in a bar in Montparnasse who was married & wanted company. After some drinks, she SAYS she dropped him off at Champs Elysees. She was happy when she returned, as she thought, he may want to use her escort services in the future also happy that she was able to attract a man quickly. She said that she may be able to use the same tactics to get customers for her Moni Clean nettoyage (cleaning) company.

Monica describes her escort gang bang evening.

Unlike her boy friends, she was happy to tell me all about her afternoon. She is due for her stomach operation soon, & she said she hoped she would be able to get the clients when she has recovered. I thought while she is in a good mood & open with me, I would try to ask whether she had had any other clients while I was away in Iran. I acted as if I was enthusiastic at the prospect of her new business. Initially, she seemed coy, but with a twinkle in her eye, I gauged that I could pursue the questioning further. I said, lying through my teeth, "You know it is alright, I am supporting you in your escort venture." She looked at me & smiled, "Really?" She said, "Why not? You gain money for what you are doing anyway, I think you find it exciting....true?" She smiled again, "I did see someone, he, well, his name is Nicolas..... he had some colleagues visiting Paris with him, they wanted someone to show them around Paris, & he was willing to pay me to entertain them for the evening...... and...... afterwards, they invited me to one of their rooms......", I waved my hands to gesture "carry-on", so she tentatively continued, "They.... said I was beautiful & they would love to see more of me, and Nicolas suggested that I take off my clothes..." I gestured that I was approving & excited at her story & waved my hands that I wanted her to continue. "So, I slowly teased them by taking off my clothes slowly. They were really pleased & encouraged me as they realised I was not used to doing that. I became more confident & stayed with just my culottes & bra on for a while. Then, Nicolas gestured to me to remove my bra, I moved towards him & turned my back to him so that he could undo my bra. He undid it & held me breast. Oh, Geoff, I suddenly started feeling so sexy as he caressed my breast in front of the other men, and then another man held my other breast. Nicolas started feeling my leg & then, with two hands, removed my culottes until I was completely naked. The men were so happy, & I felt liberated. I remember last month at 2+2, you looked liberated & happy." I said. "Yes, the next thing I can remember was Nicolas was on top of me on the bed." "Did you manage to satisfy all of them?" I enquired. She nodded in the affirmative. "I am sure you had an excellent night. Were you tired?" I asked. She nodded. "The important thing was, did you have fun & was the night worth it?" "Yes, I was happy with the night, & they paid me well afterwards because they were so happy with me". Showing approval, I said, "Good, you had fun & got rewarded for it, & …...most importantly, you have told me about the evening in detail without holding back". Monica was so happy that I was approving that she gave me a big hug & beckoned me to go with her to the bedroom.

All that description by Monica of her Escort evening with the businessmen made us both feel horny, & we had a marvellous shag. I didn't need any blue pill, for after her description of her night., By Jupiter, I shagged her with her facing me, so we could cuddle with James inserted. She bounced up & down on James, I could hold her boobs when they were not bouncing up & down with the shagging rhythm.

Monday 27th November

Monica goes in the morning to do some office cleaning before Moni Clean is registered, a black job from some "meeting" ? Dr Monet based in central Paris, Monica learnt he does plastic surgery & starts mentioning that night that maybe he could get rid of her fat stomach & excess skin since she lost so much weight.

Tuesday 28th November 2005

Monica meets the man she met on Sunday in Montparnasse, Paris, again after work. She then describes "George's" large house with a high wall around Antony near Bourge La Reine. She clams up & does not say what else happened.

Saturday 3rd December

Marina arrived last night, in the morning, while alone, Monica had a shower. I beckoned to her & showed an SMS from Jean-Guy on Monica's mobile phone, describing a sexual encounter & sexually explicit comments. She is shocked & says she suspected something in the past, but this was proof of what Monica is like. I said that being a scientist, I am a good detective, somethings that Monica says, that she thinks are plausible, but, for me, are not plausible, she believes a lie is possible. This is because she is not knowledgeable. Marina said exactly what I have said, "She is intelligent but not intellectual."

Tuesday 6th December 2005: Monica pushes me downstairs #2- Cracked rib

We have another row over her men she keeps secret from me in the evening, as I follow her upstairs. Then, she turns around, from the top of the stairs, Monica pushes me, & I fall down the stairs cracked my rib in the fall AGAIN. Again, the next few days were agony driving over a small section of cobbled road in Longjumeau near the church. This is the second time I have cracked my ribs with Monica pushing me downstairs.

Wednesday 7th December

I read her e-mails, & one catches my eye. Monica sends a message to Rebecca about meeting with Jacques at her flat for another orgy. I see a reply that Rebecca is getting jealous that Jacques is interested more with Monica now & is a bit reluctant to have another threesome.

Friday 9th December: Escort contact?

A builder called Paul phones Monica for an escort meeting. However, he wants to see her first for a coffee to see "the goods" before he commits to a proper "meeting".

Saturday 10th December

Monica met Paul, a builder, at a local hotel. However, the hour included caressing & feeling until warmed up, after which they have a good session together, Monica has happy & he paid her for the hour. She mentioned to him she would be available again after her stomach reducing operation, so she hoped to be fully functional for sex again in late December. When she told me, the story, I said that she was ambitious, I thought it may be late January; she needs to gradually ease into sex with me! Why is she so keen to have sex with others & not with me?

All the time she described the meeting & what happened she seemed happy about having an escort client & less apprehensive about escorting &, in fact, excited about it.

Tuesday 13th Dec 2005: Monica has operation on her tummy

Monica went into hospital for a tummy tuck operation on 13th December. She was told she would only be able to do light things for 2-3 weeks & fully recovered within 6-8 weeks. The operation was for reducing all the excess skin from losing weight from her previous larger size. I visited her each night after work.

Ever since she had the breast reduction operation in 2002, she has gradually lost weight making her look much better, lighter & of course sexier, however the now excess skin was an annoyance to her for her looks and was willing to pay for the operation to be done.

Friday 16th (3 days after)

I drove Monica to our home ultra carefully as she could feel every bump in the road. In the house, when comfortable, Monica tells me the doctor said she must do nothing for many weeks.

Sunday 18th December 2005 (5 days after op)

Natalie, a Rwandan friend, phones, & Monica attempts to get out of bed at normal speed, but suddenly pain from the operation stops her in her tracks. She calls & searches for me finding me in the downstairs bedroom of the new house. I made her a cup of tea as she sat down carefully with my help.

Wednesday 21st December 2005 (8 days after op)

We are expecting maybe 20 people mostly Rwandese for the Yuletide/Xmas period of 4 days. We now have the room for all these people & can put up many now. The time will be rather testing as Monica must do nothing, especially no lifting for still weeks!

Many stay for several nights with the large family room looking like a refugee area with 8 people sleeping there in an assortment of things to sleep on. Even though it is carpeted, it must be uncomfortable, but none complained; they were so happy to be with us and share the Yuletide celebrations.

Most leave on the Boxing Day, Monday 26th, while a few stay later in the day due to closer distances from their home. I shuttle many to the Massy-Palaiseau station & other to nearby transport stops.

All the women who came helped clear up the house, and this made the job much easier, especially since Monica was not allowed to do anything. Cloe stayed longer as a good friend of Monica, she is a very conscientious woman. Eventually, she needed to go home on 27th December, so I volunteered to take her. Monica was comfy & had Lennon around, who was actually being helpful & caring, so I did not need to worry about leaving Monica alone. Chilly-Mazerin, where Cloe lived, was only a few kilometres from our home. Arriving outside her flat, she looked at me as if to say "do you want to come in". Pre-empting any verbal invitation, I said I should get back to Monica to ensure she was OK with that kissed her, embraced & left after saying that I should have a coffee with her another time when Monica is better.

Wednesday 28th December: discovery of sexual foursome Rebecca, Jacques & George

Against my advice Monica goes out to Cloe's flat to deliver some things she lent us for the Yuletide period, she also expects to meet another Rwandese woman who is a friend of Cloe. She would, therefore, be away for an hour or so.

Alone for maybe some hours, I read many e-mails from Monica to Rebecca, a friend in Paris, her replies were deleted, but I recovered.

NOW, I know so much that has gone on recently with lame excuses to see friends in Paris. She has been meeting this Rebecca who obviously lives in London & has a flat in central Paris. She obviously uses it as a base when in Paris to meet female & male friends for sex. Monica obviously knows 2+2 with Rebecca & these men Jacques & George. With her escort "work", these meetings with Rebecca & company, plus Jean-Guy and her business course, November was VERY busy for Monica. No wonder she does not have time for me..... I have to be fitted in her busy schedule. All this sex with other men.....& women, & she says to me & her lovers that "I am complicated!" ....errr "hello".

All comms below have original spelling & grammatical mistakes

-----*Original Message*-----
From: Sxxxxx, Rebecca
Sent: 14 November 2005 14:24

To: '*Dawn Monica*'
Subject: RE: Today Nov 5
Oh Hi Monica

Lovely to hear from you. And yes, lets do something the afternoon (and evening if it it works Dec 9. I would prefer you and Jacques, without Geoff for the afternoon. I quite like the idea of my flat or the club at this stage want not to venture to his house just to make it easier for me. Be happy some other time. How can we get out of Geoff without hurting him? I should not have mentioned the date in front of him. Now he clearly knows and wants you and him and me together. I can always say that I can't come until later that day, but then what about the evening?

As far as George is concerned: I am so unhappy. So he is coming today and will stay in my Chelsea flat until Thu or so. We have made no arrangements to meet and I will be damned if I want to meet him at this late stage. He has also asked me whether his No 2 son Romain can be in my flat over Christmas. Of course I said yes. I don't charge for it, it is just at my expense. I will of course always have to have a cleaner come before and afterward. I must be mad. Be my guest, you can have him any time - I don't want him any more, certainly not under these circumstances. He has asked my friend Mathide to find him a new girlfriend!!!!!!!!!!!!!!!! So there we are. As you will appreciate I am upset about him. This is mad. Should I at my age have this hussle??

And what about you? So you have no one to watch over you for the next ten days or so. Are you planning anything special? I am sure Geoff only means well but he should not be so watchful over you.

Let me know please what you think about Dec 9. Gosh if only it was sooner. It seems such a long time away.
Much love
R xxxxxxxxxx

> "*Sxxxxx,Rebecca*" <Rebecca.Sxxxxxx@unitedxxxxx.com> *a écrit:*
> *Me again Monica.*

Please do not say anything to George if you are in touch with him at some stage that I was so upset. I will probably see him today, will see how I feel. He clearly has other interests but so what. I won't mind. But please remember not ever to say anything to him.

As for Geoff? If I were to go out with Ian to the club in the evening (he expects me to) would you go with Geoff? You need to give him something - or can he go with a friend and you go with a friend? Really it is all so very complicated. Next time I won't say anything, i.e. when I am coming back to Paris.

Are you well? Please let me know.

Love and kisses

R xxxxxxxx

-----Original Message-----
From: *Dawn Monica [mailto:xxxx2000@yahoo.fr]*
Sent: *15 November 2005 13:49*
To: *Sxxxxx, Rebecca*
Subject: *RE: FW: Today Nov 5*
Hi Rebecca,

I wish you good meeting with George, I haven't spoke to him since last Saturday when we went to the club with Diane. Don't worry, he will never know about our conversation. I don't phone him and he doesn't either. About Geoff, I don't want to him to come with me when Jacques is with us. He can make his arrangement if he likes. I didn't tell him that you are coming. I must to tell you something about him, when you are coming, whay I am upset with him!!

About me I am very ok but upset with Geoff, I am trying to arrange our flat (which we are selling) and he is in Iran and doesn't want to give order to do something with the floor, he did bad job before and buyer want to that job be done before the 24th of november, Geoff think that he can do that job, he dosen't want to spend many event when is necessary!! That is english (smile)!!!!

Cheers from Paris and love

Monica

Objet: RE: FW: Today Nov 5
Date: Tue, 15 Nov 2005 09:58:09 -0500
De: "Sxxxxx, Rebecca" <Rebecca.Sxxx@unitedxxxxxx.com>
À: "Dawn Monica" xxxxxx2000@yahoo.fr
Hi Monica

Thanks re George. It may not last much longer with him in any case, but there you are, I am still suffering.

Re Geoff – I think I mentioned the date either at the flat or at the club afterwards. And of course I should not have done that. We will just have to say that I can't come until later in the evening and that I am arranging to go out with Ian, which in fact I am. You with Jacques and I will be with Ian. But as we said before you could come with Jacques to the flat – I should be there around 3 p.m. as the last time. Yes, we should talk on our own at some stage. As before I will then go out with Ian for dinner (the usual arrangement – I will pay for the dinner and he for the club).

On Saturday I will probably invite Mathilde for lunch and then must go to the station back to London, around 2.30 p.m. I am getting very concerned about who is in the flat and where, i.e. Chelsea or Paris.

Re the work for your flat: I am sorry to hear the trouble you seem to be having. The man who wants to buy it has he already signed a contract? It really must be difficult with Geoff away. And of course you do not want to lose a potential buyer. But of course I can't advise either way.

Take care, will keep you posted if anything happens dramatically with George. If really of course should drop him considering the way he has behaved in the past. He clearly has a girlfriend (or two or three probably) and then drops them. In that situation the worst thing to do is to fall in love. I must be mad and that at my age.

All the best

Rebecca xxxxxxxxx

Objet: RE: News
Date: Tue, 6 Dec 2005 18:22:28 -0500
De: "Sxxxxx,Rebecca" <u>*Rebecca.Sxxxxx@unitedxxxxxx.com*</u>
À: "Dawn Monica" <u>*xxx2000@yahoo.fr*</u>
Hi Monica

All my sincere apologies, life has been and is so very hectic. At the last minute I decided to let my London painter Alex (from Argentinia) repaint the Paris flat. I am still going to Paris on Fri Dec 9 with Stefan's girl friend's mother, back to London Sat afternoon Dec 10. Janice and I will be working the afternoon of Fri to take pictures down, role up carpets, the bookshelf, etc. Janice is then going out that evening with her special man - all very complicated - I will probably collapse or have a simple dinner (with you perhaps), but I am not going to 2+2 with Ian. I need to be up again early on Sat to continue. Alex is coming midday - I am then taking him out to lunch with Mathilde who might help him whilst he is in Paris - he reckons 11 days for painting etc.

This means that all my plans for this coming trip are up in the air. Somehow we must meet. I have not made any arrangements with anyone for Fri evening - can we meet? Would love to meet your friend of course, but may be not this time, unless Fri evening. Saturday the flat will be in a real mess. I am coming back Dec 21 to put everything back in order. Have visitors in the flat from Dec 23. We clearly must talk.

Tomorrow I have a big meeting, but should be able to chat on Thursday - not tomorrow. The 10th Anniversary dinner meeting of my Intellectual Property Lawyers organisation, very important. I am so sorry about all this, somehow I got pushed into this rush of the repainting of the flat before Christmas, so must go through with it now.

Will be in Paris from Dec 29 to Jan 3, although with Ernie I am sure I can get away an evening or so. If you are in France that time, lets consider what we might do.

Much love
Rebecca xxxxxxxxxxxxxx

-----Original Message-----
From: Dawn Monica : xxxx2000@yahoo.fr]
Sent: 07 December 2005 07:56
To: Sxxxx, Rebecca
Subject: RE: News
Hi Rebecca,

Don't worry about me, but my (1st friend) Jacque wanted to meet you, he was agree to come around your flat (between 7-8 p.m) on friday. Another alternative is, you and I go to his flat (because that your flat will be full)! He is very nice and gentleman (more than George)! He would like to me in contact with you, at moment I don't have his e mail adresse, but you can phone him if you want, his telephone number is: 33 (0) 6-09-65-12-xx, he relly want to talk to you before meeting you. He speaks very good english (as frensh). About me, I am not going to 2+2 either.

Keep in tuch!
Monica

Date: Wed, 7 Dec 2005 06:43:05 -0500
De: "Sxxxx, Rebecca" Rebecca.Sxxxx@unitexxxxx.com
À: "Dawn Monica" xxxxxx2000@yahoo.fr
Hi Monica

Busy all day today but will have more time tomorrow and will then give him a call and of course keep you in touch. So many things to do before this evening.

Please tell Jacques that I will give him a call tomorrow.

Much love
Rebecca xxxxxxxxxxxxxx
-----Original Message-----
From: *Dawn Monica [mailto: xxxxx2000@yahoo.fr]*
Sent: *19 December 2005 09:41*

To: Sxxxxx, Rebecca
Subject: News from Monica
Hi Rebecca,
Juste to informe you that my operation went very well and I am recovering at home.
Cheers from paris
Monica

Objet: RE: News from Monica
Date: Mon, 19 Dec 2005 07:18:35 -0500
De: "Sxxxxx, Rebecca" Rebecca.Sxxxxx@unitedxxxxxx.com
À: "Dawn Monica" xxxxxx2000@yahoo.fr

Delighted to hear this Monica. Please carry on with your good recovery.

Much enjoyed our evening with Jacques (Frid 9th dec). If he wants to stay in my flat in Chelsea for his trip to London in January, please give him my email address so that he can give me his details for arrival and departure. I don't charge for it, but usually guests provide a bottle of champagne per night, nothing spectacular, can be under £20 per night compared with at least £100 in a hotel and of course much much nicer. Just off the King's Road, excellent location.

I am off to Paris Wed morning returning Thu evening – just to get the Paris flat back into order – I have visitors arriving on Friday Dec 23 – so must get it done. No clubbing or anything else Wed night, just a bite to eat I suppose in Le Petit Marcel. Stefan's girl friends's mother is coming again with me – this time she says she will really help me. Little last time because she met her "man". He is so complicated and I wish she could get out of that relationship.

I have George's son and girl friend in my Chelsea flat at the moment. They arrived on Thursday and are leaving tomorrow. I need the flat by 16.45 so must be sure they will have gone by then. His children are really really lovely.

Take care and don't forget to check with Jacques. I know I have his telephone number but won't call him unless he sends me a message or calls me – you know how I am – I do not wish to impose on anyone.

Much love and please do take care

Rebecca xxxxxxxxxxxx

From: *xxxxxx2000@yahoo.fr*

Sent: *28 December 2005 00:02*

To: *Sxxxx, Rebecca*

Subject: *Thank your for your card*

Hi Rebecca,

It was with pleasure to receive your card at my adresse, I was really surprise (in good) for your (gester). about me, I am recovering quickley, I have done 2 weeks after the operation and I can drive, work and dowing few things like (dance)! No sex yet and I miss that. I think that you must be in Paris at moment! Anyway I will see you mybe next year if you come (in January?). I don't have any news from Jacques because he was on holliday and will be back tomorrow. I wish you a wunderfull N.Year part and all things the best for 2006 (lot of love)!

Monica

Hi Monica

Many thanks for your message but how annoying my long reply which I thought I had sent to you from home did not reach you. Anyway basically it was to congratulate you on your quick recovery – keep it up and no doubt soon you will be able to enjoy sex as well. But please be careful.

I am taking Ernie to Paris tomorrow Dec 29 and then on Jan 3 we will travel on the TGV to the SoF returning there back to Paris on the 7th Jan and back to London on the 8th Jan. I will start work again on Jan 9th.,

Don't worry about Jacques. In fact I would prefer if you did not contact him on my behalf. If he is really coming to London in January and wants to see me and/or stay in my Chelsea flat no doubt he will ask you for my telephone number or email address. I don't want to see him unless he takes the initiative. Interesting with George I have come to a very nice friendly situation. In fact I am so far gone the other way that I really would not want to have sex with him now. I am passed that stage and thank god. I have suffered emotionally too with him and rather stay clear of the emotional aspect. He has asked me now whether his daughter can stay in the Chelsea flat in the first week in February. Fine with me. Have so far had his No 1 and No 2 sons. Very nice young men although I did not see them – George sent me a photo of them. Charming young men.

If you want a change of scenery and want to have dinner with Ernie and myself at say Le Petit Marcel, do give me a call on my mobile or send an email – my mobile just in case 00 44 70803 008 2xx. If you want to include Geoff that is fine with me – just let me know.

I am in the office today and have lots and lots of work.
Much love
Rebecca xxxxxxxxx

* Rebecca gave me a key to her flat & said <u>do not tell Monica</u> or give HER the key to her flat, she could not have trusted her?. The key was a VERY ancient type of key that would be difficult to copy by a modern locksmith!

January 2006

Monica has constantly wanted me to adopt Lennon as my son. Before I would do that, I would need to get the approval from my children Steven, Sophie & Dawn for my own peace of mind. I did not want to land them with a brother they did not want. All the kids liked Lennon, even if he was a "lazy lemon", he was fun, always happy & intelligent.

Having broached the subject with them, they were all in agreement to have another brother. I then agreed when Monica raised the question again, "OK, I will adopt Lennon. All his future brothers & sisters agree." Monica was so happy that she embraced me & gave me a wonderful hug & went out to get some Champagne to celebrate.

27th January 2006 before the Chambre du Conseil du Tribunal de Grande Instance in Evry, I legally adopted Lennon as my adopted son.

Sunday 1st January

I found an e-mail reply to Andre (Abidjan) on Monica's computer dated 30th December. She mentioned she already had two Moni Clean contracts & nearly a third! Then, she said that she would register the company soon!

She did not realise Andre was not stupid, & being intellectual, he would see that it is a lie. No company will sign a contract with another company that does not yet exist! What does she hope to gain by such stupid lies? Image is so important to her that she tells lies to enhance her image in front of others.

This is the source of so many rows we had with Monica telling stupid lies that intellectual people cannot believe.

In a roundabout way, without letting on, I had read her e-mail to him. I said to her, "Why should you lie to people & friends to enhance your image. Are you going to tell them, you see so many men with money to enhance your prowess?" Whoops! She is not happy with that statement!

Monica blurts out to me to go out with other women & then see if you are jealous of me with men then.

Sunday 15th January 2006: cracked ribs …3rd time

Training on my own at the athletic ground in the field, they put up a railing during the winter to keep any spectators from the rugby pitch that goes across the throwing circle! This morning, as usual, I vaulted over the railing; however, there was morning dew on it, & my hand slipped, & I landed on my ribs, cracking them….AGAIN!

Subsequent days in the car driving across the cobbled streets of Longjumeau near the church to work was an anticipated agony pain as the car bumped along over the cobbles. I am getting used to going to work now with cracked ribs & walking around the factory VERY carefully.

Monday 16th January

I see an e-mail from Monica to Jean-Guy. She is explaining that she is concentrating on Moni Clean & that she understands that Jean-Guy should concentrate on his wife who has had a bad accident. She says she wants to meet him again sometime in the future. Monica is always giving out the usual sob story that her husband (me) does not understand her & he (me) is complicated!

I see that Andre has e-mailed Monica & that she had phoned him yesterday 19th January, saying she will meet him anywhere to have a shag (his words "small, small" mean a shag).

Wednesday 18th January

Jean-Guy accepts that liaison is probably over & thinks Monica has been playing fair with him. He needs to concentrate on his ill wife. However, Monica requests some sensitive & confidential information on contract pricing information for tenders. He is able to give an indication of an extra €750 twice per year on performance over the contract price demanded. Monica was happy with that information.

Thursday 19th January

Monica gets up early & sends an urgent e-mail to **Casey**, an American escort client. She then says that she needs to wait to see if he has replied.

Friday 20th: Geoff takes up Monica's encouragement to see other women

With constant encouragement from Monica, I finally agree & arranged to meet a woman from the "Meetic" website. I parked as usual in the underground car park near St Michel & walked to the fountain to meet Felicia. She is Hungarian, after recognising each other, I take her down Rue de la Huchette for dinner in the St Michel Latin quarter at one of my favourite Greek restaurants. I normally take business clients when they visit JY factory to this particular resto as they have a small traditional Greek group. The waiters encourage, with some help, to get females to dance on a small moveable table & entice customers to come in the restaurant by smashing plates outside!. Felicia is slim build, about 5 feet 5 inches (1.65m) & could speak English quite well. She lived in the Vincennes area. We got on well, & after a kiss & cuddle, she said that she needed to get the metro home, not accepting my invitation to take her home. I like her, & we could chat about a wide variety of subjects, maybe we might see each other again.

Saturday 21st January

Monica still keeps wanting me to meet other women, so I arrange for number 2. I go into Paris & leave Monica again at home to rendezvous with Kaba (Central African Republic). Again, I arrange to meet at the fountain at Place de St Michel & eat in Rue de la Huchettet for dinner. Again, an introductory meeting, conversation a bit more difficult due to being in French, she again wants to get the metro home.

Monica was so jealous that she went berserk when I got home that evening. She started shouting, became aggressive when I did not respond, started hitting me on the face & then pushed me onto the bed where I aggravated my broken ribs…..oooommf that hurt!

Monica had said to me, ***"to go with other women, because if I go with other women & you will appreciate her & not worry about*** *me with other men".* However, when I did find other women, she is jealous and did not expect me to do what she suggested!

What the hell does she want?

She goes out that evening to see "Satar", a "banker", to arrange banking details & what she would need for Moni Clean. However, she wore a nice fluffy bra & top; the clothes suggested that it would be a meeting, maybe at a club, especially as she arrived home late.

Friday 27th January 2006

I leave early from work lunchtime to walk into the centre of Longjumeau to get to the Credit Agricole bank before it closes for it's 2-hour lunch break at 12.15 pm & arrange for a transfer of € 5,000 from my account to a new Moni Clean account to start Moni Clean Srl.

Sunday 5th February

Alice arrives. She is a gorgeous-looking woman with a RAVA car, living in Epiny sur Orge, & sometimes, comes to the house usually when I am not around. This day, Monica says that she is going to Alice's, but I noticed she packed a number of condoms in her bag when she thought I was not looking. Maybe, she is seeing Alice, but maybe she is meeting another man called Theo, men need condoms for sex, not lesbiens. I investigate when I get the chance & get many names from her SMS messages & e-mails. It is difficult to keep up with all her men. Theo has left a verbal message saying how sexy Monica is & cannot wait to see her again.

What am I going to do? *It seems I have to accept all these men because* **I love Monica, despite all, I still love her. What a state I am in!**

Monica says that she is going out to see Cloe for a few hours. On her return, I broach the subject of whether she has seen any men lately. Monica refuses to answer the question, however, I see a small smirk that tells me she has seen someone. Monica was tired & went to bed early, maybe she was shagged out? I research on her computer & see that she had researched hotels locally for Friday & Saturday.

Monday 6th February

I phoned Cloe from work during lunch time, & while chatting, I asked her the question of any recent visits from Monica. She said that she had not seen Monica for a week! This confirms what I suspected or EXPECTED. I then phoned Alice & arranged lunch with her one more time. I want to chat with Alice to find out more about her & her relationship with Monica & whether they do any "foursomes" involving other men or maybe it is a lesbian relationship.

Having waited a few days to allow the memory to dim, from the weekend, I purposely ask Monica how did she meet "**Theo**" the "banker"? She forgets that it is supposed to be "**Satar**", the banker, & makes some lame reason they met in "Ed" the small local supermarket. When one lies, a small test a few days or weeks later can easily reveal the truth.

Wednesday 8th February 2006

Monica goes to the local Longjumeau notaire at about 5 pm to investigate her "titre de voyage", a temporary passport, for a visit to Dubai before it is cancelled. As the visit was obviously long, I phone Monica twice, & the second time I hear a man's voice in the dead quiet background, no echo, the sound of Monica moving in a leather chair as leather made a distinct sound. On her return, she says she went to Carrefour shopping & met Pierre, the garage owner, so they had coffee when I phoned. I said, "You always lie to me; you are not telling the truth" (not telling her I could hear the leather seat noise when she moved). She pleads innocence, puts her arms around me & says softly, "You know I love you, do not worry".

Why do I melt when I am in her arms? Why am I sharing my wife with other men? Why does Monica want these other men? Why do I put up with all this? What should I do?

I ask her, "Do you REALLY love me?" "...yes, but when you agreed for me to become an escort & took photos to help me, I felt you were encouraging me to be an escort & get money for sex". She did not accept that she was looking forward & excited to see men as an escort. Anyway, I said, "What was the difference between an escort for money & seeing men for a job, contract or being "expenses" or a nice meal, as she was doing now?" She pleaded it was different & that she was doing it for us. She said her only problem was that two out of three escort clients were not turning up. Or were they? Monica never wants to admit to something, even when there is overwhelming evidence to prove it. She suggested I should find a man for her with money like some of my JY agents. She suggested Kamal, my agent & owner of JamAra in Iran & Dubai (SMT), run by his son, Robert, might be suitable because they had money, & she wanted to go to Dubai & have fun.

What is it about the lure of Dubai that so many want to go? It is a concrete jungle with innovative tall buildings and items in the same shops as in Paris or London but more expensive.

Friday 10th: Middle East tour mainly Dubai & Egypt 2006

I leave for Middle East tour incorporating UAE with Dubai & Egypt on Friday 10th & return on Thursday night 16th February. Robert, son of Kamal, the Iranian agent owner, suggests we go to a masseur. I experience a strong man looking like a giant American wrestler pounding me on the massage table, ooohh! I did not know some parts of my body were not so good. However, I found out when he applied full force! Oomph! Lunch in the Dubai golf club overlooking a lake was nice. My visit to Egypt was to see Ashraf of ISS (International Scientific services). He is a very nice & honest man & I will do all my best to help him. **I find Ashraf is probably the only honest man in the Middle East!**

Sunday 12th February 2006

Monica tells me that she got a parking ticket for blocking an access entrance in 9 Cours St Vincent, Issy les Moulineaux, department 92, on Saturday, the 11th evening, while I was in Dubai. As the car is in my name Monica knows I will get the notice, so she freely admits the parking ticket on the phone. I have seen an address in Issy before. Who is it, who is it?

She boasted and danced all night at the party in Issy. She was quite talkative & wanted to know what Dubai was like & said she would love to go there. I described the clubs & the hotels with bars full of women at the higher-end hotels, like the one I was staying at, the Jameireh (Emirates) Twin Towers. The bar at the top of the tower I was in (remember two towers) was quiet, but there was a couple of delicious women sitting at the bar drinking, with a few businessmen nearby. It was early, so I would expect the rich Arabs would arrive later that evening. I had a look around & then went out without getting a drink. I could sense I would be sucked into a situation that I might want to escape or be enticed to pay a lot of money for "something". Even though they looked delicious women, I did not want to break the bank for a bit of expensive sex when I had a beautiful wife at home. In describing the place, Monica wanted me to expand; she was REALLY interested, especially when I described the women & who would probably be frequenting the bar later. I teased her & said I would explain another time. The description of our conversation expanded a few weeks later (1/3/2006).

Thursday 16th February

Theo, one of her boyfriends, seems to be in Turin. Monica asks him in two e-mails, one being via "Serencontre" a male/female mating website about Alexi. I see also Pierre Mburo phones Monica from

Brussels, he says in an e-mail Monica promises she will come June with him. Where? I could not see any reference to where they were supposed to meet. Another e-mail from Jean-Luke.....who is he ?(see May 2006). **My brain hurts keeping up with all her meetings with men!** Why didn't I make that Excel spread sheet for all her men? I can't be bothered to look back on all my notes now to start the spreadsheet.

Friday 17th February 2006

Monica goes to CdG airport supposedly to meet a friend to give a letter & money to someone. But,I am sure she met Pierre somewhere; maybe he was in transit to Brussels & was staying in an airport hotel? Whatever, I noticed she had researched many times the Thalys Paris to Brussels trains probably to meet up with David.

Wednesday 1st March

Monica writes an e-mail to Pierre Mboro quoting him as Mr Mansard 06-115363xx. I also find two e-mails with a photo of her attached. We now have a man John escort 06 23 34 54xx & Pat Perpigna with a new photo & 6 SMS messages in 2 days!

Monica was also using a new mobile phone that she claimed was given to her by a Rwandese friend who bought it in the USA, who, by chance, realised when he got to Europe, it was not compatible. **Errrr, hello,** if it was not compatible in Europe, how come it works for her in France! Monica makes such stupid lies that are so easily disproved!

At night, we chatted about my Dubai trip, & Monica is very interested in my comments & views about Dubai. Wondering why there is so much interest, she says that Claudine, her married Rwandese friend in Epiny sur Orge, who has started a hair business supplying hair to shops in the Paris area (Isle de France), has mentioned she goes there to buy her hair for sale & gets much money from going to top hotels & attracting rich Arabs who stay the night & pay well. The first part is true rich Arabs DO pay a lot for Western women. But her second part was not true; it was just a story she made up. See 3rd March. Hair wigs & extensions come from the USA, China or India, & Claudine said, <u>she **orders them online**</u> from the wholesaler.

Monica then says to me, "Can you imagine me spending a night in a top hotel with a fat Arab?" She then says, he dislikes Arabs & their customs, separating women, no manners, etc.......... however, she kept returning to the subject of going to Dubai specifically to make a lot of money attracting Arabs in these hotels. She said perhaps she would go with Claudine next time using Emirates airline & said if she booked early, she has found it was only € 400 return. Hey, she is SERIOUSLY thinking about it ! She was excited about the thought about going to Dubai with Claudine to earn escorting services & yet she was sometimes reluctant to carry on escorting in France. She said she could make more than € 10,000 in a week. She was so excited, doing her best to whip up enthusiasm in me for her visit. I am not sure I believe it is the Claudine I know who she is talking about, Claudine loves her husband & is very domicile, not the type of person to go wandering. Maybe a man? Perhaps Pierre…or David? I will investigate.

Thursday 2nd March 2006

Unbeknownst to Monica, I had Claudine's phone number given to me at one of the Rwandese monthly meetings. Claudine could speak a bit of English, I had been able to chat with her several times at these meetings. We had also chatted much at various Rwandese parties & struck up a friendship. I had also received a package one day at my apartment that was destined for Claudine that Monica had somehow become involved. Without mentioning it, I had delivered it to the family home in Epiny-sur-Orge & met Claudine's husband, a nice, sincere man.

I decided to phone her from work & suggested we meet for lunch the next day because I wanted to chat over a couple of things, and she agreed.

Friday 3rd March 2006:   The truth about Dubai from Claudine lunch

Claudine was intrigued as to why a lunch meeting locally in Epiny sur Orge, so I told her what Monica had told me the other night. She was shocked & said she had never been to Dubai! All her hair came from the USA & China via online wholesaler. From the monthly Rwandese meetings, I had seen her general demure & that she was happily married with kids. I could not work out how she would be able to justify a week's visit away from the family to go to Dubai, when hair would come from countries that sold hair like China, India or USA. We chatted about many things, especially about Monica & her escapades with men.

While Rwandese women have no problem with cheating on white men, they drew a line with their Rwandese husbands. Monica classed Claudine as a good & close friend, but although I was cautious with what I said, I was able to slowly win over Claudine, so she could open up to me.

Claudine mentioned certain things about Monica's life back in Rwanda: her father was a policeman & then left to buy a shop. I would find out several years later from Faustin in December 2011 the truth (see note 3 & 4). This latest information backed up the truth I had suspected. This is not exactly the big transport business Monica had always told me, so it was all lies, dreams & images. She also said Monica was also well known in Kigali, the Rwandese capital, for "earning money & favours with men".

In closing, I took her back close (but not too close) to her house. Before leaving the car, Claudine said she really enjoyed our lunch meeting & would be pleased any time to have lunch again & gave me a kiss. I promised to take her up on that & then left to return to JY in Longjumeau. Interesting meeting & interesting closing comment from Claudine!

That afternoon at work, I was thinking about all the enthusiasm Monica had for going to Dubai, but it was NOT to go with Claudine to earn money being with rich Arabs! It was, therefore, to spend time with a man, but which one? What of her many men has promised to take her to Dubai? If she did manage to go, how would she suddenly earn, say €10,000, expenses paid unless one of her men was willing to pay? **OH, MY BRAIN HURTS TRYING TO THINK THIS OUT.**

Wednesday 15th March

Monica wanted to see her girlfriend at Issy les Moulineaux around 8 pm & said she had to take a top to a friend (also by coincidence in Issy), being polite she asked me whether I wanted to come, I said, "OK". She quietly drifted off, I noticed she phoned her friend & in French and said that her husband was also coming, so she could not come. Again, later she phoned her friend to say it was too late, so they rearranged the meeting for Friday.

Friday 30th March

Kelly, another of Monica's girlfriends came around the house. While Monica was cooking, Kelly told me quietly that Monica had told her earlier that one of her boyfriends had suggested to her to divorce me, so that she could be with him. Who is this boyfriend who had made this suggestion? Apparently, Monica said to him, "No, I want to stay with my husband". How come she has been so often with this mysterious man who has suggested that? Or maybe it is the constant sob story of lies she spins. I constantly get feedback from friends & e-mails about Monica trying to get sympathy through her sob stories about me not understanding her.

Saturday 1st April 2006

We visited Kelly in an expensive area of the 10th arrondissement near the Gare du Nord train station with high-class flats. Kelly came down & let us in through the various security doors & codes before entering her flat. It was rather modern & had a good view from the "nth" floor of the apartment block. Monica & Kelly chatted in French, with me chiming with my poor French when I felt it was appropriate. The body language told me they were more than just friends! Kelly mentioned she may move to the Longjumeau area because her work is on the southern side of Paris. However, I mentioned the traffic problems of joining rush hour going INTO Paris, whereas at present, she is against the flow & fewer problems. She paused for a thought & then agreed that was a point she had not considered.

6th April

I see a message Dorian F is very interested in the advantages that emerge from your Escort ad. He continues, I would like to know more about your services and prices. Sounds like an Escort client enquiry.

May 2006: Monica invited to become a Free Mason

Monica tells me that Jean-François has recommended Monica to become a Freemason. I knew from previous comms that she had been in contact with him since at least January. If she wanted to be & if they accepted her, she would be an "Orient de France" Freemason based in Saulx les Chartreux.

We start having several nights together during the month where female Freemasons come to chat with Monica, asking questions, looking around the house & chatting with me to size up the situation & Monica's candidacy for joining the Freemasons.

Tuesday 6th June: Monica recommended to join Freemasons

Jean-François comes around the house & spends the night chatting about what to expect. Jean-François was apparently 70 years old was partnered with Nathalie, who was in her 40's. He apparently knows many women & why not Monica? He will be recommending Monica at the next Freemasons meeting on 27th June. He went with Monica to Croix Blanche, an enormous out-of-town retail area south of St Genevieve des Bois, to return a large shampoo carpet cleaner that is used for the professional cleaning of carpets.

While they are out, I am cleaning a few things in the bedroom. I find Monica is reading up on sexual play borrowed from somebody, as well as an "Adam & Eve" online purchasing site selling sexual things & clothes. Not only that, I also found a fully illustrated book Monica bought me on sex & sexual arousal for the opposite sex. I also saw she had been in touch with a sexologist, "Dr Exotic", with several phone numbers. Who is he?

We know Monica likes older men, even 70 years old…Jean-Luke? Again, using her wiles, maybe in getting to be a Freemason she needs to shag him? Watch this space! I know Monica will do virtually anything with men to achieve something, job, money, favours & now Freemasons? I had noticed Monica was spending much time with Jean-François, but I put this down to preparation for the Freemasons. However, on reflection, she is always VERY early to meet him prior to any event starting. An example was the first informal meeting at 6 pm, when she met him at 4 pm at Porte Doree near the peripherique. Jean-François is apparently the only man in the female Freemason lodge & he needs to "sponsor" her. I found out he lives at an address in Rue la Bruyere, 75009 Paris St Lazare area. The building is typical "Haussman" style with 4 upper floors, probably built in the mid-1850 of stone.

Saturday 1st July 2006

Monica goes to a "Treasure Hunt" organised by the female Freemasons & leaves at 7:45 pm, although the meeting is at 9 pm at the Marie de Paris, near the river Seine. Did she meet Jean-François beforehand somewhere & do something together? Another man to add to the list, I suppose. Hey, I am running out of ink & paper!

Wednesday 26th July 2006: discovery of receipt for new furniture

While Monica has a shower, I find in her handbag an order receipt for a new table & chairs, a large sideboard with a Plasma TV space for € 4,800 dated 8th May from "Mobile de France" in Croix Blanche with delivery of early September. I quickly photocopy it before she comes out of the shower.

Thursday 27th July 2006: Row about furniture order. Monica calls police when I am in bed

After work, I went to Mobile de France in Croix Blanche to see if they had the furniture Monica had ordered on the show. Yes, they did. I took photos of the various parts of the furniture assembled.

Later that evening, I confronted her with the fact I knew about the furniture order. We have a flaming row, whereby she then attempts to stop the row by calling the police. I am fed up & go to bed as usual with nothing on. I am in bed naked when the police (man & woman) arrive in our bedroom! They asked me to get out of bed, I obliged, the policewoman quickly beckoned me to get dressed. I explained to them there in the bedroom why I was angry, and she ordered new furniture to the value of €4,800 with money she did not have. I will have to pay to stop being blacklisted as well as her. They are understanding about the situation, & after our conversation, they then chat with Monica for 20 minutes before leaving.

Friday 28th July

I went to Mobile de France in Croix Blanche to see the furniture shop manager. I said I wanted to cancel the order. However, the contract was with Monica, & they could not do it as the trial period of 10 days had expired. We tried to work out what to do, as Monica has no money, so it would be ME that foots the bill. I will have to see the advocate about HOW to cancel this order before delivery & her cheque that would bounce, giving ME a blacklisting as well as her & Moni Clean.

Monday 30th July 2006

During the lunch break, I went to an advocate in Longjumeau & fixed an appointment for the following day.

Tuesday 1st August 2006

I had a meeting with the advocate in Longjumeau after work with a copy of the order to see how we can cancel the order with Mobile de France. He says he fully understands & would write a letter to her & Mobile de France.

Monday 7th August 2006

Monica opens a letter from the advocate with a copy of a letter from Mobile de France. Monica started shouting, "It's none of your concern," when I asked if she got the letter from the advocate & read it. She started accusing me of reading her letter, how could I? She had just opened it! Anyway, I made her aware I had a copy of it, sent to me from the advocate.

I had not seen much activity with boyfriends & lovers lately in the last few months, maybe the lack of sexuality & concentration on Moni

Clean explained this? I saw she was not communicating much on her Hopesperance2000 e-mail address nor on her yahoo site address.

18th August - 27th August 2006: UK holiday with Lennon – his 2nd visit to England

Due to Monica's work, we decided I take Lennon to the UK with me alone & visit my friends & relatives. On the ferry, Lennon was impressed with the sight of the cliffs of Dover & the excitement of visiting England for the 2nd time. From Dover, we went straight up to Stoke on Trent to stay with Steven, my son. During one day's messaging, I get a message that annoys me regarding Monica's men & Paul. I get a message from him as he promised me that they "had a good time". However, when I asked on the phone, how did she get on with Paul, she said she had not seen him! I was so annoyed that I spilt the beans with Lennon regarding her affaires. He doesn't react whether in defence or astonishment, he just listens & takes it in as I unload my frustrations.

The rest of the holiday went well, & we both enjoyed our time both south, including Sophie & up north with Steven. On the first day, we spent the day locally in the Stoke area, shopping in the town centre. Of course, most nights were spent in the pub playing darts or bar billiards. Saturday night was a pub crawl, resting at the fourth one for the lock-in*.

* "A lock-in" is where, after licensing hours the land lord/lady call "last orders" then when most of the customers have departed, he/she will close the curtains, lock the doors with the "regulars" still inside the pub & then carry on drinking as "guests". No money is supposed to be exchanged...... but....

We did a grand tour, including York, a Viking city by them called Yorvik, meandering the old town with the ancient lanes & shops called "Shambles" (called so due to the local butchers in the middle ages), the famous cathedral "The Minster" & getting a ride on a double-decker bus from the "park & ride" outside the town. Near Steven, we saw the unique "Anderton canal boat lift" in Norwich, that lifts the canal barges up to a new height to the next stretch of the canal. Due to the height (50 feet / 15.2m) it would have meant a number of locks that are eliminated by this unique barge lift built 1875. Conway castle in north Wales & the subsided (& now dis-used road due to constant subsidence) Mam Torr pass on the Pennines as we meandered around the north of England.

We said goodbye to Steven as Lennon & I travelled south via Oxford & finally rested the night in High Wycombe for the evening meal with Sophie & Roo. Onto Essex, later we visited Don & Catherine, his girlfriend who had a house in a small Suffolk village & met up in Ipswich, returning to Catherine's house. Lennon liked riding a motor mower around her large garden in Bidford. We stayed with Nan in Chelmsford & took her out for a ride to Maldon, an old Anglo-Saxon burgh town where the crucial battle of Anglo-Saxon Earl Byrhtnoth in 991AD with the Vikings was lost.

My last stay on a Saturday was with my old school friend, Richard. We went to Ashford, a small market town centre, to look at the shops & see an original circa 1916 1st world war tank in the square..

Sunday 17th

We left early to catch the mid-day ferry back to France.
We returned & was greeted Monica warmly, with Lennon bubbling with explaining all the key things he discovered. We discussed much about the English & England.
It was interesting to hear the observations of Lennon about England & the English:
His observations as a foreigner were as follows:

- ➢ In supermarkets lots of fresh milk & a small area for UHT milk. In France, there are maybe 10 metres (30ft of UHT milk & about 1 metre (3ft) fridge of fresh milk

- Can buy fresh milk to drink in restaurants, cafes, snack bars, it is impossible in France to drink milk, French do not drink milk.

- Can buy cigarettes in supermarkets, which is not possible in France, only available in a "Tabac".

- Pubs are very careful regarding licensing laws Over 18 years old. Many exclude anyone they THINK is under 21 to ensure that an old looking 17 year old is not serve alcohol. However, for many city & small village pubs the "lock-in" enables one to drink until the land lord decides it is time for bed. When there is a lock–in then it is easy for under age kids to have a drink.

- Many TV ads in UK are; investment, banking, insurance, job help etc. In France rarely see anything like that.

- Old buildings preserved, renovated for all to enjoy. Rather than "……it's old, pull it down & replace it with a new building …."

- The enormous number of pubs (even though many have closed) in England, & in the middle of the countryside one can find & enjoy a drink in a pub. In towns all the pubs (on our pub crawl) were full.

- National Express coaches that go from major cities for about £10 or less return (2006, just checked 2024 & now £11).

- Especially in the north of England, the number of factories is even higher in small towns. Per person England is still an industrialised nation, even though of course the total amount of industry is greater in the USA, Germany & Japan.

- Hedges around all the fields, making narrow country roads with passing places blind & "interesting" especially with the many sharp bends.

- Southern country roads derive from old circa 700-900 AD Anglo Saxon "strip farming", where the serf had his own strip of land to work on his 7th & free day, while he worked for the lord of the manor for the other 6 days. These strips needed a path around the fields, hence the roads zig-zag, especially in Essex.

- The contrast of the beauty of the Pennines, the Welsh mountains & then the totally different southern agricultural areas of the south east & East Anglia.

- Driving on the left-hand side of the road was an experience for Lennon.

- The number of pubs & clubs in Britain where they have live bands on a Friday &/or Saturday. In the north, there are many "Working Men's clubs", derived from the "workers" in the factories clubbing together to own a club they can run & share a good time at low cost.

- Lennon was amazed at the practice of "dropping in" to see a friend or neighbour without an appointment or prior notice. We did this on four occasions all welcomed us in with the customary invite for a "cup of tea".

Monday 28th August 2006

I read Monica had had two e-mails from Pierre Buro & Andre K unread. Andre K was desperate for a shag with her & was getting frustrated at no communication for an arrangement. She had not communicated with Andre K since about March/April time when he wanted to meet her in Ghana. Alternatives were Frankfurt or London when she signed off "I love you". I am not sure whether that was sincere or just titillating him, like she does so well with men's e-mail below. Spelling mistakes not corrected

Hi Dear;

I am very busy (busyness) and forget everybody!!! How are you then? How are you doing? When are you coming over here? If you come in London, I will probably come to see you!

I love you.

Cheers

Andre kxxxxxxx a écrit :

Hi my dear

Where are you... You have been too quiet for too long. Good day

Andre K

Hi Monica

Where are you? I miss you. Send me email pliz.

Regards

Andre K

It rained heavily that night & flooded the road outside in the corner, threatening to enter house number 1, a large house on the corner. I took photos of the flood for evidence to Kauffman Broad, the builders, to correct the drainage.

Tuesday 29th August 2006

While I was still as work, our new house neighbours at number 1 came & gave us a Syrian cloth & invited Monica to go over to them. She went over, had tea there & returned before I got home. In the evening, she let slip as she had been over there several times to see the chap while the wife was out. Although I had taken photos of the flash flood in the road that mainly affected outside their large house, the Syrian chap had informed Kauffman & Broad of the situation that needed to be fixed.

Monica is constantly instant messaging Emmanuel G in Afrique Conseil in Cotonou, Benin reference Benin president cleaning project. I cannot see the comms properly now as my access has been restricted by Lennon fiddling with Monica's computer. Is this purely business or more? She was in Instant message chatting for about 30 minutes plus last night.

Previous experience tells me to get the work she wants, she will go with him alone, & eventually, go to bed with him to extract her wishes of work etc. That is the way she works: melt men with her looks, provides sex & then extracts job, services or money.

Monday 4th September

Jean Lall-Loeuillet, who lives in St. Dennis north of Paris, sends Monica a loving e-mail, saying she is beautiful. By the language in the e-mail, he has already met her or has received a photo of her.

Thursday 7th September

Andre K is on the move again & wants to meet Monica by re-starting comms between them; she is obviously keen to continue playing with him. She mentioned to Virginie in Cotonou that she plans to go to Cotonou in October, accompanied by another man from another society. Who is this? Andre K? Could this be another plan to meet again, or just a Moni Clean business colleague?

I also notice another e-mail with Jean LL, where she had sent more sexy photos of her, however, she still refers to him as "vous". By addressing him as "vous" she is distancing him rather than intimately.

I managed to recover a history of comms to & from Andre K they were arranging meetings several times when he was in Europe.

--- Dawn hope <xxxxx2000@yahoo.fr wrote:
OK. I will confirm that asap.

Cheers

Andre kxxxxxx <xxxxxx@yahoo.com a écrit :

Hi Monica

Tentatively the dates are 1 June on my way to Ghana So we can spend 1 - 3 June and on my return it will be on 15th. So we can make 15 - 17 June. We can enjoy twice n'est ce pas? I would really love to see you after such a long time. If there are any changes I will let you know... I love you trop!

Andre K

--- Dawn Monica wrote:

Hi Andre,

Frankfurt could be also convenient for me but give me the dates and I can make plan for now.

Cheers

Andre kxxxxx a écrit :

Hi Dear

I will go to Ghana for 2 weeks at the end of May or beginning of June. I will travel either through London or Frankfurt. Do you prefer London or Frankfurt.

I can make arrangements to stay for say 2 - 3 extra days so we can have real good fun. Let me know if London or Frankfurt is more convenient

Loving you trop!

Andre K

Thursday 20th September Egypt / Dubai trip

I travelled to Egypt & spent the Egyptian weekend (Friday/Saturday 21/22) with Ashraf, my agent, tour the pyramids & buy locally a ½ litre of perfume oil for Monica.

Tuesday 24th: In evening, I travelled to Dubai & stayed there on business & return home on Thursday 26th evening.

September seems a fairly quiet month with e-mail/SMS men activity & news as Monica concentrates on Moni Clean work. Although, I learnt on 22nd January 2007 that this was not so.

Friday 6th October

A chap phones at 7:30pm while Monica is still out working, asking for Monica. In my normal professional manner, I asked for his name & phone number so that Monica could phone him back. He was reluctant to leave his name & phone number, but I insisted it could be important, so he left monsieur Assenceon & the mobile number. Later when Monica returned, she said she did not know him. However, the next day, she makes a note with his correct spelling, sends a message & signs off "Je t'aime"!

Wednesday 11th October 2006

Monica meets a Freemason woman at our home & sends her CV I made for her for application to join the lodge.

Friday 13th October

Andre K is asking Monica in an e-mail why no answer from his question a month beforehand? She is rarely logging in to the xxxxxx2000 address. I know she suspects I have seen some of her e-mails, so maybe she has started another e-mail address?

Friday 13th to Sunday 15th October 2006: Monica Brussels trip

Monica leaves work early & goes to Brussels to be with friends & supposedly to see a chap about selling wine in bulk. While I could not understand why it would takes so long to negotiate buying bulk wine, she probably wants to use the excuse to see many Rwandan friends in Brussels.

Wednesday 18th October: Radisson sugar

I find in Monica's handbag a Raddison SAS lump of sugar. Where did this come from? Monica's trip to Brussels or central Paris? Watch this space…. Research finds the answer.

Thursday 19th October: Raddison hotel card

I find in Monica's work briefcase a visiting card Raddison hotel EU central Brussels, so this where the lump of sugar came from. OK, so she has been to Brussels central Radisson hotel on her last visit. With whom? When did they meet? Where did they meet? Why did they meet? The sugar must be from her last visit to Brussels.

(I would find out much later it was David Vloeberghs, Gisele's partner).

Saturday 21st October 2006

I see on Monica's mobile she met with Pat Mburo during the Friday 13th (the day she went to Brussels), I also found a label from "Victoria's Secret" something a visitor from USA might give. At present I do not know of a Victoria's Secret shop in Paris yet. I find out later it was Virginie from Cotonou who gave her something.

When you have absolutely no confidence in your wife, one becomes paranoid about everything, however, before accusations, I DO check things out, before confronting Monica with the facts.

During the rest of the month, Monica has messages from various men: Theo, Pat Mburo and Moise, all asking after her & wanting to meet her for lunch or even dinner…….or…

One SMS message to Moise confirmed what I suspected, Monica has started a new e-mail address Mxxxxx@yahoo.fr. He phones her mobile phone, while Monica is occupied having a shower & she does not see the message until AFTER I had read it. He plans to meet her in Paris. He then phones the fix number, & I ask for the man's name.

I say I will pass on any message, one suspects that not wanting to sound suspicious he gives his name & asked that Monica phones him about some business. I sent an SMS to Monica with the information. She phoned him later & said he was looking for a job in Moni Clean.

On a daily basis, I am seeing messages from men wanting to meet her for lunch, for dinner or anything that by the sign-off e..g. je t'aime is **not** business. **It is affecting me at work, I am still thinking about her various men even when I am training.** Normally I lose myself in sport when I am throwing or doing weight lifting, not now, I cannot relax. Pierre Buro keeps cropping up increasingly.

November: €5,000 loan to Agnes

Agnes arrives in France & asks for me to loan her €5,000. She needs to buy many speciality things to take back to Cotonou for her resto "Livingston". I make a cheque out for that amount to her.

Wed 15th November 2006

I read more SMS messages from Pierre about how sexy she looks & what he wants to do with her the next time they meet. That evening, we have a row. I said that it was not natural for Monica to cheat on me, be with all these men, & now we have Pierre MBuro as well as her regular boy friends like Paul & all the others. I said that I wanted her to apologise to me for possibly endangering me with somebody else's AIDS via her sexual encounters. She goes mad at me worrying about AIDS. She says "She is seeing these men for us & Moni Clean business. **Anyway, I am not stopping you from seeing other women!"** Really? What am I supposed to make from that comment, free to go with different women with her approval? How often has she said; you can go with other women if you want, then you will not keep pestering me about going out with men. She got upset the last time when I actually DID see a woman.

Thursday 16th November 2006: I ask many questions of myself

Monica goes to work & forgets her mobile phone in the bedroom. Never one to give up an opportunity, I read all her SMS comms & inspect the address list at leisure.

Reading messages from other men like "I love you & want to be with you even in the shopping mall, send more photos of you."

All this makes me feel an outsider. What is it they can provide I cannot? What is it Monica wants? She claims always it is for us, but **why am I supposed to share my wife with other men shagging her?**
Why am I accepting it?
It must be more than just love, is it some African Voodoo spell over me?

I read one message from Monica to one man, Mudeli, "Leave me alone, stop harassing me..." & then, instead of French, she finished off by writing in Rwandese Kinyarwanda. Moise was getting impatient with "appel moi!!!"

Another call message from a Jacques Latriqiu seemed keen to see her again asking for a lunch appointment, finishing off with the now customary bissous (kisses).

It seemed Monica was frustrating a lot of men by leading them on & then dangling them on a length of string for something. What for? If I know her well, it is to extract something she needs, a contract, a job, influence or just fun.

Chapter 16

Saturday 18th November 2006: Meet Rachael for the first time at an indoor athletic meeting

I had a shot put competition at an open indoor meeting at Viry Chatillon. While warming up, I saw a lovely-looking black lady with highly patterned fishnet tights under her skirt, who I saw was throwing a medicine ball to her athlete daughter. I realised I wanted to chat her up, but realised I would have to do this in French. I walked around for a couple of minutes thinking of what I would say. I mentioned to her that she was putting more effort throwing the medicine ball than her daughter. She said her daughter was doing the shot put; I said I was throwing the shot and mentioned I was a throws coach. Apparently, the clincher was I gave her my JY visiting card, nobody in France does that, she said later. She said her name was Rachael, originally from Martinique. She contacted me that night to ask whether I could coach her daughter, Zoe, the next day when I train at Longjumeau. I said that I would.

We had Rwandese family members invited for a party "chez-nous" that evening; however, Jado turned up as well, he is not family. Why did Monica invite him? In spite of this intrusion, all went well, & we spent a nice evening. Monica is happy after all the guests had left, so would I get anything tonight? I look at her like a little dog wanting a pat. She looked at me as if to say "OK, you can have your shag." I am getting used to taking Cialis that lasts 4-5 days, it had a great advantages over Viagra. Caressing her pussy started to get results then her legs opened & in goes James. She lifted up her bum so that I could penetrate further in. Am I getting fitter, is it the Cialis or is it a great performance by James? Monica is really happy at the end of it all. I could tell because she said I was getting better. Am I up to the standard of her other men I thought?

Sunday 19th November 2006

I went training as usual & saw Rachael with Zoe joining me to get some coaching for throwing. After training at the Longjumeau stadium, I returned to see Lennon, who was just vegging out as normal. I asked him if he had finished all his homework. He replies that he does not care & obviously has little intention to work. Monica & I read his letter from school about his constant late attendance. Monica is getting very frustrated with Lennon's attitude to school work. He is over-confident about his ability to get the required BAC (Baccalaureate) grades & possible further education. He is becoming very difficult to manage due to laziness & could-not-care-less attitude.

When Monica returns home, she also sees Lennon doing nothing & gets angry at him. Where was Monica today? Probably with another man? My mind thinks up so many scenarios with her & her men.

Sunday 3rd December 2006: 2nd session with Rachael & Zoe

After Sunday's training down at the stadium with Rachael & Zoe as well as my other athletes, I saw communications with Marie-Solonge about the female freemasons. She is an ordinary member, not a high-order member, but the comments between them make me suspect something, maybe nothing. Then, I have seen Monica in action with other women, so I know she likes women.

Thursday 11th December: Row over men & no €5,000 cheque Decide to take out Rachael.

Monica & I have another row over her men, "Why are you angry about me being with other men? **I do not stop you from seeing other women. Try one & then you will see I am so good for you,**" she replies.

I find out that a friend of Agnes gave the €5,000 loan re-payment cheque to Monica. She has pocketed it & won't pay me MY money that I loaned to Agnes.

I decide that I might as well do as Monica says & take her up on her offer. I will go out Saturday night to prove to her I will not stay at home watching TV & worrying about with whom she is with. I decided I would ask Rachael to go out with me on Saturday night to a local nightclub in Rungis. I phoned Rachael the next day & fixed the arrangement for Saturday.

Sat 13th December 2006: Night club with Rachael

Rachael & I go to a big Rungis nightclub bridging over A7. It has 5 dance floors, each concentrating on a different type of music as it spans the A7 dual carriageway. We left around 1am for home. I dropped Rachael off before going home. Monica had obviously gone out with some man & didn't arrive home until maybe 3 am when she woke me up from my sleep.

Sunday 14th December: Rachael wants to finish with me #1

Rachael sent me an SMS saying she wanted to stop seeing me due to me being married & that I wanted to stay married to Monica. She sees no future in the relationship. I am disappointed. We got on well, but I can understand she does not want to hear all my moans about Monica, each time we meet & are together.

Wednesday 20th December: Rachael regrets her SMS wanting to finish with me

Rachael sent me an SMS saying she regrets wanting to stop with me due to me being married & that she still wants to go out with me. All is fine again.

More comms (below) from Andre K after they had a phone call Tuesday (his computer date setting was wrong). He talked "being together as husband & wife" "*It will be sweet to have small small* once again after a long time….*" *this Andre K's terminology of having a shag together.

Hi Monica Where Are You

⬜ *Andre kxxxx <kxxxx@yahoo.com>*

Afficher   Vendredi, 20 December 2006, 14h27mn 13s

À :   Dawn Monica <xxxxx2000@yahoo.fr>

Hi my Sweetheart Monica

I was also quite happy to speak to you yesterday. I felt sweet talking to you. I had nostalgia about all those sweet moments we spent together as husband and wife. It was nice n'est ce pas?

I am happy that you are busy with your business. I am sure you feel happy and fulfilled doing something you enjoy. It appears to be a busy and well equipped business. Keep it up

I am seriously thinking about leaving the Bank. I have a plan. 1). I have two trucks making business in Malawi - I want to increase the number of the trucks; 2) I want to buy a number of buses to operate a serious bus company covering all the major towns and cities in Malawi and also doing international routes to Tanzania, Mozambique, Zimbabwe and Johannesburg; 3) I want to seriously engage in agro-business — thus buying agricultural produce, processing and selling or exporting; 4) Solar energy is another business I want to do - to install solar panels in rural schools, clinics and private homes at least those who cannot get connected to electricity.

I am busy writing a business plan so that I can secure a soft loan for my business. Once I am able to get that money I will leave the next day.

I look forward to meeting you soon. I will tell you my mission programme, so that we plan where and when to meet. It will be sweet to have **small small*** once again after a long time.

Love you plenty

Andre K

* Andre's term for sex together

Wed 27th December 2006

As I know Andre, from both my discovery of him in bed with Monica at the hotel before our wedding in February 2003 & as a Monica-invited guest, I decided to do an innocuous e-mail to Andre to find out information & try to circumvent problems.

Geoff wrote: 27/12/2006

Hi Andre

At this time of festive Yuletide season I often think of people I have not communicated for a while.....It is a long time since we communicated. How are you? Are you divorced yet? Last time I seem to remember you were contemplating the prospect as she was living in Malawi and you in Tunis and there seemed to be no feeling between you two. I imagine Tunis is still the same as before, no women except those serious to marry with all he "normal" marriage protocol in muslim countries. How do you cope with the frustration?

I am sure I would go mad!!!

So how are your missions? Do you visit interesting countries & work missions?

I travel much more now than before, always away somewhere in EMEA (Europe, Middle East and Africa), usually about 3 missions per month. I have to remind myself what home looks like!! Monica wanted me at home more, but I was absent for about 50% of the time, this year. This caused a problem when she was in Benin and me in Dubai/Saudi Arabia/Egypt, so Lennon was alone for a week and was having a wonderful time with friends at our home. When I arrived home the home was like a pig sty, even after 4 days, he did nothing to tidy up.

Monica, well she has progressed with "Moni Clean" a little by expanding her capabilities with import / export..... wine being the latest addition, but we still have problems with helping me with the mortgage due to no contributions from Monica. She is finding things difficult with negative cash flow at about € 400 per month, with income at about € 2,000 and outgoings at €2,400 per month, but always she paints a wonderful picture to her friends.....I keep quiet when she speaks with friends, IMAGE is everything with Monica.

I am not sure where she will be at the end of the financial year...... April with no salary taken and many personal expenses (for her and me) not claimed! I keep saying to her because I know more about her business than anyone else (she is not honest even with her accountant friend), I can speak the truth without prejudice, she will not speak about problems. If she does not rectify her problems she will be bankrupt by the summer.

Still she is so happy to be her own boss, even though she is still hopeless with figures (2+2=5!!.... so spend the profit of 1!! We have a saying in English "some people see things thorough" Rose tinted glasses. Monica will not listen to me as she says " I am negative " ...which hurts, because I see things as they are and not as she says they should be....She is very head strong, which has its advantages ...and disadvantages.. I like to be PRO-Active.....not RE-Active

When she does not want to listen..... What can I do?

I have appealed to several people (with the same text) for advice, now with this e-mail, I appeal to you to offer advice. She will not listen to anything I say that is different from what she thinks.

Frustrated and I look forward to your advice and.......... "General life of Andre"

Cheers

Geoff

PS Happy Yuletide and New Year!

**

Hi Geoff

My wife and I managed to reconcile our major differences. So divorce is no longer in the horizon!

Regarding your problem with Monica, I believe it requires honest, transparent and heart to heart discussion to enable her see what you are seeing and you to see what she is seeing. That way both of you will be singing from the same page, so to say...

Had a wonderful xmas and looking forward to yet another powerful New Year celebration...

Later

Andre K

2008

January 2008 JB (Jean-Baptiste) & Jeremy start to come training to me at Longjumeau stade for coaching. JB & I had met at the regular Chelles throws meets, he liked my discus technique & wanted me to coach him in that technique. He brought Jeremy, a young lad with lots of potential, with him after some while & also Yves, the French No 1 shot putter at the time. Yves wanted me to coach him more to do with discus as he had a shot coach, including his father. However, unfortunately, he died in a car crash, not so many months later.

Mon 8th Jan 2007: I started to do weights at Grigny. The facilities were better than in Longjumeau.

Tuesday 17th - Friday 19th January

Monica is away in Bruxelles to see a person supposedly to sell her bulk wine. Remember, she ordered a palette of Madiran 2003 wine. I would find out much later that this was to meet & stay at a Radisson hotel with David (remember the sugar & card).

Saturday 20th January

Jado arrives at 7 pm while a Freemason assessor is there doing, in effect, an interview for joining the Masons. Jado realised he was unwelcomed by the glare & off-hand reception he received from Monica, & he left quickly after I made him tea in the kitchen. Why did he come?

I notice that Monica goes to "Croix Blanche", a large retail park, often in the last weeks since the start of the New Year. Does she meet him there? I then remembered he was the only non-family member to be invited at the party 18th November. He was like a "fish out of water" because he did not know anyone, remembering it was a family party. Why did Monica invite him, is he some local boyfriend, what does he have to offer Monica? He has no charisma, it was some 2-3 years ago that Imogen, Monica & Jado went off somewhere. He must be able to offer something Monica wants.

Sunday 21st January

I went to training, as usual, meeting Rachael & Zoe. Afterwards, I went to her place in Grigny & then we walked around Viry Chatillon Lake chatting all the time about all different subjects.

Jean-Pierre from Switzerland phones, who is he? Is he the Swiss escort punter back in Nov 2005? During Monica's stay in the other bedroom last week, she re-visited the secretary medical books. Why is she looking for a new avenue of work?

Monday 22nd January 2007

I phoned Claudine, she said during our lunchtime conversation that Pierre, Jado & Claudine had dinner at our house when I was in Dubai in September 2006. However, Monica never said there were three of them, and she had said it was Claudine & Francoise...... that is VERY different. I also asked what was Jado & his relationship with Monica. Apparently works for Etam in the Chatlet area in Paris & was originally in the Congo & is a friend of Pierre Mburo. Pierre & Claudine left separately before Jado..........mmmmm.

Sunday 28th January

I went to training, as usual, meeting Rachael & Zoe. Afterwards, I went to her place in Grigny & then we walked around Viry Chatillon Lake, discussing various subjects again, Monica & her affairs being the foremost subject, but also my impending Middle East trip.

Friday 9th February

Julienne is invited to come chez-nous that night to sew professionally my suit that I need for Saturday. It has some damage. I am going away again on Saturday to the Middle East for ArabLab exhibition in Dubai. I need to be there to help set up the exhibition for

Sunday. The first day of the week in the Gulf states, I will go to various Middle East countries & as part of the 2 week trip.

Agnes has a cash flow problem again & asks me for a short-term loan Transfer of £6,700 (~ €10,000 at the time) to Agnes

Sat 10th Feb 2007: Middle East tour KSA

The first leg, as usual, was Kuwait for my first working day on Sunday (equivalent to Monday in occidental lands). At the time* the Gulf states' weekend was Friday/Saturday & KSA (Kingdom of Saudi Arabia), & Iran was Thursday/Friday. For this reason, I would plan my 2-week tour to coincide with these differences to maximise my time there. I would always move to Al Khobar in Saudi Arabia via Bahrain** & taxi on Thursday night. A day off on the holy day of Friday, ready for work on Saturday.

* Saudi Arabia has since realigned with other Gulf States with their weekend to Friday/Saturday

** To arrive in KSA by plane can takes anything from 2-6 hours in the queue waiting at the immigration desk, (a colleague found out later waiting 6 hours in the queue, ignoring my advice). I found that flying to Bahrain & then get a taxi across the causeway was much quicker with less than 30 minutes at immigration & then a one hour ride to Al Khobar.

Tuesday 13th February 2007: Dubai

I had booked up my usual Dubai hotel, the Marco Polo. It is not as expensive as many more first-class hotels, but I prefer this one for several reasons. 1) It is less expensive, I don't like wasting money even if it is at company expense. 2) It has 4 nightclubs within the hotel & thus is able to sell alcohol. I usually go to the nightclub that had a resident Sri Lankan group that is pretty good, & eventually, over the years, got to know me well. I sometimes went to the Russian bar where the ladies sing, sometimes to the Indian bar & once to the Pakistani bar, all for a change. I usually went up to my room at about 11pm local time as I normally have a hard day's work the next morning.

I phoned home from my hotel room & got no reply from the home phone nor Monica's mobile phone, I eventually gave up. I went to bed but couldn't sleep, wondering what Monica was up to. I decided to phone again at 10:30pm French time. Monica answered & said she had been with Julienne. I later checked with Claudine, who, by chance, rang me on Wednesday 14thFeb, while I was at the ArabLab exhibition. She said Julienne had been with us on Saturday but had not mentioned meeting Monica again so soon afterwards. Why does Monica ALWAYS lie to me.

16th Feb

I communicated, while in Dubai, with Agnes about Monica stealing the €5,000 cheque, & now I had a cash flow problem, so I needed the latest loan of €10,000 urgently that Agnes promised to repay me quickly. I never got a reply to pay me back as requested.

De: Agnes Mxxxxxxx   REDACTED

A: xGxxxxxx@aol.com

Sujet: RE: Money € 10,000

Date: Lundi, 23 Février 2009 17:33

Hi Geoff

I just read your message (im in south africa right now), I'm planning to be in France in March and i will bring your Cheque and Monica promised me she will give your 5 000 euros back at the same time. I'm very sorry for the late payback and am very upset that Monica didn't give you the cheque. For the rest, I don't know what really happened...I will contact you once i am in France (a few weeks from now)

Regards,

Agnes

To: mxxxxxxxx@hotmail.com

Subject: Money € 10,000   REDACTED

Date: Mon, 16 Feb 2009 13:24:35 -0500

From: xGxxxxxx@aol.com

CC: geoff.tyler@jobinyvon.fr

Hi Agnes

since I have been in direct contact with Monica's family & friends, I have learned much about a VERY shady past. The history she told me about her family being massacred in the Rwandan war was fabrication, for example her father died of AIDS/SIDA in prison as a genocide perpetrator ~ 2001 & that may explain why she did not want to identified by those who know her past in Rwanda (amongst other activities). I am researching her past in Rwanda & reading e-mails written in Kinyarwanda I now find that she planned from the beginning to marry a rich white (sucker) & drain all money from him by various means & then dump him for another. She said so in an e-mail to a dear friend of hers, that I have recently had translated from Kinyarwanda to French. She has said to several "friends" her intentions AND what she did, that now I am investigating through a web of lies & false declarations. I am finding that she will accuse me of various things that really upset me to think how desparate this woman is & to what depths of lies to keep the house....her dream.

Monica stole my € 5,000 cheque & she has NO INTENTION of giving back to me....that is the way she is. This leads me to the urgent cash flow problem question I have. Agnes, I lent you € 10,000 late Nov 2006, with the intention that I was going to get this back max 2 months later approx January 2007. It is now Feb 2009 & I am not getting "good vibes".

Can you not borrow the money from David to pay me back.? Monica I am sure will pay YOU the € 5,000, but not ME.

I could speak with David if you like.

At least can you photocopy the cheque stub so that I can use this in police action.

I have the tribunal March 19 & now as time is short I will be cutting corners to get information quickly to prove her past & lifestyle as a prostitute that she was & still is (but more sophisticated). YES, she boasted that Germans pay more than the French! & was keen to go to St Tropez for rich clients. Does this sound too improbable? I have so much information including her secret e-mails to clients. I have been shocked to the core to what I have discovered in the last 3-4 months as family & "friends" have opened up on the real Monica. God I was a sucker & Sooooooo much makes sense now.

She is chasing at present David the "common law wife" of Gisele. In Monica's greed for a big house & money & influence as part her "IMAGE" of success she is upsetting many people. She has always upset her "friends" when they no longer serve her purpose. I am sure the only reason she wants to be friends with you is your house in South France & maybe....just maybe steal David. Oh YES, she could try that VERY easy. Remember she USES people....... men & women & they are classed as "friends". I must go home, all this makes me feel so gullible (or as my advocat said a "pigeon").

cheers & regards to all

Geoff

Mon 19th Feb: While in KSA, Rachael sends SMS final decision to finish with me 2nd time

I received a long SMS from Rachael while in Saudi Arabia saying that she does not want to see me again. This **time, it is final;** she does not want to see me again. She says she realises I am never going to divorce Monica, so what is the point of being a woman having an affair?

Tues 20th Feb

While in KSA, I have time to reflect & make a comparison of problems.

I have so many problems: what with Monica & her men, finances with Monica stealing my €5,000 cheque, spending & now Rachael doesn't want to see me…what else can go wrong?

I give Monica a printout of my list & comments below

Monica & Lennon are similar

20 Fevrier 2007

Monica	Lennon
Does not listen to people who know better, e.g. Geoff	Does not listen to Monica or Geoff
Does not realise the critical state of business	Does not realise the critical state of his schoolwork
Does not realise closeness to business failure	Does not realise closeness to exam failure
No sense of Priorities	No sense of Priorities
Usually not self-motivated to keep pressure on herself	Usually not self-motivated to keep pressure on himself
Not Proactive, leaves everything to the last moment, e.g. doing expense claims, prospecting.	Not Proactive, leaves everything to the last moment, e.g. homework, getting books ready.
Monica puts pressure on others to sort out her problems because she didn't do what was required immediately, e.g. leaving docs to be posted, photocopied.	Wants help due to not doing things at the last moment & then needs help getting presents at the last moment.

Spends money before it is earned. "Doesn't care about money," except the things it buys!!!	
Irresponsible: orders Table & chairs without consultation & without the means to pay for it! Wastes €1400	Irresponsible: doesn't care about the house when he is in charge, e.g. when Monica & Geoff were away, had a party & left the place a mess for 4 days & let "friends" drink all our spirits
Day dreamer: talks about dreams as if reality tomorrow. Loss of credibility with her friends, when they find out fallacy of lies e.g. telling friends that she was earning 45,000 per month!	Talks of University as if it is a done thing
Untidy to the extreme, like a little 7-year child	Untidy to the extreme, like a little 7-year child
Wants to do what she wants to do, like shopping for clothes, shoes, and anything without thought of priorities, like getting prospects & making a business successful.	Wants to do what he wants to do, going out at night and playing football, rather than get his priorities right, like schoolwork.

> ➢ Doesn't tell friends or colleagues the truth & therefore, people do not realise you need help.
> ➢ Too proud to admit mistakes & inadequacies "Pride goes before a fall."
> ➢ Geoff knows more than any other person your mentality & state of Moni Clean, & I "try" to help you with advice. Do you appreciate it? NO!!! Too proud & independent.
> ➢ An international athlete pushes him/herself more than a club athlete.
> ➢ Successful business people push themselves more than failures. Pressure has to be WITHIN yourself. BUT, it helps to get someone to push you before you are capable of self-pressure. Spending half the day shopping is not helping your business …or our bank

- balance for paying the mortgage.
- Remember: you have worked this first year for no money, & when the social stops, Moni Clean will make a loss that will lead to bankruptcy. Turning prospects into clients is a TOP priority… not shopping, getting up at 9 am or phoning friends during PRIME TIME.
- Like Lennon, you are running out of time.

20/2/07 Budapest

Monica,

I want you to succeed & be successful for both of us. I cannot & will not stand by & watch you do/not do the things you NEED to do.

Does an athlete shout at his coach because he is criticising his technique or his lack of work required to get the top? NO!

So, why, when I point out the TRUTH, you get annoyed & start shouting at me? You lie to YOURSELF, just like Lennon, about how much work you do & need to do.

Remember, if you lie, you need to be credible; often, you are not so many people have told me, "Why does Monica lie so much?" You lie even for simple things, e.g. I bought this leather coat in Auchan for 50 Euros; these shoes were given to me by Julienne because they did not fit her. People are not stupid, especially your husband. Some days, you are organised & work hard, but many days, you are NOT ……that's the truth. I see by the clothes & shoes you buy & then claim are given to you!

I have tried to help you get organised:

- Keep a book to note all phone calls/numbers & actions. Have you ever used a method used by ALL business people? NO!
- I have advised you over a year ago to make a database of possible workers with location & other details to help you organise a particular client, especially when you have an illness

or new contract possibility. Each time you find a temp job or contract possibility, you keep asking a business friend for a favour. One day, they may not be available or want to be bothered by you…then what?

➢ Put your expense receipts on A4 paper rather than stuffing them somewhere. I noticed you found receipts I had stuck on A4 paper just the other day that were your summer expenses!

Whenever I tell you the truth, you do not see you are getting good advice. Let us see whether you will read all of this message or delete it without reading any of it. **Do you love me?** Simply answer that in your reply, yes or no? That is the test, & you never answer me.

I do love you.

Geoff.

Monica Reply 21-2-07: *(original English – no corrections)*

Geoff,

I appreciate your help but you put me on pression every time (that is your nature)!!!! Everything you have written in your message is what you keep telling me every minute!! I have shown you that I am working hard and I am determined to do things but do not put me on pression!!! You can advise me without pressurise me! and when you see that there is tension between us and when you I tell you to stop the conversation because of tension, you keep presser and shouting!! Please, let me do my business and when I need help the first person I will ask will be you! Pression on the person like me (who has problem for business, who has Mum between death and live, who has a son of 17 yr does nothing at andchool and husband who pressurise anybody even at work) that doesn't help me!!!

About your question, I do love you and that is not a test for you

Monica.

Wednesday 21st February

I finish Wednesday evening in KSA, fly to Cairo, stay overnight & then go with Ashraf, our Egypt agent, to see customers. I was working all day in Jedda and then left the late afternoon for a flight from KSA to Cairo. Ashraf picks me up, we go to my favourite fish restaurant. In that restaurant, we get to choose the fish we want from the large slanting shelf, they weigh them, & then we sit down for them to be cooked with our non-alcoholic drink.

Thursday 22nd

Egypt visits with Ashraf before getting the late afternoon flight back to CdG, Paris.

I arrive home late Thursday 22nd night from Cairo knackered: 14 days of work with not a single day's rest.

Friday 23rd February 2007

On my return, I decide to contact Julienne the next day, Friday. She confirmed my suspicions, no visit or meeting with Monica. So, we have another mystery, what boyfriend was she out with? She always lies, not knowing I am a good detective. Let's see who it could be THIS time. I remember Monica saying she had a "present from Mobile de France manager to me." Obviously, he is one suspect, especially as recently, she has been going to Croix Blanche (a giant retail park near Genevieve des Bois) a lot recently. Why for just one account? Monica said one evening she was delivering some wine that she was selling, but again, being a detective, I had made sure I could count & identify any missing bottles from the pallet; none had gone. Each time, Monica usually returns at about 8:30 pm.

Another possibility was Pierre Prost. I met with Monica in a bar in Paris 75015. I noticed that on the receipt, his name was Pierre. A suppose another could be Doric with his bar near the Marie de Paris, whom she got close to. Then, of course, I had found in her GPS an address, 49 rue Daniel Niord, Savigney, near the A6 autoroute. Who was this? Could this be the Mobile de France manager's house? I will find out one day to see what this house looks like.

Monica is often going out "to see clients" looking sexy. She contradicts herself when seeing REAL Moni Clean clients & says she cannot look sexy for clients. All this suggests either ONE regular boyfriend or a number of different boyfriends. If it is one regular boyfriend, then almost certainly she is having sex with him.

However, I DO know she loves being with many men; she is fit, so maybe, maybe not. Oh, my head hurts thinking about the permutations; I cannot relax.

All these suppositions & lies are driving me mad. I try to accept that Monica is just seeing boyfriends, having sex with some to gain some advantages (Moni Clean contracts, discounts, things, money) & getting benefits for us as a family. However, all I see is that my wife is being shared around with different men.

I keep thinking of the book, "**Women who stay with men who stray**" **by Debbie Then.**

In that book, she says: Some women do not want to know and just accept their husbands going with the same or different women, while other wives **want to know** *but still accept the husband's infidelity.*

I always say with me, it is Men who stays with a women who strays! Either way it is a stress that if it were not for sport and work, I would go MAD. I guess I am in the latter category, **I want to know,** *but accept it, if only she would admit and tell me.*

Friday 23rd 2007

Having returned home last night Thursday 22nd, Monica phones me at 7:15pm to say she is at Port Versailles & that traffic is light & has done shopping at Carrefour & is returning home. I phone her back at 8:50pm, she is somewhere indoors. There is no noise, then she moves, & I can hear her high heels clip-clopping across a tiled floor indoors. Did I hear a soft man's voice? I asked where she was, she was evasive. Some 7 minutes later when I phoned her, she was in her car driving & said she had been around a new shop built that needed cleaning & did I want to meet her. I declined, within 2-3 minutes, she was home! However, I did visit the new build the next day, it was still a construction site still, where tiling would not be done for a while until near completion. Therefore, she was NOT there when I heard her high heels on a tiled floor.

However, she was probably within a few minutes of the 2nd phone call, I checked out on Saturday 24th with the GPS Savigny address, this was 6-7 minutes from home.

Lie #1   She claimed to be Porte Versailles on the peripherique, & yet a bill I found later was 18:44 hrs

Lie #2   She was not outside as she claimed; she was INSIDE a room with a tiled floor that resonated with her high-heeled shoes when walking.

Possible locations had to be local, very local.

When Monica got home, she was not wearing her bra. Upon taking off her high-heel boots, her boobs fell out of her low-cut dress. When she was in the loo, I looked in her bag, there was no sign of her bra. Given the opportunity, I looked in her car, and there was no sign of her bra. Did she go to see the boyfriend without a bra to start with?

I said to her, why didn't she stay longer with her boyfriend? She got upset & was in a bad mood due to my accusation. However, she quickly forgot her anger & put on the charm.

I often notice when she is with a boyfriend & has had sex, she is often horny. This time, she was VERY horny. Tonight was no exception, why do I just melt & want her? I cannot resist her smile as she turns me on. I can not understand her desire for different men. Tonight was doggy night; oh, I do like the doggy position. I can also see her boobs swing when looking in the mirror.

Obviously, sensing I know a lot that she had been with a man that night, Monica started to open up after the fun while resting in the bed. Monica told me that men having lunch with her who fancy her is not wrong & does not constitute an affair. I said lovingly, "I know you are going out with different men. Do you have sex to get contracts or money for us as a loving couple? You know I do not mind like Paul. I know you do it for us, but I just want you to tell me & not hide it. Remember, I have seen men shag you before, so it is nothing new." This was a ploy to get her to admit to having sex with men.

Monica looked into my eyes inquisitively, not sure if I was sincere or whether to lie as normal, "Is he old, rich or young?" I enquired. "No, he is not young. He is about 50 years old," realising she was opening up with information, she hesitated to say more until I said, "Does he shag you better than me, if so, you need to instruct me how I can improve." With such an invitation she opened up more, "He is about 50 as I said, & he is a manager of a site where I hope to get a contract." "That is good," I encouraged her. "Yes, he has the power to award contracts for my Moni Clean & has a big house, bigger than our house." "Wow, so it is a really big house. Is he married?" I interjected. "Yes, it is a big house. His wife is really bad continually spends his money & goes on holiday a lot. He is really unhappy." "So, he is happy being with you, & you please him? "What does he like most?" Monica continues, "It is not just sex. He wants to chat & have a friend to open up to about his problems. I am a good listener, & the sex is just a way to relax him so that he can feel he can please someone." "Sounds a bit like Paul in some ways," I said. "Yes, I suppose you are right. He hadn't had sex with his wife for so long, so when he saw me, he said he just wanted to be with me, chat, open up & feel me. He said he likes my legs." "I would expect he would also like your African bum & those lovely boobs," as I held & caressed them. She smiled, "Of course all men like my bum & boobs." "Me too," as I continued to hold them gently & caress them with special attention to finger rolling her nipples.

Monica keeps giving me permission to meet other women again & have an affair.

Oh, Monica does love attention & flattery. "You do not realise I am special, condoning you being with other men. You would not want me with other women would you?

Monica replies, **"Why not find other females & have fun? I do not want you to feel frustrated because I am with other men."** Well that was interesting statement & question. "Do you think if I went with other women, they would want to talk or just have sex?" I answered. **"Well, why don't you find out?"** she said. **"Err, so you would not mind me going out with other females?"** I spluttered. She smiled, **"Of course not. You would not then be jealous of me being with other men."**

Now no longer meeting Rachael, I have to decide what I have to do. Monica has her men friends, & of course, Paul. The lack of someone to unwind my frustrations is telling on me. I do not want to divorce Monica. **In spite of all our problems, I love her.** What to do? We chat. I mention she has Paul & meets other men, yet I am alone except for male friends from the athletic club & work at JY.

I found out the next opportunity the next day. I had to search her things, a Carrefour petrol receipt at Ville de Bois (5 mins from Longjumeau) time-stamped 18:44 hrs, allowing for loading her car & getting to her boyfriend at approximately 19:00 hrs. She probably phoned me outside his house.

23rd Feb: 2007: Comms from Agnes about re-payment of €10,000 loan

I receive a reply e-mail from Agnes (see 16th Feb original):

Postscript: I never got either the €10,00 from Agnes nor, the €5,000 from Monica. Being married to David, a ginger-haired Brit, I felt completely comfortable giving the loan. I am now retrospectively wondering if Agnes and Monica worked in collusion to help Monica with her secret money problems.

Sunday 25ᵗʰ February 2007:   Rachael hot & cold. What to do? Start looking?

I arrange to pick up Sophie B from Rachael's for training, I am able to chat with Rachael. While being friendly, she is not sure about going out with me again. On returning Sophie B to her Grigny house after training, I am able to take Rachael out to the Viry Chatillon Lake for a long walk, as often we have done before. I have to be patient as Rachael is quite reluctant to pursue a relationship.

Rachael seems to be hot & cold, on & off. I can understand, in some respects, that she does not want to be a "bit on the side" from a bad marriage & relief from Monica all the time. I need to think and accept Rachael's rejection & move on. Should I make efforts to look?

> I just read your message (im in south africa right now), i'm planning to be in France in March and i will bring your Cheque and Hope promised me she will give your 5 000 euros back at the same time.
> I'm very sorry for the late payback and am very upset that Hope didn't give you the cheque.

If I do that, Monica will go mad, I am sure, even though so she keeps encouraging me to see other women ! It is like a game for her to play with me. While she can go with other men, I am sure she would not accept me with other women, as proved before when afterwards she goes mad. I suspect Monica knows about Rachael & is not happy. I am so frustrated with what is going on; I cannot sort my head out.

My salvation is throwing the discus shot & doing weight lifting. When I am doing these activities, I can lose myself in the event & forget about my problems. This has been a major advantage for me even when I was with Lyn, my first wife. An alternative was work, & there was plenty of that for Varian in Australia, now, in JY in France. My family, sometimes, got hit in the crossfire of Lyn & I. Taking the kids out up the Dandenong hills outside Melbourne in Victoria, Australia, or the Pennines in England would give us time to relax together as nearly a family, be with the kids & forget Lyn. Lyn never wanted to come with us anyway, always making some lame excuse, like I am tired. (see Note 1)

Wednesday 28th February 2007

When I returned from work at JY to change & go training, I found evidence Monica had gone to the Montparnasse area several times & bought high-heeled, high-length boots near 2+2 club had some light food & coffee at Bistro Linois 89 rue St Charles 75015. I also found in a new diary of Monica a 26th February entry: "Alain & Emily 2+2 tel 06 62 38 79 xx" Did she go with someone else to 2+2, was it with Alain & Emily? Or is this somebody else?

Bateaux Rouges manager

Monica fixes an appointment for a chap who manages the "Bateaux Rouges" boats with the possibility of a cleaning contract. She goes out with him to ensure the contract. Did she suggest a 2+2 club?

Thursday 1st March

I arrive home to find Paul is there, we chat about where to go together. He suggests Monica finds a female to accompany us to the 2+2 club, and he wants to make arrangements. However, Monica says that she does not want to go to the 2+2 & is adamant she does not want to go again with me. Interestingly, she DID go with someone a few weeks ago in February. I found a diary entry on 22nd February with Alain at Bistro Linois, the meeting cafe, before entering 2+2. Did I find another receipt for Bistro Linois with waiter Pierre's coincidence? I also found a card for Chez Anne at Regis, Savigny sur Orge. It is only open Tuesday to Saturday, all day. Was there a probable lunch with a local boyfriend, or another one?

Just had a thought, could this be Pierre Prost 75 Rue St Charles, Linois Bistro, maybe also 89 Rue St Charles, so was she chasing a rendez-vous for the Bateaux contract? In which case, Pierre waiter is just that.

Friday 30th March 2007

Monica arrives home at 9:25pm. It is getting later & later than her initial 8:30 pm arrival timing. She says she is speaking with shop managers, when things get quieter in their shop. She is in a BAD mood, does she expect difficult questions from me? However, I am nice understanding, & soon, she turns on the sexy posture. I ignore the fact that Lennon may come downstairs & slowly remove her sexy clothes & reveal a nice lacy bra that comes off easily. She quickly loses inhibitions as well, so my clothes come off, with all revealed, she caresses my penis, "James", gently as I sit back on the settee. On her knees, she sucks me ever so gently with increasing depth of swallowing; the sucking, in & out, puts me in ecstasy. Oooh, the pressure is building up as she smiles more & more. She looks into my eyes and sucks in & out. WAIT for it..... uuurrhhh, I cum with a power of a volcano into her mouth. All this time, she is smiling that mischievous smile. By now, cum is oozing out of her mouth around my penis. She loves it; I love it, oh what joy. As the pressure is released & the excitement subsides, she sucks any excess cum, swallows, licks my penis like an ice cream, making sure no valuable cum is wasted and finally, swallows the last of it. How satisfying is that?

We cuddle with her still on her knees. "I bet no girls I would find would satisfy me like that," I said. Smiling, she replied, **"Find out, why don't you? You may find shagging another woman may improve your performance with me."** "Maybe, you are right, but I do not know anyone willing, since I have been married to you," telling a porky* reply.

* "Porky pie", is Cockney rhyming slang for lies.

With Rachael seemingly out of the picture, I am now alone & with no prospect of female company except Monica & her friends. I have to be careful with her Rwandan friends, they can talk to each other. I think I know who will & who will not talk, but then again, I am not sure. I have no problem meeting someone alone like Cloe, Charlotte or maybe Claudine, but for now, no further than amicable terms with others.

Monica is happy that I am not with Rachael, why, I will never know but she **wants me to see other women. She helps & encourages me to inscribe on "Meetic"**. "Why don't you go on a mating website like "*Meetic*" & "*Serencontre*"? "Oh, are you sure? I do not want to go out with a female & make you angry again with me for going out with a female?" I said. She suggests that I find a woman on the "Meetic" meeting site. I said to her, "I am sure you will not condone me going with other women." "Not at all. You need to meet women who can satisfy you when I am not around." "Do you really mean that? I do not want to pay money to inscribe on Meetic & then find you are jealous about me being with another woman," I said. "By going with different women, you will be in a better mood when we are together. Just give it a try," she replied. "OK, will you come with me to the computer & I will inscribe?" "Sure, I will help you." she replied.

The two of us went to my laptop computer upstairs & with Monica at my shoulder, she helped me inscribe onto the Meetic mating website. We both looked at the possibilities, with her suggesting various good-looking possibilities. I carry on looking over the possible women I fancied, & within an hour, I have a number of females interested in contacting me. After that first half hour, I chatted with the different women. Monica is content she smiles & leaves me to carry on while she goes to bed. I start to make some arrangements with several women.

I realised that **she did not want me with Rachael & was happy that I no longer was seeing her.** Monica wanted to encourage me to go with many women and make sure Rachael did not reappear in my life again & prevent a complete marriage breakup. Why did Monica specifically not like Rachael and felt that no other women would be a danger to her married life? **This has always been a question I could never work out, even now. They had never met, except at the final notaire meeting, nor had Monica ever seen any comms between** us. **A perennial puzzle.** I fix up three female appointments for the coming 7 days.

I then decide, while having a coffee, to check the usual places Monica puts her things. I find a torn up publicity for something at the Astoria hotel in Chilly Mazerin (3 minutes from Longjumeau), would this be a meeting place only 6-7 minutes away? I then discover many phone calls on Moni Clean Fix telephone line with a Champlan number again, only 6-7 minutes away. The number is **not** the phone number for the Creche job she has at present in Champlan (again, about 3 minutes away from Longjumeau). I then research & find it is the same number that started in October last year 2006, usually in the morning, with increasing frequency through to March.

Saturday 7th April 2007:   Johanne, the first "Meetic" lady

I mentioned to Monica that I am going out with my first lady appointment, Johanne. We met at the fountain at Place de St Michel & then went out for a meal in Rue la Huchette in St Michel Latin quarter. Johanne was rather short & not thin, but not fat, sometimes referred as "built for comfort rather than speed". We had an enjoyable meal with live music, we walked back to my car parked underneath Place St Michel. I drove us back to her flat up on the 5th floor just off the Avenue Jean Jaures 19th arrondissements. I found it amazing we went through THREE sets of security doors, each one requiring a different code before entering her flat with a key. We chatted for a while and exchanged information about our jobs. She worked for the government & mentioned something that shocked me.

In France, women working in private companies have up to 3 years of maternity leave after having a baby to return to their job at the same level. In Government & municipal jobs, the new mother can return at ANY time. One lady she knew returned when her son went to university, i.e., 19 years old, & therefore, 20 YEARS after she had stopped. They had to re-train her for nearly a year before she was up to the standard required to be a supervisor again! Imagine the difference in computer technology, software & working practices in 20 years!

We had a kiss & cuddle as I departed for home. While we got on well, I was not sure whether I wanted to see her again, so I decided to sleep on it.

On arriving home, Monica was watching TV, smiled & asked how did it go? I told her that it went Ok, but I was not sure whether I wanted to see her again.

Sunday 8th April 2007: Stella lady #2

I mentioned after training that I would be out later to try lady # 2. Monica smiled & said, "Good, I want you to enjoy yourself." Later, early in the evening, I met Stella at the same place at the fountain of Place St Michel. She was late, making me nervous that she would not turn up. Eventually, Stella appeared in a short skirt & low-cut blouse. She was above-average height with a nice figure & originally came from Central African Republic (often referred to as simply CAR). We walked around the Notre Dame cathedral & then the city region. We found a resto & had a nice meal.

We returned to the car parked usually underneath Place St Michel. I drove Stella back to her place off Rue de Sevres. In her flat, the parking was underneath, requiring the normal code to access the parking. Back in her flat, we chatted as she prepared the coffee, boiling the water in a saucepan as so many do in France, they do not seem to realise a kettle does the job much better.

Talking in French about various subjects is always difficult for me, but Stella seemed impressed with me & sat next to me on her settee over coffee. The small chat seemed difficult, as my eyes started wandering at her legs & chest. She noticed that. As I have noted in books about female body language, she **crossed her legs <u>towards me</u>** in the inviting direction. I had to say it, "tu est tres beau." She smiled, reciprocated with compliments & then leaned over to me, the cleavage being more visible. My eyes became fixated at her cleavage, "t'aimes ça?" (you like that?) I replied, "Oui, j'aime ca." She then slowly pulled up her skirt enticingly, "t'aimes ça?" "Oui, j'aime ca."

Oh, my blood pressure was rising, & she noticed movement in my trousers. "ça grossit." Before I could say, "oui", she placed one of her hands on my trousers over my growing penis & then with her other hand took my hand to place it on her top covering her boob. I investigated further down her top & bra to hold her boob, caressing & pulling one boob out of her bra. She stopped & started to undo her blouse buttons. Now, her red bra was fully visible as she invited me by turning around to undo her bra. I did it with pleasure and removed her blouse. Her boobs were fully open for handling by my eager hands. Caressing them & playing with her nipples, she started to heave deep breaths. She then proceeded to undo my belt & unzip my trousers; she removed my trousers & popped out my penis from my pants. Caressing my penis (James), she made him stiff was determined to enjoy it. Dropping down on her knees, she placed James in her mouth. Up & down deep inside her mouth, I tried to hold back; I succeeded for a few minutes, but when a volcano blows, one cannot stop it. POW, James blew inside her mouth, she carried on up & down without any sign of lost cum. She must have a technique to hide her swallowing my cum. She continued until James's size subsided to a withered example & then she licked all around to make sure nothing was wasted. I then proceeded to feel down her culottes to give her pleasure and removed her culottes. After some 10-15 minutes, I was able to make her cum. We cuddled & kissed with both of us tired from non-penetrating sex.

I must remember to bring some condoms when I have these female matches from Meetic. I never know what to expect from my rendez-vous. Eventually, I excused myself because of work tomorrow. Stella was keen to meet me again, & me to see her again.

Returning home at about 11:30 pm, Monica was again watching TV after being out herself with Cloe. She smiled & said, "How was your evening? I mentioned I had a good meeting with the second lady. Monica gestured for me to expand, so I said I had a good evening & that I needed to buy some condoms because I was not expecting women to be so keen. She said, "Just keep trying different women. You may find some even more forward & enjoyable. You do not need to see the same female each time. See, you like trying different women, eh? Did you not take some condoms?" "I did not expect to have sex so quickly, but she did a blow job," I replied. "Good, I am glad for you, and now you will not feel so bad when I see my different men". I could only nod in agreement.

Slow progress on Bateaux Rouges – Is HE playing Monica?

I discover several meal tickets just off the Eiffel tower area 75015. Is the Bateau Rouge manager Pierre Prost? Monica says they are working together, and she hopes to get the contract soon. I sense she takes him to 2+2.

Wednesday 11th April 2007: Francoise Meetic, female #3

I left JY's work early at noon & drove Massy to meet another "Meetic" female encounter. I arranged to meet at the local shopping centre in a cafe. About 40-ish, with brown hair, **Francoise** was slightly built & about 5 feet 6 inches (1.68m), white & French. We had a nice meeting, & I conversed in my poor French. I told her I was married & that did not perturb her at all. She was single & wanted company. We agreed to meet again, and she would phone me at work.

After work, I went down as usual to do weightlifting at the weightlifting gym down the road. On my return, Paul was there, we had a beer or two before the normal "witching hour", when he left for home to arrive before 8 pm.

Friday 13th April 2007: Alison, Meetic female #4

I had already mentioned to Monica I would arrive late & arranged to meet another female at a bar in Corbeil-Essonne by the river Seine. **Alison** was from Nigeria, medium height, maybe 5ft 7 inches (1.7m).

While not at all fat, she had a rounded face, an African bum & nice pair of presented boobs. I could tell she was out to impress with body language, it was difficult not to be impressed. She was intelligent & worked in a bank locally that had some exchange arrangement for a year. She liked France & would rather stay in France than return to Nigeria at the end of the year. She spoke English as well as French, and we both found it easier to converse in English. As we were on her home turf, I asked her whether she wanted dinner & if so, where, as she was the local person. She suggested a resto within the old town, we had an enjoyable evening talking about a range of subjects, which was a change. If Monica did not know about any subject, she would change it.

On completion & bill payment, Alison suggested I come round to her apartment for coffee. Sure, I was up for that, I enjoyed her company & looking at her. We got into my car & drove maybe a kilometre or so & arrived at a block of apartments with a large car park. Through the car park & some bushes, she held my hand to guide me to the doorway & entered the entry code for the building. Up in the lift to the 4th floor, she opened the door to her apartment. It was one bedroom, with a really small kitchen, something I found usual in France & a lounge with enough room for a settee, TV stand & dining table. The French windows opened up to a small veranda that overlooked the town. Too early in the year to stay outside, I placed my hand on her shoulder, indicating it was a bit chilly. She held my hand & agreed, so we returned inside with her still holding my hand that was on her shoulder. She closed the French windows, turned to me, looking into my eyes, "What would you like?" My thoughts were I would like to get closer to you, but I refrained from being so forward. "Errmm, do you have tea?" "I have everything," she replied. I thought nor arf (London Cockney for half) you have.

In the dim standard lamp light, she was looking wonderful. She noticed my difficult-to-hide gaze at her nicely presented boobs. "Do you like them?...... my boobs." "Eeeerrr yes, they look lovely," I spluttered. "Would you like to hold them?" she followed & beckoned me to feel down her bra as she undid a few buttons on her blouse. Oh wow, I did not expect anything so quick. Next thing, Alison was fondling my bulging trousers. I carefully undid another button on her blouse, watching for any adverse reaction, only smiles & facial encouragement, until only her bra was in position. She stopped fondling briefly & undid her bra with the flexibility only females have to reach back that far up their back. Oh, what a wonderful pair! I must admit I am a boob person (I like nice bums as well), they were a delight. My hands were fondling them as she proceeded to undo my shirt & trousers. My turn, as I felt for the zip on the side of her skirt, & hey presto, down it fell. Oooohh, what a body, culottes need to come off as well as my pants. Oh shit, I forgot a condom! What to do? Already she was having difficulty getting my pants off the fully erect penis. In desperation, I asked, "Do you have a condom?".... A little shake of the head indicated no. Oh shit, I never anticipated this so quickly. Alison could see my anguish & said, "Do not worry about tonight; you can please me another night," & with that, she indicated me to recline on the settee. She then proceeded to give me a blow job. Gee Whiz, her mouth was as tender against my penis as she swallowed up & down that I was able to hold it for a while. However, all active volcanos must blow their lid & mine did just that, with a mouthful of cum quickly brimming & then oozing out around what minute gap there must have been until she took a swallow. She was smiling & looking into my eyes all the time to gauge my pleasure. What is it with Africans? They like to look up at my eyes & gauge the pleasure of a blow job, or is that a natural thing for females? Anyway, Alison was similar to Monica in that not a drop of precious cum was lost, all was licked up like an ice cream, & he, James (penises are male, I call mine James), was fit to put away with a tissue.

Alison now sat astride me with her boobs dangling down in front of my face. I held one & kissed, fondling it with my tongue & then did the same with the other. She loved it & quickly placed a boob into my mouth to suck. I duly did with all my romantic possibilities, tongue-licking her nipples, hard sucking & then swapping, so that the other boob did not get jealous. By this time, of course, while she was sitting astride me, my willy (James) was deflated & posed no possibility of going up the nearby pussy. A shame & a relief.

We played for ages, all the time she was astride of me, but gradually, all the movement of her pussy in the region of James was starting to get him excited again. Noooo, what would I do if he starts rising again? I try to think of other things not associated with sex, but I am cuddling a lovely body, feeling, licking and sucking her boobs, which is a turn-on. Shit, THINK! "Do you have you a boyfriend here or in Nigeria?" I ask. "No, I had a couple in Nigeria, but I did not feel they were for me, so I finished with them." "I cannot believe you have been alone for over 3 months," I said. It is working James's pressure is receding, I thought. "I like intelligent men with whom I can chat about different things without feeling like they only want one thing: pussy. You never made any overt approach; it occurred naturally, maybe even a bit of help from me," she confided. "I do understand, I have never forced myself on any female. If women do not want me, then OK, we can still be friends. A woman has got to want me for me to do anything," I said. "I admire that & love you for that, I could also tell by the way you did not want to shag me without a condom, I think you were worried when I felt your penis was starting to get excited again!" she remarked. "You are observant about my penis getting excited again." "Is that why you started talking about my past boyfriends?" "Yes," I replied. "I was really afraid I would not be able to resist when your pussy was so close!". She bent forwards and held my head with both hands & kissed me. "Thank you for being a perfect English gentleman" & then got up. Wow, that pussy looked so lovely. Next time! "How about that cup of tea?" I asked. She smiled "You English & your cups of tea, yes, of course."

We got semi-dressed, enough to hide private parts; her with her culottes, and me with pants, sitting on the settee, drinking tea & talking about life in Nigeria & comparison with England. Eventually, I left for home.

Well, after that meeting, I will forget about female no. 1 & cancel female no. 3 previously fixed. I need to explore Alison more!

Tuesday 10th April

Monica puts in the waste paper bin some comms of Sunday with Mathias. She obviously was afraid I would see it, unaware I check everything!

Mathias, husband to Jutta, whom Monica met in Cotonou, Benin, in September 2006, are communicating privately & wanted to rendez-vous in Cotonou again. Monica was hoping to go to Accra, where Agnes has a second Livingston bar resto (the first one being in Cotonou). Monica invited Mathias to go with her, but, of course, there are many assumptions here, as I have found in the past, many of her schemes fall through or are not serious.

Friday 27th April 2007

Monica receives a phone call, obviously from a boyfriend because she spoke softly & closed the door. I carry on making arrangements for taking out Alison tomorrow.

Sat 28th April: Alison

Monica wanted me to go with her to see her friend, but I said I had already made arrangements to meet Alison. She smiled & said, "Good for you, where does she live?" I told her Corbeil-Essonne & then departed. I rang Alison's apartment number, to let me in, when let in, I went up in the lift to her 4th floor flat. WOW, she looked lovely! When I gave her a kiss, she took one hand around my neck & other hand immediately felt my penis. That is some welcome, rubbing him made him excited, I started to kiss her passionately. I could not help myself, I started unzipping her dress at the back while she was undoing my trouser belt & unzipping to pull down my trousers.

A wiggle, & her dress fell down. She pulled off my shoes & trousers. Within seconds, we were both naked as she led me to her bedroom. Down on the bed, she laid on top of me. Almost doing a McKensie* exercises with straight arms sitting back on me. James was being rubbed up & down against her pussy. Damm, I left the condoms in my trousers. "Whoops, Alison, I left the condoms in my trouser pocket. You will need to get off." She looked with a glint in her eye & quickly moved position & sat on James so that he disappeared up her pussy. Oh Shit, her rhythmic bum up & down was getting James really excited. Sitting upright, she bounced up & down. I held her hips to try to lift her up, but she was too upright & heavy to do a straight arm curl with her. Realising what I was hoping to do, she transferred both my hands to her flopping boobs while bouncing up & down on James, & now nothing could stop us. Have you ever enjoyed something you really did not want to do? WOW, what a shag! We were both panting at the end of the session & flopped sideways with exhaustion. That was wonderful! As good as anything Monica had with me or even better! It was several minutes repose when we both embraced each other in thanks. Then the horrible thought crossed me as brain started to think normally, what if I made her pregnant? Nothing more I can do now, let's enjoy the moment & the evening.

We eventually got dressed & departed for a local resto. Returning afterwards to her flat, we were up for another shag, we cannot resist each other. If I did not make her pregnant the first time, then a second shag so close to the first, will not matter, so again no condom was used.

* McKensie exercises are for sciatica & other back problems (search Google to see many examples of McKensie exercises with diagrams).

When I got home, Monica was there & asked me how was the meeting with Alison (I told her the names of each woman I met, I did not want to be a hypocrite). Monica asked for more details, & I supplied them. She then asked, "You did use a condom?" When I said that things got out of hand & we did not, Monica went balmy. "What if you have made her pregnant?" "I know, I am concerned about that myself," I said.

She then wanted to know more about Alison. Monica started to say she was after getting a child to be able to stay in France due to the child being half-British & born in France. That thought had occurred to me, even if the circumstances seemed innocent.

Monday 30th April

We receive many visitors with Marina again from Nantes & others. Monica goes at about 6 pm to Massy "to get some pills" and returns at about 8:30 pm with many Nespresso coffee capsules, which cannot be bought locally in any 24-hour shop. So, she must have seen a boyfriend locally or, maybe, the notaire whom she is now cleaning their office? Monica does not care that she has guests when she sees these men.

Wednesday 2nd May 2007: local boyfriend identified as Julian Baptiste

Monica returns home with a "new-looking" 2nd hand tower computer & latest type of LCD screen for the new salesman/Raymond joint Moni Clean project. She says she was given it. When I had the opportunity, I saw underneath it and found it to be formally a property of Notiare XXXXXX in Longjumeau. It was not just any old PC, it was a powerful PC tower & in very good condition. Soooooo, who is the benefactor? Research showed it had to be either Julian Baptiste or YYY because ZZZ was no longer there. Further research revealed it must be Julian Baptiste. Obviously, Monica had asked Julian for the PC as a gift. I think I have identified one of the local boyfriends, maybe this is the address on her GPS in Saux les Chatreuse, a village next to Longjumeau also the person close by she has been seeing since October. Everything is starting to fall into place from my notes: high heel noise in an office, Astoria hotel in Chilly Mazerin and local Saux phone number.

Friday 4th May

Monica leaves the house at 6:30 pm & then phones me within 5 minutes for something. I could hear a busy street; it must be Longjumeau. I went to Place de Steber, Longjumeau car park, & voila, Monica's car was parked there. I park hidden from her potential view & note her car is there until about 8:45 pm. I missed her departure because of a parked lorry obstructing my sight for about 15 minutes…. drat! She apparently then went to Carrefour afterwards to do some shopping for the monthly Rwandese "Tontine" reunion.

I walked around the back to where the notaire's park their cars with a barrier & pass. One vehicle is still there, I see a large grey Renault Velsatis. I wait for a short while & then an elderly & distinguished man with a raincoat over his shoulder walks to the car. After the barrier lifted, he turned left down the road & went into the Massy & Saux direction. Things are starting to fall into place as to who is the local boyfriend. The profile fits exactly the type of man Monica seduces, e.g. like Paul, a man with power & influence.

I tried to contact Alison, but no reply, so I instead fixed up a meeting again with Stella

Saturday 5th May 2007

I managed to find a receipt for Hotel Codran, Cafe Ladoux 3 Rue General le Clerc, Longjumeau. The receipt seems to be paid by the notaire at 14:37hrs on Friday 27th April. Voila! Customers do not take the supplier out for a long lunch-time. They also do not give good computers to their customers, unless a payment in kind like a shag!

I met Stella again that night, I couldn't get hold of Alison. I met Stella from near her appartement. I had to stay on a "no parking" part of the road, but Paris police do not seem to worry about illegal parking if you are in the car waiting, they walk straight past! Stella arrived, & we went out to a resto in west Paris. We returned to her place eager to have sex. No need for niceties; both of us took off each other's clothes quickly & played with each other's private parts before Stella put on a condom. She turned her back on me to penetrate doggy style. She stood up in front of the mirrored wardrobe so that she was able to see me mounting her. With my hands on her ample hips, I could see her boobs swing to the rhythm of me shagging her. I was able to hold back long enough for her to be close to climax before I could no longer hold it. She squealed with delight at a climax of a good shag. Now, I have a comparison Stella, Alison & Monica!

Sunday 6th May 2007: Rachael walks with me around lake back together again?

I picked up Sophie B (Rachael's eldest daughter) as usual, for training & tried to entice Rachael to walk with me around Viry Chatillon Lake. Rachael agrees, we spend an agreeable hour walking around the big lake. The lake was an old stone quarry, extracting a special porous hard stone used extensively in the area for house building. When it was disused, it filled up, & for some time, people used to swim in it. However, eventually it was banned & left to be a nature reserve with a cycle/walking path around all of it. The lake actually is a series of inter-connecting lakes with a roadway between the major ones. One day, walking to the external throwing area, I actually saw an Otter. Some weeks later, there was a litter of baby otters with the parents; I had never seen otters before.

Monday 7th May: Monica extracting too much money from joint account.

Monica & I have a row about money because she is taking too much out of the joint account. I will have difficulty paying the direct debit for the large house mortgage if she keeps extracting so much money. For her, it is not a problem; for her, **Geoff will work harder to get more money!** Monica decides to sleep in the large family room.

I tried again to communicate with Alison, but still no news from her and no answer to calls or SMS. Why not?

Tuesday 8th May

I find Monica spends 3 hours with Julian the notaire & arrives late with some lame excuse. Without admitting it, I now know who the new boyfriend is. I am so unhappy that money problems crop up again, so we row about money again. She simply does not care about how much she spends and thinks it is MY responsibility to earn more money for her to spend. Monica sleeps in bedroom no. #3 this time.

I've decided I will see Rachael tomorrow night, I need to talk to someone to keep my sanity.

Wednesday 9th May: visit Rachael's house

I visit Rachael at her home in Parc des Aiglons, Grigny village, a nice village spoilt by giant apartment blocks nearby called Grigny-2. Her 4-bedroom council house is full of people: 3 daughters, a daughter of Rachael's ex-boyfriend living in the same house & ex partner as well. We go out to the local Viry Chattion Lake again to walk around it & chat. Afterwards, I drive back up the hill to Grigny village & her house to say goodbye to Rachael, the extended family before driving home. I am not sure whether Rachael is still keen to see me again regularly as a friend. I need to keep my options open for the moment.

Thursday 10th May 2007

I left work at 6 pm & waited in the Place de Steber, Longjumeau car park. At around 6:30, I see Monica arrive with just her bag, looking sexy. I was hiding in a position, so she could not see me. She parked her car & proceeds to go over to the notaire's office opposite. After ringing the buzzer, Julian lets her in & locks the door again looking around.

From experience, I guessed she would be a couple of hours, so I went home for those hours. I returned at about 8:45 pm, & back in my strategic position, I would be able to see Monica come out of the front door. Within 15 minutes, I see Monica leave as he locks the door behind him. She got into her car & drove off. I proceeded to walk around, where I could see the only car left in the private car park at the rear was the same large, grey Renault. When I saw him exit, a suave elderly man, wearing slung over his shoulder a coat, I quickly walked to my car on the other car park in Longjumeau. I had parked it there to avoid Monica seeing my car in the car park opposite the notaire, being a distance of maybe100metres. I saw his car go, however, by the time I got into my car, I could see he had gone in the direction of Massy, but by the time I arrived by the hump of the bridge over the railway, I had lost him. Where did he go? I drove on further & then backtracked & investigated a few side roads, but after not seeing his car, I gave up & returned home. Monica was still out, she later said that she was at Carrefour to get some shopping as we unloaded the carrier bag. In general chit-chat, I enquired why she was late & she told me she had a dental appointment! Why does she lie with a stupid lie that is not believable? What dentist is open at 9 pm?

Friday 11th May: BBQ at Longjumeau stade

I left again work at JY to check on Monica arriving at Julian the notaire. She arrived as normal, around 6:15-6:30 pm. immediately after she went to Julian, I went to the athletic club' BBQ at the Longjumeau stadium with Longjumeau AC. The club had a number of BBQs & AGMs to use up excess money, yes, excess money! Conseil general distribute so much money the various clubs do not know what to do with it! What a difference to the UK! I left just before 8:30 pm & parked at the opposite car park & saw Monica's car was still in the car park opposite the notaire. Waiting from a safe distance, Monica comes out to her car at about 9:00 pm. I went back to the athletic BBQ to enjoy the rest of the evening. When I got home, Monica claimed she was working & came to the BBQ but could not see me, so she came home. I did not say anything that I had proved she was lying. She was with Julian, the notaire.

No news from Rachael, she still seems not interested in me, so I will see if I can fix up a RV with another Meetic female. **Monica keeps encouraging me to meet different women & not get too hooked onto just one.**

Still no news from Alison: no answer to calls or SMS. Why? Has she had her period? I am tempted to go and see her and find out why the absence of contact or news.

Sat 12th May 2007

With constant encouragement from Monica the previous night on using Meetic to meet different women, I met Natasha, a white French woman. We arranged to meet me at the St Michel fountain, my usual meeting place & then went for dinner in the Latin quarter; a rather difficult dinner getting her to converse. Afterwards, I offered to take her home by car, but she said she loved our evening, but needed to get the train & went.

Bateaux Rouge

On general chat about Moni Clean, Monica explains she is still expecting the Bateaux Rouge cleaning contract. I said, I think HE is playing her. For a change, think that the man is using YOU. He is promising the contract if YOU give him sex. She is NOT happy with that statement, but I think it has made her think. I said it is not natural to make a promise of a contract within a few weeks & then NOTHING, no valid explanation except excuses that were not believable; it is not happening, nor is he trying to really explain the delay over many months. Monica started to realise over the next weeks, maybe I was correct. Now starting to realise that I may be correct, she pressed the case of the contract. But, he always he gave lame excuses. NEXT!

Thursday 17th May

She is seeing Julian a lot & always lying about him. We have a row, I blurted out that I would fix an RV with Julian. "Who is Julian?" she said. REALLY, can you believe her statement!

Friday 18th May 2007: Notaire Julian with Monica -Truth Day

Monica discusses this with Paul, who is angry that she lies to me & him as well. She asked me to come to Palaiseau bar immediately to discuss things with Paul because he wants us to discuss our situation. I left work immediately & arrived within 15 minutes. With the three of us in the back room, we discuss the fact that she continues to lie to me & Paul. She does not admit to being with Julian, the notaire.

She acts like a perfect escort, listens to all we said, says she needs constant help, plays the lost female & needs shagging to keep her life happy. She then, by mistake, says Julian provides her with a job & gifts, e.g. tower computer. She said it started in February, she was protecting his professional position. She admits SHE made the first approach. She said he is providing unofficial (illegal) inside information on bankruptcy & introductions for contracts for Moni Clean. Monica tells me all that night that I must not contact Julian as it could ruin him & make him lose his licence as a notaire. I wasn't going to; it is not my nature to ruin someone's life, with maybe his family & career.

That evening after we return, Monica reads one of my e-mails from Rachael, where I open up with all my worries about Monica & her lifestyle. Monica is upset & angry & says that she thinks I love Rachael more than her. I say nothing & walk away.

Saturday 19th May

Still no news from Alison, no answer to calls or SMS. Why? Has she had her period? I have a free day and decided to go to her flat in Corbeil-Essonne in the afternoon. To get to her flat, you need the code to get into the building. I buzzed her number, no reply. I try phoning her, no reply. I hang around hoping someone will come out or in, so I can enter the building. Eventually, someone comes out, so I am able to enter. I press the door buzzer and try knocking, no reply. Frustrated, I wonder what to do. As I ponder, I see a neighbour & ask her whether she has seen Alison as I am concerned. She says she has moved out earlier in the week! On asking her, she didn't know where. She moved out quick, why? Where? This is bizarre, I did not know what bank she was supposed to be working in, unless I go into every Corbeil-Essonne bank & hope to see her. It may be a lot of fruitless effort, especially if the bank is not in Corbeil-Essonne.

I decide I should just keep trying to phone Alison & SMS her in the hope of receiving her response.

Mon-Frid 4-8th June

Monica visits Julian each night, arriving at about 6:15pm when all other employees have gone & leaving at about 9–9:15pm to enable him to tell his wife that he is working late.

We are now each night rowing about money. Monica is not paying towards the high house mortgage payments & she is spending money without a thought of where it is coming from. Maybe she just does not care because I am paying for everything. I am her money tree.

Monday 11th June

Unless Monica has something special on, for example, Free Masons or a friend visit, she is going to Julian every night.

Another month of fruitless calls & SMS to Alison. Ok, seems like Alison is history, pity I liked her.

Sunday 17th June 2007

Monica invited me to join her at her Fitness First at Croix Blanche enormous retail park. She could invite me with no charge for 2 free visits. We went together in her car, after a gym session, we had something to drink & snack at a local bar.

Sunday 1st July

I went training & picked up Zoe (Rachael's middle daughter) for coaching. We threw the discus at Viry Chatillon, where there is a throwing area outside the stadium that is open for all to use.

Monica has invited a friend Bernadette to stay with us. While Monica is out that night, I chat to Bernadette about our marital problems. Bernadette said that when she & her husband have disagreements, they would say nothing in front of others but discuss in the evening all night, if need be, until they had resolved the problem. I said I would love to be able to do that, but every time I want to discuss a problem, Monica would say, "I am tired, or we discuss in the morning," always demain, demain, demain.

Often, **I am like a fly on the wall**, she will ignore me with people around & if the discussion is not to her liking when I am talking, she will change the conversation with people.

Monday 2nd July 2007: Monica, dare divorce me

Bernadette phones Monica & told her all we had discussed last night. Monica phones me up to meet at lunchtime, she is livid that I discussed our problems with her friend. I said we need to talk, "What about?" "You always keep saying, "Demain, demain, demain, but tomorrow never comes, and we never discuss problems. "We meet at a large cafeteria in Massy. I said I am getting to the end of my patience with Monica with all our problems, both financial as well as men.

She dares me to divorce her by saying, **"You know you love me & I love you.**

"You say I am spending too much money, but the problem is, you are not earning enough money! I see & go out with these men to help you, me & Lennon. These men help us, so what is your problem?

You are now free to see other women & good luck with your meetings, I am sure when you are together they help you forget our problems eh? I think you are just frustrated because you cannot satisfy a woman. I have given you Cialis & that does help with your erection …yes?" While we talk for some time probably 2 hours over the lunch break, I needed to get back to work. We decide to arrange for a pub meeting with Paul, I left that with Monica.

Wed 3rd-Frid 6th July: Hungary trip

I attended a small Hungarian seminar conference arranged by our Hungarian agent, Francoise, a dynamic little woman who lives west of Paris. She was always with two mobile phones hanging from her neck, one her Hungary phone with a local SIM card for local customer calls & the other French phone for other calls. After the seminar & dinner that night with key customers, she then took me the next day to visit customers in the Budapest area, including the Hungarian Geological Institute, where I got to know the head of the department. Chatting about his research work, I offered to give them publicity by using their data.*

*I was able to arrange for their analytical work to be sent to me. I made PowerPoint lectures & wrote an article in the Horiba magazine quoting their data, Horiba JY paid both him & his chief assistant €250 each. He, as head of department said that was almost one month's salary for him & more than a month's salary for his assistant!

BBC News broadcast changed my sales strategy for concentrating on the Middle East

One night in the hotel, I listened to BBC world news on the radio & listen to a VERY interesting broadcast based in Irvine, California. The BBC radio world news article in **July 2007** was about the calamity with the housing market in Irvine, California & soon to encompass all USA. Mortgages could be obtained by the estate agents within 2 hours on the phone **without** investigation or consideration of other loans like car or boat loans. After 6-9 months, people would realise they could not afford the house mortgage, car & boat loan repayments, so they would post the keys through the post box. The value of the house would depreciate in value from purchase by maybe $100,000. The reporter interviewing the estate agent chap said he had 5,000 houses on this estate agents books 5,000 x $100,000 amounted to more than

$500m lost just in Irvine, CA! Imagine multiplying this all over the state of California & then all over USA!

Well known saying, *When America sneezes, the rest of the world catches a cold*. I realised the rest of the world would suffer....BADLY, so I immediately planned to concentrate on the Middle East market as this was full of potential & at the time was a miniscule order value in my regional responsibilities, especially having been banned from selling to Iran due to the increasing political problems.. My plan was it could compensate for loss of European business that was bound to happen. The middle east would be less likely to suffer compared with fall in Europe & Africa sales, anyway, Africa was mainly South Africa & Egypt business. If I did not change strategy from mainly Europe to the Middle East, my sales would be a disaster & that would affect production & people's jobs in JY. I would need to find better agents in most Middle East countries & visit them at least 4-5 times a year with a concentrated 2 week tour. Researching to find good agents for several countries like KSA took some months.

Game-changing BBC programme on impending financial crises in July 2007

My position as EMEA (Europe, Middle East & Africa) sales & operations manager starting in 2005 progresses well after being an ICP-AES product manager since I moved to France in 1998. When I got back to the JY factory, I started to investigate potential new agents, especially for KSA (Kingdom of Saudi Arabia). We had only ever sold one ICP-AES in the country, & we had no idea of its status. I eventually appointed NSC (National Scientific Co) based in Al Kabar East KSA.

I made my plans in late 2007-early 2008 to start having a 2 week Middle East tour incorporating Kuwait, Dubai (UAE), KSA (Kingdom Saudi Arabia) & finish of in Egypt. I implement my plan with 4–5 trips per year 2008–2011. Business increased so that sales expanded exponentially, especially in a region that previously was virtually zero.

This increase in Middle East business happened just as the world banking "sub-prime" crisis started to bite mid to late-2008 into the world economy & affected JY European sales.

Thank you, BBC World Service!

Friday 6th July 2007: List of grievances with Monica – cannot go on for much more

I decided to make a list during work on the subjects that were eating into me with Monica.

1) Money Spending what we do not have & not contributing to the mortgage

    a. I have looked at Moni Clean business & it is not making a profit & yet she spends money like profits are good. At the present rate, the business will fold into bankruptcy (it did).

2) Ask a simple question requiring a simple "yes" or "no" or "name", but no, she explains over minutes all the things I do not needed with excuses; or "I need to go to the loo" or " I am tired" or "demain".

3) "Fly on the wall" she will speak in French all the time to people & ignore me.

4) In the company of others, e.g. a party or a gathering I may be chatting with people & she will leave her group, come over to my group & purposely interrupt us & say they are not interested in what you say. Another example, we are together, & the subject is not one she knows anything about, again she will change the subject,

5) Will not teach me French to be better. Always "demain, I am tired." I believe the real reason is that I will not understand talk or written information that is detrimental to me or what she is hiding from me.

6) Monica does not put herself out for anyone UNLESS it is of advantage to her. She will even refuse ME to help others, e.g. Cloe and Stanley.

7) IMAGE is so important for Monica, she always puts on a show to impress people, telling lies in the process

    a. Giving false information on the success of Moni Clean business & showing off the house that we have money.

8) Monica is not interested in what I have to say or my views. She is not interested in me.

9) I am not sure Monica loves me, I think she just loves what I can provide....**Money, status, Image.**

10) I have to accept all of her affairs, & usually, she is not interested in me in bed.

I meet Paul & Monica in a Novotel in Massy, we discuss all the points I had written down. Some points she disputes like money, while she promised to be more loving & let me shag her more. I said to both Paul & Monica, *this cannot go on for much more. My love for Monica was getting fragile.*

Tuesday 10th July 2007

Monica phones me at 5:45pm while I am driving to Viry Chatillon to train & coach. I phone her back when I arrived to find out what she wanted. She said it was urgent and if I could drop everything off immediately to pick up a chap Abdule, who is doing a job for her at a block of flats being cleaned by Moni Clean prior to letting, the building was in Chilly Mazerin Abdul cannot drive. I said I could do that when I have finished & not before. Monica was not happy with my reply. I finished training & coaching at about 7:45pm & went around to the apartment block in question. When I arrived on the floor, Abdule was still working & just starting to clear up! Monica wanted me to waste my time. She wants to muck up all my plans & fit in with what she wants me to do, like a servant puppy dog. Why was she lying about the time when he needed a lift? She knew he would still be working for several hours.

On the way back home, I popped into Longjumeau centre & saw Monica's car still in the car park opposite Julian's notaire office. Why does she lie about wanting to be with Julian? She made her usual story of how tired & busy she was. When she spoke to me, she was in Chilly Mazerin, which was not true. I stopped listening & walked away to the kitchen to make a cup of tea.

Wednesday 11th July: Don stays again

Don, my cousin, came & stayed with us at Longjumeau a 2nd time without saying how long he would stay. He said he was thinking of moving over to France. He floated that idea last time & stayed 3-4 weeks.

Most nights after work or training, we would go for a walk & always discuss the subject of Monica, Rachael & my marriage & Lennon's problems of being lazy & poor school work. We chatted in depth as we walked.

When the opportunity arose, we would drive around the region where maybe he would like to live. I am not sure he was too serious. An example, when we saw an estate agency in a nice area west of Longjumeau, he would not come in the office, but stayed outside, perhaps worried about the questions they would ask. Don's excuse was that he could not speak French, but seeing that I would do all the talking, his reluctance to enter the agencies was puzzling, unless he was not serious about moving to France.

Sunday 22nd July 2007

When I got home that morning after training, I realised I had left my computer open whereby Monica had read my e-mails to Rachael. Monica was really upset with comments like, "I think I love Rachael more than Monica". She also saw I had investigated Monica's secret money income, she was claiming from the social security, for Epilepsy for Lennon! Monica could go to gaol for that fraud! Alternative would have been paying back €800/month, what she had de-frauded*. Monica is annoyed that I found out, not that she is doing something illegal!

* Much later, I found documents in the house when clearing it out for sale, that she had to pay back €16,000 in total, adding to the enormous debt she accrued. This in turn delayed her application for French nationality, this came to light when Monica had a fight with Gisele in a shop, August 2011 in Brussels & both were arrested. Gisele said Monica had to show her Rwandan passport.

Wednesday 25th July 2007: research on boarding school

For some weeks, Monica has been saying that Lennon is not working hard enough. I agreed with Monica that he is too easily distracted with his friends around. She said that a boarding school would be the answer whereby he would HAVE TO do the homework with few distractions. I thought it was all talk until that night Monica thrusts in front of me a document to sign. I asked, "What is it?" She responded that it was the document for Lennon to attend a local residential boarding school. "So how much is it?" "Read it," she responded, expecting me to ask her what it said. However, my written/reading French is much better than speech or listening. I read it & could see that Monica had put a deposit of €100 to inscribe Lennon without mentioning costs. I refused to sign it, we had a row. I noticed on Friday that a cheque had been banked for €100.

From the snippets of information Monica had mentioned over the past few weeks, I surmised it was local & started researching local residential boarding schools. I found one that ticked all the boxes of information that I remember Monica saying to me. At lunchtime, I researched & went to a school up on a private road near the Villebon-2 commercial area, a small single-track road Rue du Baron de Nivière, 91140 Villebon-sur-Yvette, a few miles from Longjumeau.

It was by chance I found the director there, lucky because it was the school summer holidays. Expecting & confirming the large fees required, I explained that Monica had no money and that her company was close to bankruptcy, with no chance of me funding Lennon to be a residential student. He suggested that if residential schooling was too expensive, it would be cheaper to attend daily. I said Monica wanted Lennon to be residential to enable him to be detached from his friends so that he would work harder. Daily attendance served no purpose; he was already at a good school, Lycée Jacques Prévert, on our road just 100 metres from our house in Longjumeau! The director saw my logic & agreed to cancel the inscription & return the money.

That night, another row occurred when I told her I had been to the school, seen the director & cancelled the inscription. Here was another example of stupid expenditure with money we did not have. It does not matter; Geoff will pay, and we have just one life; spend it.

Saturday 28th July 2007: marriage end is nigh – Nicky to resume relationship?

I went around Rachael's to pick up Zoe for training & coaching down the hill by Viry Chatillon Lake where the stadium was located. I had been giving messages to Sophie B, Rachael's eldest daughter when training & coaching that I was seeking a divorce from Monica. Rachael agreed to meet me again & resume our relationship. That night, I returned to Rachael's house in Grigny village to pick her up & then we went to a restaurant locally. Afterwards, we quickly booked & stayed in a local hotel for the night. WOW! Rachael could perform, all those worries with me being married or not, she showed me what was on offer if I did get a divorce. Good job I had taken Cialis in case! This position, that position, James was so happy that night, up & down, in & out, his volcano kept erupting, much to Rachael's pleasure.

Monday 30th July: separate bedrooms agreed holiday all together cancelled

After work, I went to Grigny to see Rachael with her family around for a quick chat, but I left as there were too many people around, she was also rather busy cooking. Returning home, Don & I went for a walk around the Longjumeau area. The new house at the back just fields and & a large wood beyond and, was a small walk away from Ballainvilliers village. Returning home, we had dinner & then went to bed.

Monica & I quietly chatted in bed for some 3 hours. Monica was not happy I stayed in a hotel with Rachael Saturday night. We decided to cancel the planned holiday in Sanary-sur-Mer with David & Agnes's at their holiday house all together. We also decided to sleep in different bedrooms & only be together when visitors came to say with us & not to tell anyone of our problems except for Don of course.

One question Monica asked me was a good one about Don. He stayed with us last time for a month; now, he has been with us for 3 weeks without any desire to search for a house here in France, as he says, or where he will go when he returns to England.

Having said our family holiday would be cancelled, I did not know what to do regarding a holiday. I knew Rachael had an aunt in Biarritz — maybe we could go other together?

Tuesday 31st July: what are Don's plans? A rolling stone

I went after work to Rachael's house & told her my planned holiday with Monica was off & asked if she would like to go on holiday with me. She immediately said "Yes," & we started talking about the possibilities. Apparently, the aunt in Biarritz was not keen on visitors except the kids, so she had another idea. Sophie B was Rachael's eldest daughter, her father Paul B was living in a village near the Pyrenees called St Girons. Rachael said she would phone Paul to see if we could stay there for 2 weeks. I returned home after maybe an hour because Don was still with us.

Don a Rolling stone

On our usual evening walk, I asked Don about his plans. He did not know. I said he was like a rolling stone. No home, yet he owned two houses rented out in Chelmsford. He was floating around lost. Ever since he left Germany 20 years previously, he was rather lost in England. I said he needs to put some roots down to say this is "home", even if he goes on holiday & sees friends much of the time. He was already having to jostle paperwork, bank address, tax etc around the fact he had two houses without one being his "home". I suggested he moves in one & then decide what to do from there. He agreed. Within a week, on 7th of August, he left for England with a better idea of what he needed to do with his life. Within a few weeks, he decided to sell one house & buy a bungalow in Suffolk. He saw what he wanted, managed by cunning & trickery at the estate agent, got the bungalow owner's address. He offered a quick sale of £140,000, paying in cash. Therefore, no delay or possibility of any deal falling through. With his persuasion, he bought the bungalow even though the owners had accepted a previous offer via the estate agent. This is why in England NOTHING is certain about a house sale UNTIL all the documents cross signed by BOTH parties.

Wed 1st to Saturday 11th August

I moved some of my clothes into the upstairs bedroom #4 & keep the rest in "our" bedroom. I still have a shower in "our" en-suite & neither of us cares much about the privacy one would have with strangers. We now often pass like strangers, even when neither of us is fully clothed. I have not seen any other women other than Rachael on Sundays, & I have lost much interest in following Monica's exploits or of course, pursuing any females on Meetic.

Friday 10th August

I started packing my suitcase for the next day, Monica hadn't fully realised what she had agreed on several weeks ago & couldn't face up to the fact I had cancelled the Sanary-sur-mer holiday on the Mediterranean coast & would be going with Rachael on holiday. I feel peculiar that I am not with my wife but going on holiday with my girlfriend. All the time I feel guilty, I should be going with Monica, my wife.

Sunday 12th August 2007 – Saturday 25th August: Holiday with Rachael -St Girons near the Pyrenees'

Rachael & I leave early for St Girons to stay with Paul B (Sophie B's father) & partner, Elaine. We arrived early evening at this small town with their ground apartment floor overlooking the river below.

Paul was a very interesting character. Born as the son of a French ambassador, he was fluent in four languages and very intelligent but wanted to escape from the "rat race". He could have been in a high position in diplomacy or anything, but rejected all including his parents, who were so disappointed with him. He only worked enough by painting & sculpture-making to pay bills & then veg out. I could see why Rachael decided when Sophie B was less than 1 years old to leave him. A really nice man, but he had no "get up & go". He just wanted to live a hippy life and smoke the weed he grew.

He grew his own weed/pot (marijuana) plants on the balcony over the river. I mentioned that people could see his pot plants. Oh, there is a river between us. "Yes, but the path on the other side of the river is only 20 metres away. I suggest you put some cloth over the balcony to hide the plants." He agreed & put some old bed sheets over the railing. I found it easy to talk with him for a whole range of subjects as I really enjoy an intellectual conversation.

Rachael & I had a nice holiday with Paul & his partner, going to various interesting places like Beziers*, Château de Montségur, a mountain-top ruined 13th-century castle & various walks.

* On 22nd July 1209 Bezier was attacked initiated in the Kingdom of France at the behest of Pope Innocent III, the idea was to eliminate the growing Cathar religious movement that challenged the Catholic Church. The Abbot of Citeaux, Arnaud Amalric, ordered every single person in Beziers to be killed with the famous edict "**Kill them all, God will know His own**" *he later wrote, "…….Our men spared no one, irrespective of rank, sex or age, and put to the sword almost 20,000 people. After this great slaughter the whole city was despoiled and burnt, as divine vengeance miraculously raged against it…….*"

The small road in front of their apartment has a large gully gutter that one needed to park the car into to enable other cars to pass the narrow town side road. When walking down the road, one needed to walk carefully with eyes serious fixed on the ground because the road was full of dog shit where dog walkers just let their dogs shit anywhere, I called it, « la capitale du monde pour le caca ». (The capital of the world for shit), much to the amusement of all.

While on holiday, I used to go to a cyber café* to pick up e-mails on business & any personal ones. I received an angry e-mail from Monica, saying that Lennon had broken his leg & that I was nowhere around but was off with my girlfriend. Funny, I don't remember Monica coming to see me in the hospital when I was only 500 metres away from our house. I supposed she was angry that Lennon needed her attention, & this was restricting her men's activities. I found out much later, she still saw her men anyway.

* No WiFi in those days

Sat 25th August: back in Longjumeau, Lennon's broken leg

We return home, & after unpacking the car of Rachael's things, I leave to go back home. Rachael says, "Why are you going back to

Longjumeau?" "I live there, Lennon has broken his leg; I need to look after him," I replied, gave her a kiss & drove off. I could see Rachael was perplexed & disappointed.

I arrived home with a frosty reception from Monica. Looking at Lennon with his leg in plaster, she says, "Look after your son, like you should have done during the last week." I have an appointment soon. Within an hour, Monica departed, leaving me to unpack my suitcase in my bedroom, now bedroom #4 & spend time with Lennon.

Sitting in the lounge, Lennon starts to tell me things that had happened during the 2 weeks I was away. The accident where he broke his leg & then he says things that obviously favoured his mother Monica. He starts saying things like, we would not be able to sell the house; Monica does not want to sell, so with me (Lennon) here, you would never be able to sell. She would make things so difficult that you would have a nervous breakdown etc.

I started getting agitated at his stance, eventually, I said that his mum was a prostitute and that she was always going out with different men and I also knew of most of her sexual affairs & that it was driving me nuts. Remember, she has gone out, who do you think with? MEN, she is always seeing men & getting money, favours, contracts etc, for sexual return. Lennon did not argue, or defend her actions but then just stayed quiet; he knew I knew much more than him.

As a scientist, we make VERY good detectives. I know MUCH more than Monica thinks I know. Maybe that was what he was referring to that I would have a nervous breakdown for.

Sunday 26th August 2007

Monica arrives home about 1am Sunday morning from a long Saturday night out. She wakes me up in my bedroom. Monica wants to talk. So still in bed, she sat on my bed, we chatted & chatted & chatted until 8am! She was still angry that I had cancelled her holiday in Sanary-sur-mer (David & Agnes's holiday house) with Lennon. I said I wanted to sell the house, but this house was her dream, & there was no chance of her agreeing to that. She said that I could not sell the house without her agreement & that would NEVER happen. I replied that I was the only one that was paying the mortgage & with all other expenses, I was having problems with money while she was paying nothing. One way or another, either we sell the house with a profit, or the bank forecloses with unpaid mortgage payments. If the bank sells, they will sell VERY cheaply just to get their money quickly, & we would get virtually nothing out of the sale to share.

Monica thinks hard & then proposes, after some hours, that she would contribute to the mortgage & that I can live with Rachael.

Monica will not face up to the fact that Rachael is NOT the cause of the marriage problems and breakup. I said it was an accumulation of so many things together that are causing the problems. I said remember, I have made notes I gave you for you to think about. She just ignored what I said & carried on accusing Rachael as the source of the problem. Monica really has a mental problem of assimilating information & then bending things to her mindset. She is starting to think her dreams of living in this house are numbered & is clinging on to anything she can think of. She will not accept that, at some point, she will need to sell the house.

She then starts when the threat becomes clearer, "Are you going to put Lennon & me on the street?" I repeated that the profit from the sale of the house would be divided among both of us. She can buy what she wants like Lyn did some 11 years previous. Whether she could afford another house when considering the real financial state of Moni Clean business is another question.

Monica keeps harking back to the fact in her eyes that it was Rachael who was dividing us. No matter what I say, it is like talking to a brick wall. She is not listening or wanting to listen. I said, "Monica **I love you,** but I cannot carry on with our marriage as it is. You are driving me nuts with worry on so many issues. Why do you not understand? My health will suffer with the mental strain unless I do something."

Monday 27th August 2007: Rachael shock – it is finished between us #3

Rachael sent me an SMS it said, "*Goodbye, go back to your wife and adopted son. We are finished. I do not want to go with you again. You will always want to return to your darling wife, Monica and your son. You will never divorce her.*"

Oh, shit, what to do now? Where to go now? I am in a state of shock!

I leave work early to go to Rachael's house. On opening the door, one of the kids shouts for Rachael, "Geoff est ici." Rachael come to the door but stays at the door opening. She explains in more detail what she said in her SMS: I am married to Monica, that I still love her & still care for her & that I am not really serious about leaving her. She said that she did not intend to be hanging on waiting for me forever, while I stay with Monica. Sorry to say, this is goodbye. Seeing the resolution in her eyes, I turned slightly, waiting for a come-back reaction but none came, so I slowly departed.

I got home about 7pm, rather lost & watched TV with Lennon sitting there with his leg in plaster. Monica arrived home about 7:30-8 pm. I only greeted her with a sad "hello", she reciprocated & saw I looked a bit dazed & sad. "What's the matter?" I was reluctant to say anything & tried to evade the question & asked whether she wanted a cup of tea. **Monica may not be intellectual, but she is intelligent, astute & can read people well.** She pursued me in the kitchen. "Are you OK? What's the matter?" She could see in my eyes that I was sad. She embraced me & lovingly looked into my eyes, "You know you can tell me." "I know, but…… Rachael has finished with me." Monica's expression was one of surprise & happiness while trying to appear sad & concerned for me. She cuddled me more, there was a pregnant pause before she said softly, "Do not worry, my dear, I can help you. We can work something out. I promise I will try to make you happy". I wanted that cuddle & did not want to let go; I was so sad. Eventually, eyes so watery, I used my hand & sniffed & I said, "Ah, you wanted a cup of tea?" "Oh, yes, make me a cup of tea while I change."

At that point, she went upstairs to her bedroom to change. I followed her upstairs to change myself as well. I do not like relaxing in my work suit, even though I have always had to wear a suit, shirt & tie all my working life. I HATE ties or anything around my neck, I always want to find tops that have a low neck line. Why do they provide low neck line for woman & not men, except occasionally, I find one. I went in "my" bedroom to change, Monica heard me & called out to me to help her. I had only just taken off my tie & trousers, but I had not put on some shorts, it being still hot. Not thinking & still in a daze, I went into "her" bedroom, where she indicated me to undo her dress zip at the back. I pulled down her zip ready to depart, when she turned around, "Do you like to look at me still?" "Of course," I said. "What is it you like when you look at me?" "Well, you have a lovely face, beautiful body, lovely boobs, lovely bum &…." Each time I made an observational comment, she would smile. "Do you want to see my boobs again?" "Of course." So, she turned around for me to undo her lacy bra. Having done that she turned around, "There, these are what you have been missing. I am your wife, & these are yours…….if you want them." Indicating her boobs, I caressed them & fondled them. She then smiled a mischievous smile, "Forget about Rachael, I am much better, & **I love you & you love me**…" I started to breathe heavily as I caressed & fondled her boobs, she started to stroke my culottes with James rising up. "You love me, don't you?" "Yes, you know I do" I replied as she sat down on the bed, removed my culottes, started to stroke James up & down with her hand & then bent down to put James in her mouth. I forgot all about my problems as Monica sucked & squeezed James with her mouth, harder & harder until the explosion happened with cum oozing from her mouth as she carried on the up & down action until the final reduction to a shrivelled walnut was achieved. All that time, she was looking at me with a lovely smile of satisfaction. I flopped on the bed beside her, we cuddled a bit until she got up & went to the en-suite bathroom.

Well, that was some homecoming, I thought. Nice holiday with Rachael, then she finishes with me again. Monica feels sorry for me & turns on the charm to seduce me & gives me a blow job to smooth things over. Now what do I do? Do I seek divorce? Or ….see how things progress? My mind is now so confused, & so many things whizzed around in my head. What the hell am I going to do?

Tuesday 28th August 2007

Monica sent me a message when I was at work, asking me how I was and if I were. I replied that I was OK, thanked her for last night & understanding me. She comes back with an idea to go out for dinner somewhere. I agree, she finishes work early to be home by 6pm. After changing, we went to a resto I know in a local village St Michel sur Orge. It was good to get out & talk about different things other than problems. I was saturated with them. Monica had put on a sexy lace blouse, skirt & high heel shoes. She was very nice to me & didn't raise once any hint of what had proceeded. Was this a new leaf of the book?

Returning home, Lennon was in his bedroom, we had tea & then Monica beckoned me to follow her upstairs into "her" bedroom. She invited me to undress her, & quickly, I was in her spell. **It is like she has a Voodoo doll that she can manipulate me at will.** Another great night with me mounting her doggy style, this time as she & I prefer. I slept well that night. Monica says as things are now "normal" and that we are back in love together, I could come back into our bedroom. So, I transferred what I had moved back from my temporary bedroom #4

Voodoo or what?

What is it that Monica has me under her spell? Am I under some Voodoo spell that even if I am angry, she can twist me quickly around her finger? When we are not at war, we can talk about any personal things so easily.

Sept 2007

Things start to settle down to the usual story of appointments with men & finding money being spent frivolously. I feel trapped with Monica, & a strong feeling of impending financial problems due to Monica began to loom over me. I don't have Rachael to fall back on; however, the pressure of financial ruin, the constant stream of men she meets & her sexual evenings are starting to take their toll again. If one more major thing happens, I will take the leap into divorce.

I am able to see Moni Clean docs, finances, & her plans. I start analysing the dire situation:

Average loss per month (last 6 months) = € 940/m

Secret Comments made Sept 2007

- Moni Clean has small window cleaning contracts €100-200/m & sometimes one or 2 /day jobs paying sometimes €500-600.
- It is losing money WITHOUT the extra expense of the new office she has taken (admittedly, this is low cost €350/month), but she spent about ~ €800-1,000 on office furniture.
- The plan is to take on a women as secretary/logistics this week. She would cost a min of €1,000 (assuming she paid ~ €700 plus statutory charges that are > x1.4 salary).
- Job description: to do quotes, take phone calls & organise from the office the logistics of each contract requirements.
- This means she will have ~ <u>€1,500 **extra** expense per month.</u>
- September 30th **account** could be negative by as much as €1,000

- ➢ She has two extra contracts worth €450 & €650 = total €1,100/m starting mid Sept

- ➢ Promise (always lots of promises) of 2 more contracts worth €1,200 (End Oct) & €1,100 (end Sept) (total €2,300/m). Monica runs her business on promises. (e.g. Marie de Paris, Bateaux Mouches).

- ➢ We still have some 300 bottles of wines unsold in the garage (being reduced by private use: give aways, taste to buy personal consumption…)

QUESTION

- ➢ Monica draws NO SALARY, why is the cash flow going down?

- ➢ Is she getting contracts at a net loss?

- ➢ She has had to pay off two employees that the client (Champs Ellysse doctor) did not like.

- ➢ Monica has sometimes cash flow problems paying "black". Where does the "black" money go?

Friday 14th: Trawling Meetic encore with Monica's encouragement in September 2007

With Monica fully occupied with her various men, I need to find a woman. With Monica's enthusiastic encouragement, I go online again on Meetic. I fix up a meeting with Agatha, a Nigerian living near Aulnay sur Bois, for the next day. We arrange to meet at a café she knows, giving me the details of its address.

Saturday 15th 2007

I meet Agatha in the evening at a local bar she knew first & then went to a resto. She was about average height, had a rounded Nigerian face & probably a fair handful of boobs well-hidden. It was a pleasant evening. I drove her home, & she invited me back to have a nightcap.

Up a lot of stairs because the lift was not working, we went into a dingy flat. We drank tea on the tatty sofa, she put her hand on my thigh. She explained in her African English accent that she had only just gone onto Meetic that week, so I was her first man to meet. I did not volunteer the fact she was one of many I had met. I explained my relationship with Monica that I was unhappy, also that Monica had given me permission to meet other females so long as I stayed with her. She was rather shocked at Monica's attitude. Normally, I see the female's cleavage with low-cut tops or dresses, but Agatha's were well hidden, she was shy. However, it did not stop her from caressing my leg and getting closer to my groin. I reciprocated caressing her thigh in her trousers. We gradually got closer to both our private parts, as I switched to feel her boobs on her fluffy pullover. With approval, I went under & felt her boobs on her bra & caressed them. Yes, there was a good cleavage.

Suddenly, the doorbell rang, & Agatha got up with a start. Embarrassed, she went to the spy hole. Upon recognising the person, she opened the door. It was a friend of hers, she entered. We made pleasant greetings, & the friend started talking incessantly without realising she had interrupted something. Agatha slowly started to answer any questions & started a conversation that left me out of it. After some 15 minutes, I excused myself with Agatha embarrassed & gesturing for me to call her again. With the state of the flat, I was not sure I wanted to pursue Agatha again.

24-28th Sept 2007: Poland-Estonia trip

I made a series of sales visits with the Polish agent in Krakow, Lodz and Plock & then the night of the 27th stayed in Tallinn, Estonia, to see a few client possibilities on the 28th before flying home that evening.

Sat 29th September

Just before my birthday, I have "reached the last straw" with another financial action of Monica. I discover more money spent by

Monica, with an average of €5,000-7,000, disappearing in the last few months as she used our joint account to pay into Moni Clean. She will ruin me* unless I do something drastic. I need to divorce Monica.

* When clearing out the house in January 2012, we found debts of €410,000 for the year 2008. WOW, I could not have made a better decision. Perhaps I should have decided earlier!

Monica doesn't want to discuss the hopeless financial state of Moni Clean & repeats those now famous words **"It's not me spending too much money; it is YOU not earning enough!"**

Sunday 30th: Saddest birthday

It is my birthday, but *it is the saddest birthday ever.* I go training to de-stress about the situation, but I constantly thought about the financial situation and going bankrupt with Monica extracting so much money to prop up her loss making company, PLUS, of course, her men & keeping it secret. I decide, die is cast, I must seek a divorce. On returning from training, I tried to avoid Monica as much as possible until she went out for another appointment with a man. Who? I really do not care now.

You can push an Englishman so far, until finally he says… NO MORE! Then, NOTHING will stop his resolve.

First Lyn, then Anne & now Monica have found that out

Mon 1st Oct 2007: Advocate – the die is cast - Geoff seeks divorce

The die is cast. I research an advocate dealing with marriages from work. I phoned for an appointment & see the advocate, Haussmann, based at an office on the A7 Attis Mons, to file for divorce.

I went home & told Monica. Monica is shocked & screams that I will never get her out of this house and that it is hers! Monica asked whether I was still seeing Rachael. I said, "No, that is dead." "So you will need to find someone new then?" "Yes, I will start anew & look."

Monica suggested I pursue the "Meetic" website. I agreed that would continue to be the first starting point.

Due to possible clashes, I agree to move out of our bedroom into bedroom # 4 across the corridor again.

During my research of various documents, I discovered for the divorce case that money was stolen by Monica via a VERY complicated means when we bought the house, loads of docs & loans all in French with only Monica to try to explain, always "I will explain tomorrow I am tired..."

- *Between €50 -90k disappeared via fraudulent drafts,*
- *My money transferred from the UK is now deemed inadmissible to my ownership*
- *child support to pay for Lennon €5k who was at the time nearly 18 years old,*
- *other stolen money €5k,*
- *€5-7,000 being transferred from our joint account to pay for Moni Clean losses*
- *Spending approx €1.5k each month on her alone & her company, I funded what was a loss-making company that was the money laundering method to get my money.*

Wed 3rd – Frid 12th Oct 2007: UK trip

I visited England for the week and stayed with Nan, who was living in dad's house. I had promised dad on his death bed via the phone to the nurse that Nan could stay there until she needed to move. Little did I know, she would survive quite some years before she needed to go in a care home for her last couple of years; she died aged 101 years old. I finished the tour of clients up in the Manchester area before driving down south to get the ferry home. The UK visit gave me time to relax from the situation & think hard as to what I would be doing in the future.

During the interval between trips in October & November, I tried to be as nice as possible to Monica to avoid clashes with her. I would have meetings at €600/ visit with advocate Haussman, providing him with the information he requested, but also any information I felt would help me get the divorce done.

Sunday 21st – Sat 27th Oct 2007: South African trip

I flew to Jo'burg Sunday to stay at a guest house, Melville House on 4th Ave, Melville, near a nice street of restaurants & bars for entertainment. The owner, Heidi Holland, was a writer and knew President Mugabe well when he first became president after Britain negotiated the transfer of Ian Smith's illegal Rhodesia UDI to true legal Zimbabwe independence. However, over the years, Heidi saw how his attitude had changed, so she wrote a book about his years as President Mugabe, "From Hero to Tyrant", she signed a copy of her book I bought from her.

I then got an internal flight to Durban, staying one night on 23rd for visits to Richards Bay & Durban & then flew onto Cape Town the night of the 24th. Customer visits in Cape Town & Stellenbosch. I was taken around that weekend by Paul de Plessis, meeting his family. It was a nice weekend visiting Kalk Bay, a small beach town near Cape Town & then more customer visits before finally flying back home. The trip was a nice change from the stress of my life at home at the time.

Sunday 28th Oct

I went down to the stadium to train, even though I was tired from my trip. I don't see much of Monica except to say good morning & good evening. She was out all day, which suits me fine; we both want to avoid conflicts. I don't ask where she is going, and I don't care anymore as she would lie anyway.

Thursday 1st Nov 2007: Club Med Bercy, Paris with Monica

Monica invited me to meet her at a fête being held in Club Med, Bercy village, with her friend, who was a Club Med member, she could get us in free with her visitor's pass. The club was in Bercy village, a nice touristic precinct near Bercy peripherique junction. It was an enjoyable day, Monica was very friendly to me as if trying to change my mind on divorce.

Friday 2nd - Tues 13th Nov: Resigned to divorce or possible reprieve?

Monica is still thinking and hoping, I guess, that I will stop the divorce process. She is friendly & seems to be wanting to be on my good side. We go out for a drink, if she needs a company with relations & close friends, I am by her side, still as her "husband". We are, to all the world, still Mr & Mrs.

I am effectively single again, so now I am online on Meetic in contact with various females. It is a case of meeting some of these women when I want. I don't need Monica's approval, but every time I am on the computer, Monica seems to glance at the screen & see "Meetic" moves away pleased. She lives in hope.

Wed 14th-Thurs 15th Nov 2007: Sweden / Finland trip

My trip started with Sweden seeing Dag Seden, the GammaData president, to visit a GDS prospect in Finespong north of Stockholm. After our visit, I get an evening flight to Helsinki. On arrival, my Finland agent drove westwards as we needed to traverse the whole breadth of Finland. For many hours we see trees, lakes, soggy ground, trees, more trees, more lakes & trees, it seems never-ending. We eventually arrived late, about 10.30 pm, at a small hotel in a small community. When we checked in, the receptionist/owner told us that we had missed the weekly great community social gathering & entertainment. The next morning, we drove onwards to the coast to Norilsk Nickel, after our meeting with the lab manager. Up early &

again some hours drive to arrive on the coast. I had a meeting with the lab manager regarding the possible sale of a new ICP-AES to replace his old Spectro ICP & then lunch before we made the return journey back to Helsinki airport & home. A very long day in the car & then a flight; I was knackered when I got home, with only Lennon there. We briefly chatted before I needed to go to bed

During the interlude period from **16th to 28th November**, I wasn't having much luck fixing any female appointments with anyone I fancied. I met Paul on several occasions at our normal Palaiseau pub, he suggested I use a couple of female phone numbers he had hidden away.

Thursday 29th November: Marina -nymphomaniac in club 2+2

Paul had recommended a Caroline & Marina whom he had met various times. I contacted Marina on the Thursday & suggested we meet at a bar in Montparnasse & then go to 2+2. We entered 2+2, I forgot to remind Marina she must wear a skirts or a dress. She turned up in trousers, so I paid €10 for Marina to change from her trousers to a skirt that I rented. It seems a bit silly, because once we had another drink at the bar, we went upstairs & then everything comes off anyway! I had taken Cialis before I left the house, and I was ready.

Marina was a slim African lady from Togo, about 35 years old & well-proportioned in the right places. She said she had a boyfriend only, but I found out from Paul later when I next met him that she was married. Several men eyed her up & down, ready to pounce, before I took charge, led her to a couch & played for a while before she put the condom on & invited a doggy-style shag. Once the performance was over, I moved off to rest & sit down, thinking she would do the same. No repose for her; her suitors eyed her again. With an acceptance look, one was quickly playing with her & shagging her. Wow, that was quick between shags. Other men saw how quickly she accepted their looks, and they played the game when he had finished. With eye-to-eye language to number 2 man, Marina indicated a rest, said her back was aching, because the couch reclining back was too far away & asked whether she would lean against me as I was sitting up. I shrugged OK, & then man number two started feeling her backside while she held my shoulder. I was able to be in a good position to caress her boobs while she was being shagged by number 2.

By now, several men were looking and admiring Marina. So, when number 3 looked at her, she looked back to suggest "go ahead", and he was quickly in action. I let her boobs swing from time to time, as the rhythm of shagging is quite erotic. Wow, no wonder Paul liked her & said she shagged well. By now, there seemed to be a queue to try her out. I could see all from my position sitting on the couch in front of Marina who was facing me. How many more shags, one after the other could she take? Well, number 4 was already fully erect, & she had to tell him to be more gentle with inserting his plonker. He was impatient as he was already ejaculating over her backside...... does that count as a shag? Well, number 5 certainly counts: gentle, slow insertions. The rhythm of her boobs showed a slow acceleration until they were flopping in all directions. She certainly moaned with excitation this time. She has cum. It only needed 6 consecutive shags! NOW, she needed to rest, sitting beside me & disappointing the queue of men.

Marina went to the loo, & while I was sitting there, a blond-haired lady came up to me & placed my hands on her boobs. She intimated they needed a massage, didn't they? She obviously felt my tool needed a massage as well. After a time of massaging, James started to grow much to her satisfaction & then with condom at the ready in her hand she slipped it on & sat on me slowly. Ooh, her movement was ever so gentle & then got off! She then turned around & sat on top of me again, but that was difficult where we were, so then smiling, her legs went up over my shoulders. Oh, c'est plus bon, full penetration. She wiggled her bum. I, with my restricted movement, doing what I could, I was able to pull her & push her shoulders holding around her armpits. No time or opportunity to hold her boobs I had a "job in hand! This is difficult, I thought, and she must have thought as well. Throwing her body forward, I was able to stand up, she moved her legs around my waist, & now mine around her back. We were in a better position for sex. "…Tu es plus fort..", & with that, I was able to get a good hip thrust, well, all that snatch, clean & jerk weight-lifting hip thrusting had to come in handy for something else! Climax came, she seemed satisfied &, eventually, slipped off me to stand up. "Merci, c'est incredible!" & with that, she disappeared to the ladies' room.

Unbeknown to me, Marina had returned & was looking at me with astonishment & did a thumbs up & patted the couch next to her. While I think her fanny was well worn & needed a rest, she was keen to cuddle, kiss me & have her boobs massaged. That was good. I am not used to two shags like that. However, as I caressed her boobs, the nipples got harder more erect & she started showing interest in what I had that was a bit shrivelled below. It was like a walnut at the time. It is amazing what a bit of attention & gentle caressing can do, "by joves." James is smiling again, ready for action? I was afraid of disappointment, but we moved to a bar facing a mirror, & there I could see her mischievous smile. She slipped on a condom over a sort of erect James – yep, Cialis is THAT good.

Facing the mirror, I could see her boobs slowly swing as I slowly used that hip thrust again. She squeezed him tightly & relaxed from time to time until we had a "go situation". Funny how silly thoughts come into one's head; I was thinking of a NASA space rocket ready for launch. We are ready for lift-off, 5,4,3,2,1 ….WOW, here we go again! God, my snatch should be good next weightlifting session, I thought as I pounded away & finally climaxed. While an orgasm is always good, this time, it was tinged with relief. I had made it without disappointing her. The inventor of Cialis should be given a Nobel Prize in a special category, "service to mankind".

She stayed with her hands still holding the bar, looking in the mirror, looking at the men around. One caught her eye, within a wink, he was tooling up with the condom & making a slow insertion. My god, another invited gang bang? What an appetite! I can't believe it; second session number 2 arrives & shags her. I waited for number 3...... but she has had enough. I guess by now, her fanny must be on fire & nearly worn out. We both had a shower & relaxed in the bar before parting company.

That was an experience to remember. However, do I really want to keep going out with a girl who just wants sex with anyone? Conversation (in French) was minimal, so I decided I would just keep her number handy just in case I REALLY wanted sex & nothing else. I doubt it!

Sun 2nd -7th December 2007: Belarus & Ukraine trip

Belarus:

I arrived at the airport customs & immigration, and all the officials looked like they were in the Soviet Union with their distinctive soviet caps & their stern faces with not a nano metre of a smile. Irina, my main agent contact, was there to pick me up & ensure I was booked in OK in the Hotel Minsk before leaving. The next day, I was giving a seminar that we had 55 people held at the local university. All the equipment in the labs was mid-1950s to 1990, and they were VERY inventive in being able to maintain them in good working order since they were so old.

There are many things that strike you as you arrive in another country. The first for me when I arrived in Belarus was everyone was so miserable & stern-faced that I wanted to say to tell the officials to SMILE! I mentioned this when I met our agent, Irina, & she confirmed the fact that everyone has a miserable face. The following evening, we had dinner with the owner of our agent company for Belarus. In conversation, I mentioned the dour faces of everyone in Belarus; he confirmed that when he goes to Western Europe, he sees people with a multitude of faces, many smiling & then after a few days, he gets used to this & then it is a shock when he returns to Belarus!

Due to the effects of the 2nd world war, Minsk was new & totally rebuilt after 1945. This allowed them to build wide boulevards & a ring road around the city that makes for no traffic jams (another reason is they cannot afford new modern cars, so there is a business importing 2nd hand cars....some via USA!).

While there are shops, there are relatively few of them & only one major shopping mall underground in the centre of the city. Shops rarely have large shop windows, so there is little chance of being enticed inside by what is on display! There is no atmosphere to entice one to shop, and one has to walk far to see just a few shops along the boulevards (I am using this terminology to give you an idea of the vast size of the roads).

Traffic lights are good & similar to Ukraine, Egypt & Iran...to name a few in that give pedestrians & motorists a countdown of how long to wait & when the lights will change. NOTE: I saw for the first time that they have started to appear in the UK around 2017. Also, guiding dotted lines for the 2 or 3 lanes on the curves for a left or right turn at traffic lights, dotted guidelines is something I saw in Australia & a few other countries. Pity in UK they do not incorporate both these ideas in most countries to avoid accidents & people getting annoyed at being cut-up when turning!

One night, I went to the Minsk Bolshoi ballet to see "Swan Lake". Now, while I have seen a modern ballet (in Moscow), I never thought I would like a classical ballet...but I did. There were 4 Acts & it lasted from 7 to 10:30 pm. I was amazed at the variety of music that Tchaikovsky wrote for the ballet... the famous part is just a miniscule part of the whole ballet!! In Minsk, families go to the theatre, ballet etc, as it is cheap ($10 each) compared to a restaurant meal at $40 each.

Apparently, all the churches in the western part of Belarus are still there due to the fact that until the war, Belarus was part of Poland & catholic, whereas the eastern part was part of Russia & communist therefore, all the churches in the eastern part were demolished as an act of communist Stalin atheism.

Anyway, I was able to give my seminar to 55 people & lay the foundations for business in 2008 & 2009. We walked to the <u>Minsk forensic department</u> & I was amazed at the fact we were able to just walk in & with a brief shaking of the client's hands, walk straight up into his office & then give a presentation without any security checks, badges, etc. Perhaps they are so used to the fact it is safe there!

Ukraine:

Kiev & Ukraine observations

Quite a difference between the two countries. The atmosphere is more "western" & less "Russian" but there are still the "taxis" that will not give you a receipt…… so I took my camera out & took a photo of the number plate for my expenses!!

It was sub-zero for the time I was there & yet most of the young women wore mini dresses & many just jacket-length coats….now, I should add that I would normally be looking at a nice pair of legs…but most of the Ukrainian women I saw had broomstick legs… no meat! One thing I like about Monica's figure is that there is meat in her legs. I did notice that people smiled in Kiev, so there was less effect of Russian communism here…I think!

The shops were more often open late, & people seemed to be shopping more in them. The shops had Western French fashion shops with many clothes, boot & shoe shops with the occasional fur coat shop. The electrical & electronics shops had the normal array of Japanese goods, but I noticed they are more expensive by about 10-20% than say France, that would mean it would be cheaper still in USA & UK. I wandered along the shopping street & often went in if, for no other reason than to warm up; it was COLD, probably at least -10c to -15C (14F - 5F)!

The buildings were older (apparently, although Stalin ordered the buildings to be uninhabitable for the advancing German army during WWII), but they have been renovated so the city does have an older look & atmosphere than, say, Minsk. However, there are always advantages & disadvantages….the roads are pitted with potholes, so speed bumps are not required!!

The traffic was more like a "normal" city….traffic jams & many cars. It was interesting that there were ads for Jaguars, & apparently, one sees many exclusive & expensive cars owned by the many "oligarchs". Many cars, as in Belarus, are modern 2nd hand cars imported from the West. However, here, there were old trolley buses (electricity powered from cables overhead via a connecting pole), which are still seen in many Eastern European countries, but disappeared in the UK in the 1950s.

I noticed many construction sites, & my immediate reaction was similar to that of South Korea & Dubai, that of progress. But on walking around the streets in sub-zero conditions, I discovered that many of these construction sites had pedestrian safety walks that were years old, & many sites showed the stain of liquid rust on the concrete below. I saw, in most cases, no workers working & no signs of any work for some time. Money is a big problem in Ukraine for all walks of life. Many I asked did not feel that the "orange revolution" had achieved anything except freedom of expression.

One night in the hotel bar, there were the customary "beautiful women giving their customary glances", but then one man arrived with an obvious "minder" (his neck was about the same size as these Kiev women's waist). He arrived & met some friends at the table near me & had a nice evening for an hour & then left. It was interesting that when the man moved more than 2 metres (~6 feet), the minder got up & moved to cover him. I was told he was probably an "oligarch" rather than a gangster. Either way, I would not want to mess with his minder!!!

I gave my seminar at the local Academy of Sciences & technology Kiev & noticed that, as with Minsk, all the scientific equipment was communist era (before 1990), which in itself was way out of date for the time. Nothing was less than 20 years old, knobs & dials where computerisation even in 1987 had taken place in the west. Some were doing excellent work with such primitive equipment. When I think of the effort, I made in coming to Ukraine for business purposes, I think the lack of money & the long budgeting cycle means it will take some years for my efforts to be felt. Of course, with time, those efforts will be diluted.

2008

January: I am effectively single

I re-start researching online on Meetic for a Female rendez-vous

I had a number of meetings with different women in January. It seems like when I first looked online in 2000 few native French looked online, but now the difference was with Meetic, they would all be resident in France. I made meetings with various women that sometimes I would see more than once, others I would see, and they just wanted money even if nothing happened. I am sure, it is like with Monica with some of her men. I am using Meetic, so I am now meeting women locally, rather than when I used "AOL at Love".

Thurs 3rd Jan

I contacted a lady, Celia, from Cameroon, living in Melun. I picked her up, & we went to a bar & chatted & returned to her place in a large apartment block on the northern side of town. We chatted & then she made overtures & with my help, undressed, revealing some ample breasts. She said she went to the gym once a week, and while her body was not fat, she could have lost a couple of kilos around the midriff. She slowly took off my clothes, not wanting to be forceful, by the time my culottes were removed, James was growing to a decent size. We played & then, with the aid of the condom, she was ready for mounting. Unusual for a woman, she was easily brought to climax & was within the window of my climax.

Afterwards, we chatted and had a drink & then she did something I had been prepared for, with some Africans, she asked for money. I had only a €20 note, so I gave that to her. OK, I will not be seeing her again! I had been warned by Monica (funny that) that Africans usually ask for money at the end of an RV. Although she never said it, I think Monica did the same with some of the men, but probably in a more subtle way.

Frid 4th Jan: Carole & Carin

I was not happy with last night's RV, so I immediately made an RV with Carole, another Cameroon lady living on the main RN20 (Route National, now downgraded to D920) on Ave Aristide Briand in Cachan, a Paris suburb banlieue on the south side. She was more a family type of woman with two grown-up daughters, one in the Paris area & one in Cameroon, while the husband lived permanently in Cameroon. Although she did not say, it seems that they were separated, except when he came back once or twice a year. She did not care much for him, & he had his life in Cameroon & she just accepted; that was her life. We chatted in French & English a lot & went out locally to a bar on the main road not far away from her flat. When we returned to her flat, she offered some tea, & we sat down & chatted, kissed & cuddled. She said she could have her daughter pop in at any time. I was pleased she did NOT ask for money. She gets a "browny point".

Carole was keen to see me again, so I arranged to see her again, & we started going either to a restaurant or a bar, depending on the day & time I arrived. Never once did she ask for money & that was a BIG plus for me. Carole was amorous, hugging me, kissing me passionately & was keen. I feel her ample boobs, she would guide my hands to finger her pussy, still with clothes on, in case her daughter Carine could arrive. I could sense she was worried her daughter could arrive any time & we wouldn't be dressed. I never pushed a woman; I just needed a woman's company at that time with my divorce going through the motions.

7th Jan 2008 onwards: I started to visit maybe 2 evenings a week to see Carole

Her daughter Carine was there sometimes when I came, & I realised with two young children & no job; she could arrive any time to have the company of her mum to chat with. She seemed to almost live there, Carole seemed to want to stay with her all the time, so I sensed a feeling of guilt if I were to ask Carole out one weekend. We shall see, slowly, slowly, no rush.

Carine was fairly slim, well-proportioned, & a good pair of boobs up top, nice good African bum, really good looking, about 30 years old, about 1m 65cm to 1m70cm (5ft 5"-5ft 7") and usually wore a pullover & trousers. With the two young kids, Carole would help look after them when Carine needed to go out shopping, etc. to have some peace from the kids. Carine lived locally within a 20-25 minute walking distance of her mum in Cachan, south Paris banlieue, with her two young kids alone. I did not ask who or where the father was, but I guessed gone.

Carole was disappointed that Carine did not have a man, due to the young kids & could not get out to enjoy herself, except when Carole looked after them, which apparently was very rare. Carine was basically quite shy, so I guessed she would have problems initiating a conversation to attract a man, even though she was very good-looking. I could see, Carole was sad Carine did not have a life, except being stuck at home with the kids. Maybe in Cameroon (?), being stuck at home is normal, but Carol, having been here in France for some time, realised there was more to life than having babies, cooking & looking after your man. While Carole did not have a problem with staying at home, having two adult daughters, she felt Carine needed a life & did anything to let Carine have a happy life.

Sometimes, I arrived while Carole was still out shopping, Carine would let me in & make a cup of tea while I waited for Carole. She could speak only in French, so I would make small talk that I thought may be of interest to her. She would respond quite well to that & chatted back on different subjects.

I will have little time to see Carole soon as I prepare in the coming weeks for a lot of trips with lectures & presentations planned for them. I phoned Friday to arrange to see Carole. She suggested Saturday is better.

Saturday 12th Jan

I went around Longjumeau market as usual to get my weekly horse meat before setting off for Cachan. This particular day, I was let into Carole's apartment by Carine, who was there & expected the customary cup of tea while I waited for Carole. However, on this occasion, while drinking tea & chatting while I waited, I found Carine becoming increasingly sensuous, fingering her boobs & this time, she was wearing a low-cut dress instead of her normal pullover & trousers. Being English*, I tried to hide my glances. However, sometimes, she knew I was looking.

* A French minister said on TV something like: English men were not interested in women because they don't look intently at good-looking women like French men do (they ogle). A British minister, when asked by a reporter for a comment, replied, English men **DO notice** good-looking women **but hide their glances**, taking in the information within fractions of a second.

Continuing to finger her exposed skin, she saw I was gradually fixated on what she was doing. She started more & more as she chatted about personal thoughts about what men like & asked about what I liked. She told me what she was doing to get fit, as she knew I was doing athletics & that body fitness was important. While I was at ease with Carine, I kept thinking of what Carole would make of the obvious sexual approaches, constantly fingering her skin & cleavage. She started to be bolder & asked me more personal questions. In French, she would ask, do I think she is good looking, "mais oui, tres belle". "tu me trouves sexy » (do you find me sexy?). The answer was obviously "Yes/oui", but how do I answer that without inviting a BIG problem between her & her mother? I was thinking more & more about what to say in French when suddenly words just ejected from my lips, and I said, "bien sûr, tout la monde trouve tu es tres sexy" (bad French). She understood, "Of course, anyone would find you sexy." This was just what she wanted to hear from me. Is she fancying me? She moved closer to me, looking me in the eyes, puffing her upper body out so her boobs were in the proximity of me……. Oh shit, what do I do now? If Carole arrives? I was almost praying for her to arrive.

First sex with Carine

She then drops a bombshell, "maman n'arrivera pas avant au moins une heure ou deux, pour nous permettre de mieux nous connaître," I understood enough to translate: (mum will not be arriving for at least an hour or so, to allow us to get to know each other better.) She asked, "peut-être que tu m'aimerais" - maybe you would like me! Bloody hell! Carole is happy, even encouraging me to be with her daughter! Surely, I cannot be with mother & daughter? All these thoughts go through my head as she takes my hand & places it on her boob. What is it with Africans that they can be so sexy? Carine already had a low-cut dress, so with her guidance, sliding my hand down her bra was not difficult. I have melted; my hand is feeling a nice warm, smooth boob with someone who has a look of expectation. She smiled, "ouvre mon fermeture…open my zip". I used my other hand to undo her zip, with a movement of her hands & shoulders, her dress dropped down, revealing a nice set of boobs in a red bra & scanty culottes. "Tu aimes?" You like? "Mais oui, je…. je veux". She took off my shirt, tie & then slowly unzipped my trousers, with me removing my shoes with my feet only. "défaire mon soutien-gorge s'il te plaît…undo my bra please… ». Undoing it, her boobs were revealed in all their glory. Soon, my culottes were being removed as she crouched down & gently held my ever-growing penis (James). She looked at me with a smile before inserting him into her mouth. Oh! I did not expect this when I arrived, & certainly not with Carine! I held her shoulders, & now, all my inhibitions were gone as she made James penetrate deep into her mouth & out with a rhythm that would surely soon come to a climax. Would she stop or keep going to the point of me cumming? I did not have to wait long….. POW, like a volcano, I cum, & she still was still working hard, in & out. I could see my cum eventually oozing out of her closed mouth.

When all had subsided, she looked up at me smiling, cum now around her lips, dripping & running down her chin. She opened her mouth full of cum & then swallowed. She now stood up, with arms around me, she passionately kissed me. I now could taste my own cum. We stayed embraced, kissing for a while & only parted for her to place my hand on one of her boobs to caress. "Tu aime ca? You love it?" "mais oui".

She dressed & looked at me, smiled then went to her phone & sent a message. Who was she sending a message to so soon after she was dressed? I did not have to wait long, maybe for 15-20 minutes, when Carole came in & greeted me warmly, but in a different way….as if to say "thank you". Carole had done some shopping & invited me to dinner. As I had nothing special to do, I accepted. After dinner, Carine said she needed to go home to get the kids in bed & went to leave us alone. I offered to give her a lift home, but she was insistent that I stay with her mum. We chatted, but the ambience was different, she was almost happy that she had arrived late. Did Carole purposely leave Carine & me alone to "get acquainted", as Carine had claimed?

First sex with Carole

Carole was now so happy. She embraced me, kissed me & fondled my crutch. Oh, my…. Would James come alive again? He started to wake up as Carole worked on him. While we were kissing, she let go of me to undo her blouse to reveal her bra & ample DD boobs contained within them. With the extra mobility that females have, she undid her bra. I was seeing something that I had wanted for some weeks, but because of possible intrusion, it had never happened. This time, there was no stopping Carol or myself, except I did not have any condoms with me. No problem, Carol liked blow jobs & wanted "69". Oh yes, I licked her pussy while she swallowed James, & I am not sure who came first, but we both had a good time.

On leaving, Carole asked me when I would come next. I thought a bit & said I could come that Friday straight from work, maybe 6:30 pm. I said I should phone from work to give a more accurate time. She smiled, kissed me, & I departed.

Friday 18th January 2008: first penetration of Carine

I left work when I decided I had finished what I needed to do at work. I gave Carole a ring & then departed for Cachan along the N20. It was only a 20-minute drive for the 17km distance, as I was going in the opposite direction to the traffic coming out of Paris. I arrived, Carine let me in and she offered me tea as usual. I noticed again no kids: "pas les enfants. No kids," I asked. In French, she said her mum had taken them to the supermarket, and she had many things to buy……. she smiled & put her fingers down the crevice of her low-cut top & then, with my eyes glued to her boobs, she put her arms around me & kissed me. Oh, if the first time was a bit of luck & planning, this was certainly a planned departure of Carole to leave us alone.

Carine quickly undid my belt & trousers, I removed my shoes. She helped me take off my shirt. Her lips looked at me, a glance down to her breast told me I needed to undress her. I unbuttoned her low-cut blouse then around her back to undo her red bra & "hey presto", we now had a wonderful sight of Carine's sleek figure. Must not forget her skirt as it quickly came down her legs. She took my hand, led me to the bedroom & then pulled down my culottes …two naked bodies.

I caressed her boobs, & she did with my penis James. She pulled me down onto the bed, & kneeling, swallowed James with a rhythmic gusto. After a while, she stood up & then put my hand on her fanny so I could caress her as she started to enjoy the experience. She got more & more excited, and all the time, James was free to imagine what was close by. She then slowly pushed me back on the bed & kneeling inched up towards my head. She stopped as her fanny approached James & then she sat on him! He entered so quickly with her juicy pussy that there was no need to be a gentle injection. Oh, where is the condom? Shit, I could have a problem here. She raised herself up & down with James fully home & then slightly out again. What do I do? I want to shag her now this instant, she wants me to shag her, but if she is "on heat," I may make her pregnant. That is not in my plans at present. I could feel James's pressure mounting; if I do not take some drastic action, I am going to shag her without a condom. "Est ce que tu as un condom pres de nous" Do you have a condom close by?" I asked desperately as the pressure was near to release. With a small shake of the head, I decided to use my weight training to my advantage. As she lifted herself up in her rhythm, I lifted her up completely & put her down to my stomach. WOW, that was a close shave! She now started knee-walking closer to my face until her fanny was in my face. Within a nano-second, I was licking & sucking her pussy. Her enjoyment had not stopped since James went inside her, & now, she was close to a climax with my tongue in & out. The groaning was getting really desperate for the event & suddenly, she screamed in delight she had her orgasm with female cum over my mouth & face. I carried on until she had subsided & flopped beside me. "Oh merci, merci, je suis tres heureuse," (I am very happy). She looked at my face & then, with her finger, removed some of her cum & licked it herself like a chef does when tasting one's dish they are preparing to ensure the taste is good. Suddenly, she realised she had not satisfied me, so she proceeded to play with James, & without too much effort, she made him cum & then, with her finger took some of it from her face & put her finger in my mouth so I could taste it. We were both exhausted, but eventually, we both cleaned up & dressed, then Carine sent her phone message for Carole to come back home.

Carole appeared on cue within 10 minutes with the kids. Before Carine left, she chatted with Carole, I heard the word "condom" & knew they were discussing our predicament. Why did I forget to buy some condoms?... Too busy at work...you idiot! I should have guessed a situation may have arisen like that at some time.

I had visited Carole on-spec sometimes previously to avoid any conflict of interest with daughter & mother. However, it was sometimes difficult to imagine what was going through my head when Carine arrived now. Now, I needed to phone beforehand to ensure their special arrangements could be made.

Hectic time ahead. I had much work to do with a lot of consecutive trips planned, so with lectures & presentations to prepare plus fitting in training, coaching &, of course, the ongoing separation & divorce.

Saturday 19th January: Carine & Carole

After going around Longjumeau market as usual, I went to Cachan. It's not far away, only 20 minutes from Longjumeau. Carole & Carine are there with the kids. I suggest we go for a walk somewhere, they suggest a park 10-15 minutes away. We all walked there & then, on arrival, let the kids play.

We sat down on a bench, watching the kids & chatting, Carole on one side and Carine on the other. Carole placed her hand on my leg as we chatted & telepathy told Carine to place her hand on my other leg. Oh, WOW, this is interesting, mutual affection from mother & daughter. Facing me, Carol says "si tu veux, je restes ici avec les enfants et vous allez chez moi », (if you like, I will stay here with the kids, & you can go to my place). No chance for me to respond, Carine, like lightning, said, "OUI, bonne idee" & immediately grabbed my hand to help me up. Carole smiled, "dit me quand tu es prete" (phone me when you are ready). Carine held my hand as we walked back to Carole's flat.

On arrival, no playing around, Carine immediately took off her clothes & helped me with my trousers. She was not mucking around. She knew what she wanted & it was NOW!

Carine had bought some condoms in case of a problem. With James sticking out horizontally, she rubbed it gently, placed the condom on, pushed me gently on the bed, crawled up & sat on me, whereby James disappeared into a cavernous wet pussy. I could hold her lovely boobs while she gently lifted herself up & down, pushing on my legs to help her. Oh, what is it that makes these African females so good at making pleasure? James was having the time of his life, up & down. I was making Carine's nipples really hard again, & we started to increase the speed of the rhythm. Now it was so fast I couldn't hold her boobs; they were bouncing too fast until the last crescendo, and they were flopping all over the place. I came with a final set of thrusts, James erupted & then she came….WONDERFUL! I had given her pleasure as well as she did to me. I think it is important to give females the same amount of pleasure as females do to us men. We stayed like we were for some minutes until I could feel James was now walnut size. As she got off, the condom was still up Carine's pussy, so I pulled it out, yep it was still full. We lay on the bed beside each other for a while, "merci je t'aime" she said. She then got up to phone her mum to start back home.

By the time, Carole arrived home, we were presentable, we all had a cup of tea & then Carine said she needed to get back home, to what, I thought. It did not take long for the answer. It was Carole's time with me! Carole undid my belt & unzipped my trousers. OK, I know what is coming next, I thought. I was already in just my socks, so my trousers were off. She pulled down my pants, & James was out, full of beans & ready to go again…I looked at him & thought what a godsend Cialis was. No blow job this time. Carole wanted a shag, doggy style. With a condom on, I was ready to mount her & start the game with the slow rhythmic swing of the boobs in sight that slowly but surely increased rhythm as my pelvic thrust increased until the final thrusts made her boobs flop all over the place. I love to see boobs swing & finally flop while I am shagging a woman. Carol was keen to stay in this position for a while until I dismounted & removed the condom & its contents. Cup of tea time & then after some chatting, which included Carol explaining she was pleased I like Carine & that I could keep her happy as well as her. I said I enjoyed both their company & ….sex.

Eventually, I left for home, Monica was there when I arrived. She was getting things ready to go out later. I said I had gone to Cachan to see Carol & her daughter. Is she good-looking she enquired? Yes, both are? Oh, how old is the daughter, I told her about 30 years. Monica looked into my eyes, "Old enough for you, then," I couldn't stop myself from saying, "Yes." "Did you take a condom?" "Yes," I replied, "Which one did you shag?" "Which one do you think?" "Depends. What nationality are they?" "Cameroon," Monica looked in my eyes, "You didn't, did you?" I nodded. With a big smile, she said, "Good for you."

Sun 20th Mon 21st – Tues 22nd Jan 2008: Israel trip

I flew to Tel Aviv Sunday evening to be ready for work Monday. As usual with my trips, our agent had a board up with my name & when greeted, he took my luggage & put it in the car. We went straight to my hotel. It was late, so he left after arranging a pick-up time for the next day.

We visited Jerusalem to see an influential customer, Joe Brenner, who, as an expert on ICP, it was important for me to visit to discuss a collaboration work I envisaged. I had already worked with him when I was with Varian. We spent most of the day there, so engrossed were we talking about ICP, it was now late. I was disappointed I could not go around the old quarter that was just around the corner from the resto we had been at for some 4 hours or more.

In the late afternoon, we went to Haifa, where we went to a seafood resto. The agent explained A & B may not be kosha, not A & C either, but A & C could be!….Mmmm, OK? No, I could not get it.

"Don't worry, nor do many Jews, so we have a "Kosha hotline" where you can phone up & explain what you would like to eat & they will explain if it was kosha or not or HOW to adapt to make it kosha". I don't think pork chops are ever on the menu though!

"Now, for example, you said a crustacea meal may not be kosha", I said, "Yet we are eating at a nice seafood restaurant by the sea," a slight shake of the head, " but I told you, we Jews are pragmatic!" Boom, boom, no answer to that one!

We made a couple of customer visits including a visit to a customer who has JY ICP's in the desert where they have a secret nuclear research station. They had some old JY ICPs in the middle of nowhere. We chatted in the foyer about how they were getting on with the instruments & any possibilities of further purchases.

Back to Tel Aviv & that evening I got a flight to Istanbul.

Wed 23rd – Frid 25th Jan 2008: Turkey trip.

I visited Istanbul to see my new agent, Kutay, whom I had just appointed. I am booked into a small old hotel within 50m of an ancient Galata tower, a restored 14th-century tower and former prison overlooking the Bosphorus with a top-floor restaurant. This is in the centre of the city centre. I was able to easily wander around the old streets nearby. We visited a client across the large Bosporus straight bridge. Then on one day onto Izmir & stay overnight near the beach. We saw a client there before returning back to Istanbul.

I got back home late Friday night & Monica was already out to see one of her boyfriends. I unpacked & phoned Carole about coming around her place the next day. Yes, for sure. She was happy to hear me again. With tomorrow Saturday sorted, I relaxed in the lounge chatting with Lennon after he had returned from seeing his mates.

Sat 26th Jan

Going to the local market first, I made sure I went to the chemist to buy some condoms before I journeyed to Cachan. I was equipped with condoms & popped in a Cialis. I am prepared, I am ready for action!

I arrived about 11:30 & everyone was there, Carole, Carine & the kids. I embraced both Carole & Carine with passionate kisses. No need to hide my relationship with both now! Cup of tea & chat about my trips to Israel & Turkey. I then posed the question about what we should do this afternoon. Both shrugged their shoulders, looking at me to suggest something. Thinking hard about the kids, I suggested maybe a park somewhere for the kids to play? I suggested we could all get in my car to go out somewhere away from Cachan for a change. Some discussions ensued & finally, we agreed to go to Bois de Boulogne, not too far away (15km), about 40 minutes away by car. Bois de Boulogne is a massive park, including a hippodrome, a lake where one can hire boats & of course a giant wood (bois), café etc.

We spent a pleasant afternoon, the kids enjoyed themselves & we then returned late afternoon. Shops close earlier than in the UK, usually 5:30 pm, so I could see there would be a problem with what excuse the two girls would hatch up to get the kids away, especially as they were getting tired after the whole afternoon out playing. I could see from the nodding of heads that after their discussions, they had agreed on a plan. Carole asked whether we could all go to Carine's flat; I said no problem, I had not seen it anyway. We all got in the car & went to Carine's flat & went up to the 2nd floor. I was shown around the 2 bedroom flat with the typical small kitchen. Customary cup of tea while Carine fed the kids & got them ready for bed. Carole & I chatted with Carole's hand holding mine as if not to let go, or let me go! She said she was so sad Carine did not have a man or go out at all, so today was nice & she was so happy I was here. I could hear the general chatter of the kids slowing diminishing until all was quiet & Carine appeared & softly said, "Ils dorment." (they are sleeping). With a movement of the head, Carole indicated to Carine to go to her flat, so she picked up her handbag & said to me "allons y", so off we went back to Carole's flat.

Once in Carole's flat, I did not need to hesitate to take off my shoes as we passionately kissed. Carine was keen to lead me to Carole's bedroom, where we could strip. Oh, Carine does have a lovely body, all the curves in the correct places &, of course, even though fairly slim, she has a lovely African bum. I caressed her boobs as she caressed James, who was quite solid. I felt we needed to move positions in case James became too excited too soon, so I decided to lie on the bed. Which way would she go, on her back or on her knees? She lay back with that ever-so-inviting look as I lay on her, kissing her. Oh, James is being naughty; he is looking for a pussy as Carine was trying to manipulate my body into the best position. I remembered to take out a condom, & she looked at me with a funny look …..as if to say oh really, do we have to? In resignation, she slipped it on & now James was protected as he slid up & disappeared. She started to move her legs past my arms so a better penetration could be achieved with her leaning back with me holding her. Oh, boy, was James & pussy happy. As we both were hip thrusting hard until that climax was achieved, my bum subsided with little extra thrusts, I looked up into her eyes. They were shut in a sort of contented glaze. We stayed in this position for a while until I could feel that James was now so small he was slipping out, condom intact, so we moved to lie next to each other. We cuddled & kissed encore. She was a good, passionate kisser, tongue deep in my mouth, & I think I was giving her pleasure as well. We just lay there together on Carole's bed, both exhausted from our efforts & happy. "Je t'aime » she said, I replied « moi aussi, je suis très content. » (me also, I am happy). We could not stop caressing each other's body, hugging & kissing. Eventually, she suddenly had a thought & said, "Peux-tu me ramener à la maison et ramener ma mère ici" (Can you take me home & bring my mum back here?), bien sure I replied.

We slowly dressed, hugs, kisses & then we left the flat & I took her home & we returned to her 2nd-floor flat. Carine knocked softly so as not to wake the kids. Carol opened the door, and she looked at Carine's happy, beaming face. Carol let us in, hugging me as I entered & whispered in my ear, "merci". The thought crossed my mind, how many mum's going out with a man will thank him for shagging her daughter as well? Carine made a cup of tea for us three as we sat on the settee. We chatted about different things, but the subject returned often with Carine filling her mum on events at home, each time Carol looking at me lovingly & face of thank you.

I instinctively looked at the clock at some point & Carole said perhaps you should take me home. I gave Carine a big hug & kiss then we left for Carole's flat. Once inside, Carole took hold of my hand & led me to her bedroom. While I was not surprised, it was the determined speed she took me there. She couldn't wait, unbuckling my belt, trousers off, my shirt eased off, blouse off, skirt off. She meant business. I helped with her bra & massaged her ample boobs, while down below, James was being shown affection. He was being guided between Carole's legs. Carole hugged me closer with James still between her legs. She squeezed him, released him & moved closer. Ooooh, condom time; they are over there in my trousers. I looked & indicated at my trousers as if to say condoms are in my trousers. She released James by opening up her legs, allowing me to get a packet. She indicated she would open it as she gently pushed me onto the bed & indicated to lie back. She crawled onto me on her hands & knees & then took James with one hand rubbing him against her thigh, then her pussy & then stuck him up there as she then carefully fell onto me, cushioned by her boobs against me. She started to move her hips & James was happy, but I needed to put that damm condom on. Carole was still holding the packet, and I indicated she needed to open it as she arched her back to get the condom out of the packet. This movement was making James happier. "S'il te plait", I said, & she moved off to place the condom on James & then, quick as a flash, he was back home again inside. She slowly moved her hips & mine started too as well. Now, she did a press-up on my chest so that she could get a better hip movement. We both were patient, as gradually, both of us got more & more excited. The hip movements became fast & faster, and her boobs were swinging and were now starting to reach that critical speed whereby each boob flops independently. The final hard hip thrust & James, I could tell, had exploded. Carole gave a muted squeak of ecstasy as she came as well. I was so pleased that I had made her cum as well; that was satisfying for me. She wanted to stay there forever, but by this time, I sensed James was finished & totally shrivelled. I was right because when she got off, the condom was still there, with only a small part showing as I extracted it, full of my juices. We lay together exhausted & just cuddled & kissed. WOW, two shags on the same bed, one a mother & the other her daughter, in collusion for sex with me!

Carole, on getting dressed, offered me a cup of tea & we sat on the settee chatting about the day & how both Carol & Carine had really enjoyed the day out. She said she was especially pleased Carine had an opportunity to get out of the locality. I enjoyed the day with having a day without stress & having people around who <u>wanted</u> to be with me. All the stress that Monica was giving me & the divorce was getting to me. Eventually, I left, knowing I had a trip next week.

Wed 6th Feb 2008: Finland demo in Longjumeau lab

I picked up the Finnish customer from Norilsk Nickel Mining company, who had arrived at the Hotel du Lac a Longjumeau hotel Tuesday night for his demo of our ICP-AES in our factory lab. We were able to demonstrate the instrument & analyse all his samples during the day. We had lunch at a local resto & then when finished we got Rodrigues to take him back to CdG airport late afternoon.

I received notice today from the Tribunal dated Tuesday 6th February 2008, stating **I have 3 months to move out** because Monica has a "child", Lennon who, at the time was 18+ years old! Ah, French law!

Thursday 7th Feb

With both my advocate & Monica's advocate informing us of the tribunal decision yesterday, Monica mentioned to me that night that she has a Moni Clean contract working on some nice brand new apartments in Montrouge within walking distance of the peripherique & Porte d'Orleans metro & these apartments are very good. She says to me what documents would be required if I wanted to rent a flat. She said they were now cleaning up & some would be available in maybe a month's time for the first clients. She invited me to meet her at the apartment building to have an initial look. I left work early to meet up with Monica at the address & went down the open underground car park. We looked over the buildings & in particular, the apartments that would be available soon. I went into a number of the different flats & decided it was a good location close to Porte d'Orleans metro.

Frid 8th February 2008: Inspection of Montrouge new flats

I left work at lunchtime & decided to have a better look with Monica at the flats on Boulevard Aristide Briand in Montrouge. She had her Moni Clean employees & herself working there all day. All doors were open for finishing work to be done, so inspection could be done without the need for estate agents to give me a key. Yes, they were good, with many bedrooms, a sizable lounge & kitchen. We inspected the flats that were of interest & close to completion. I decided on the tenth-floor flat with a long veranda curling around the building & a view of Paris with the Eiffel Tower hidden by a building a distance away. Monica needed to get back to her employees. I went alone into the sales office opposite & said I wanted to rent an apartment. I asked how much the flat I had chosen would cost, the lady said it was €1,340/month. I asked what documents I would require. I went home first to get all the required documents before returning to the office.

Leaving work later that afternoon, I arrived at the apartment sales office with all the required documents, & a different lady at the counter, she was surprised that I knew so much about the building, the flat I wanted & that I had all the documents in my briefcase & money via a cheque. Within 45 minutes…..DONE! I signed a one-year contract to be renewed each year. I had chosen a flat on the 10th-floor, with a large surrounding balcony maybe 5 metres long & wide enough to get a table & three chairs for people to sit & eat. My new 10th-floor flat was on 68 Ave Aristide Briand in Montrouge, less than 500 metres from Peripherique of Paris, rent at € 1,340/month. It was only 600m from Port d'Orleans metro station, useful for getting into Paris centre. Once finished, I found Monica on-site to tell her all was done & gave her a big hug & said thank you.

Sun 10th -Thurs 14th Feb 2008: Middle East trip

Normally, I had my customary ArabLab Middle East tour of 15 days touring the other Middle East countries (Kuwait, Kingdom of Saudi Arabia & Egypt) to raise the profile of JY & hopefully get some sales. However, this time, I just did the ArabLab exhibition in Dubai & incorporated just a few local UAE visits, then off to Cairo Wednesday night to visit a customer there with Ashraf the next day. We went to my favourite fish restaurant. No long tour this time; I needed to get home to move house.

Thursday 14th Feb: No Monica -off to Benin

Ashraf took us to Alexandria to see a client, the roads are awful, massive potholes need a large route around them. Farmers in their fields doing much as they have done for thousands of years. We arrived late, but that does not matter in Egypt, all smiles & welcome with a tea & figs. Then back again to drop me off at the airport on the northern side of Cairo. I arrived home late Thursday night, 14th February from my trip, to find Monica had suddenly gone to Benin to stay with Agnes & David & her their "gold mine" resto "Livingston" restaurant. This resto apparently the centre of social life in Cotonou, anyone, but anyone goes there. David was the managing director & general manager of a French cement manufacturing plant. He told me one day the situation when he was in another country, the regime decided to take over the plant. He had been fore-warned & decided to take the keys to everything, including all documents pertaining to the operation of the plant. When the government troops arrived, they could not get in & when they forced their way in, they had no idea how to restart the plant that had been shut down. By this time, David had also transported all the finished cement products for export, leaving nothing worth taking.

Frid 15th February 2008: Collect keys to 68 Boulevard Aristide Briand Montrouge

The apartment owners were keen to get some cash flow & as workers concentrated on finishing some flats quickly while others still needed finishing. They had Moni Clean also concentrate on getting these flats ready for occupation. I was informed at work, so I went to the sales office to collect the keys & signed the final confirmation documents in an office in "La Defense", a massive above-ground region. To describe La Defense west of Paris is difficult; it is like some science fiction depiction of a city above ground, a mile by maybe ¾ mile in size, with massive office blocks, shopping mall area all in 1980-90's concrete, with the western Paris main arteries highways underneath.

As all was cleaned by Moni Clean, I have brought some things with me to put in my new flat & look around with a new view of possession.

Over the weekend, I start to ferry things from the Longjumeau house to my flat, including all my weight lifting equipment & small breakable things. I have been given a storage area down near the garage & I have my own numbered underground garage space, accessible by a "zapper". Although I was sorely tempted to invite Carole & Carine to help, I started to think with the kids & the need to have an empty car, it was best to wait until I moved.

Geoff moves house: - Tues 19th / Wed 20th Feb 2008 move to Montrouge

I moved into Montrouge while Monica was still in Benin. In doing this I could take what was mine without arguments on property rights. I asked an associate of Monica called Nomal, whom I knew who was an associate company, that sometimes worked with Moni Clean. Nomal was based in Antony & he got two men to help me move. They charged me €120 for the labour while I hired the van from Grigny. All was done within the day, so I was able to sleep in my new flat that night. I took a carload of more personal things the next day & now I could avoid problems & live a single life again without Monica asking questions about possessions.

On her return from Benin, Monica was a bit "miffed" at me moving everything while she was away. "Why did you not wait for me to help you?" I replied that I just wanted to move away & out of her hair, not to mention that I also wanted to avoid a row about who owned what. The golden rule: possession is 9/10 of the law!

I would enjoy my time in Montrouge, and I had local shops for normal living things I needed like food etc. I could go into Paris whenever I wanted by walking just 600m to the Porte d'Orleans metro. I now had the freedom without worrying about what Monica was doing or Monica around me.

Saturday 23rd Feb

I invited Carole, Carine & the kids to come to the flat to have a look around; rather than me picking them up, they chose to walk from their respective homes to rendez-vous at my place; they must have met somewhere because they arrived together. They had to ring the flat number to get in the building & then again when on my floor to my flat door. The two loved my flat as I also did. I felt free of Monica's antics.

After I made them a cup of tea & chatted for a while, I suggested we get the metro & go into town. We walked around the Chatelet les Halles & les Marais areas, seeing the different types of shops & people in those areas. The latter area I found out later was a gay area & in a boulangerie, we see a crafted loaf of bread in the shape of a penis & two balls! We laughed, but the kids were perplexed, but we just carried on walking, not explaining to them.

After walking a lot of the afternoon, the kids were tired, so even after a M'cDo (M'cDonalds) for the kids, they had had enough excitement, so we got the metro. On the way, I could see the two women discussing what to do. It was decided I could tell we all go onto my flat & then I take them all to Carole's flat in Cachan. The kids would stay the night with their grandmother. We arrived at Carole's flat, the kids fed & then were put to bed by the two girls until asleep. Carine as keen to sleep in my bed in my new flat. Parking the car underneath, up to my flat on the 10th floor, we gazed over the panoramic view of Paris, hugging each other in the cold.

Eventually, Carine wanted to go inside. I offered some tea, but she had other ideas. She started to take her clothes off & gestured me to do the same. I went up to her & said "elle a dit que me déshabiller était son travail" (undressing me was HER job). She smiled and loosened my belt & trousers to reveal James under my pants/culottes. James was ready to play, I fondled Carine's boobs to make her nipples stand out. She guided my other hand to caress her pussy, and within some time, she was breathing heavily & eyes glazed. She was enjoying every second & slowly, we collapsed on my double bed. I was on top as I tried to keep the pussy caress going, difficult when on top. She somehow managed to get hold of James, who was worried he would be snapped in two. By the position we were in, she realised poor James was rather squashed & promptly made him disappear! No "James can't go there until he has his "coat" on.

Meanwhile, Carine's pussy was happy & so was James. As she started moving her hips & "involuntarily", so did my hips. I needed to reach my bedside cabinet where I had put some condoms. Long arms & determination all the time Carine was moving her hips. I reached a packet & then retracted for her to be disappointed, before I put on the condom & resumed our enjoyment. The condom & the "rest period" had delayed my climax & that gave time for Carine to reach hers. We lay there, me on top for ages & ages, just relaxing in the position, cuddling & kissing, with no thought of moving at all. Eventually, we moved, & I went to remove my condom. It is not on James, and I looked at Carine's pussy, and I could not see it there. Where is it? Carine started to look as well, so I beckoned her to open her legs wide. I used my hand to play & open up her pussy more to see if the condom was still there. Opening up her cave, I finally found it deep inside. Phew, that could have been nasty!

Carine was amused by our antics "moins de problèmes sans préservatifs (less problems with condoms)" « peut etre (perhaps)» I said. We then resumed our cuddle until we both dropped to sleep.

Sunday 24th February

The next morning, I found Carine had made me a cup of tea, & we drank together in bed. I don't like drinking & certainly not eating in bed. I hate it, but I was not going to tell her that. It was still early. Having got dressed, we got into my car for Cachan. The kids were boisterous with grandmother trying to control them. I could hear Carole asking Carine how was your night "magnifique!" Carole turned to me, then came up to me & gave me a big hug & a kiss. Mum is happy that her daughter is having fun…at last. I excused myself as I needed to go training & coaching my athletes, with JB & Jeremy coming from the other side of Paris, taking some 1.5 hours, so I could not let them down.

Tues 25th February: Carole & Carine on the way home

To get home in Montrouge from HJY work in Longjumeau, I could go either via N20 onto Ave Aristide Briand or use the A6 auto-route to my flat in Montrouge. It was easy to pop in to see Carole if I took the N20 route. Sometimes I saw just Carole & we chatted, other times Carine was there as well. Both would say why don't you ring us to say you are coming? I explained it was difficult to know when I would finish work, and mine was not a 9-5 pm job, and I had people phoning me all day & people coming into my offices wanting my advice. Lectures to prepare, etc.

Under pressure, I promised I would phone when I was coming, often 10-15 minutes to clear up & make notes of things to do the next day, then drive the 20 minutes to Cachan…… but who should I phone? Obviously Carole, but Carine wanted me to SMS her at the same time, especially when it was earlier, before the kids needed to be in bed. I complied & as I expected, Carine was alone in the flat. We kissed on my entry & quickly, Carine wanted to take off my jacket. I took off my jacket, she undid my tie & then unbuttoned my shirt. She was wearing a very low-cut top, especially I guessed for me, exposing her nice cleavage. She smiled as I looked down to see her boobs, "You like?" she said in English. I was taken aback by Carine speaking English, "Yes, I did not know you could speak English." She said in French she had bought an English book & practised that phrase. I laughed & said "mais oui". We hugged, caressed & quickly, various clothes came off us both until we were both naked.

I caressed her boobs & she caressed "James," & then she took my hand & took me into the bedroom. Quickly she lay on top of me & with James now erect, her pussy was coming closer to him. "Oh shit, the condoms are in my jacket", "les Durex sont mon veste". She softly put her finger to my lips & moved so that James entered her pussy. Oh, such joy, but I must be careful; perhaps, if we just enjoy for a minute & then retract? I have done that before. Sexual pleasure increased with both of us until I could feel the pressure was just about to explode. I quickly lifted her frame above me like a bench press & my cum squirted around her pussy area. She quickly moved to suck James off his juices & give me final pleasure. "je suis desole, je suis tres prudent," I said. She smiled a wry smile, & I felt guilty.

When dressed, I took her back to her flat, expecting to ferry Carol back. Carine indicated to leave her there because Carole would spend the night there at her place, so I left for my Montrouge flat. Interesting, why didn't she offer me to come up to her flat & have a cup of tea? Are Carole & Carine now trying to get me to lose interest in Carole & concentrate all attention on Carine; .it seems so; I see so many small signs.

Thurs 27th February

My daily visits to Carole would become more & more visits to just see Carine. I had not had sex with Carole for a while & it seemed that Carole was trying more & more to take a back seat, she seemed much more interested in getting me to want Carine & not her. Why would a 30-year-old be interested in a 60-year-old? I never feel my age, I act like I am much younger & go for women much younger, due to most women my age looking to vegetate or not be active like Lyn, ex-wife #1. I know Carole was unhappy with Carine's status of being unmarried & with 2 young kids by a father who was absent. Carine had no life & probably no prospects, so my coming along would be an opportunity to make Carine's life happier & maybe something else. It was inevitable I was getting more attached to Carine. I was seeing so much more of her & of course, having sex.

That night was no exception. I entered Carole's flat & within minutes, we were naked on the bed, caressing each other. Before she would sit on me, I could lift her off when needed to put on the condom & carry on. My weight training has to have other uses, not just for athletics. James is so happy these days with Carine. She likes him, she plays with him & deep throat kisses him. James loves Carine & her large cavernous wet pussy. She seems to emit a homing signal & he is able to find it so easily.

Carole was now making all sorts of excuses to be absent when I came to her flat. Carine would be there waiting for me. Carol was increasingly absent from my visits, trying not so much to avoid me, but doing everything to ensure I enjoyed Carine, with less & less Carol, by being absent.

I like Carine, and I think I will ask her out to a nightclub & see what happens. I will have a busy time preparing for a tight schedule of foreign trips for March, so it will have to be when these trips are finished,

Tues 4-Wed 5th March 2008: Czech trip.

Living as I did now in Montrouge starting 15th February & working in Longjumeau, also training in Longjumeau, it was not difficult to take the RN20 route rather than the A6 autoroute to Paris.

The Czech trip involved giving a seminar in a hotel tucked away in the woods above Bruno to about 40 potential clients. We went to a resto afterwards that had model trains with trucks that could carry two glasses of beer, delivering the drinks to the table. When waiters/waitresses need to get to certain tables, they would lift up the flap that separated the bar from the surrounding tables. The flap had the connecting track on it; if up & therefore no connection, trains stopped.

We made a client visit on the way to the airport & my departure in the evening.

Thurs 6th March

A quick phone call before I left work & a quick visit to Carole's flat to see everyone, have a cup of tea, kiss & cuddle with both, before I needed to get home to prepare for the next day's arrival of Sophie, my eldest daughter.

Friday 7th – 9th March 2008

Sophie & Roo visit me in my Montrouge flat. Sophie was worried about me & the divorce with me now out of the house. We were able to have dinner on the balcony & could see over Paris because except for Montparnasse, there are no tall buildings in Paris, no approvals are ever given for tall buildings, except for the Montparnasse monstrosity of a square tower block & shops underneath; I wonder how many backhanders led to that approval?

We spent a nice weekend where I was the guide in Paris together before they left back to London on Sunday afternoon.

Monday 10th -16th March 2008: South African trip

Early morning flight to Jo'burg, we made various customer visits over the next days. On the weekend spent time with Selwyn's (Peterson) family. Selwyn has been with Wirsam Scientific for many years, he is still there as of 2025 & was a key person for both Wirsam & the person covering the Jo'burg region. I always got on well with Peter Wirsam, the owner & Vicky, the daughter. Sometimes I was invited to them having large group family dinners. Later, Vicky took over as managing director of the company. I stayed again at Melville with Heidi Holland's guest house. I prefer this compared to the golf club, which is too remote for someone alone. I could walk down the road to the shops area where there were various bars & restos. I always walked in the middle of the side road in South Africa it is much safer to avoid a man suddenly jumping out of the dark roadside paths & attacking you.

Mon 17th March: another fun night

Phoning as now usual beforehand at the office, I popped in to see Carole & Carine Monday night. As usual, when I call to say I am coming, Carole is out "shopping" with the kids. I entered the flat with now a normal, passionate kiss & cuddle as the door was closed. She is wearing tight jeans & a hug fitting T-shirt. I took off my jacket as usual over the settee & Carine undoes my tie. She is not bothering with a slow striptease. She quickly takes off all her clothes & beckons me to either hurry up or occasionally help me when I am slow. This time, I remembered & went quickly to my jacket pocket, produced the packet of condoms and exclaimed, "Voila!" She smiled & I followed her into the bedroom. She has a typical lovely African bum & ample boobs I like so much, nicely rounded wide hips & as she bent over to pick up some clothes on the floor, my urge to caress her pussy from behind was too much.

As I touched it, she immediately shuffled her feet wider to help me with access to caress it. I took her left shoulder to be sideways & enable me to play better. "James" was now getting excited so was Carine. She now had both hands on the bed to support her & now I was in a doggy position. I needed to put this damm condom in my left hand. I was having difficulty, so I asked her to "ouvre le paquet, s'il te plait", she took the condom packet & opened it & then, turning around, placed it in position on "James", before resuming her original position. I love doggy style & so did she.

I would have taken it off the shrivelled James afterwards, but we loved the position so much. I had, not for the first time, had to extract the condom from her pussy. She turned & smiled "merci, je suis heureuse". We lay on the bed quietly, cuddling and caressing each other's parts. She rolled on top of me so her boobs were on my chest. Looking into my eyes, she said, "Je suis heureuse avec toi, tu es gentil" & lifting up her groin, she picked up, "James", "il est heureux?" "mais Oui." I said as she fingered & stroked him. We both looked as he started to grow bigger & bigger & bigger until he was full of life again! She smiled that smile & promptly sat on him, so he disappeared up her pussy. She now started to ride him like those cowboys on a bucking bronco. Ooooh! My eyes were dazed with ecstasy, her rhythmic thrust swaying her boobs, I lay helpless with only a little help from my hips. Riding me with one hand occasionally on the bed to support her, I was putty in her hands. More & more she rode me, until she slowly accelerated the rhythm, boobs bouncing more, pressure building up inside "James", I had not the strength, even if I could reach her, nor the inclination to stop! Oooh, I have cum; it feels great. She is riding me now so hard; her boobs were bashing against each other, groaning in joy as I was as well. Gradually, we both slowed down our movements & after some while, she flopped on top of me & kissed me. With my arms around her, I kissed & cuddled her. With all the excitement I had forgotten all about another condom & did not even remember even afterwards we had had sex without one, I was so happy & deep in thought about things like, asking her out to go to a night club.

When we relaxed for a while & started dressing, I said, "peut etre, nous irons au club dancing?" in my best French (which is not good, but she usually understood.). She lit up & said « mais Oui, c'est une bonne idée ». OK, ce Vendredi? "Yes," she replied in English, we fixed a time I would pick her up at 7:30 pm. I did not need to ask whether Carole could look after the kids. I got to know all would be OK, because Carol was encouraging our relationship. I knew she would love the excellent nightclub traversing the N7 near Rungis not far away, which had 5 dance floors with separate DJ's playing different types of music: Salsa Latino, 1960s, 70s, 80s & 90s, rock, techno, house & variable.

Tuesday18th & Thursday20th

My visits were fleeting as I needed to get back to do some things. My daily night visits were great, but I was ignoring basic things in the flat I needed to do; I did not want to think I was using Carine to clean the place.

Friday 21st March 2008

I arrived early, as I like to do, never late. Carole opened the door beaming with pride (as if to say I knew you would like my daughter). I had an open neck shirt & trousers with a green corduroy jacket that was my favourite. The kids were still awake & still in normal clothes, which I thought was odd, noting that kids that age should be in bedclothes. However, I knew French, Spanish & Africans often let their kids up late, so I thought no more about it. Carine was still doing "woman things" to get ready. About 10 minutes later, she appeared from the bedroom.... STUNNING !: short silver dress with a low neckline & high heel shoes. "WOW tu es manifique, absolument manifique," I exclaimed. She beamed with pride, & Carole also was very happy. She took a shawl & a small matching shoulder bag. I reflected as I drove to the nightclub. She probably bought the dress shoes & handbag for the occasion.

We arrived outside the club & being early, I was able to find parking nearby (it was always difficult to park later, so we always see when I have left the club before, there are cars parked everywhere). We went inside, Carine was like a dog with two tails, looking at everything. We left our jacket & shawl in the cloakroom, & I kept the ticket. We, at first, just wandered around so that Carine could get a feel of the place & where the "loos" were. We started dancing in the 60-90's dance hall & stayed there for maybe 20 minutes, then moved to the Salsa room & danced for a short while. I am at home with all types of music, but Salsa I find it difficult to get any variation that I like to make when dancing, so we quickly went to the 60-80's music dance floor & spent most of the time there, but also trying some 20 minutes or so in each dance floor. The electronic house music dance floor would be for maybe 15-20 minutes before returning to the 60-80's music floor.

We stayed until we were tired and around 2 am & came out into the chilly night air, cuddling me as we walked, she said, "merci pour ce soir, je suis tres heureuse." "de rien" (your welcome). The journey home only took about 20 minutes, I parked the car on the N20 as usual. Carine had a key to let herself in, all the lights were out. No doubt Carole is asleep. Carine put the lounge lights on & asked whether I wanted a cup of tea (she knew I preferred tea to that concentrated French coffee). I spoke softly so as not to wake Carole, especially as the bedroom door was open. "pourquoi parlez-vous si doucement?" Carole is asleep, I said in French. She laughed, «Non maman elle va dans mon appartement avec mes enfants pour ce soir. tu dors ici ce soir», Oh, that was planned well by the girls, I thought.

When the saucepan* with water had boiled for our cup of tea.
* very few French have a kettle, reminiscent of when I first arrived in

JY, I brought in a kettle into my office for tea or coffee; colleagues asked me what it was. A "kettle" I told them, so they found the word in French "bouilloire »

We sat down with our tea on the settee. Having restricted myself to beer all night to be within drink/drive laws, I was thirsty. We had small talk as she slipped off her high-heeled shoes, & I took off my shoes. We finished our drinks, then once we had put the cups in the kitchen, she turned around & took my hand as she led the way to the bedroom. Inside, she turned around so I could undo her dress. She took off her earrings as I took off my shirt & trousers, and we faced each other. "James" was bulging in my pants/culottes, she stroked him outside & down came my culottes. now, he was standing upright like a soldier.

I put my arms around her to undo her bra at the back & then I bent down to remove her culottes. There was a thin pad with a slight amount of blood on it, and she smiled to indicate it was OK. Her pussy was so inviting I caressed it & fingered her inside, and she moved her legs apart so my fingers would go up easier. She shuffled towards the bed & then when we arrived, she sat & then turned over to lay down on her tummy. I was drawn down beside her on the bed, pleasing her until she was groaning. She turned over then grabbed hold of me so that I was over her as she gently pulled "James" towards her. He went & disappeared as she held her legs up in the air. I took hold of her "love handles." As I have said, Africans have lovely wide hips & it made for pulling me towards her as I thrust away. In this position, I could see her boobs now reasonably flat, wobbling in rhythm to my thrusts.

Eventually, my volcano erupted inside her, & she squealed with delight. Eventually, a depleted "James" popped out, & I lay on top of her, supported on my elbows so as not to crush her with my 100kg of weight. We rolled over, she was now on top of me with her hands supporting her arms on the bed to see into my face. Her boobs were now hanging down in front of me & moved my head to kiss one &

suck it & then the other. She liked all the attention to her boobs & always had an enigmatic smile when I paid attention or looked at them. A series of cuddles, & it was sleep time. Lying there before I dozed off, I kept thinking of the fact that I originally was seeing Carole & she was encouraging me to be with her daughter. Now, I was sleeping in HER bed with HER daughter on a regular basis! We were too hot to have any covers on because Carole always had the heating on high.

Saturday 22nd The next morning upon waking up, I found Carine looking so sleek & slim with her boobs hanging to one side as she was awake & leaning over on her side looking at me. "Bonjour", " bonjour" I replied. She looked at me & then down at something starting to grow. "Morning glory" is the expression; perhaps doctors can explain it, but I can't. In this case, "morning glory", with James fully erect & looking at a beautiful naked black beauty, was an intense combination. She smiled & stroked "James." Oh wow, he wants fun! Carine moved over & then sat on me & "James" disappeared from sight. Oh! Carine would be good riding a bucking bronco I thought, as she again rode me. She decided to ride slowly to prolong the ecstasy until, inevitably, I came to a climax. By that time, I was grabbing her hips to maximise the feel for both of us.

Carine stayed sitting on me for a long while after the event, just looking at me with loving eyes as I stared at her, scanning her body & gently caressing her all over.

We eventually got up & started dressing. Carine sent an SMS to Carole to say she could come with the kids. About an hour later, she arrived & looked very happy. "On peut aller faire du shopping? J'ai besoin de choses pour la semaine?" Can we go shopping as I need things for the week? So, as we were all ready, we went to the Casino supermarket nearby on Ave Aristide Briand & filled a shopping trolley with loads of bags, and I could see that I was to pay.

Once we were back and all the things were put away, I suggested we go for a walk. With a bit of gentle persuasion, we all went out. We went to a local park area, parc Rasail, where the kids were able to run around & adults could relax with a gentle stroll. Carole was not fit, so she found a bench, Carine & I continued walking & chatting. She was interested in what I did at JY. However, trying to explain in bad French the complexities of ICP-AES was problematic to someone who had just elementary knowledge of science and chemistry in particular

On arriving back at Carole's flat, we had a cup of tea & then I made excuses that I needed to get back to sort out things at my flat. Carine looked at Carole, she quickly read her body language & suggested Carine go with me as she could look after the kids the day or even return home tomorrow. I was stumped for a reply other than "errr, OK."

Carine went into the bedroom, followed by Carole, the two spoke to each other in whispered voices. After some minutes, Carine appeared with a shopping bag filled with different things & her handbag.

She explained to the kids that she would be away for the day & their grandmother would look after them. They seemed OK with that, & off we departed, both of us kissing Carole goodbye.

Carine was excited to be able to see my flat again. As we arrived at the entrance, I zapped the automatic door to open to the apartment block subterranean car park. I had a reserved parking place, & after picking up things, we went up to my flat on the 10th floor.

Carine was still in awe at the new flat & the view from the balcony, and she put her arm around my waist. After some minutes, I suggested we go into town & find somewhere to have a drink; Porte d'Orleans metro was only about 600m away. I sensed she felt there might be more, so she said she wanted to change into something nicer for going to Paris. I showed her the bedroom, she went in & reappeared some 5 minutes later in a nice floral, low-cut short dress with a thin jacket as Paris can be chilly in March.

We walked the 600m to the peripherique & Porte d'Orleans metro station. Even in winter, this particular metro station at the end of line 4 is always hot & it runs the oldest trains in Paris with rubber wheels. We got off at St Michel, and there is lots to do there, with the river Seine, & many sites all within walking distance, & of course, a multitude of restos. We walked along the Seine looking at the little street sellers with their small 2 by 1-metre lock-up storage spaces that open up. Books, paintings and souvenirs all in these little spaces & then onto Notre Dame Cathedral on an island in the middle of the river Seine. Being a Saturday, there was a long queue to enter Notre Dame*, but as it was moving quickly, we joined the queue & were within 5-10 minutes inside the cathedral. The famous rose-stained glass window was great above the enormous organ. We spent 20 minutes inside, & I noticed Carine did a "cross the heart" sign that Catholics do when looking at the altar.

*This obviously was before the great fire in April 2019 destroyed Notre Dame's cathedral. Since renovated, it is as of now 2025, open again.

We walked around various sights and had walked a lot, so I suggested we stop at a bar to have a hot drink to warm us up. By now, late afternoon / early evening, I suggested we had dinner. We could eat in the Old Latin Quartier. There are numerous cheaper restos there & I quite often took women or JY clients to a Greek resto on Rue de la Huchette. We ate early evening & had a good time, especially watching women dancing on a one-metre square wheeled table, part of the entertainment as the musicians played Greek music. I could chat better with Carine now as she had opened up from her shyness & was making great strides in her English. A visit to a nearby souvenir shop & then back to the metro & my flat.

Returning to my flat, I asked whether she wanted a cup of tea. She came with me to the kitchen to watch me making us both cups of English Earl Grey tea using a kettle. Like so many French & Africans, they were intrigued by the kettle (bouilloire). We sat down on the settee, Carine was so happy she kept thanking me for the day out. I could see now that she had not seen much of Paris, even though she lived 20 minutes by metro, as the kids occupied all her time. However, she could go out only when Carole babysat them. Carine was not a naturally outgoing woman, rather shy, so probably she had few friends. In France, it is not the usual thing for "girlie nights out" like in the UK or USA. She was now getting much more open about her feelings, what she wanted & the subjects of common interest. With my poor French & her now-improved-but-still-poor-English, we were really hitting it off really great.

I got up to take the cups, she got up as well & followed me into the kitchen. Once put down, Carine, who was behind me, put her hand around me to feel my crotch, gently stroking it. I turned slowly, looking into her expectant eyes. "je pense nous irons au chamber," she said as she took my hand & slowly led me to the bedroom, looking deviously at me from time to time.

Carine was losing her shyness now very quickly with me. We moved to my bedroom in what seemed an eternity of anticipation. She held my belt & undid it, then dropped my trousers, with a slow extraction of my private parts from my pants, I was feeling so horny. I put my hand around her to unzip her dress and reveal her red bra; she loves red bras. How can I remember the red bra? She liked red, & each time I saw her bra, it was a different bra in red. I fingered her exposed breast, so soft, so expectant, heaving up & down. She felt down my pants/culottes& "James" was expectant as well. I reached down to remove her culottes, & she did likewise with me.

We moved onto the bed, I lent over to my bedside cabinet to pick up a condom. However, she rolled me over so she was on top & quickly sat on James, up he went & disappeared. I gestured her that I needed to get the condom, but she just smiled & started riding me harder. I looked in desperation as her boobs moved up & down to the rhythm & saw her pleasure & I felt mine with every movement of her buttocks riding me, leaning back to maximise the sexual pleasure for both of us, also so I could not lift her off me in that back leaning position. I felt helpless, Carine had taken total control of me, & in a few seconds, I was sure my volcano would explode. Oooh, it is coming, ooooh, yes, I grabbed her legs to maximise my thrusts as I cum, thrusting hard as I could in that prone position. She carried on riding me even when I had subsided my thrusts & ejaculation was mostly complete. Oh, that was wonderful, I feel fantastic, euphoric. Within a minute or so, she moved over, as she could feel James was so small, he had slid out of her wet pussy.

We lay together, her smile of satisfaction of pleasure & pleasuring me. But what would be the consequences? She surely was not having a period; that was the other day....I think? I was now worried about making her pregnant. Was this her goal? She has two kids at the moment. Does she want a mix kid with me? Am I fish she wants to catch, or is it just she loves having sex with me? Remember, I am now 60 & she is 30-ish; I am too old to start having a family. I did not want one with Monica & anyway, I do not want one now. I had said the same to Monica years before Monica had her operation to remove her fibroid, & at that time, I was married.

As I lay there on the bed exhausted, my mind was in hyper gear. She stopped me from getting the condom and chose to ride me in an upright position, so I could not get up easily to stop our sexual intercourse. She knew that because I was able to stop her previously by lifting her off in a more prone position. She learnt by riding me and leaning back, I couldn't do anything. Is Carine playing a game of fishing, where I am the catch by hooking me with a child? All the time looking at her & her enigmatic smile, I was trying to read what was behind in her mind. I need to find out what she thinks. Does she want a child with me? Is she trying hard to have a child with me? I need to find out before that happens…unless I have already made her pregnant this evening.

I asked her why she stopped me from getting the condom, and she replied she wanted true, natural sex with me. However, I replied I could make her pregnant. "Is that such a bad thing?" She replied. Oh dear, alarm bells were ringing. I was thinking of a reply & slowly thinking hard about what I wanted to say in my bad French. I asked, "Was that what she wanted? A baby with me?", "Oh yes, I would love to have a baby with you". Bloody hell! I looked shocked & lost for words, especially in French "sacre bleu" was all I could blurt out. She smiled, rolled over onto me & kissed me. All the time she was kissing me, I was thinking what have I done? I need to monitor when she is due for her next period.

Sunday 24th March

The next morning, I got up & said I needed to drop her off at home as I would be training & had athletes waiting for me. I was feeling a bit different to Carine this morning compared with last night. I don't know how to think; I like her so much.

Thurs 27th March 2008: last meeting with Carine - she wants a baby with me!

I was busy at work, so other than a couple of phone calls, I did not see Carine or Carole until later in the week when I phoned while at work & popped on Thursday 27th. Carine was there with the kids & Carole, I sat down with the kids playing. "Would you like some tea?" in English, Carine asked, "Oh, oui, s'il te plait," I replied & got up to go to the kitchen with Carine. She filled the saucepan with water and put it on the stove. She put her arms around me & we passionately kissed. She apologised that we could not have any fun tonight as she was having a heavy period. "pas de bébé cette fois » «cette fois ?» I replied. She lovingly looked into my eyes, « Je t'aime et je veux ton bébé ». Then, she embraced me harder, kissing with her tongue deep into me. Taking a breath, she said, "Je suis sûr que nous ferons un bébé adorable, est-ce que-tu d'accord mon amour». Totally flummoxed, I could only say, "eeerr Oui." She was pleased and quickly replied with a smile of approval & said "c'est bon ça." Thoughts raced through my head. While I am sure we would make a lovely baby, I do NOT want another baby, not at my age!

The saucepan of water was boiling & making cups of tea for us. We sat down on the settee with Carole in the armchair opposite & the kids still playing. After chatting about nothing particular for a while, I excused myself, & we kissed goodbye. Outside, as I walked to the car, I thought, "OK, that is the last time I will see Carine. I can see BIG problems, that I do not want, I certainly do not want to start another family at my age & all the expense of the baggage".

Why do women think that having a baby will attract a man, especially at my age? Back home in my flat, I decided I would not contact Carole of Carine again. I really like Carine, but now things could get too dangerous! If she promised to take the pill, how or when would I know she hadn't taken it to just become pregnant? Damm!

WHY did she have to spoil things for us? I wrote a loving but final message to Carol & Carine, sent by SMS that I adored Carine, but now I could not trust her to not try to get pregnant when we had sex. Be it a seduction without a condom or purposely failing to take the pill, having a baby would be disastrous at my age, I cannot & will not take the gamble of that occurrence. I am sorry, really sorry, it has to be goodbye. I made sure I got a good French translation from a colleague friend & sent it. I really was sad about what I had to do.

Frid 28th 2008: Carine pleads for me to return.

As I expected, Carole & Carine separately tried to change my mind with SMS messages. Carine came on the phone crying that she wanted me so much & promised not to let pregnancy happen by seeing the doctor prescribe her to have the birth pill.

I felt so guilty at making Carine so upset, but re-starting our relationship could instantly turn bad by me making her pregnant if she were cunning. Carine could simply stop taking the pill without me knowing until one day, she announced she was expecting our baby.

Lyn, my 1st wife, did a similar thing, but in that case, it was to keep me & our marriage together. I was to find that out many years after we were divorced, when Dawn told me Lyn had confided in her.

In my mind, I wanted to go back, I really wanted to go back, but logic told me NO! That would be stupid.

It took a week or so of being sad about what I had to do, but reluctantly, I went online for the first time in ages & started looking again for women.

April 2008: Anne opera singing girlfriend

I made an RV with a nice, fairly short French-Chinese lady, Anne Sing, who was fairly small in stature. He had a teenage daughter & lived in Vitry sure Seine on the D5 road just off the southern part of the A86. Her house could be accessible also from the southern part of the peripherique.

We went to various resto's & bars around the area & only had sex when the daughter was not there. Mostly, I would come after work, so there would be only a few opportunities. However, on those occasions, blow jobs & frontal approaches were really good without being memorable. The relationship lasted about a few months, with certain question marks as to how long I wanted this to last.

She was nice but could be a "firebrand" & blow up on some little things. An example was she used to flush the loo with a bucket of water because the cistern was broken. We went to "Bricorama" a DIY shop; I chose the replacement system & was about to buy a new mechanism for €40 when I saw a special offer of a loo complete with cistern for €50, so we got that. I installed it & everything was fine. Next visit, she blew up because there was a slight leak inside the bowel. All that was needed was a pipe to be tightened further. I did not have the tools with me that day to fix; however, all hell let loose, and she went ballistic. With my tool case I fixed it next visit within 10 seconds. I decided I could not live with that. I had previous experience with Lyn & Anne

#1 in England & in France….no thanks, so Anne mark #2 became history.

30ᵗʰ Sept 2008

I held a 60ᵗʰ birthday party at my flat. Those invited were: Rachael as a friend; Sophie "B", her eldest daughter, Jude her youngest, plus her sister Claudine & her kids; Lennon with his girlfriend, athletic friends JB (Jean Baptiste) & his wife, Clare; Jeremy, Helene & her mum Claire. We all had a good time and had a buffet. Some refused further food when offered, "We are leaving space for the cake". "Oh," says Rachael, "Geoff does not eat cake, so there is no cake!" They were astonished … bizarre Englishman!

I am still single, no girlfriends, I need to search more for female company.

I still have withdrawal symptoms from missing Carine, & from time to time tempted to phone her. I searched online, but at the moment, my heart is not in it. I have not fixed any female meetings.

I am seeing Rachael to pick up Zoe & or Sophie B for training. Rachael is friendly but not amorous; she has dumped me 3 times, so I have to be patient as to whether we are able to get back together sometime in the future. We are spending more time together even when the girls are not involved. Amical friends, not sexual partners, I want to hang fire on seeing other females as to where this latest friendly phase may lead.

Very slowly, Rachael & I are seeing each other as friends; she helps me when I meet various professional people where I need to know exactly what is being said. Rachael's presence was also useful when Monica's former friends wanted to confide in me. My limited French prevented me from fully understanding a given conversation without a fluent French speaker present.

Oct 2008: Rachael & myself see a Notaire. After a second visit, he says he is the wrong type of notaire for adversary divorce cases.

Monica does not want a divorce & obviously would disagree on finances. Official recognised divorce proceedings had started.

Dec 2008: I know that Gisele has an axe to grind, so not everything she says can be taken as gospel. Be-friending Gisele is proving to be a mine of information as Monica's Rwanda life is being exposed. I phoned Gisele from my Montrouge flat & as Rachael was there, we would get more information from Gisele. We are gaining so much information about Monica in the early years & the latest news. David's hussiers (bailiff) business is falling apart due to him being lazy & extracting too much money from the business. Monica is angry on the phone at me because I had told Gisele that Monica was now in the FreeMasons. Gisele tells David, who hates the masons!

Jan 2009: we find out Moni Clean is near bankrupt & is heavily in debt. She needs to sell the house to pay off creditors. Rachael & myself got together again

Feb 2009: I moved out from Montrouge to live with Rachael in Grigny.

As of, 2025 we have been together, I have not attempted to seek another woman since.

Summary of proceeding months of divorce & information

I have made a précis as bullet points of the following months & years, as I did not make comprehensive notes like I did when living with Monica, so events seem to be haphazard. It will also enable you, the reader to not get bored with some details.

- Sept 2008 — Notaires contacted
- Oct 2008 — Divorce documents officially approved
- Dec 2008 — Gisele gives background to Monica in Kigai, Rwanda
- Dec 2008 — Rachael speaks with Gisele for nearly 2 hours.
- Dec 2008 — Monica is livid as David learns from Gisele what I had told her., about FreeMasons
- Dec 2008 — Gisele learns that Monica is pushing her out from David.
- Jan 2009 — Geoff gets back with Rachael
- Jan 2009 — Monica cannot pay her half for the Longjumeau house mortgage
- Feb 2009 — Geoff moved from Montrouge flat to Rachael's house
- Feb 2009 — We learn Monica is heavily in debt.
- March 2009 — Faustine researches Monica's Rwanda & Cote d'Ivoire background
- May 2009 — Evidence, questions as to Lennon's real father?
- May 2009 — Monica wants to sell the Longjumeau house to pay off debts

- May 2009   Lennon moves to Bruxelles, but NOT in David's house
- 2009   BODACC Moni Clean declared bankrupt
- 2009   Monica attempts to use my bank RIB to pay her gas bill. I involve the police to give me immunity
- 2010   Realise my advocat is a charlatan & is doing nothing with my information, but accepts €600/visit. .
- June-Oct 2010   Divorce approved
- 2011   Divorce papers come through
- April 2011   Monica wants me to buy her out for €70,000 to enable urgent debt to be paid off
- June 2011   Hussiers break in to Longjumeau house & take Monica's car & all valuables.
- August 2011   Monica & Gisele fight in Bruxelles shop, police called
- August 2011   At Police station Monica had only Rwanda passport, not French as she claimed
- Nov 2011   Geoff has hernia operation
- Dec 2011   Geoff starts cleaning the house & clearing out Monica's stuff.
- Jan 2012   Geoff discovers Monica was in debt to €410,000 in 2008!
- Jan 2012   Estate agent says VW asked for Monica, she paid one month for a new car & has disappeared with the car without further payments. I said she is Belgium & gave David's address
- Jan 2012   Geoff discovers Monica's Cote d'Ivoire driving licence, not valid there!

- 2012   Nicky says she is adopting an African child, then discovers parents were selling him for €500!
- 2012   Geoff & Rachael spend 2 weeks in Martinique.
- 2013   Geoff & Rachael (plus her 2 younger daughters) move to England

Finally - a conclusion - divorce

I will finish with the question I posed at the start:

"Why did Geoff stay with Monica when all the evidence was she was bad, very bad for him?"

I really think it was a blind, or intense love for her.

It was like a Voodoo spell Monica had over me & maybe still has. I want to know more about what she does these days & what she looks like. Is it just curiosity or something else?

With absolute devotion & love for Monica, my main requirements she refused to give were;

1) Give me (or maintain) your love for me.
2) Tell me when, who & what she was doing with various men.
3) Tell me the truth, no lies.
4) Control her spending within our financial means *(it was this that finally "broke the camel back")*.
5) Don't treat me like a fly on the wall; involve me in your/our life with friends.
6) Don't try to belittle me to try to enhance yourself with friends & conversations. *"Tall poppy syndrome"*

I was willing to put up with all her numerous men IF ONLY she would admit each time to me. What I could not accept was lies, lies — lies about her men & money.

Monica's lesbian affairs were interesting, especially as I was to witness some of them in public, or our home.

As some friends have observed, if Monica had been smarter & more patient, she could have totally ruined my future life & made me penniless. Although, she never wanted a divorce, she liked the image of being married to a white successful "cadre supérieure".

How smarter? Monica could have told me about her men in advance & afterwards, I would have accepted it. **I loved her so much**. I said so many times, tell me about who you are seeing & what you are doing if it is sex OK, but I want to know, yet she tried to hide them from me & where she was going. "She cooked her goose" or "shot herself in the foot".

Monica could have involved me more with her friends like she did in the early days of us going out together. However, I was later to be a "fly on the wall" to be swatted. If I happened to be chatting with others about subjects, she had no idea about & therefore could not contribute to the conversation, she would just change the subject. In other cases, she would leave her discussion group & come over to mine to interrupt to belittle me or not want others to be impressed with me. Known in Australia as "Tall poppy syndrome". *This means that, if you cannot aspire to rise up to a higher level, then cut others down to your level.*

If I asked a simple question, she would spend ages explaining why she could not answer & say I will get back to you, "Demain". In some cases, it was a simple question of "yes" or "no", but that was too complicated!

Monica purposely did not want to teach me French, so if my French was bad, I would need to ask her & she would redact what she did not want me to know when explaining things to me. However, my writing & reading in French is much better than spoken or, worst of all, listening. It is the listening that is worst due to the liaison of words used in French that makes it flow together, but difficult to understand. English words are separated, & therefore, easier to understand.

Monica never put herself out for anyone UNLESS there is an advantage to her. Give a lift home to have a favour in the future or sex for a contract, job or position. What amazed me was that if, there was nothing to be gained, not only would she not do the favour, but she would attempt to stop **me**. Examples were giving a lift home at night to Cloe or another time to uncle Stanley both could not drive at the time.

IMAGE was & I am sure even now, MOST important for her. I would hear gross lies about various things, including the success of Moni Clean (to Andre) even though Moni Clean never made a profit or our wealth, she would splash money out on trivial things to show wealth.

One day, 2nd July 2007, Monica sums up much of the problems as she saw them from her perspective.

"……..She dares me to divorce her by saying; "you know you love me and I love you. **You say I am spending too much money, but the problem is you are not earning enough money.** *I see and go out with these men to help you, me and Lennon. These men help us, so what is your problem? You are now free to see other women and good luck with your meetings. I am sure when you are together, they help you forget our problems, eh?…….".* She repeated that so many times.

Stealing & wasting my money was & still is, a red line for me. With Monica & occasionally, a source of conflict with Rachael. I did not & do not want to be a "sugar daddy".

It could have been so different, yet maybe culture or just Monica's personality destroyed a relationship I really wanted & tried hard to keep.

I was a man who stayed with a wife who strayed until finally, "the hair broke the camel's back" – **finances**, I decided on divorce being the only option.

Oh, I forgot, Monica had at least 10 sexual affairs that I discovered & numerous > 25 other men she would try to extract favours / jobs & money, of course, as an Escort girl. (see **Note 5** for a known list) She just could not stop wanting to see other middle-aged or elderly men who could help her.

Being a person who talks about my problems to numerous people helps my sanity, they can give alternative views & advice (some better than others). They all said, I should write a book. I have decided I will do this & make an autobiographical novel (names changed to protect the innocent!) and to also include some fictional wishful thinking.

When one is <u>unhappy,</u> then one can go "off the rails", be it through drug, alcohol or seeing women. With Monica's constant encouragement, I maybe started to become like her, seeing these women.

However, once in a good, stable relationship, I have always been good. I always try to help others & that is where often I can come unstuck, especially financially. Over the years, I have helped so many people financially in times of need & most still owe me money that I have mentally written off as a bad debt.

So, what is your verdict?

- ✓ Was I stupid?
    - o Am I gullible to female wiles?
- ✓ I was determined to make this marriage, my 2nd work.
    - o I never give up, be it relationships, athletics, or work.
    - o Would I re-marry? No !
- ✓ Was I so blindly in love that I could not help myself? Yes.
    - o I have been asked; "do you still love her ?" Well ?
    - o I proved yet again, I am very tolerant, even of physical abuse.
- ✓ Did she, has she, got some Voodoo type control over me?
- ✓ I obviously lost my morals for a while, eventually with **Monica's encouragement** going with other women & going to these sex clubs, while married with Monica.

- ✓ I have not made any attempt to see another female since late 2009, when back with Rachael.
  - o One can recover one's morals.
- ✓ Do I regret marrying Monica - No.
  - o We had some wonderful times. I appreciated different country cultures & nice people. We had good times as well as bad times.
  - o I am still in contact with many of her friends.

Note 1: Lyn, my first wife

Throughout the early years, I was worried about her short temper & what would happen if we had children. I waited until I thought she had quietened down when we were both 26 years old. I realised, after married about 10 years, there were gross problems with the way she treated Steven & Sophie. I started to become more engaged with athletics & work to compensate for my stress, the kids being too young to discuss with them.

Lyn guessed things were not going well, & in typical female fashion, she confided in Dawn many years later. To keep me & ensure we stayed married, she planned to become pregnant in 1984. It worked in that I was unhappy but accepted my lot & never strayed even though on my business trips, it would have been easy. Lyn stayed at home & did nothing but read what I called "Noddy books", Mills & Boons sloppy love stories of approx. 150 pages of tripe & TV. Another thing I found out only decades later from former neighbours: drinking. She loved the image, especially when we bought "Brookhouse" a very large Georgian manor house circa 1820 in Macclesfield. She once joked at a party that she always wanted a girl so that she could be her little slave. Oh, how true that "joke" turned out to be; Sophie despised her mum for a number of reasons.

It was only when an Australian colleague's wife visited Lyn one day to find her drunk with sherry bottles scattered around. He told me the next day & with Steven's help, we searched the lounge & found 13 sherry bottles, mostly empty or half-empty, as well as the unpaid bills stuffed down the settee cushions. About A$ 1,500/month was going missing, PLUS bills not paid.

I was to find out decades later from Sophie especially & also Dawn what was happening while I was working, Lyn was treating the girls as little slaves, doing all her housework, while she read her "Noddy" books & TV. The memory of her constant jokes to friends came flooding back.

I was scared about Dawn as she was so young, Lyn would indoctrinate her that I was bad & the guilty person for anything wrong with the marriage. I confided in Allison McAdam a female athlete I coached who became a dear friend of the family about all my problems that were so evident to all who knew us. She became almost Dawn's adopted mother giving the attention Lyn should have given. Only when Dawn was about 11 years old & the situation with irretrievable with events in Australia (another story in itself) & nothing improving once back in the UK, did we agree to divorce. I felt free & even more so when I got the approval of Sophie & Dawn, who was now mature enough to understand things, especially when explained by Sophie.

Lyn planned to stay in Australia & get Australian nationality for the three of them after Steven & I had moved back to the UK via Switzerland. I needed to see my new boss, Gilbert Essieva, Varian vice president for Europe. Remembering the school year in the UK started about 1st September, I quickly organised via our secretary, Vicki Mann, for Sophie to join us & before Lyn could think Sophie was gone. That thought in July & quick action saved us all being together* back in the UK.

Lyn had a few affairs in the 5 months Lyn stretched out staying in Australia, selling the house, before returning just before Christmas 1995. I arranged a weekend in an exclusive country club 5 Lakes, in Essex, to try to get back on track, but it was obvious it was only a matter of time before we would agree to divorce.

The time arrived quickly in the new year when, in the Winsford rental house, I arrived home to see Lyn in a brown frock, looking like a granny. I said the golden words, "You look like a granny in that old brown frock". "That's it, I want a divorce." "Good," was my reply. We slept in separate bedrooms, One day Lyn wanted money quickly to buy a house near Stoke on Trent. I agreed to release the money she needed to get her house.

* Dawn met an Australian & desperately wanted to return to Australia. She did so in 2005 with her partner, Al Heyer.

Note 2: Anne #1

Jealous of any other woman & very possessive

Anne was a girlfriend I brought to France & caused me much pain when I moved to Longjumeau with HJY. I had threatened to dump her a number of times when I was living in Haslington, Cheshire. On arriving in France, I brought Anne with me, who could not speak a word of French (at least I could crudely) & had constant jealousy & paranoia of any other woman. She was an insecure woman who was in a fantasy world, lying about her qualifications, what she did previously, her assets & even where she lived previously.

I was to find out in small conversations with her son Craig, who tragically died, that she was not to be trusted. When only a teenager, Craig moved in with his father rather than live with Anne, his mother. We got on well, I learned much from him, but I thought maybe I could change her. Lies were one thing, but she was paranoid that either I was seeing another woman or other women were after me. Upon seeing any new woman, she would immediately give me the "Spanish inquisition," & when I would tell her the truth that nothing was happening, she would beat, punch & slap me around the face. Now, being an athlete & strong, it is not in my nature to hit out, especially if I did hit anyone, I would probably put them in the hospital! I use my patience & wit, which for Anne infuriated her even more, so she beat me more!

At HJY, she would imagine all the French women were "after my pants." She would say she had spoken with this person or that person in the factory & they told me XYZ, so after about 12 months of this, I laid a trap. I had not mentioned one woman, Olivier, in the office whom I did some marketing with & while very good at her job was not a raving beauty. I mentioned this particular day, I had spent 3 hours with Olivier on a marketing project. Without fail, the next night, she said she had spoken to various HJY female colleagues & they said I was attracted to Olivier & she was "after my pants". She went on & on all night wanting me to admit to some affair, of course, I denied every accusation.

At some point, I gave up, got up from the settee and passed by her. She bent both her feet & with them, pushed me over the coffee table. I damaged the table as I flew over the table & landed on the floor on the other side banging my head & elbow badly. "That's it, this is the last straw. You are going back to England!" I ordered the ferry for the following Friday night, all the time during the week & the journey up to Haslington, she pleaded with me to return to France. I let her stay in my Haslington house (vacant at the time) for 3 months to allow her to find a home in Cheshire near her daughters. She got some of my foreign friends' e-mail addresses & started to send lies that I had put here in England on the street & needed money. I got into her e-mails, once I read, I countered her lies by giving the true story as an update, <u>without</u> letting on I had read her messages. That saved my friends' money through her lies.

After I broke up with Anne in 1999 & took her packing back to the UK, I started looking for someone in France. JY had given us all AOL e-mail accounts, so I looked on <u>love@AOL.com</u> & found, to my surprise, very few French women, but mostly American females & a number from Africa. I think the reason for the poor response from French females is that few speak English & this is mainly a English-speaking American internet provider.

Note 3: Monica's real Rwandan story.

Monica, according to a former close friend, even when young, maybe 8 or 9 years old, grew big boobs. It was no surprise, therefore, that when I met her, they were enormous melons. Monica always told me a different story of being 15 with small boobs & prayed to god for bigger boobs. Several sources said she had sizable boobs at 10 years old.

Monica went to Rwanda before our marriage to get the required false documents. I also got information from a former Rwandan politician & former prime minister, Faustin Twagiramunga, much later that put everything Monica told me about her life in Rwanda on its head. We met Faustine when Rachael & I were invited by Gisele to stay at David's house while Monica was with David at our house! One of the guests at dinner was Faustin, who was interesting, very knowledgeable & obviously kept close ties with Rwandans in Rwanda & Cote d'Ivoire. On my request, he investigated many questions I had about whether Monica's stories about her family & early life were true & what happened in Abidjan, Cote d'Ivoire.

Faustin's research uncovered (see e-mail & my reply below) many lies Monica made about her past. Firstly, while her father was a policeman for a while, he owned a small shop. Her story was he had a large business that included four articulated lorries. She claimed they had a large house with large gardens that she did gardening from time to time as well as having a permanent gardener. I knew she did not do gardening was false, because she threw out some flowers with bulbs into the dustbin at rue des Amandiers house. I saw holes in the garden one night returning from work where they had been & I had to retrieve them from the bin. She said they were finished & threw them away in the bin, not knowing they were bulbs & would flower again next year.

She was supposed to live at this large house with all her four brothers & she claimed that all four brothers, except for Gilles, died in the genocide. Instead, they died beforehand. Apparently, Monica was well known in Kigali, but for being "on the game" near the "roundabout" region. When you are not rich but not poor, you may have desires to have a better life by selling your body. This is a tough question for millions of women throughout the world.

She claimed to escape with Lennon & her husband out of Rwanda & fly to Cote d'Ivoire. Her story was that they dug a hole with a covering in the garden & the three of them hid in the hole for several days while the Hutu butchers were around & then made their way to Kenya. How she actually escaped, I do not know, maybe Stanley was instrumental, as he was a former justice minister.

The husband (or convenient partner?) was a forest manager & when they moved to Cote d'Ivoire went up country on a job in Cote d'Ivoire & died probably of meningitis. He died quickly & apparently, at the funeral, Monica wore a short mini-dress & was jovial. It's not the normal way to behave at a funeral of your husband.

Questions for me abound with:

i) What is Lennon's father's real name? I saw several documents with differing versions of his name: Mozambigwi or **Mbanzarugamba** or Banzarugamba. Faustin is insistent that the 2nd version is correct.

ii) Did Monica marry him or just a partner?

iii) Monica always used XXXXX (redacted) surname for herself & more recently, XXXX surname (redacted), also for Lennon before becoming my adopted son.

iv) Who is Lennon's father? This chap or Stanley?

Once in Cote d'Ivoire, Monica got a job at ADB (African Development Bank) & got a small rental house with a maid who looks after Lennon. She said she ran a bar/snack place in the evening, with Stanis named because the owner, because ADB does not allow two jobs at the same time.

Rachael & I were in constant contact with Gisele, so she invited us to David's house one weekend when David would be in Longjumeau with Monica. I then met Faustine, a guest & friend of Gisele, at David's house when Gisele was still living there. David was with Monica at our house, so Rachael & I stayed the weekend in Bruxelles. Rather amusing, eh?

My follow-up e-mail to Faustine several years later, Faustin mentioned to me that he would like to go back to Rwanda when we visited Gisele at David's house south of Bruxelles in late 2011. Later, Faustine said he planned to go to Rwanda, and I said he would be mad to try to enter Rwanda again. The news from an article I found below proves I was correct. **Wikipedia** entry is also below.

1st Dec 2011

GT   *Hello Faustin*

It is a long time we have communicated, so I will start by updating you on my news

Monica (Monica XXXX (redacted) said originally "never will I leave this house" (her dream), but increasing debt to people all over the place change her attitude whereby by 2010 she changes to wanting to be bought out. I know her position, because various organisations cannot get money from her, so they get huissiers (bailiffs) to contact me for money. I was harassed by various huissiers for over a year. Monica uses illegal tricks that required me to go to the police to get a "courant a main" document when she uses my RIB (guarantee) to pay her gas bill of € 2,500. !

The tribunal approved my application for divorce in July 2010, but I am not informed officially until September (things work slowly in France). October we saw a notaire, after a 2nd private meeting he says he is the wrong type of notaire for adversary (no agreement of splitting of the estate), so I went back to the advocate and he appoints another notaire adversary.

Again nothing happens until August (normal for France), when I finally after asking all the time for name and information on the notaire I provide MANY documents that I had given to the other notaire. One month later (Rachael phones him for me to find out what is happening? He says nothing, he received the documents and did not know what to do with them! (typical French attitude…put to the bottom of the file, do not ask questions …it may involve work !)

Lennon moved into Brussels Belgium autumn 2010. Because he got kicked out of EICAR Media College because Monica does not pay the bill, he inscribes for a short course in a Brussels media college. Gisele has seen Monica and Lennon several times there was a big fight in a shop, when Gisele saw Monica wearing her jewellery the police arrived and took them all down to the police station, where it transpired that Monica never received French nationality as she claimed to me. I find out many lies of Monica I keep the information to myself. An example was that Monica eventually got French nationality after being refused the first time due to stealing from the state (false claim of monthly payments accumulating to € 6,500). The police station where details were required lead to Monica admitting she still had refugee status not French nationality.

In October 2011, we had a big meeting with both notaires my advocate, Monica, Rachael and me in attendance. The notaire meeting was interesting and lively affair especially when I ask some questions, it was evident that Monica had not given her notaire any facts including owning a company called "Moni Clean" or a car etc. She replied that Moni Clean was not on the agenda, because it was HER company....."anyway is no longer exists..."

By waiting to say goodbye to my advocate and waiting to say goodbye to Monica (a total of 10 mins) Monica and her Notaire were deep in conversation outside regarding certain information she had not given, as we passed them Rachael overheard she had no accounts for Moni Clean.

Moni Clean was compulsorily wound up (admitted by Monica) at Notaire meeting 14th Oct 2011.

*Subsequent research and letter confirmation from the chamber of commerce, is that Moni Clean had **NEVER** given accounts during its existence! This is illegal! More trouble for Monica, much labour Monica used was paid black money.*

So now I have figures for my notaire to make an offer, because in typical French fashion he was waiting for Monica's notaire to make an offer, which would never happen because he does not have the facts.

So what news from you? Did you go back to visit Rwanda?

Comms with Faustin 20th March 2009

Dear Geoff,

I am so sorry for the delay, since I got your message before you travelled to Turkey.

I was not busy, but I was absent from Belgium for a while, and I could not get time to concentrate.

Also, it was not easy to get in touch with a friend of mine now working in Chad who knew Monica well, when they were both working for ADB (African Developing Bank) in Abidjan, Ivory Coast.

It appears from the information obtained that Monica has not finished High school. She may be intelligent, but as you mentioned to me, she is not an intellectual. And again, what does it mean to be intelligent? Is it to be a crook, hypocrite, liar and malicious? Is it to abuse the trust and confidence of others?

GT   *Yes, she is excellent at lying, but many times, her lack of education showed things or scenarios not feasible, so I investigated*

Nobody knows whether Monica got married officially to Mr. MBANZARUGAMBA or whether they lived together as "partners" or friends in Rwanda.

GT   *Stanley e-mailed me to say he was there as a witness at the wedding. I do not know whether to believe him because Monica and Stanis have been close and according to Gisele: Stanley is not her uncle but a previous lover……. I cannot verify this, and so at present, I must "take the comments with a pinch of salt…"*

No one was able to tell me whether her son, Lennon, whom you have adopted (as I was informed) is **MBANZARUGAMBA**'s son. Can she prove it? It could be. But hardly, I suppose.

She fled with "her husband" to Abidjan, like some other Rwandans, just after the genocide in Rwanda. Her "husband" worked outside Abidjan in a company or a state organisation dealing with timber. I was told that **Mbanzarugamba** later died of malaria or aids. Nobody knows what exactly has been his illness.

GT   *Interesting fact on the name. This shows the death certificate I have a copy of (below) that was used for our wedding is false. Does this mean the wedding is invalid? Monica told me he died of Meningitis (I have attached the death certificate, which does not define the cause of death).*

While he was working in the forest, Monica found another "husband" from Sierra Leone

GT   *I think this was Emmanuel Samah whom she got engaged.*

I was told that she made a lot of boyfriends while working in ADB
GT   *yes, I can confirm this; she probably had an affair with George Taylor-Lewis, a big manager whom she visited often, even Lennon remembers him visiting often.*

It has also been reported to me that on the day **MBAZARUGAMBA** was buried, she did not show any emotion. She was dressed in a miniskirt, trying rather to seduce people with her buttocks, that same day of the burial.

She made arrangements to obtain fake documents to get to France with the assistance of "her husband" from Sierra Leone (fiancé Emmanuel Samah).

GT   *I met her on holiday in August 2000 when she went back home, the situation in Ivory Coast had deteriorated. She said she immediately turned Lennon back to stay with a friend in the south of France while she sorted things out got a plane 3 weeks later. But since I have seen documents that show she arrived 2 days BEFORE, she claimed to take Lennon to Montpellier then returned to play as if she had just arrived.*

I do not know what documents she used because when she arrived, it was in Abidjan, Ivory Coast en route to London via Paris. She said she gave her Rwandan passport to another passenger to send to my address then got off claiming refugee status. I picked her up after many hours of waiting at CdG airport Paris with her luggage a few days later. She stayed with me for a couple of days then she wanted me to drop her off in Paris to be able to phone the authorities that she needed a room. I was never involved with giving her any documentation, as she was living as a refugee at various hotels for some 9 months before she moved out to Melun to the refugee centre. She moved in with me at my apartment in June 2002.

In France, nobody knows how she got the refugee status.

She obtained refugee status fairly easily due to a policy of Rwanda genocide by the French govt.

But what my informer knows is that she managed to get in touch with a British who later married her and adopted her son. He also told me that she married the British while the gentleman from Sierra Leone still believed that he was also her "husband".

GT   *Certainly, Emmanuel Samah was angry sent a letter to me via Bibiane, a friend of his and Monica that she was a cheat a liar. They were engaged he planned* to go to Europe marry her; he set up a bank account for her at Sociale Generale Bank. I wish I had listened to him!!

When the latter learned that Monica was officially married to a British, without his knowledge, he angrily said that Rwandans were "escrocs!"

The father

I know the father. He, like his daughter, did not finish his high school. He was trained as a policeman in a kind of African standard police course. When the police were dissolved after the coup d'Etat of 1973 and replaced by the "gendarmerie", he became a trader. His name is George Rumongi.

GT   *Interesting that Gilles (Monica's only surviving brother?) is Gilles Rumongi. Gilles lives in Holland, and I still keep in contact with him.*

Mr Rumongi was trading in foodstuff in Gisenyi and then afterwards moved to Kigali. NB: He was not an important "home d'affaires". He was just someone who wanted to live decently on his own by making those impossible small businesses.

I was informed that he divorced his first wife, who I think is the mother of Monica.

GT   *YES, Monica says that her real mother lives in the south near the border and has a bad face cancer that needs an operation. She has been trying to get a visa for her to have treatment in France for the last 2 years. It has been refused several times. Monica claimed she did not know her real mother existed until she was about 13 years old; she thought previously that the 2nd wife was her mother.*

After he divorced, he married, or lived with another woman who is the sister of Mr MBONAMPEKA.

It could be that Monica's mother is still alive

GT   *Yes, see above.*

I was informed rather that Mr RUMONGI and his second "wife" died of aids before the genocide... No precise date has been given.

NB: 1. The name of her so called husband is not BANZARUGAMBA, but **MBANZARUGAMBA**, and it makes a lot of difference.

GT *Yes, but what difference would it make to the wedding validity? Interesting question.*

2. Monica's father was not a police officer nor a junior police officer but a simple policeman.

3. Monica's father was not a businessman but a poor local foodstuff dealer.

4. It is agreed by many Rwandans that Monica is an intelligent and "escroc" prostitute.

5. Monica is better known as XXXXX (redacted nickname). People don't know her last name as it is not Rwandan custom to have his own father's last name.

Yes, many "friends" call her "Moni *" short for Monica. *
Name changed to preserve secrecy

Faustin

GT *Thanks for the notes it makes interesting reading. If I could get some black and white evidence on a few crucial points, e.g. name of the dead "husband" death certificate different from that (see below) used for our marriage, that would be excellent, but like so many things, I would think that would be most difficult.*

Cheers, Geoff.

Faustin Twagiramungu

Faustin Twagiramungu   From **Wikipedia**,

6th Prime Minister of Rwanda

I In office
19 July 1994 – 28 August 1995[1]

President	Pasteur Bizimungu
Preceded by	Jean Kambanda
Succeeded by	Pierre-Célestin Rwigema

Personal details

Born	14 August 1944 Gishoma commune, Cyangugu prefecture[2]
Nationality	Rwandan
Political	Rwandan Dream Initiative party
Spouse(s)	Maria Assumpta Taigga[2]
Mother	Anizi Nyahizumwami
Father	Jean Gishumgu
Residence	Brussels, Belgium
Education	McGill University[1]

Faustin Twagiramungu (born 14 August 1944) is a Rwandan politician. He was Prime Minister from 1994 until his resignation in 1995, the first head of government appointed after the Rwandan Patriotic Front (RPF) captured Kigali. He then exiled himself to Belgium.[3]

I read one day in 2014 in an on-line article the following:

In 2014, the Belgium intelligence gathered credible information that prove that the Rwandan government was plotting to assassinate exiled former Rwandan prime minister Faustin TWAGIRAMUNGU who is living in Brussels. A close protection with an armored car were urgently dispatched to ensure he is protected.

In 2010, Twagiramungu founded a "new political trend" called the Rwandan Dream Initiative (RDI). [27] In early 2014, RDI teamed up with three other parties (PS-Imberakuri, UDR and FDLR) to form the Coalition of Political Parties for Change (CPC). The inclusion of FDLR was a point of controversy. [28] The coalition was reportedly falling apart before the end of the year. [29]

On 4 April 2014, only two days after Kagame had visited Brussels, Twagiramungu was informed by Belgian police and state security that his life was in danger, and his house was provided with police protection for four days. The Globe and Mail reported that "there is mounting evidence that Mr. Kagame's (Rwanda president) agents are involved in organized efforts to kill exiled dissidents".

Note 4: Rwanda

The story of Paul Kadame & possibly/probably being responsible for the former president Juvénal Habyarimana & the Burundi president Cyprien Ntaryamira being shot down by a missile on the 6th of April 1994 is well known. This started the genocide of 800,000 to 1 million Tusi & politically moderate Hutu's. Paul Kadame escaped from one of the previous wars to Uganda, then, with his army Rwandan Patriotic Front (RPF) backed by Uganda, he took power & finally became president.

This raises the question throughout Africa: is a good dictator better than a crooked democracy with corruption, or a bad dictator? Certainly, President Kadame has been good for the stability of Rwanda, and all foreign aid actually goes where it is supposed to go (UK government finding of UK aid to Rwanda). Transparency International voted Rwanda the 5th cleanest out of 47 countries in Sub-Saharan Africa & 55th cleanest out of 175 in the world — that is some achievement.

Hutus & Tutsis are now living & working together for the common good of a stable country. Discussions with Rwandese during our monthly meetings & various parties did show there was a common consensus that Kadame was good for Rwanda; however, many would disagree, including Monica.

However, I was introduced later to the ex-president Habyarimana's wife, Agathe & her family several years later; obviously, she hated Kadame for killing her husband. The location of her home & family was kept a secret from the general public, although the security forces knew the location. The "house" was actually a double fronted semi-detached joined together inside. The separation wall of the two houses had been knocked down to make the large single house. Her house was like a mausoleum to her late husband, portraits of him, photos & souvenirs. Fearing her possible influence on domestic politics in exile, President Kadame tried unsuccessfully to get her extradited to Rwanda after initially being permission for extradition in 2011.

Rwandans all speak Kinyarwanda, with about <5% also speaking French (declining to forget the role France played in the genocide) & now, increasingly, English is spreading beyond the present <15% to enable international trade better. Kadame spoke English, having escaped to Uganda in the 1980s to build up an army there. Having been president for many years, English has become the 4th official language as well as Kinyarwanda, French. & Swahilli.

In the year 2018, one sees that Rwanda is shown to be a prime example of a country being able to progress & work united with all tribes working together for the common good. It has increased it's wealth for the common good. Is this an example of a good dictator?

However, there is growing evidence of political assassinations of Rwandan political figures and foreign nationals (By Alfred Antoine U. and AMS reported www.jambonews.net) interested in Rwanda's social and political affairs in foreign countries across the world is not a hoax. It is a reality that is disturbingly ongoing.

In 2014, Belgium intelligence gathered credible information (see article before) that proved that the Rwandan government was plotting to assassinate exiled former Rwandan prime minister Faustin TWAGIRAMUNGU, who was living in Brussels & whom I visited twice in David's house when he was with Monica. Rachael & I visited Gisele & had several meetings with him to discuss research on Monica's past in Rwanda). Close protection by police gendarmes with an armored car was urgently dispatched to ensure he was protected.

More recently 2019, an article showed that in Rwanda, living standards are good, there is peace between tribal factions & all funds sent to Rwanda are REALLY used as described to improve the country. 13/4/2019 **"i"** newspaper (UK) article by Clement Uwiringiyimana.

Rwanda is funding **"M23"** gorilla forces in DRC & guarding illegal mines of Coltan the ore of tantalum, a key element in modern phones, computers, etc. so that <u>without any mines in Rwanda</u>, it is a <u>key exporter of Coltan</u> !

Note 5: Monica's affairs, men & women

List of **known** **affairs, men meetings** & online contacts via male/female sites

    # = identified sex

1) Paul   #
2) Andre   #
3) George-Taylor L   #
4) Pierre Car   #
5) Arend H   #
6) Claude   #
7) George (via Rebecca.)   #
8) Julian Baptiste Notaire   #
9) Pierre Mburiro Bukavu   #
10) Jado   #
11) Unknown others arranged with Rebecca

Escort work
I. Business - gangbang   #   French Antilles
II. Dorian Faust   #
III. Jurgen   #   Switz
IV ??

Various lunch/dinner meets (+maybe a few sexy exchanges)

a. Pierre R   maybe # ?
b. Jean Claude   maybe #?   Ref. irate wife
c. Jean L
d. Jean Marie
e. Jean Guy
f. Mensiah.
g. Kasi
h. Pierre Bora
i. Kris San Lennon
j. Pierre Lombard

k. Asare
l. Theo
m. Tenereux
n. Luis
o. Fabrice Der
p. AlMasi
q. Big Bill Billou
r. Jen-Marc Coz.
s. Cedric Aubert.
t. Pierre Don Quichotte..
u. Doucoure Kaidiatou Kadi.
v. Cisse.
w. Regis R. via Serencontre ad
x. Satar   .
y. +++…?.

Women lesbian sex
1) Imogen
2) Rebecca
3) Kelly
4) Alice
5) Marina
6) Maria
7) Naomi
8) Jemma
9) +++…..??

Note 6: Business trips catalogued

2003
- 28-31 July UK trip
- 7-12 Sept Granada, Spain conference

2004
- 6-10 Jan   Plasma Winter Conference Fort Lauderdale, Florida, USA
- 1-6 June   JY annual world sales conference, Biarritz, SW France
- 21-25 June   Japan   Yokogawa, HP

2005
- 7 -12 Feb 2005   ArabLab, Dubai
- 8-15 May   South Africa
- 5 – 10 June   Libya
- 13 – 15 Nov 2005   Iran

2006
- 13 Feb 2006   ArabLab, Dubai
- 6-10 March   UK
- 21-25 March   Sweden
- 10-12 May   Poland
- 24-25 May   Hungary
- 14 June   JY world sales conference, Bormes, South of France
- 9-13 July   Hungary
- 7 September   Holland
- 21 Sept   Egypt
- 24th Sept   Dubai
- 11 Oct   Turkey
- 26 Oct   Portugal
- 30 Oct   Holland

2007
- 12 Feb   Middle east, ArabLab, Dubai, Egypt
- 20-22 Feb   Hungary
- 14 March   South Africa
- 21 May   UK
- 14 May-16 May   Poland & Czech republic
- 6 July   Hungary
- 24-25 Sept   Poland
- 4 -12 Oct   UK
- 22-25 Oct   South Africa
- 14 -16 Nov   Finland
- 3 5- Dec   Belorus
- 6-7 Dec   Ukraine

2008:   Rachael's 1st visit to England
- 21 -22 Jan   Israel
- 24 – 26   Turkey
- 5-6 Feb   Finland
- 14 Feb   Egypt
- 4 – 5 March   Czech Republic
- 10 -14 March   South Africa
- 13 July 14-15, July 16-17, 19-23, 24   Middle East tour: Qatar, Kuwait, Dubai, Abu Dhabi, Saudi Arabia (KSA), Egypt
- 9, 11-13, 15-20 Nov   UAE, Kuwait KSA.

2009:
- 7 Jan, 9-11   Middle East: KSA, Turkey
- 12-14, 25-26, 28-March-1April, 2 April Middle East: Kuwait, UAE: Dubai, Abu Dhabi, KSA, Egypt
- 24 April   Sweden
- 30 May-1 June, 2-4, 6-10, 11   Middle East: Kuwait, UAE, Oman, KSA, Egypt
- 12-14 Oct   Holland

- 17-26, 29 Oct   Middle East: KSA , Egypt

2010
- 9-12 Jan, 13-14, 15-20, 21   ArabLab Dubai, Kuwait, KSA, Egypt
- 10 – 12 March   Czech republic
- 26 -27, 27/28, 29 April, 1st -5, 6 May   Middle East: Kuwait, Dubai, Qatar, KSA, Egypt
- 10-11, 12-13, 16-21, 22 Oct   Middle East: Kuwait, UAE, KSA, Egypt

2011
- 1-2 March, 2-10, 12-16, 17 March   Kuwait, ArabLab Dubai, KSA, Egypt
- 14 -19, 24-27, 28-29, 30 May   KSA, Kuwait, Dubai, Egypt
- 1-5 Oct   KSA

2012
- 21 –22, 23-29 March   Egypt, ArabLab Dubai
- 13-14 April   Norway
- 12-14 Nov   Russia

2013
- 3-4, 5-6, 7-13, 15-20 March   Egypt, Kuwait, KSA, ArabLab, Dubai,
- 23-24 April   Russia
- 28-29 May   Spain
- 17-19 Sept   Belorus

www.ingramcontent.com/pod-product-compliance
Ingram Content Group UK Ltd.
Pitfield, Milton Keynes, MK11 3LW, UK
UKHW021037210325
456568UK00007B/740